Susanna Gregory is a pseudonym. Before she earned her PhD at the University of Cambridge and became a research Fellow at one of the colleges, she was a police officer in Yorkshire. She has written a number of non-fiction books, including ones on castles, cathedrals, historic houses and world travel.

She and her husband live in Carmarthen.

Visit the author's website at: www.susannagregory.co.uk

Also by Susanna Gregory

The Matthew Bartholomew Series

A Plague on Both Your Houses
An Unholy Alliance
A Bone of Contention
A Deadly Brew
A Wicked Deed
A Masterly Murder
An Order for Death
A Summer of Discontent
A Killer in Winter
The Hand of Justice
The Mark of a Murderer
The Tarnished Chalice
To Kill or Cure

The Thomas Chaloner Series

A Conspiracy of Violence

BLOOD ON
THE STRAND

Susanna
Gregory

sphere

SPHERE

First published in Great Britain in 2007 by Sphere
This paperback edition published in 2008 by Sphere
Reprinted 2008

A CIP catalogue record for this book
is available from the British Library.

ISBN: 978-0-7515-3759-8

Typeset in Baskerville MT by Palimpsest Book Production Limited,
Grangemouth, Stirlingshire
Printed and bound in Great Britain by Clays Ltd, St Ives plc

Sphere
An imprint of
Little, Brown Book Group
100 Victoria Embankment
London EC4Y 0DY

An Hachette Livre UK Company
www.hachettelivre.co.uk

www.littlebrown.co.uk

For Michael Churgin

Prologue

Matthew Webb was cold, wet and angry. The rain, which had started as an unpleasant, misty drizzle, was now the kind of drenching downpour that was likely to last all night. Fuming, he adjusted his hat in the hope of stopping water from seeping down the back of his neck, but the material was sodden, and fiddling only made matters worse. Cheapside was pitch dark at that late hour, and he could not see where he was putting his feet, so it was only a matter of time before he stepped in a deep puddle that shot a foul-smelling sludge up the back of his legs. He ground his teeth in impotent rage, and when the bells of St Mary-le-Bow chimed midnight, he felt like smashing them.

It was a long walk from African House on Throgmorton Street to his handsome residence on The Strand, and he should have been relaxing in the luxury of his personal carriage, not stumbling along the city's potholed, rain-swept streets like a beggar. He cursed his wife for her abrupt announcement that she had had enough of the riotous Guinea Company dinner and was going home early. And how dare she forget to send the vehicle back for him once it had delivered *her* safe and dry to Webb Hall!

It was not just a thoughtless spouse who had earned his animosity that night, either. There were also his Guinea Company colleagues, who had seen his predicament but failed to come to his rescue. It was true they were drunk, because it had been a long evening and the Company was famously lavish with wine at its feasts, but when everyone had spilled noisily out of African House at the end of the dinner, it had been obvious that Webb was the only one whose coachman was not there to collect him. Surely, *one* of his fellow merchants could have offered to help? But no – they had selfishly packed themselves inside their grand transports and rattled away without so much as a backwards glance.

Webb had certainly expected Sir Richard Temple to step in and save him. The seating arrangements that evening had placed them next to each other, and they had talked for hours. Cannily, Webb had used the opportunity to do business – he owned a ship that brought sugar from Barbados and Temple was thinking of purchasing a sugar plantation with money from the rich widow he intended to marry. It was obvious they could benefit each other, and Webb was always pleased to be of service to the gentry. Of course, the agreement they had reached – and signed and sealed – would see Temple all but destitute in the long run, but that was the nature of competitive commerce. It was hardly Webb's fault that Temple had not noticed the devious caveat in the contract before putting pen to paper.

The merchant's ugly, coarse-featured face creased into

2

a scowl as he recalled the reactions of some Company members when he and Temple had announced their alliance. The loud-mouthed Surgeon Wiseman had declared that *he* would have nothing to do with men involved in the heinous industry that used slave labour, and several others had bellowed their agreement. Wiseman's medical colleague Thomas Lisle was among them, which was a blow, because Lisle was popular and reasonable, and men tended to listen to him.

Not everyone had taken the surgeons' side, though: some had the sense to see that sugar was needed in London, that the plantations required a workforce, and that slaves were the cheapest way to provide it. The wealthy Brandenburger, Johan Behn, had attempted to explain the economics of the situation, but most members were too drunk to understand his complex analysis, and had cheered when Wiseman, in his arrogant, dogmatic manner, had declared Behn a mean-spirited bore.

Then Temple had stood and raised his hand for silence. If people wanted affordable sugar, he had said crisply, they would have to put squeamish sentiments aside. Even Wiseman could think of no argument to refute *that* basic truth. Unfortunately, a foppish, debauched courtier called Sir Alan Brodrick had spoiled the victory by 'accidentally' hitting Temple over the head with a candlestick. Debates at Guinea Company gatherings often ended in violent spats – or even duels – and members were used to a little blood. Their guests were not, however, and Webb recalled the shock on the Earl of Bristol's face at the way the disagreement had been resolved.

Webb turned into Paternoster Row, swearing viciously as wind blew a soggy veil of rain straight into his eyes. A cat hissed at him as he passed, and in the distance he

3

could hear the cries of bellmen, announcing that all was well. Webb grimaced. All was *not* well. He had never met the Earl of Bristol before, and he had been delighted when the man had accepted the Company's invitation to its annual dinner. Being low-born – Webb had started life as a ditcher – it was not easy to break into the exclusive circles of the privileged, not even for those who had become extremely rich. However, Bristol, who had no money of his own, had a reputation for socialising with anyone he thought might lend him some. Webb had cash to spare, and saw the impecunious earl as his route to the respectability and acceptance he craved. He had intended to befriend Bristol that night, and the acquaintance would open doors that had hitherto been closed to him.

Webb had spent an hour hovering at the edge of the bright throng that surrounded Bristol, waiting for an opportunity to make his move. Unfortunately, he had made the mistake of taking his wife with him, and Silence Webb had heard some of the things the witty but spiteful Bristol had said. She had found them amusing and laughed with the rest, until he had made the quip about the decorative 'face patches' that were all the rage at Court. Every lady of fashion stuck one or two false moles to her cheeks, and Silence, eager to prove herself as cultured as the rest, had managed to glue fourteen of them around her ample visage. Because of this, Bristol's casual remark that an excess made their wearers look like victims of the French pox had been taken personally. Proving to the entire Guinea Company that her Puritan name had been sadly misapplied, Silence had forced her way through the crowd and placed two meaty hands on Bristol's table, leaning forward to glare at him.

'I do not like you,' she had said loudly, stilling the frivolous chatter that bubbled around the man. 'I prefer your rival, Lord Clarendon, because *he* is a man of taste and elegance.'

It was not every day an earl was harangued by an ex-ditcher's wife, and for once Bristol's famous wit failed to provide him with a suitably eloquent response. 'Madam, I . . . ' he had stammered.

'You are fat, and your doublet is twenty years out of date,' Silence had continued in a ringing voice, so her words carried the length of the hall. People began to turn around to see what was happening. 'And you stink of onions, like a peasant.'

'Well, there you have it, Bristol,' drawled the dissipated Brodrick. He was Lord Clarendon's cousin, so always ready for a chance to snipe at his kinsman's deadliest enemy. 'Clarendon *never* smells of onions, so he has the advantage of you in this dreadfully serious accusation.'

People had tittered uneasily, and Webb had taken the opportunity to haul Silence away before she could say anything else. Bristol had not smiled, though, and Webb knew he was angry. The merchant stopped for a moment, to shake water out of his hat; under the thin soles of his expensive shoes the road felt gritty with wet soot and ashes. Yet perhaps all was not lost. He had already lent Bristol several hundred pounds through a broker, so they were not *exactly* strangers to each other. He would call on the Earl the following morning, to apologise for Silence's comments, and at the same time offer to lend him more – at a rate of interest that would be irresistible. Gold would speak louder than the insults of imprudent wives, and Bristol was sure to overlook the matter. He and Webb would be friends yet.

5

Webb took a series of shortcuts – he had been born in the slums known as the Fleet Rookery, and knew the city like the back of his hand – and emerged near Ludgate. His fine shoes rubbed his soaked feet, and he began to swear aloud, waking the beggars who were asleep under the Fleet bridge. His knees ached, too, as they often did in wet weather – a legacy of his years in the city's dank runnels. He thought about Silence, and wondered whether she was angry with *him* because of Bristol's remarks. Was that why she had failed to send the carriage back to African House to collect him?

He reached The Strand, limping heavily now, and heard the bells of St Martin-in-the-Fields announce six o'clock; they had been wrong ever since a new-fangled chiming mechanism had been installed three months before. He heaved a sigh of relief when he recognised mighty Somerset House and its fabulous clusters of chimneys. The newly styled 'Webb Hall' was next door.

Suddenly, a figure loomed out of the darkness ahead and began to stride towards him. Although he could not have said why, Webb knew, with every fibre of his being, that the man meant him harm. With a sick, lurching fear, he glanced at the alley that led to the river. Should he try to make a run for it? But his ruined knees ached viciously, and he knew he could not move fast enough to escape a younger, more fleet-footed man. He fumbled for his purse.

'Five shillings,' he said unsteadily. 'I do not have any more. Take it and be gone.'

The fellow did not reply. Then Webb heard a sound behind him, and whipped around to see that a second man had been hiding in the shadows. And were there others, too? Webb screwed up his eyes, desperately peering into the blackness, but he could not tell. There was a blur of movement, and the merchant felt a searing pain in his chest. He dropped heavily to all fours, not knowing whether the agony in his ribs or to his jarred, swollen knees was the greater. He was still undecided when he died.

The killer handed his rapier to his companion to hold, while he knelt to feel for a life-beat. Then a dog started to bark, and the men quickly melted away into the darkness before the animal's frenzied yaps raised the alarm. There was no time to snatch Webb's bulging purse or to investigate the fine rings clustered on his fat fingers.

The mongrel was not the only witness to the crime. A figure swathed in a heavy cloak watched the entire episode, then stood rubbing his chin thoughtfully. There was little he could have done to prevent the murder of Matthew Webb, but that did not mean it was going to be quietly forgotten. Someone would pay for the blood that stained The Strand.

Chapter 1

Hailstones as large as pigeons' eggs pelted the royal procession as it trooped down King Street from the palace at White Hall, and any semblance of dignity was lost in the ensuing scramble for shelter. Horses pranced and bucked at the sudden commotion, and the Earl of Bristol was not the only courtier to take a tumble in the chaos when the cavalcade reached Westminster Abbey. His retainers dashed forward to drag him upright, but not before his red, ermine-fringed cloak was irretrievably stained with the dung and filth from the road. His bitter enemy, the Earl of Clarendon, allowed himself a small, spiteful smirk before tossing the reins of his own mount to a waiting servant and hurrying up the steps to the abbey's great west door. Clarendon's massive new periwig, made from the hair of a golden-maned Southwark prostitute, had been expensive, and he did not want it ruined by the weather – not even when it was to gloat at the gratifying sight of his rival wallowing in muck.

A handful of flustered trumpeters did their best to

produce a regal fanfare when King Charles leapt from his saddle, but His Majesty was disgracefully late, and most of the musicians had grown tired of waiting and had wandered off. They came running when they heard the clatter of hoofs, but too late to do their duty. Meanwhile, it had been raining hard all morning and water had seeped inside the instruments of those who had remained, so all that emerged was a series of strangled gurgles. One youngster had had the foresight to keep his horn dry under his hat and proudly stepped forward to prove it, but in his eagerness, he forgot what he had been told to play, and graced the royal ears with a lively rendition of a popular alehouse song. The King shot him a startled glance, and Thomas Chaloner, who had been assigned 'security duties' for the day and was in disguise as a raker – a street-sweeper – struggled not to laugh.

Somewhat belatedly, a bell began to chime, but an administrative hiccup had seen the ringers provided with their barrel of refreshing ale far too early in the day, and most were now incapable of performing the task in hand. The man who had been assigned the largest bell hastened to make up for his colleagues' shortcomings, and produced a deep, sepulchral toll that was more redolent of a royal funeral than a celebration to mark the third anniversary of the King's coronation. Yet if any Londoner did think the monarch was dead, he shed no tears: in the three years since Charles had been restored to the throne, his Court had earned itself a reputation for debauchery, vice and corruption, and Chaloner was not the only one to think England might have been better off under Cromwell and his sober Parliamentarians.

Courtiers, barons and members of the Royal Household hastily followed their ruler's example by abandoning their steeds and scurrying inside the church to escape the battering of icy missiles from the sky. Chaloner was astounded by the number of people who were taking part in the procession, and thought it small wonder that the King was always clamouring for money to maintain them all. There were grooms, pages and gentlemen of the Privy Chamber, masters of hawks and buckhounds, ladies-in-waiting, and keepers of the King's wine cellars, jewel houses, kitchens and laundries, all combining to make a dazzling spectacle of red, blue, gold, purple and silver.

The most glorious of all was not the King, whose taste in clothes was comparatively modest, but the ebullient Duke of Buckingham. Buckingham was the brightest star of the dissolute Court, and one of its leaders in fashion and mischief. The man who bore the brunt of his spiteful waggery tended to be Lord Clarendon – Chaloner's master. The Duke was always jibing the older man about his obesity and prim manners, and their paths seldom crossed without some insult being traded. That day, Chaloner watched Buckingham give a fair imitation of Clarendon's short-legged waddle up the abbey steps. The voluptuous Lady Castlemaine laughed uproariously at the performance, but no one dared rebuke her – as the King's current mistress, she could guffaw at whomsoever she liked.

Behind Buckingham stamped the Earl of Bristol, swearing furiously under his breath – poor horsemanship had nothing to do with his fall into the mud, of course; incompetent servants and the weather were to blame. He was a handsome, although portly, man with thick brown hair and a thin moustache, like the King's. He hurled his soiled cloak at one of his retainers, revealing that underneath he wore an overly tight doublet with ruffs, and the kind of 'bucket-topped' boots that had been popular during the civil wars. Either he could not afford fashionable clothes, or he did not care that he had donned an outfit that would not have looked out of place thirty years before.

Next to Bristol, his face an aloof, impassive mask, was Joseph Williamson, head of the country's secret service. Before the Earl of Clarendon had offered him work, Chaloner had entertained hopes of being hired by Williamson. He had been a spy for a decade – a long time in an occupation so fraught with danger – and was an accomplished intelligence officer. The only problem was that those ten years had been in the service of Oliver Cromwell's government, and Williamson was naturally suspicious of agents who had been employed by the King's enemies; the fact that Chaloner had only ever plied his skills against foreign powers, and had certainly never spied on the King, was deemed immaterial. Williamson wanted nothing to do with him, and Chaloner was lucky Lord Clarendon was prepared to overlook his past.

At the top of the stairs, the King offered his Queen a solicitous hand across the treacherous carpet of hailstones, although Chaloner thought there was scant affection in the gesture. There was, however, a great deal of fondness in the arm he proffered to Lady Castlemaine. The royal paramour wore a triumphant smirk as she strutted inside, head held high. When she had gone, the King and Queen turned to salute the assembled masses together. The King had insisted on doing this, despite rumours that someone might try to assassinate him that day, because he liked to think of himself as a man of the people. He had even declared a public holiday, so work would not prevent the citizens of London from coming to see him.

The citizens were mostly elsewhere that inhospitable Friday morning, however, and the 'crowd' that had gathered to watch him ride from White Hall to Westminster Abbey was pitifully small. There was a smattering of merchants representing various city companies, along with a few Royalist fanatics who were always present at such occasions, and a gaggle of beggars who hoped someone might throw them some coins. When the King had returned from exile three years before, London's streets had been packed with cheering, jubilant supporters, and Chaloner was amazed that Charles and his Court had managed to alienate the population quite so completely within such a short period of time.

Knowing a lost cause when he saw one, the King disappeared inside the church almost before he had finished the royal salute, but the Queen lingered. Chaloner raised his hand in greeting, because he thought a raker would probably do so, and was surprised when she waved back. It was the second time she had smiled at him since his arrival in England a few months earlier, and he was oddly touched.

'There is no need to go overboard,' snapped Adrian May, the agent with whom Chaloner had been assigned to work that day. 'And while you leer at the Queen, an assassin might be priming his gun.'

Chaloner resisted the urge to point out that an assassin could prime all he liked, but the King was now inside the building, and so safe from danger. He nodded noncommittally, reluctant to quarrel.

May was a thickset man with a smooth bald head and a vast collection of wigs to cover it; Chaloner had never seen him with the same hairpiece twice. That day he sported a cheap grey one, because he was in disguise as an abbey verger. May not only held high rank in the government's fledgling intelligence service, but was a Groom of the King's Privy Chamber, too. Combined, these made him an influential figure in the world of British espionage. Sadly, he had scant aptitude for the business, and Chaloner disliked both him and his dangerous incompetence intensely.

Meanwhile, May disapproved of Chaloner because he had been away from England for so long that he was a virtual stranger in the country of his birth – after the civil wars, Chaloner had completed his studies at Cambridge and Lincoln's Inn, then had immediately been assigned duties overseas. He had returned to England after the collapse of Cromwell's regime, only to find himself regarded with suspicion and distrust by almost everyone he met. And May's suspicion and distrust were the most fervent of all.

Pushing his antipathy towards May to the back of his mind, Chaloner began another circuit of the abbey, plying his broom as he went. Hailstones cracked under his feet, although the storm had abated and the deluge had dwindled to a hearty drizzle. May grabbed his arm and stopped him.

'How many more times are you going to walk around?' he demanded. 'Williamson's informant said the assassination attempt would be made *during* the procession – and the procession is now over. After a few prayers, everyone will go his own separate way, and the King's life will be the responsibility of the palace guard again.'

'He still has to come out, though,' said Chaloner, too experienced to be complacent. 'And that will be an ideal time to attack.'

'But we have already searched for lurking killers,' argued

May, falling into step beside him. Chaloner wished he would go away – real vergers would not keep company with rakers and any would-be regicide with a modicum of sense would know it. 'The streets are clear. Besides, there are a dozen threats on His Majesty's life each week, and few ever amount to anything. We are wasting our time.'

'You just said an assassin might be priming his gun,' Chaloner pointed out, unwilling to let him have it both ways.

May's voice became mocking. 'I suppose the great Spymaster Thurloe taught you to be ever cautious. However, a *good* agent knows which threats are real and which are hoaxes, and only a fool treats them with equal seriousness.'

Chaloner did not reply. John Thurloe, who had master-minded Cromwell's highly efficient intelligence network, *had* taught him his skills, and his decade-long survival was testament to the fact that he had learned them well – too well to be cavalier about matters as serious as threats to the King's safety.

May grimaced in annoyance when Chaloner declined to discuss the matter. 'You are not very talkative today. What is wrong with you?'

Chaloner pointed to St Margaret's Church, a hand-some building of pale-yellow stone that stood between the abbey and Westminster Hall. 'See that beggar? He has been loitering in that porch for the last hour. Perhaps the threat of assassination is real after all.'

Rain pattered in the mud as May regarded Chaloner in astonishment. The deluge had turned his wig into a mass of sodden strands that reeked of horse, and his shoes squelched as he walked. An explosion of laughter came

14

from a group of palace guards, who were waiting to escort the King back to White Hall. Their leader, Colonel Holles, hastened to silence them, afraid they would disturb the ceremonies inside the abbey. Meanwhile, May's surprise at Chaloner's statement turned to disdain.

'It has been pouring all morning and beggars shelter where they can. As I said, you must learn to distinguish between real menaces and imagined ones, Heyden. You are a fool if you see anything sinister in that fellow's presence.'

Tom Heyden was Chaloner's usual alias, and only a handful of people knew his real identity – because he was kin to one of the fifty-nine men who had signed Charles I's death warrant, Chaloner was a name best kept from Royalist ears. The older Chaloner had died of natural causes shortly after the Restoration, but there were still plenty of Cavaliers who would be delighted to wreak revenge on a member of his family. It was unfortunate, but there was not much Chaloner could do about it, except wait for the righteous anger to cool.

'Look at his boots,' he said shortly, becoming tired of May's condescension. As they were obliged to work together, the man could at least try to conceal his antagonism. Chaloner had managed it, and he expected the courtesy to be returned, so they could concentrate on the task in hand. 'How many vagrants do *you* know who can afford such good-quality footwear?'

May raised a laconic eyebrow. 'I saw one with a fine lace waistcoat yesterday, which had clearly been filched from someone's washing line. Decent boots are more indicative of a fellow's morals than his designs on the King's blood.'

Chaloner was not so sure. 'I am going to talk to him.'

May moved his coat to one side, revealing the dag – a heavy handgun – he had shoved into his belt. 'Go on, then,' he jeered. 'And if you do learn he is a dangerous fanatic with a musket under his rags, rub your nose with your left hand. Then I shall put a hole in him for you.'

Chaloner made his way towards the beggar, sweeping his brush back and forth to clear a path among the sodden litter of old leaves and rubbish that carpeted the ground. May leaned against a wall, affecting a relaxed attitude by removing a pipe from his pocket and tamping it with tobacco. The operation took both hands, which meant he would be unable to retrieve the gun very fast in an emergency. It made Chaloner realise yet again what a dismal intelligence officer May was, and was surprised Spymaster Williamson tolerated such flagrant ineptitude.

He moved closer to his quarry, keeping his head down to conceal his face, but at the same time watching the vagrant intently. The man's face was far too clean, and the stubble on his chin indicated that although he had not shaved that morning, he had certainly done so the day before. He was about Chaloner's own age – early thirties – and his demeanour was that of someone in a state of high agitation. He lay on his side, in an attempt to look as though he was sleeping, but his knuckles were white as he gripped the hem of his cloak, and his dark eyes were full of unease as he stared at the abbey's door – through which the King would emerge within the hour.

Chaloner pretended to notice him for the first time. 'You cannot stay here,' he said, prodding him with his foot. The dagger he always kept hidden in his sleeve slid into the palm of his hand, and it would be embedded in the fellow's heart long before May could draw and aim his gun. 'Go and sleep somewhere else.'

16

The 'beggar' made a show of coming awake, rubbing his eyes. 'It is raining,' he whined, trying without success to disguise a voice that was cultured. 'Do not oust me until it eases. I mean no harm.'

But Chaloner had detected a bulge under the man's cloak that could only belong to a weapon. Since few regicides hatched their nefarious plans alone, he knew Williamson would want to question this one about his associates, which meant taking him alive. He made a half-hearted swipe at a patch of sludge with his brush, then let the broom handle slide from his hands. It dropped into the man's lap. He leaned down, as though to retrieve it, then made a grab for the gun instead. The vagrant was no match for his speed and dexterity, and Chaloner had him disarmed in an instant. The fellow's jaw dropped in horror when his own dag was pressed against his temple.

'This is not how it appears,' he gabbled in alarm, promptly abandoning his rough speech. He was round and plump, with an ancient scar above one eye that looked as though it might have been earned in the wars. 'It is nothing to do with the King. I need to speak to Spymaster Williamson, but his servants refuse to let me see him, and I am desperate. All I want is a few moments of his time. Please!'

'That can be arranged,' said Chaloner, thinking the fellow would be speaking to Williamson now, whether he wanted to or not. He stepped away and indicated with a jerk of the gun that his captive should stand. 'What do you want to talk to him about?'

The vagrant struggled to his feet. 'There has been a misunderstanding that *must* be put right. I am accused of dreadful things, but I am innocent, and Williamson is the only one who will believe me.'

17

Chaloner raised his hand to summon May, but his colleague's attention was focused entirely on his pipe: the rain was making it difficult to light. He was glad he was not rubbing his nose in a frantic plea for help. 'That verger will—'

'No!' cried the beggar urgently. 'Your "verger" is a spy called Adrian May – one of the men who refuses to let me speak to Williamson. Do not call him, I beg you!'

'He will not stop you from seeing Williamson now,' said Chaloner dryly, indicating the weapon he had confiscated.

'I *know* I should have devised another way, but my wits are too frayed for sensible thought,' said the man miserably. Chaloner was under the impression that he was speaking more to himself than to his captor. 'It occurred to me to throw myself on Lord Clarendon's mercy, but his secretary is even more protective of his master than Williamson's minions are, and he guards him like a jealous dog.'

'What is your name?' Chaloner placed his hand on the fellow's shoulder and began to propel him towards Colonel Holles – as Master of the Palace Guard, it fell to Holles to transport suspects to a place where they could be interrogated. But before his prisoner could reply, May became aware that the situation had changed while he had been preoccupied with tobacco. He dropped his pipe and hauled the dag from his belt.

'He is going to shoot!' cried the beggar, stopping in horror. 'He is aiming right at me!'

'May, wait!' yelled Chaloner, watching his colleague cock his gun so it was ready to fire. He held the confiscated weapon aloft, to show him there was no danger.

'He has a knife!' bellowed May in reply. Chaloner

glanced at the beggar's hand and saw it was true, although it posed no danger. Chaloner still held his own blade and, if he missed, handguns were designed with large, bulbous butts that could be used as clubs. There was no possibility of him being bested in a scuffle.

'He is going to kill me!' shrieked the vagrant, becoming more agitated as May ran a few steps nearer, dag held in both hands. 'I meant no harm – my gun is not even loaded. Look for yourself.'

Chaloner did not need to look. First, the weapon reeked of burned oil, and he knew such a very dirty gun was unlikely to work. Secondly, the powder pan was empty, which meant there was nothing to ignite the charge and make the missile fly. And thirdly, there was no ball in the barrel anyway.

'Disarm,' he called to May, knocking the blade from the beggar's unresisting hand. May was now quite close. 'He is harmless.'

May took a firmer grip on his dag and squinted along the barrel. The beggar grabbed Chaloner's arm and cowered behind him. With a sense of shock, Chaloner saw May intended to shoot anyway.

'Terrell is not what he says,' stammered the vagrant, desperately trying to shield himself. 'Tell Williamson that, but no one else. And then save Dillon.'

'What?' Most of Chaloner's attention was on May, who was jigging this way and that as he tried to get a clear view of his intended victim. If he did shoot the fellow, it would be cold-blooded murder, and Williamson would be furious that an opportunity to question a possible assassin had been lost.

'Dillon,' repeated the beggar, tugging Chaloner's coat hard enough to make him stumble. It was a stupid move, because it exposed him to May. 'You *must* save Dillon, and Burne is another who is—'

There was a sudden crack, loud enough to startle a flock of pigeons and send them flapping into the air. Immediately, Holles appeared with a sword in his hand, looking around wildly. Next to Chaloner, the beggar dropped to the ground, while May shook the smoke from his gun and replaced the weapon in his belt.

There was a moment of silence, then pandemonium erupted. So many soldiers rushed from the abbey that Chaloner wondered whether any had remained behind to guard the King. He thought about the danger of diversions, and suggested some went back inside. No one listened to him.

May was the hero of the day. He maintained a cool, dignified poise as the palace guards clapped him on the back and congratulated him for dispatching a would-be assassin. Colonel Holles snatched the gun from Chaloner, eager to inspect the weapon that was to have been used. He did not approve of regicide on his watch, and was incensed by the notion that a plot might have come close to succeeding.

'This dag is a disgrace,' he said with a good deal of professional disdain. 'It is not even loaded – and probably would not have worked if it had been. What sort of murderer was he?'

'A dead one,' said May smugly. 'And one we shall not have to pay the executioner to hang.'

While May basked in the glory of his achievement, Chaloner bent to examine the vagrant. He moved the ragged jacket aside to look at the hole caused by the ball, and was surprised May's gun had caused such massive damage – it was not a large-bore weapon. Of course, May *had* fired from very close range, and Chaloner had seen enough death on the battlefield to appreciate the deadly power of firearms when their victims were only a few yards distant. A red splatter on his own cloak indicated how near to him the beggar had been standing, and he glanced uneasily at May, wondering how confident he had been of his own marksmanship.

'It would have been better to keep him alive,' he said in an undertone, when the soldiers' attention had moved to Holles and the deplorable state of the felon's weapon. 'Now we do not know his name or the identity of the man who sent him – assuming he *was* an assassin, and not just someone who wanted an innocent word with a member of His Majesty's government.'

He was not sure what to believe about his brief conversation with the beggar, although he was unwilling to share details with May – the man would assume he was trying to undermine him, and he did not want the animosity between them to escalate any further.

May was dismissive. 'He was not working for anyone. You can tell from his pathetic disguise that he was a rogue fanatic, acting alone. If you were familiar with London – as a spy should be – then you would be aware that these lunatics appear at regular intervals.'

Chaloner was unconvinced. 'Now he is dead, we will never know, will we?'

'He had a knife,' argued May. 'And do not tell me you had seen it already, because I saw your surprise when I pointed it out. I saved your life, and you should be thanking me, not criticising me.'

Chaloner was astonished May should have drawn such a conclusion. 'I was in no danger—'

'That is not how it appeared to me,' said May icily. 'And I shall say so in my report to Williamson, along with the fact that *you* bungled the arrest. If you had searched him properly, he would not have drawn a dagger and I would not have been obliged to kill him. This death was *your* fault.'

Chaloner sighed, knowing May would do exactly what he said. And he was loath to admit it, but May was right: he *should* have looked for other weapons on his captive. However, that did not detract from the fact that May had been very eager to open fire. Chaloner wondered why. It would certainly not have been to protect his colleague from harm.

May smiled unpleasantly when he made no reply. 'I saw him muttering to you before I dispatched him. What did he say?'

'He was begging not to be murdered, because he had important information to pass to the Spymaster General. Will you include that in your report, too?'

May did not believe him. 'How could a low villain like him know anything to interest us?'

'He was not a "low villain". He was well spoken and he talked about White Hall as though he had been there. I suspect you have made a grave mistake by murdering him.'

'If you say it was murder once more, I shall bury you next to him. You were bad enough in Ireland last month – we could have crushed that rebellion in half the time if you had not been so damned cautious.' May became aware Chaloner was barely listening to him, so said something spiteful in an attempt to regain his attention. 'Williamson will never hire you, you know.'

Chaloner was inspecting three pale bands on the beggar's fingers, which suggested the man had worn rings until recently. What pauper habitually donned jewellery? 'I do not need him to hire me – not any more. I am perfectly happy with Lord Clarendon.'

May sneered at him, unconvinced. 'The feud between your new master and the Earl of Bristol means you will *never* be promoted to the secret services. You see, if Williamson does employ you, it will look as though he is taking sides – trying to harm Clarendon by depriving him of a useful retainer.'

'I doubt Clarendon sees it like that,' said Chaloner, sure it was true. He was useful to the Earl, but a long way from being indispensable. He wished it were otherwise, because courtiers were constantly being urged to ease back on their expenditure, and he was always worried that the Earl might see eliminating the salary of his spy as an easy way to cut costs.

'We shall see. Do not think you will come to Williamson as long as *I* am his friend, anyway. He listens to me, and I shall oppose any application you make.'

Chaloner turned away, not dignifying the threat with a response. He thought about what the beggar had said before he was shot, and wondered how best to communicate it to the Spymaster. Finding a way to Williamson's White Hall offices without May's knowledge presented no great challenge, but he suspected that appearing unannounced would not be a good idea – Williamson was likely to have him arrested before he could speak. He would have to find another way to pass on the information.

Or should he? The vagrant's words had meant nothing to him, and if they were meaningless to Williamson, too, then was there any point in relaying them? He decided to make a few enquiries first, to see if he could unravel their meaning. Repeating garbled sentences verbatim was likely to make him look stupid, and he needed to provide Williamson with solid, useful intelligence if he wanted to make a good impression – and despite May's warnings, Chaloner *would* apply for work with the government if his earl ever dismissed him. Therefore, he had to determine why Terrell was not what he claimed, who Burne was, and why Dillon required saving.

So it was decided. Only when he had answers would he ask to speak to Williamson.

It was still raining when the royal party emerged from the abbey, and there was an undignified scramble for horses and carriages. The King and Lady Castlemaine were first away, eager to escape the damp chill of the medieval building. Buckingham and the Queen were quick in following, but Bristol took rather longer, hopping about with one foot in the stirrup when his lively horse would not keep still as he tried to mount it. Eventually, he took a second tumble. Clarendon happened to be watching, and this time he sniggered openly. Bristol scowled in a way that made him look dangerous.

Williamson nodded to May, silently ordering him to assist the wallowing noble, although Chaloner could not tell whether he did so from compassion, friendship or pity. Virtually the entire Court had taken sides in the Bristol–Clarendon dispute, but no one knew where Williamson stood. Chaloner assumed he was waiting to see who would win before committing himself, which was the sensible option for any ambitious politician.

Eventually, all the courtiers had been helped on to horses or into carriages, and Colonel Holles came to stand down the security detail. His Majesty had been pleased with their diligence, he said, especially when it transpired that an assassin had indeed been waiting. As an expression of appreciation, he had provided a few shillings for ale, so they could drink to his health that evening. There was a cheer, which faltered somewhat when it transpired that the King's idea of 'a few' was two, which would not go far among so many men.

Chaloner knew his earl would want an eyewitness account of the beggar's death, so he decided to stop at White Hall on his way home. The streets were strangely quiet, and the churches, which had been compelled to hold special services of thanksgiving for the three-year anniversary, were mostly empty. The stalls that lined busy King Street were dutifully shuttered, although their owners had been furious at the royal decree prohibiting trade that day – Fridays were always good for commerce because of the many markets taking place. Dogs scavenged among the rubbish that carpeted the cobbles, and a preacher stood on a box and informed passers-by that the world would shortly be consumed by fire and brimstone, so folk had better repent while they could.

The sprawling Palace of White Hall, London's chief royal residence, had been built piecemeal as and when past monarchs had had the money and the need, and the result was a chaotic settlement with dozens of separate buildings, few of which seemed to bear any relation to their neighbours. Thus ancient, windowless halls rubbed shoulders with flamboyant Tudor monstrosities, and dark, grubby alleys sometimes opened out into elegant courtyards fringed with glorious gems of architecture.

Chaloner was still dressed in his street-cleaner's disguise, which was simultaneously an advantage and a drawback. On the one hand, no one would recognise him, which was always a good thing, but on the other, he was more likely to be challenged as an intruder. Relishing an opportunity to practise his skills, he made his way undetected through the maze of yards, halls, sheds and houses, coming ever closer to the sumptuous apartments that overlooked the area of manicured grounds known as the Privy Garden, where the Earl of Clarendon had his offices.

Like most good spies, Chaloner worked hard at being nondescript. He was of medium height and stocky build, with brown hair and grey eyes. He had no obvious scars or marks, although his left leg had been badly mangled at the Battle of Naseby, and he tended to limp if he was tired or had engaged in overly strenuous exercise. That Friday had been an easy day for him, however, and he walked with a perfectly even gait along the corridor that led to the Earl's offices. He opened the door quickly, using a thin piece of metal to assist him when he found it locked, and stepped inside to wait.

It was not long before Lord Clarendon arrived. He stood in the hall outside, congratulating May for shooting the wicked traitor who had come so close to murdering the King. Williamson was with him, and his softer voice added its own praise. Chaloner grimaced. People were assuming that May had acted correctly, which meant any attempt to tell them what had really happened would look like sour grapes on his part – they would think he was making excuses for not killing the man himself. Eventually, Clarendon finished the conversation and bustled into his rooms. In his wake was a short, smiling man with bushy brown hair and dimples in his cheeks.

The Earl of Clarendon, who currently held office as Lord Chancellor of England, had gained weight since the Restoration. The Court's rich food was unsuitable for

26

a man who tended to fat and whose working day revolved around sedentary activities. Chaloner had even noticed a difference in the Earl's girth between the time he himself had been dispatched to Ireland to help quell a rebellion back in February and his return five days ago. the Earl knew he was expanding at an alarming rate, but blamed it on a nasty brush with gout, which had confined him to his bed for much of the past three months.

He had dispensed with the enormous blond wig he had worn in the procession, and had donned a smaller, more practical headpiece. He had also removed his elaborate ceremonial costume and wore a pair of peach-coloured breeches and a coat of dark green – although there was more lace on it than Chaloner thought was possible to attach to a single garment, and he hoped the man took care near naked flames. the Earl was chatting to his companion about a popular new cure-all called Venice Treacle, asking whether it might help with the residual pains in his lower legs.

When several minutes had passed, and the two men had still not noticed him in the shadows near the curtains, Chaloner cleared his throat. the Earl almost jumped out of his skin. He spun around in alarm, and then closed his eyes and rested a plump hand on his chest when he recognised the intruder.

'I wish you would not do that,' he snapped. 'One day my heart will leap so much that it will stop and never start again. And then where would you be?'

'I am sorry, sir,' said Chaloner, contrite. the Earl had asked on several occasions not to be startled, but noisy, attention-grabbing entrances tended to be anathema to a spy.

'I think *I* might be able to do something about a stopped

27

heart,' said the other man comfortably. 'I am a surgeon, after all, and intimately acquainted with that particular organ.'

'This is Thomas Lisle,' explained the Earl to Chaloner. 'He is Master of the Company of Barber-Surgeons, here to help me with my gout.'

'And you are a raker,' said Lisle, his eyes crinkling in a smile. 'However, as you have made your own way to My Lord Chancellor's rooms, and as he is not surprised to see you here, I surmise you are actually something rather different, and I shall enquire no further.'

'He is Thomas Heyden,' said Clarendon, obviously feeling an explanation was in order anyway. 'He has been at Westminster Abbey today, protecting the King against assassins.'

'We live in a wicked age,' said Lisle, shaking his head sadly. 'No one can be trusted, it seems.'

'You are right,' agreed the Earl sombrely, 'although Heyden has proven himself loyal to me twice now – once in retrieving some missing gold, and once when I sent him to Ireland with some of Williamson's men to thwart the Castle Plot. He acquitted himself admirably both times.'

While the Earl was speaking, Lisle produced several flasks from the bag he carried looped around his neck, and began to mix them in a goblet. He barely reached Chaloner's shoulder, and had the look of a gnome about him, with his brown face, kindly eyes and slightly stooped posture. He wore the red-trimmed gown and hat that identified his profession, and he hummed under his breath while he worked. When he had finished, he handed the cup to Clarendon with a conspiratorial grin.

'The apothecaries will be after my blood if they learn I am dispensing medicines – tonics are their domain, and they jealously defend their sole right to concoct them – but I refuse to watch a patient suffer when I can help him myself. The head of a young kite boiled in wine is the perfect remedy for gout, although you will not find an *apothecary* who will ever share such a closely guarded secret.'

'Thank you,' said Clarendon, wincing as he swallowed the draft. 'It was kind of you to come the moment I experienced a twinge. The damp weather must have aggravated my condition and I am eager to nip it in the bud this time. I do not want to be laid up for another three months.'

'Keep your legs warm and dry,' instructed Lisle, packing away his empty phials. 'And apply that poultice I gave you before you retire tonight. There is nothing like an ointment of crushed snails, suet of goat and saffron to ease your particular trouble.'

'Lisle is a good man,' said Clarendon, when the surgeon had left. 'The only thing I do not like about him is his association with another *medicus* called Johnson, who is a loud, blustering fellow, full of wind and unfounded opinions. *He* openly supports that vile heathen, the Earl of Bristol.'

'Lisle does?'

'Johnson does. Lisle is like Williamson – he declines to take either side – although anyone with an ounce of sense will see that *I* am in the right and Bristol is wrong. However, as Master of the Company of Barber-Surgeons, Lisle will not want to offend half his members by declaring an allegiance with me.'

'It is a sorry state of affairs, sir,' said Chaloner in a way that he hoped would discourage further confidences. Clarendon had ranted at him about Bristol before, and the tirades were difficult to stop once they had started.

He tried to think of a way to change the subject, but nothing came to mind.

Clarendon looked pained. 'Bristol is *determined* to destroy me, you know, Heyden.'

'You are Lord Chancellor of England, sir,' said Chaloner, when he saw the matter was not to be avoided, 'while Bristol holds no official post whatsoever. You are in a far stronger position to fight any battle than he.' He wondered if it was true – the gay and witty Bristol was much more popular at Court than the stuffy, respectable Clarendon.

'I suppose so.' the Earl pulled himself together and forced a smile. 'You did not come to talk about my troubles, though. I assume you are here to give me your version of today's shooting?'

'I thought you might have questions.' Chaloner did not like the way the Earl had phrased his question – it made it sound as though he was expecting to hear something other than the truth.

'I do – especially since Colonel Holles told me what *really* happened. He saw you apprehend the beggar without incident, and thinks someone was overly hasty with the trigger. He has a point: it does seem to be a pity that we have lost the chance to interrogate a would-be regicide.'

'Will Holles tell Williamson this?' asked Chaloner hopefully.

Clarendon shook his head. 'I said he should keep it to himself. May has a wicked temper, and we do not want him thinking *you* have been going around questioning his actions to all and sundry. As I have told you before, your old mentor Thurloe sent you to me on the understanding that I am careful with you. And while

Thurloe lost *most* of his power when the Restoration saw him dismissed from his posts as Secretary of State and Spymaster General, he still has teeth and claws aplenty. I do not want *him* coming after me because May has skewered you in a silly duel.'

Chaloner tried to conceal his exasperation. When he had arrived in London the previous year, penniless and desperate for employment, Thurloe had indeed recommended him to Clarendon with the stipulation that his life was not to be needlessly squandered. However, the 'request' had been issued at a time when other spies had been murdered while working at White Hall, and that particular danger was long over. the Earl's continued unease about what Thurloe might do if Chaloner was harmed was beginning to be a nuisance.

'With respect, My Lord, I can look after myself – especially against May.'

'So you say, but your profession is a risky one. How many elderly spies does one ever meet? None! And it is not *you* I am worried about, anyway – it is me. Thurloe has too many old friends like you – dangerous men who will still do anything for him. I have no intention of crossing him.'

Chaloner was astonished that the Earl should consider him dangerous, sure he had never given him cause to think so. He ignored the comment and addressed the slur on Thurloe's character instead. 'He is not a vindictive man, sir.'

the Earl raised an eyebrow. 'You do not serve seven years in government without learning something about neutralising your enemies, believe me. But let us return to today. Did you manage to talk to this beggar before he died?'

Chaloner decided he was unwilling to divulge the vagrant's gabbled claims to anyone at White Hall until he had at least some idea about what he had been trying to communicate. 'A little,' he replied vaguely. 'He claimed he had information to impart, but declined to confide in me.'

the Earl stroked his tiny beard – a thumbnail-sized patch under his lower lip; it matched his little moustache. 'Do you think May shot him to prevent this information from being passed on?'

Chaloner frowned, puzzled. 'Why would he do that? The beggar seemed to think the government might be interested in what he had to say.'

the Earl raised his hands in a shrug. 'Because of what Holles told me: that the fellow was killed *after* you had relieved him of his dag. May is a devious fellow, with fingers in a great many pies. Perhaps he has his own reasons for wanting to still the beggar's mouth before it started flapping.'

It was an intriguing notion, although Chaloner was wary of embracing it too eagerly; he did not want his dislike of May to lead him astray. 'If Williamson is worth his salt as Spymaster, he will have reservations about the necessity of the execution, too.'

'May said he did it to save your life, and Williamson believes him. This beggar had a knife.'

'He posed no danger, and May should have known it. Besides, I suspect Williamson would happily sacrifice me for the chance to converse with a would-be assassin. Perhaps you are right, My Lord: May *did* want to silence him before he said anything incriminating.'

'What did the fellow say to you?' asked Clarendon curiously. 'Holles says he saw you chatting for several moments before the shot rang out.'

Chaloner hesitated. the Earl could not always be trusted to keep secrets – not from any desire to cause trouble, but from his tendency to be overly trusting of the people he met – and if his suspicions about May were correct, then Chaloner would be safer if no one knew the beggar had died reciting names. 'He was declaring his innocence – telling me he was no king-killer.'

'And what do *you* think? Did he intend to shoot the King?'

Chaloner considered the question carefully. He had believed the man's claim that waylaying Williamson had been his main objective, and the weapon had been in no state for a serious attempt at regicide anyway. 'Not everyone in possession of a gun is bent on murder,' he said eventually.

the Earl walked to the window and stared out at the wet garden. The wind blew misty sheets of rain across the perfectly symmetrical flower beds and the tiny clipped hedges. Chaloner went to stand next to him. He did not like the artificial neatness of White Hall's grounds, and preferred the tangled, chaotic jumble of places like Lincoln's Inn, where long grass grew among wild flowers, and where trees were gnarled and misshapen with age. It was some time before the Earl spoke.

'May brought the body to White Hall, and it looked familiar to me. I am sure he was no vagrant.'

Chaloner was startled that Clarendon should recognise the man. 'Where might you have seen him before, sir?'

the Earl shook his head slowly. 'That is the annoying thing: I cannot recall. Perhaps I am mistaken, what with his stubbly chin and his dirty clothes. Yet there was some-thing about him . . . '

'Would you like me to find out who he was?'

Clarendon shrugged. 'If you like. I do not have much else for you to do at the moment, and it may transpire to be important, I suppose. Yes, carry on, if you cannot think of anything better to occupy your time.'

He could not have sounded less enthusiastic had he tried.

One of the advantages of having a monarch, rather than a Commonwealth, was that His Majesty's subjects were often allowed inside White Hall to watch him dine, should they feel so inclined. The Earl of Clarendon *was* so inclined, because that Friday was a special occasion, and the King's cooks had been ordered to produce something suitably impressive. As a man deeply interested in food, Lord Clarendon was keen to know what they had devised. Chaloner borrowed a cloak to conceal his raker's rags and accompanied him to the Banqueting House, where the spectacle was due to take place. Personally, the spy failed to understand the appeal of the event – as far as he was concerned, all it did was make him feel hungry.

The Banqueting House gallery – a raised wooden structure that allowed observers to look down on the floor below – was so full that Chaloner wondered whether it was in danger of collapse. Between the jostling onlookers, he caught glimpses of a table laden with gleaming silver dishes and platters. The King's dark wig bobbed this way and that as he conversed with his fellow diners. His Queen sat beside him, although she ate little, and seemed more interested in watching the flirtatious antics of Lady Castlemaine than in doing justice to the splendid repast that lay in front of her.

It was difficult to see much, so the Earl, becoming

bored, began to ask questions about Chaloner's recent visit to Ireland. Chaloner tried to point out that a crowded gallery was not the best place for a briefing about such a sensitive matter, but the Earl dismissed his concerns with a wave of his hand.

'You arrived home five days ago, but when you gave me your initial report, I was preoccupied with a nasty remark Bristol had made about me. Tell me again. What did you say the Castle Plot was about? Discontented soldiers, who had bought estates during the Commonwealth, but who had had them confiscated when we Royalists returned to power?'

Chaloner nodded as he glanced around him. No one seemed to be listening. 'The disinherited farmers took exception to the ruling, so they decided to storm Dublin Castle and kidnap the Lord Lieutenant of Ireland – hold him to ransom until their land was returned.'

'But unfortunately for them, the plot was doomed, because Spymaster Williamson had wind of it months ago. He sent secret agents to infiltrate the rebels, and I lent him your services because he needed all the intelligencers he could get – even ones who once worked for Cromwell. Did *you* tell me William Scot was among the government's army of spies, or did I hear it from someone else?'

'Someone else,' replied Chaloner, a little indignantly. He was not in the habit of braying about his colleagues' exploits to those who did not need to know about them, and Scot was a friend. Not only had they known each other since childhood, but both had been in Thurloe's pay during the Commonwealth, and Scot's father, like Chaloner's uncle, had been a regicide. Wisely, Scot had taken the precaution of changing sides *before* Cromwell had died, so was not regarded with the same suspicion

35

as was Chaloner, and he was currently in Spymaster Williamson's employ.

'May told Williamson that the revolt failed because of the ingenuity of one man: May himself,' the Earl went on. 'Scot's brother Thomas was one of the conspirators, and it was *May* who persuaded Thomas to betray his fellow rebels. The affair ended with a whimper, and no lives were lost on our side.'

Chaloner nodded cautiously. The plan to 'turn' Thomas had actually been Scot's, although the notion had been mooted in such a way that May genuinely believed it was his own. It had allowed Scot to save his brother from a traitor's death, while simultaneously protecting himself from any later accusations of favouritism towards a kinsman. May, of course, had been more than happy to take the credit that should, by rights, have gone to Scot.

'So, Thomas sold his fellow insurgents in exchange for a pardon,' the Earl concluded. 'And there was a happy conclusion to the affair – for everyone except you and the plotters.'

Chaloner regarded him uneasily. Secretly, he had been sympathetic to the rioters' complaints. His own family had given every last penny to the Roundhead cause, and had been compensated with land when Cromwell had won the wars. But now the Royalists were back, those estates had been reclaimed – along with others legally purchased during the Commonwealth. He appreciated the fact that the original owners wanted what was theirs, but some farms had been bought for a fair price and worked for twelve years, and he felt ownership was not always a straightforward matter. However, he had never confided his opinions to anyone, so there was no way the Earl could know his real thoughts.

'You played too small a role in crushing the revolt,' elaborated the Earl, much to Chaloner's relief. 'Others – like May – claimed the glory, while you stayed in the shadows. Why?'

Chaloner felt he should not need to explain the obvious – and he had actually worked very hard in Ireland, successfully completing a number of tasks that the other intelligencers had deemed too dangerous or impossible. 'If I had exposed my identity by clamouring for recognition, I would be no use to you, sir. Spying and fame are not good bedfellows.'

'May does not seem affected by the attention,' argued the Earl. 'And neither does William Scot.'

Chaloner tried not to sound patronising. 'Have you *seen* Scot, sir?' the Earl thought for a moment, then shook his head. 'That is because he left for Surinam as soon as the Castle Plot was unmasked, and although people know his name, no one knows what he looks like. He has maintained his cover.'

'May has not.'

'No,' agreed Chaloner. 'May has not. And every rebel in England knows him.'

the Earl dismissed his point by flapping his plump fingers. 'His report said you were no help at all, and Williamson believes it – I heard the Spymaster say he expected no less from a former Parliamentarian. However, *I* am prepared to give you the benefit of the doubt, and that is what really matters. *I* know you, and you are not a fellow to shirk his duties.'

'Thank you, sir,' said Chaloner, wondering what he could do to make May stop his libellous campaign. Such documents had a habit of reappearing at awkward moments, and he did not want to be permanently tarnished by one man's spiteful writings, especially given their inaccuracy.

Suddenly, the Earl tensed and seized his arm in a painful pinch, his attention fixed on the King's table. '*Bristol* is dining with His Majesty. Look!'

Chaloner freed himself, wincing. 'So he is.'

'How dare he!' raged Clarendon, working himself into a temper. 'I am Lord Chancellor of England, and *I* was not invited to be there, so why should he be? It is insupportable! He is like a filthy bluebottle, always showing up in places where he is not wanted.'

Chaloner refrained from pointing out that Bristol looked anything but not wanted – the King was obviously enjoying his company, and even the Queen was smiling. As if he sensed their gaze upon him, Bristol glanced up at the gallery and his eyes lit on the outraged earl. With calculated insolence, he raised a lace-draped hand and waved. Clarendon gaped at him, then turned and shouldered his way outside. Immediately, Bristol threw back his head and laughed, making sure he did so loud enough for his enemy to hear.

'Horrible man!' snarled Clarendon, when he and his spy were alone again. 'Did you see how he mocked me? How can His Majesty sit beside him and permit such low antics?'

'He had no idea what Bristol was doing,' said Chaloner soothingly. He had seen the puzzled look the King had shot in his companion's direction at the sudden explosion of mirth.

Clarendon regained some of his composure. 'No? Well, that is something at least. Did I ever tell you the origins of the quarrel that has turned Bristol so violently against me?'

38

'Yes, sir,' replied Chaloner, trying not to sound bored or insolent. As far as he could tell, the dispute was far from black and white: Bristol had done some very nasty things to Clarendon, but Clarendon had reciprocated in kind. 'You debarred him from holding any official post because he is Catholic. I can understand why he finds that annoying.'

'*You* take his side against me now?' cried Clarendon in dismay. 'I expected more from you! And it was not *my* decision to ban him – I was merely following the law. It is illegal for papists to hold political positions, and it would have been remiss of me to overlook the matter of his religion.'

Chaloner had never liked the notion of religious suppression, mainly because history showed such tactics tended to breed fanatics. 'Such a rigid stance will bring you trouble, sir,' he warned.

'It has already brought me trouble. Bristol hates me, and is recruiting like-minded villains to stand with him. His latest ally is the *Lady*.' Clarendon's voice dropped to a disgusted whisper when he made reference to the King's favourite mistress. So intense was his dislike of the Countess of Castlemaine that he could never bring himself to utter her name.

'I am sorry, sir.' Chaloner *was* sorry; *he* would not want Lady Castlemaine as an enemy, and thought the Earl was in deep water if she had thrown in her lot with Bristol.

'Did you know that Bristol spends so much time with the King – playing cards – that I am obliged to make appointments days ahead when I need to see him on important affairs of state? *And* he reeks of onions!'

'Onions?' asked Chaloner, nonplussed.

'He has a penchant for them, although I cannot imagine why – they are peasants' food. Perhaps he likes them because he is a papist.'

Chaloner did not know what to say to such a distasteful remark.

'I cannot forget that mocking laugh he just directed at me,' Clarendon went on worriedly. 'Do you think it means he knows something I don't – he has instigated some plot that will see me harmed?'

Chaloner was sure of it – a clever, ambitious man like Bristol was not going to let himself be deprived of lucrative honours without recourse to some kind of revenge. 'You might be wise to be ready for—' he began.

'You are right. Forget the beggar – or better yet, investigate him in your spare time – and concentrate on learning what Bristol intends instead. That is far more important now. You must adopt a disguise and infiltrate his lair.'

Chaloner's pulse quickened. He liked disguises. 'Do you have anything specific in mind, sir?'

the Earl was thinking fast. 'My London home – Worcester House – is due to be redecorated, and I have asked several famous artists to submit plans. Bristol's abode on Great Queen Street is also in need of refurbishment, which means he is sure to try one of two things: poach the man I hire in order to cause me inconvenience, or try to recruit him to spy on me.'

'You want me to pose as a decorator and—'

'We call them upholsterers, Heyden.' Clarendon rubbed his plump hands together gleefully. 'This is an excellent plan! Why did I not think of it sooner? A spy in his own house! What could be better?'

But Chaloner could see problems. 'It *is* a good plan,

40

sir, but there is one flaw: Bristol is notoriously short of funds, and cannot afford the services of an upholsterer – or be able to bribe one to spy on his enemies.'

the Earl was not listening, however. 'And because you know nothing about interior design, you can make a mess of his house at the same time. You speak Dutch like a native, so you can be Kristiaan Vanders from The Hague. I wrote inviting him to visit, but he is indisposed.'

And there was another problem. 'That would be in-advisable, sir,' said Chaloner gently. 'Vanders died three years ago. Can we choose someone else?'

'No. This is a brilliant idea. My mind is made up, so do not argue with me.'

Chaloner fell silent, thinking it was a good thing that Williamson was in charge of the intelligence services, because the Earl would be a disaster. His skill in diplomacy and politics was legendary, yet Chaloner had seen him make some astoundingly idiotic decisions where spying was concerned. When he saw no further objections were forthcoming, the Earl continued, somewhat defensively.

'*I* had not heard of Vanders's demise, so the chances are that no one else will, either. It is a perfect disguise for you, with your knowledge of Dutch affairs. Find out all you can about Bristol, because if I lose my war against him, I will not be his only victim – who will employ you if I am in the Tower?'

Chapter 2

At first, Chaloner was unhappy about the task he had been allotted, because he was painfully aware of his lack of knowledge about the Court and its political alliances, and such places could be dangerous for the uninformed. Then he realised that disguising himself as a foreigner would explain his ignorance to anyone who might be suspicious of him. His concerns began to evaporate, and he saw the assignment might even be turned to his advantage – it would give him an opportunity to rectify his appalling unfamiliarity with English affairs. He took his leave of the Lord Chancellor in a thoughtful frame of mind, busily analysing ideas for the deception.

He could not walk directly to the main gate, because a street-sweeper so near the royal apartments would be sure to attract unwanted attention – the palace guards had been trained to shoot first and ask questions second where the King's safety was concerned – so he followed a tortuous route through storerooms and servants' quarters instead. He was crossing a yard occupied by the Queen's laundresses and their steaming boiler houses when he saw a familiar face. He smiled, feeling his spirits lift even further. Eaffrey Johnson had been a Royalist spy in Holland, and although she and Chaloner had worked for rival factions, they had often shared information when they felt an alliance would better serve their country's interests. For a while, they had been lovers, too, although the affair had floundered when she had followed the King to France and Chaloner's duties had kept him in the Netherlands. More recently, she had been in Ireland, with a remit to seduce high-ranking rebels, but Chaloner had not known she was back in London.

She was talking to the Countess of Castlemaine, whose stomach bulged with the King's next illegitimate child. 'The Lady' was generally acknowledged to be the most beautiful woman at Court, although Chaloner thought her face was too spiteful to be truly attractive, and her infamous temper was already scoring scowl marks around her eyes and mouth. She might well be lovely when she smiled, but he had only ever seen her angry.

'And he still has that diamond ring from the French ambassador,' she was saying when Chaloner edged closer, plying his broom and keeping his face hidden under his broad-brimmed hat. 'I told him I wanted it, but he always makes excuses when I order him to hand it over.'

'You order him?' asked Eaffrey, in an awed voice. 'You *order* the King?'

'Of course I do. He had better not pass it to the Queen, not when he promised it to *me*.'

'I doubt he would be so rash,' said Eaffrey ambiguously. 'I hear you are to move to new quarters.'

Lady Castlemaine laughed, although it was not a pleasant sound. 'I am weary of dashing across the Privy Garden in my nightshift each time I feel like Charles's company, and the new arrangement will be much more

43

convenient for our nightly frolics. The rooms are better, too – nicer than the Queen's.'

When she had gone, Chaloner shadowed Eaffrey until she reached a narrow lane sandwiched between the river and the series of ramshackle sheds known as the Small Beer Buttery, then darted forward to grab her arm. A knife immediately appeared in her hand, but her face broke into a grin of delight when she recognised her assailant. She flung her arms around his neck and kissed him.

Although not classically pretty – her face was too round and her eyes far too mischievous – there was something captivating about Eaffrey. She was in her twenties, but possessed a cool self-assurance that made people assume she was older. Chaloner gestured to her clothes, which boasted a neckline that plunged indecently low and skirts that clung to her hips in a way that ensured everyone would know exactly what lay beneath.

'Has Williamson set you to bewitch some hapless courtier and make him reveal all his secrets?'

Her eyebrows shot up in amusement. 'Are you implying my costume makes me a whore?'

He shrugged. 'They set you in Lady Castlemaine's camp of loose women. My Lord Clarendon railed about them at length yesterday.'

She pulled a disapproving face. 'All is sobriety and prudery with your earl – he is worse than the Puritans. Personally, I hope Bristol *does* manage to rid us of the tedious old bore! I like Lady Castlemaine's light-hearted gaiety, though, and I am delighted that she has taken me under her wing. She has taught me a lot about the Court and its customs.'

Chaloner was not sure Lady Castlemaine's advice would be the sort of knowledge most decent women would want to own, but he was deeply fond of Eaffrey, and was loath to offend her by revealing his conservatism where the Court was concerned. He looked to where the Lady was screeching abuse at a servant who had splashed her with milk from a pail as their paths had crossed. 'She seems to have developed a powerful yearning for the King's jewellery,' he said instead.

'His Christmas presents, to be precise. Surely you must have heard how she cajoled him into parting with them? Well, it is true, and the only thing he has managed to keep for himself is a diamond ring – but I do not fancy his chances of hanging on to it for much longer. Why are you dressed like a vagrant? Is it something to do with the coronation celebrations?'

'Someone told Williamson that the King might be shot at today, and every available agent in London was detailed to protect him. I was working with our old friend Adrian May.'

She grimaced her disgust. 'That toad! He is a dangerous fool, as we both saw in Ireland – the rebels *would* have succeeded in kidnapping the governor had you not stepped in and put an end to his stupid antics. And now he hates you for exposing his ignorance, so you should be wary of him.'

'I know.'

'Of course, the *real* reason for his dislike is that he knows you are a better spy than he – and that if you ever do work for Williamson, it will only be a matter of time before you displace him. He will do anything to avoid that, including wielding a sly dagger in a dark lane. Just yesterday, William heard him telling a courtier called Willys how he would dearly love to be rid of you.'

'William?' asked Chaloner, unconcerned with threats

45

issued by the likes of Adrian May. 'You mean Scot? I thought he had gone to Surinam.'

She grinned, showing small white teeth. 'That is what everyone thinks, but he is here, in White Hall, busy with his latest assignment for Williamson. If you meet a bumbling Irish scholar called Peter Terrell, you will know he is a friend.'

'Terrell?' Chaloner had heard the name, but it was a moment before it snapped into place: the beggar had mentioned it – 'Terrell is not what he says.' He had obviously seen through the disguise.

Before he could ask her about it, Eaffrey laughed, the tinkling, sunny sound he remembered so well. 'Speak of the Devil and he will appear. May I introduce you to this raker, Mr Terrell?'

Chaloner shook his head in mute admiration when a tall figure approached, knowing he would never have recognised his old friend had Eaffrey not given him away. He tried to remember when he had last seen Scot as himself, and decided it must have been fifteen years ago, during the wars. He could not say what colour his hair might be, because it was never the same shade twice, and his face had been so variously marked with scars, warts and freckles that Chaloner had no idea which were real and which were the result of pastes and plasters. Most of what Chaloner knew about disguises had been learned from Scot, who was ten years his senior.

That day Scot was dressed in a fashionable coat of deep red, which was enlivened with a sash of yellow satin, and there was an exotic flower pinned among the frothing lace at his throat. Under his arm, he carried a book entitled *Musaeum Tradescantianum*, a catalogue of the remarkable collection of artefacts and plants held in

46

Oxford. His cheeks had been shadowed to make them appear sallow, and he had somehow lengthened his nose. The only familiar feature was his pale-blue eyes.

Scot peered at Chaloner, then laughed. 'I trained *you* well – I did not recognise you at all! I saw a rough villain follow Eaffrey to this secluded alley, and I came to protect her virtue.'

Eaffrey showed him her knife. 'Your chivalry was unnecessary, although appreciated.'

'I hear you are posing as a scholar,' said Chaloner, nodding at the book Scot held.

Scot nodded, eyes gleaming with a sudden and uncharacteristic passion – he was not usually an effusive man. 'Williamson asked me to explore accusations of fraud in the Royal Society, but I quickly learned there is nothing amiss. However, I have neglected to tell him so, because the Society's meetings are so damned fascinating – especially anything to do with botanicals. Would you believe I have actually read this book and enjoyed every word?'

It did not sound very likely, and Chaloner doubted such a dry subject would hold Scot's bright mind for long. Scot sensed his scepticism.

'I mean it, Chaloner. I am weary of espionage and its dangers, and the sooner I can take a ship for Surinam, where I shall spend my days studying its flora, the better.'

'Why are you here, then?' asked Chaloner. 'You could be on your way now. Or is Williamson reluctant to release one of his most experienced and valued spies?'

Scot smiled. 'I have not told him my decision to leave yet, although he will be peeved when I do. He has come to trust me, despite May's constant whispers that former Parliamentarians should be banned from the intelligence services. However, the reason I am still here is

47

my brother – I cannot leave as long as Thomas is a prisoner in the Tower.'

Chaloner was intrigued. 'You intend to help him escape?'

'Christ, no! We are talking about the Tower here, Chaloner, not some city gaol! I want him out, but I have no desire to be killed in the process. I shall rescue him by diplomatic means – by oiling the right palms, and by bringing pressure to bear on those with influence. I *will* prevail – hopefully soon – and then I shall leave England for good.'

'I shall be sorry to lose you,' said Chaloner, meaning it.

Scot looked away. 'And there is the rub. I will miss my friends – and you two most of all.'

A dank, dripping lane in the nether regions of White Hall was no place for friends to exchange news, so Chaloner, Scot and Eaffrey went to the Crown, a cook-shop on nearby King Street. It was not a very salubrious establishment, and its owner, a man named Wilkinson, had a reputation for being rude to his customers. The Crown had once been a tavern, but had started to sell food when Wilkinson realised there was a palace full of hungry courtiers opposite. It was a large building, filled with the scent of baked pies, spilled ale and tobacco smoke. Eaffrey, Scot and Chaloner ordered beef pasties with onions, and something called a 'green tansy', which Wilkinson declined to define, but which transpired to be a mess of eggs, cream, spinach and sugar.

As they ate, Chaloner and Scot discussed their families. Chaloner's was maintaining a low profile in a quiet part of Buckinghamshire, patiently waiting for Cavaliers to tire of baiting old Roundheads. Meanwhile, Scot's father, executed for regicide, had been Thurloe's predecessor as Spymaster, and his two sons had followed him into espionage. Unfortunately, Thomas was not very good at it, as his incarceration in the Tower attested. Finally, there was the daughter of the house.

'And Alice?' Chaloner asked cautiously. He was always uncomfortable when discussing the one member of the Scot family who did not much care for him. 'How is she?'

Scot clapped him on the shoulder, laughing at his unease. 'She still has not forgiven you for fighting that duel with her first husband, and spits fire every time your name is mentioned.'

'He challenged me,' objected Chaloner. 'I was willing to overlook the fact that he had been selling Cromwell's secrets to the enemy, but *he* was the one who insisted honour should be satisfied. He was lucky you were there to plead his case, because I should have killed him for what he had done.'

'The fact that he was in the wrong makes no difference to Alice,' said Scot, still grinning. 'But her wrath will fade eventually, especially now he is dead. Incidentally, her period of mourning is over now, and she is on the prowl for a replacement. However, I categorically refuse to give my blessing to her current choice. Sir Richard Temple is *not* a man I want as a brother-in-law. He is corrupt, greedy, selfish and – worst of all – a politician.'

'Leave her alone,' advised Eaffrey. 'A woman her age does not need a meddling brother telling her what to do.'

'The meddling brother does not want her hitched to a man who is only after her money,' retorted Scot tartly. 'I despise Temple, and will do all I can to prevent the match.'

Chaloner recalled that Alice's first husband had been rich, and she had inherited everything when he had died. 'Surely her wealth will attract someone more suitable? There must be hundreds of decent, but poor, men who might . . . ' He thrashed around for a more polite alternative to 'put up with her'.

'She says Temple is the only one who fulfils her exacting standards,' explained Scot. 'God alone knows what they are, because they certainly do not include looks, character, integrity or charm.'

'I have a lover,' said Eaffrey casually, after a brief silence during which Wilkinson brought more beer. 'His name is Johan Behn and he is a merchant from Brandenburg. I shall marry him soon.'

Chaloner was amazed. Eaffrey's lifestyle – like his own – was not suited for serious relationships, and she had always declared that she would never give up her freedom for something as mundane and repressive as a husband. He supposed her opinions must have moderated over time, and recalled her mentioning someone special when they had been in Ireland. They had been too busy to discuss it then.

She smiled dreamily. 'I missed him dreadfully when we were in Dublin, and I find myself happier in his company than at any other time. I suppose that is love. And he is very handsome.'

'Rich, too,' added Scot impishly. 'Which is far more important.'

'That is probably what this Temple thinks about Alice,' said Chaloner. He changed the subject before he could land himself in trouble – Scot was fiercely protective of his siblings. 'What do you know about my Earl's feud with Bristol? So far, I have only heard one side of the story.'

'I can imagine,' said Scot wryly. 'Clarendon holds forth to anyone who will listen and, as his spy, you can hardly ask him to talk about something else. However, while *he* is decent and honest – albeit deadly dull – there is something a little knavish about Bristol.'

Eaffrey ate some tansy. 'He kissed me last week, and I thought I would faint from the reek of onions. I swear he eats them raw! And his clothes are horribly unfashionable. Yet even so, I prefer him to Lord Clarendon and his moralising.'

Chaloner regarded her askance. 'You are in love with your new beau, but you let Bristol kiss you?'

She pushed him playfully. 'I still need to earn a crust, and Spymaster Williamson wanted information only Bristol could provide. It was not easy to flutter my eyelashes at one without the other noticing, but I have always enjoyed a challenge.'

'I wish you would not take such risks,' said Scot unhappily. 'Now you have captured Behn's heart, you have no reason to court danger on Williamson's behalf.'

'Bristol is hardly dangerous,' said Eaffrey contemptuously. 'Not to me, at least – although Lord Clarendon should watch him. Do not look shocked, Tom. I have always said that lying with a man is the easiest way to make him part with his secrets, although I would not recommend *you* try it. It is best left to women, who know what they are doing.'

'I am not shocked,' said Chaloner, who knew perfectly well why Eaffrey often succeeded where her male colleagues failed. 'I am concerned. White Hall is a breeding ground for gossip, and it will only be a matter of time before someone tells your Johan about Bristol. You may lose him . . . '

51

She flapped her hand impatiently. 'He will never find out. Try this tansy. It is rather unusual.'

'Sugar-coated spinach is rarely anything else.' Chaloner tried again to make his point. 'If your lover learns that you and Bristol—'

'Did you hear about that murder on The Strand three weeks ago?' interrupted Eaffrey. She ate more tansy, not seeming to care that the landlord had provided them with some very odd victuals. 'A wealthy merchant was reeling home from the annual Guinea Company dinner, when he was stabbed.'

Scot grimaced. 'I inveigled an invitation to that particular feast – as Peter Terrell – because my would-be brother-in-law is a member of the Guinea Company, and I wanted to watch him on his home turf. It was a tedious occasion, and I shall devise another way to spy on the fellow in future.'

'You found it tedious?' asked Eaffrey. 'Johan was there, and *he* said it was overly lively. He reported several violent arguments, three of which were settled by duels the following morning.'

Chaloner watched her eat. 'Is that what happened to the man killed on The Strand? He lost a duel?'

'I have no idea – I only mentioned him as a means to stop you passing judgement on my personal life. It was the first thing that came into my head. The second is William's brother: how is he surviving in the Tower?'

'Why is he still in prison at all?' asked Chaloner curiously. 'Surely he must have told Williamson everything he knows by now? And anyway, I thought the agreement was for him to reveal the identities of his conspirators and then be allowed to live out his days in peaceful exile.'

'So did I,' replied Scot bitterly, 'but unfortunately, some

senior officials are now saying Williamson did not have the authority to make such a pact. I wish you were not so keen to follow a career in intelligence, Chaloner. Now is the time to leave the spying business, not immerse yourself more deeply in it.'

'The beggar May shot today mentioned you before he died,' said Chaloner. He did not have the luxury to make the choice Scot was suggesting, because he needed to earn a living and was qualified to do very little else. 'He told me Terrell is not what he says.'

Scot regarded him uneasily. 'Obviously he is right, but how did *he* know?'

'He must have discovered that "Terrell" is an alias.' Eaffrey finished the tansy with a satisfied sigh. 'Someone in Williamson's office has been indiscreet.'

Scot was thoughtful. 'The only spy I do not trust is Adrian May, but even he has more sense than to gossip about such matters. However, there is a fishmonger called Peter Terrell – I have never met him, but I am told he is a terrible rogue. Perhaps this beggar was talking about him.'

'I need to identify him,' confided Chaloner. 'The beggar, I mean.'

'When I heard the body had been taken to White Hall, I tried to inspect it.' Scot smiled at Chaloner. 'I thought May might use the incident to harm you – by telling Williamson that it was your fault he was shot before he could be questioned. I wanted to see if there was anything on the corpse that might exonerate you.'

'Was there?' asked Chaloner, not surprised by Scot's course of action. They had always looked out for each other, and had their situations been reversed, he would have done the same.

'I only managed a glance before May ousted me. He had wrapped the fellow's head in a sack, so I could not see his face. However, I was able to observe that his clothes – his *disguise*, I should say – had chafed his clean, soft skin. *Ergo*, I suspect your "beggar" was a person of some standing, used to better-quality attire.'

'Then I shall have to follow the lead provided by the gun,' said Chaloner, disappointed there was not more. 'The manufacturer's details were on the barrel: Trulocke of St Martin's Lane. Perhaps *he* can tell me the name of the man who bought it, because it was a relatively new weapon.'

Scot's handsome face creased into a frown of concern. 'Did this "beggar" say anything else? I do not like the notion that strangers know secrets about me.'

'He mentioned Terrell and Burne, and was insistent that Dillon should be saved.'

Scot thought carefully. 'I have never heard of Dillon, although it is a fairly common Irish name. *You* know someone called Burne, though – Gregory Burne.'

'I do?' It rang vague bells, but Chaloner could not place it.

'Come on, Chaloner! You were never so slow witted in Holland – and you will not last long in this pit of vipers if you do not pull yourself together.'

Chaloner looked to Eaffrey for help. She appeared equally blank, but suddenly snapped her fingers. 'It was the name May adopted in Dublin. He could not use his own, because *everyone* knows Williamson hires a spy called May, so he made one up.'

'Christ!' muttered Chaloner, wondering how he could have been so dim – although in his defence, he had only heard May's alias once. The antagonism between them had been so intense that he had tried to stay out of the

54

man's way, afraid it might harm their operation. Foiling the Castle Plot had been far too important a matter to risk over personal rivalries.

'So,' mused Scot, seeing understanding dawn in his eyes. 'It seems your beggar *was* referring to me and not the fishmonger, since he knew May's alias, as well as mine. How did he come by such information? And who is the Dillon you are supposed to save?'

Chaloner was thoughtful. 'May claimed the man was working alone, but I had a feeling there was more to him than a lone gunman. This investigation might be more complex than I anticipated.'

'It might,' warned Eaffrey. 'And you do not know where it might lead, so watch your step.'

Scot stood. 'There is a Royal Society gathering tonight – Robert Boyle is going to talk about the proportional relation between elasticity and pressure, which promises to be exciting. Good luck, Chaloner – and please be careful. Far too many of our colleagues have died spying over the last decade, and I do not want to lose any more.'

The daylight was fading by the time Chaloner left the Crown, so he decided to go home and consider how he would discover the identity of the beggar *and* carry off his disguise as the Dutch upholsterer. The streets were still relatively empty as he made his way along The Strand, but it was just late enough for a different kind of citizen to emerge and slink along its manure-coated cobbles. His raker's disguise meant he was ignored by the pickpockets who prowled in search of easy prey, although a rumpus near the Savoy Palace indicated that others were not so lucky.

Home for Chaloner was a pair of dingy attics about halfway up Fetter Lane, rented from a landlord who was mildly eccentric and blissfully incurious about his tenants. Fetter Lane boasted a mixture of buildings. Some, like the house in which Chaloner lived, were dilapidated, and their owners should have invested money in replacing rotten timbers and sagging roofs. Others were new and pristine – although they would not stay that way for long in London's smoke-laden air. Opposite Chaloner's home was a large tavern called the Golden Lion, which had a reputation for turning a blind eye to all manner of seditious activities. In addition, its landlord ran an unofficial post office, which Chaloner found convenient as a means to collect and leave messages without revealing his own address. Farther south was the ugly Fetter Lane Independent Chapel, and from his bedroom window, Chaloner could see the roofs of several famous Inns of Court.

He reached his front door and climbed the uneven stairs to his garret, wondering whether the dark cracks that jagged through the plaster were new, or whether he had just failed to notice them before. A bucket placed to catch drips from a leaking roof suggested there was certainly something amiss. He reached his sitting room, noting the way the floor sloped to one side, something it had not done before Christmas, although his landlord told him there was nothing to be worried about. Chaloner was not so sure, but the rooms suited him for several reasons – they were centrally located, the neighbours did not object to him playing his viol, and they were cheap – and he was loath to give them up over something as inconsequential as imminent collapse.

As he shrugged out of his costume, his mind teemed with questions. He knew he needed to settle his thoughts before he attempted any sort of analysis, so he went to his bass viol, or viola de gamba, and began to practise a piece by the contemporary composer Matthew Locke. Chaloner was not the most talented of players, but music soothed him, concentrated his wits, and there was little he enjoyed more than joining like-minded people for an evening of chamber music. In the five days since he had returned from Ireland, he had been invited to join three such events. The Locke was planned for the next gathering, and Chaloner was looking forward to it.

After an hour, he lay on his bed and stared at the ceiling, thinking about the tasks he had been allotted. First, there was the beggar. The fellow had known details about Williamson's spies that were supposed to be secret, which suggested some connection to White Hall. What had he wanted Williamson to know? Was it just that Burne and Terrell were aliases – and the man naively imagined the Spymaster was unaware of the fact? Who was Dillon? And perhaps most important of all, why had May shot him when it had been obvious he had posed no threat? Had May known what the man had intended to tell Williamson? According to the beggar, May had already refused to grant him an audience with the Spymaster, so they had clearly met on a previous occasion – something May had neglected to mention. Why had May been secretive?

Chaloner thought about the beggar's behaviour during his last moments on Earth. He must have been desperate to secure an interview, because it was foolishness itself to loiter around royal processions with a firearm. The fact that it was not loaded would have been deemed irrelevant at any trial, although it suggested to Chaloner that the fellow's purpose had not been murder. He decided to visit Trulocke's shop as soon as it opened the following morning. Handguns were expensive, and he doubted many were sold, so it should not be too difficult to find out who had bought one.

The second assignment was spying on the Earl of Bristol. Chaloner knew he would have no trouble eavesdropping on sensitive conversations, because it was something at which he excelled. The challenge lay in knowing whom to stalk, because he was not sure which courtiers had taken Bristol's side, and who had remained loyal to Clarendon. He cursed his lack of knowledge about British politics: identifying the right men would take time, which might be something his earl did not have.

He turned his thoughts to his disguise. He recalled Vanders from Holland, a wizened, white-bearded ancient who spoke eccentric English. Chaloner could not make himself small, but he knew how to appear old and stooped, and he supposed poor English might encourage people to say things around him they might otherwise keep to themselves. He only hoped no one had either attended or heard about the upholsterer's lavish funeral in The Hague three years earlier.

Chaloner awoke to another grey day, already thinking about Vanders. The upholsterer had been wealthy but mean, and people had mocked his slovenly appearance. Chaloner rummaged in the chest where he kept the materials for his disguises, and emerged with an unfashionably short jerkin and a pair of petticoat breeches – an item of clothing so voluminous that it was possible to put both legs in the same hole and not notice. In a city where the current fashion was for long coats, knee-breeches and elaborate lacy socks known as 'boot hose', he knew he would stand out as suitably outmoded, while at the same time not looking so disreputable that he would not be allowed inside White Hall.

He found an ancient horsehair wig, and ensured all his own hair was tucked well inside it – it would only take one strand of brown to expose him as a man thirty years younger than the fellow he was attempting to emulate. Then, using a trick Scot had taught him, he glued a light coating of lambswool to his cheeks and chin to produce a tatty white beard. He applied powders and paints to construct some very plausible wrinkles around his eyes, and spent several minutes practising Vanders's crabbed, arthritic walk. He disliked being in White Hall without a sword, but Vanders had never worn one, so reluctantly he set it aside. He did not dispense with the arsenal of knives he kept concealed in his clothing, however. There was a limit, even to the best of disguises.

He went to the larder for something to eat before he began his day, but was not very inspired by the wizened turnips or the sack of wheat that sat amid the smattering of mouse droppings. He closed and locked the door, then clattered down the stairs, stopping to greet his landlord, who was waiting to ask whether he had seen a raker loitering around the house the previous morning. Fortunately for Chaloner, Daniel Ellis had not yet associated the appearance of some very odd characters with his tenant's vague explanations of what he did for a living. Ellis gazed curiously at Chaloner's attire.

'That is an odd assemblage. It makes you look three decades older.'

'Good,' said Chaloner. 'My brother wants me to meet a woman with a view to marriage.'

Ellis tapped the side of his nose in manly understanding.

59

'Well, that costume should certainly put her off. She will not want to wed Methuselah.'

The clocks were chiming six o'clock when Chaloner stepped out of the door on to Fetter Lane, and the city was wide awake. Carts rattled up and down, laden with wood, coal, hay, cloth and country-grown vegetables for the markets at Cheapside and Gracechurch Street. The harsh voices of street-sellers echoed between the tall buildings – a baker offered fresh pies, although they were black with dried gravy and dead flies; a milkmaid had cream in the pail she carried over her shoulder; and children tried to sell flowers they had picked before dawn in the nearby villages of Paddington and Stepney. It was a dull day, the sky a mass of solid white above. It was darkened by smoke from the thousands of fires lit to heat water and bread for breakfast, and the drizzle that began to fall was thick with soot.

There was no point in going to White Hall straight away, because no self-respecting courtier would be out of his bed until at least nine o'clock, and Chaloner did not want to roam deserted corridors and attract unnecessary attention. It was also too early to visit the gunsmith, as such places tended to open later than the stalls that sold foodstuffs. Instead, he headed for Hercules's Pillars Alley, a lane running south from Fleet Street, opposite the Church of St Dunstan-in-the-West. Just before he had left for Ireland, his friend Temperance North had bought a house there, and he had not yet been to see how she was settling in. It was an odd hour to call on anyone, but Temperance was a devout Puritan who always rose early for chapel, so he knew she would be awake.

Temperance had been left destitute and pregnant when her parents had died, but Thurloe had tackled the law-courts to salvage some of their estate for her. He had done better than anyone had anticipated, and although grief had caused Temperance to miscarry, she had rallied her spirits and spent her fortune on a rambling three-storeyed house taxed on fourteen hearths. It was a large place for a single woman, but she had enigmatically informed her anxious friends that she had plans for it.

On the chilly February day when she had taken him to inspect the building, Chaloner had thought it gloomy and unprepossessing, but three months later it was transformed. Gone were the rotten windows, and in their place were fresh, brightly painted shutters and flowers in pots on the sills. The roof had been re-tiled, and iron railings fenced off a small yard at the front of the house, paved with flagstones and shaded by a dripping tree. He was impressed by the speed with which Temperance had made her changes, and saw she had not allowed herself to wallow in self-pity.

He was about to approach the door, when it opened and two well-dressed men reeled out, although their drunkenness was not the boisterous kind. Chaloner ducked behind a water butt when he saw they were accompanied by a man called Preacher Hill, a noncon-formist fanatic who did a great deal of damage with his loud opinions and bigotry. Chaloner waited until they had gone, then tapped on the door, pondering why the three men should have been visiting Temperance at such a peculiar hour. It was hardly proper, and he wondered whether Thurloe had been right to help her move away from the kindly widow who had looked after her following the death of her parents.

The door was opened by Temperance herself. She was a tall, solidly built woman of twenty, with a large, homely face and gorgeous tresses of shiny chestnut hair. These had been concealed under a prim bonnet when her mother had been alive, but now they were displayed for all to see, and Chaloner was sure even Lady Castlemaine would covet them. She had dispensed with the plain black skirts favoured by her co-religionists, too, and wore a tightly laced bodice that did not flatter her stout frame, with billowing skirts of green satin. She looked prosperous and confident, and her hazel eyes had lost the endearing innocence he recalled from a few months before.

She looked him up and down appraisingly, then gestured that he could enter. 'You have come at an odd time. Most men prefer evenings, but I shall see what we can do, since you look respectable.'

Chaloner was bemused by the cool greeting. 'What are you talking about?'

Temperance peered into his face, then released a bubbling chuckle of pleasure. 'Thomas! I did not recognise you under all that paint. Are you engaged on another assignment for your earl? Where have you been these last three months? You sent a note in February saying you were going overseas, but since then I have heard nothing. I thought perhaps you were never coming back.'

'You did not recognise me, and yet you invited me in?'

Temperance laughed again. 'Only because you looked too old to cause any trouble.'

He had no idea what that was supposed to mean, and when he made no reply, she took his arm and led him into a warm, steamy kitchen at the rear of the house. As he passed the large room that overlooked the courtyard, his eyes watered at the fug of stale tobacco smoke. Dirty goblets and empty decanters were strewn everywhere, and spilled food had been crushed into the rugs. He glimpsed a furtive movement on the stairs, and glanced up to see a half-clad woman. Other voices told him she was not the only female in residence. Gradually, it began to dawn on him that Temperance's plans for her new life had revolved around establishing some sort of bawdy house. He was not usually slow on the uptake, but Temperance hailed from a deeply devout family that believed even innocent pleasures like reading or singing were sinful, and the abrupt transformation was unexpected, to say the least.

'Have you come to collect the shirts I offered to mend before you left?' she asked, directing him to sit at the table. Pots and pans were everywhere, and there was a mouth-watering scent of baking pastry. Piles of plates sat washed and draining near a stone sink, and a heavy, comfortable matron sat next to a roaring fire, toasting bread on the end of a poker. 'I confess I put them away when you disappeared, but I shall see to them today.'

'Leave them to me,' said the older woman, whose powerful arms and strong hands gave her the appearance of a milkmaid. She leered at Chaloner. 'And I shall lace them, too. You are sadly dowdy, and in desperate need of a lady's touch. I shall add so much lace to your collar, sleeves and cuffs that the King himself will ask where you purchased such magnificent garments.'

Chaloner did not recall the shirts, and did not like the sound of the 'improvements', either. 'That is not necessary, ma'am.'

'It is no trouble,' she said, fluffing her hair as she winked at him.

There was a merry twinkle in Temperance's eyes. 'Were he to remove his beard and wig, you would see he is far

63

too young to warrant your interest, Maude. I harboured an affection for him once, until I realised life is more enjoyable without a man telling me what to do. What husband would permit the kind of civilised evenings *we* have enjoyed these last few weeks?'

Chaloner did not try to hide his concern. 'This is a respectable neighbourhood, Temperance, and if your . . . your *enterprise* is too brazen, you may find yourself in trouble.'

'We are always quiet, so do not fret,' said Temperance, making a dismissive gesture with her hand. 'Would you like some coffee? Maude knows how to make it.'

Maude heaved her bulk out of the chair, and set about heating water for the beverage that was fast becoming popular in London. While she was waiting for the pan to boil, she took some roasted beans and pounded them vigorously with a pestle and mortar. She tossed the resulting powder into a jug, along with a vast quantity of dark sugar, and added hot water. A sharp, burned aroma filled the kitchen when she poured her brew into three dishes. It was black, syrupy, and tasted like medicine. After a few moments, Chaloner felt his heart begin to pound, and he set it down half finished. It was too strong, although Temperance and Maude did not seem to be affected.

'Are you going to chapel?' he asked, recalling how Temperance had never missed morning prayers when they had been neighbours. 'Perhaps I can escort you there?'

She shook her head after Maude, taking the hint, grabbed a basket and muttered something about going to the market for eggs. 'I do not hold with all that any more – I go to St Dunstan's on Sundays, and that is enough. It is good to see you, Thomas. I was beginning to think you might have forgotten me, which would have been sad. I value our friendship, and would not like to lose it.'

'I have been in Ireland, and only returned a few days ago.'

Her face filled with alarm. 'Ireland? I hope it was nothing to do with the Castle Plot – that sounded horrible! I wish you would abandon your work with that Lord Clarendon. Clerking would be much safer. If you are interested, I could find you something here.'

'You are in a position to employ me?' asked Chaloner, startled. 'Your business is lucrative, then?'

'Very,' said Temperance with a satisfied smile of pleasure. 'And I am in sore need of a reliable manager of accounts. Are you interested?'

Chaloner had questions of his own. 'Why was Preacher Hill here? If you have abandoned your old religion, then why continue to associate with him? His wild opinions make him a dangerous man to know, and he may bring you trouble.'

'He has been extruded – prevented from conducting religious offices in his own church – so he works for me now, as a doorman. He is rather good at it, and the position leaves his days free for spouting sermons in public places. The arrangement suits us both. Do you really disapprove? I thought you were opposed to discrimination on religious grounds.'

'I do, but that is no reason . . . ' He trailed off, seeing there was no point in pursuing the matter. He could tell from the stubborn expression on her face that she was not going to change her mind, or listen to advice from him.

'Dear Thomas,' she said after a moment, shooting him a fond smile. 'You have not changed.'

She had, though. 'You have grown up. I was gone a few weeks, and you are different.'

She nodded, pleased he had noticed. 'I think the word is "liberated". For the first time in my life I can do exactly as I please. I wear lace. I see plays. I read books that are nothing to do with religion. I feel as though I have woken up after a long sleep, and I am happier now than I have ever been. I grieve for my parents, of course – they raised me in a way they thought was right – but I prefer my life now. Will you teach me French? I would so like to speak that particular language.'

'I am sure you would,' muttered Chaloner ungraciously. 'Brothel business always sounds so much more genteel when conducted in French.'

Even after an hour with Temperance, it was still too early to visit White Hall or to interview gunsmiths, so Chaloner crossed Fleet Street and walked to Lincoln's Inn. Although his thoughts were mostly on Temperance, an innate sense still warned him of the thieves who saw him as an easy target. He was obliged to side-step two pickpockets and flash his dagger at a would-be robber before he was even halfway up Chancery Lane. He slipped through Lincoln's Inn's main gate when its porter was looking the other way, and headed for Chamber XIII in Dial Court. It was here that John Thurloe, his friend and former employer, lived when he was not at his family estate near Oxford.

Dial Court was one of the oldest parts of the ancient foundation for licensing lawyers and clerks, and comprised accommodation wings to the east and west, and the new chapel to the south. To the north were the gardens, a tangle of untamed vegetation, venerable oaks and gnarled fruit trees. In the middle of Dial Court was the ugliest sundial ever created, a monstrosity of curly iron and leering cherubs. It had been installed in a place where it was in the shade for most of the day, which somewhat defeated its purpose.

As a 'bencher' – a governing member of Lincoln's Inn – Thurloe was entitled to occupy a suite of chambers on two floors. On one level was his bedchamber and an oak-panelled sitting room, full of books and the scent of polished wood; above was a pantry and an attic that was home to his manservant, a fellow so quiet and unobtrusive that he was thought to be mute.

Thurloe was sitting next to a blazing fire, even though summer was fast approaching and most people had blocked their chimneys in anticipation of warmth to come. He hated cold weather, and his chambers were always stifling. The man who had been one of Cromwell's closest friends and most trusted advisor was slightly built, with shoulder-length brown hair. His large blue eyes often appeared soulful, but there was a core of steel in him that had taken more than one would-be conspirator by surprise. He had single-handedly managed an intelligence service that had not only monitored the activities of foreign governments, but had watched the movements of the exiled King and his followers, too. Chaloner suspected the Commonwealth would not have lasted as long as it had, if Thurloe had not been its Secretary of State and Spymaster General.

Thurloe was not alone that morning, because a thin, stoop-shouldered mathematician–surveyor called William Leybourn was visiting him. Chaloner had met Leybourn the previous winter, and they had become friends. Leybourn owned a bookshop on Monkwell Street near Cripplegate, and Chaloner had spent many happy hours browsing his collection while listening to him expound all manner of complex and mostly incomprehensible geometrical theories.

'Who are you?' demanded Leybourn when Chaloner started to walk inside. He tried to haul his sword from its scabbard, although as usual he had not bothered to oil it, and it stuck halfway out. Leybourn always claimed that time spent on maintaining weapons was time that could be better spent reading. 'What do you want?'

Thurloe came to stand next to him, and his normally sombre face broke into a rare smile when he recognised the grey eyes. 'Thomas is playing a game with us.'

Leybourn's jaw dropped, then he started to laugh, amused by the fact that he had been fooled. 'Is this for our benefit, or do you have another perilous mission to fulfil for Lord Clarendon?'

'I would never wear this wretched thing for fun,' said Chaloner, indicating the wig. It was hot and itched in a way that made him sure it was host to a legion of lice. He said what was uppermost in his mind as he pushed past the surveyor and went to warm his hands by the fire. 'Have you seen Temperance recently?'

'I am a married man, so her establishment is anathema to me,' said Thurloe distastefully. 'I would never visit her there, although she comes to pass the time of day with me here on occasion. I am pleased to see colour in the poor child's cheeks at last.'

'She is blooming,' agreed Leybourn cheerfully, struggling to replace his sword in its sticky scabbard. 'And *I* have visited Hercules's Pillars Alley on several occasions. She runs an excellent show, although it can grow a little wild in the small hours. She has promised to introduce me to a few decent ladies, because I do not have much luck with the fairer sex, and I would like to be married.'

68

'I doubt you will find a suitable match among the women in Temperance's employ,' said Thurloe disapprovingly. 'I know you are not particular, but there should be limits to how low you are willing to stoop, and a bordello – even an elegant one – should be well beneath them. You would do better frequenting funerals, and keeping an eye out for a respectable widow.'

Chaloner rubbed his eyes tiredly. 'I am gone three months and return to find the world turned upside-down. Temperance has become a madam, Will is trawling brothels for a wife, and *you* are dispensing some of the worst advice I have ever heard.'

Thurloe was stung. 'My advice is perfectly sound. He is likely to meet a better class of person in a church than in a bawdy house. However, if you have a better suggestion, then let us hear it.'

'Temperance's place is not just a bawdy house,' said Leybourn, giving up the battle to replace his sword in its scabbard and giving it to Chaloner to sort out. 'Men visit her for witty conversation, too. It is like a coffee house that admits women, and not all its patrons are desperate for a whore. Do not tell her you disapprove, Tom. She thinks the world of you, and it would be a pity to spoil her happiness.'

'She could be arrested,' said Chaloner unhappily. 'Prostitution is illegal, and so is owning a brothel.'

'This one should be safe enough,' said Leybourn. 'It is already popular with influential courtiers like Buckingham, York and Bristol. And once word is out that *they* visit the place, it is only a matter of time before others patronise it, too, to show they are men of fashion. Buckingham took Lady Castlemaine one night, and an excellent evening was had by all.'

'Christ!' muttered Chaloner. It was not that he disapproved of bawdy houses – on the contrary, they were useful places for collecting information, and for relaxing with women he did not want to meet again – but it felt sordid when Temperance was involved.

'You have grown thin,' said Thurloe in the silence that followed. Chaloner did not believe him, knowing the ex-Spymaster could not tell what he looked like under the layers of powder and grease. 'So, I shall provide you with breakfast. My servant is ill, and has gone to stay with his sister, so I am obliged to order victuals from the kitchens myself these days.'

'I came to keep him company,' said Leybourn, when Thurloe had gone to collect the food. 'You know how he likes to walk in the Inn's grounds each morning, as dawn breaks? Well, there are plans afoot to remodel them in a way that will make this a thing of the past. He is very upset about it.'

'There have been rumours about a new garden for as long as I can remember,' said Chaloner, 'but the benchers are united in their opposition to change, and since they are the ruling council, they have the final word on the matter. Nothing will happen to Thurloe's orchard.'

'That is no longer true. William Prynne, who is Lincoln's Inn's most famous bencher—'

'A deranged bigot,' interrupted Chaloner. He had met the elderly lawyer several times, and had been deeply repelled. 'He writes bitter diatribes on matters he does not understand – *The Quakers Unmasked* was so sickeningly poisonous that I could not put it down. Appalled disbelief kept me turning its pages.'

Leybourn laughed. 'That is how I feel about some of the pamphlets the government asks me to print about mathematics. But Prynne's literary talents are irrelevant. The point is that he marched into White Hall, told the King what he wanted, and His Majesty was so taken aback by his effrontery that he signed a letter ordering Lincoln's Inn to see the plans though. The foundation is in the unenviable position of either defying its King or going against its own wishes.'

'Surely they can find a way to procrastinate until Prynne loses interest? These are lawyers, Will – making a lot of fuss while actually doing nothing is what they are trained to do.'

'Not with Prynne sending daily reports to White Hall about progress, or lack of it. The gardens mean a lot to Thurloe – he loves those old trees – and Prynne's project will see them all uprooted.'

'You are talking about my orchard,' said Thurloe, as he returned. Behind him was the Inn's tabby cat, and a servant carrying a tray. 'Have you heard what Prynne intends to replace it with? An expanse of plain grass, crossed by two paths with a dovecote in the middle. It will be as barren as a desert – and the dovecote is not for decoration, but so the hapless birds can be bred for the table. I will feed them in the morning, only to have them grace my dinner plate at noon. Damned Puritan!'

Chaloner and Leybourn gazed at him in surprise. Thurloe was a deeply religious man who seldom swore – and he was a devout adherent to Puritan principles himself. He was about to continue his tirade when the servant gave a howl of anger; the cat had jumped on to the table he was setting, and had made off with a piece of salted pork.

'What do the staff think about Prynne's designs, Yates?' asked Thurloe, waving a hand to indicate the cat was to be left alone with its prize. 'Do they approve?'

71

'We are afraid that a great square containing nothing but grass will take a lot of scything in the summer, sir,' replied Yates. He was a small, lean fellow, unremarkable except for pale-brown eyes that roved independently of each other. At that precise moment, one was fixed balefully on the cat, and the other was looking at Thurloe. 'Mr Prynne said the labour will be good for our souls.'

'He can mow it, then,' said Chaloner. 'And reap the benefit for his own soul. God knows, he needs it, given all the odious vitriol he has written during his life.'

Yates was thoughtful. 'I wager Mr Prynne cannot tell the difference between seed for grass and seed for flowers. My sister owns a cottage in a remote village called Hammersmith, and *that* is full of seeding flowers at this time of year. If you take my meaning, sir.'

Thurloe regarded him conspiratorially. 'How long will it take you to reach Hammersmith?'

Yates grinned. 'No time at all, sir.'

'I hear you were involved in a shooting yesterday,' said Thurloe, when Yates had gone and his guests had been provided with a cup containing something brown.

Thurloe was often in ill health – or claimed he was – and was always swallowing tinctures, potions and tonics that promised wellbeing and vitality. He sometimes tried to inflict them on his friends, too, and Chaloner had been the unwitting victim of several experiments in the past. The spy sniffed the cup cautiously, then declined to drink what was in it – he had no intention of imbibing something that contained a hefty dose of gunpowder. He explained what had happened as he ate bread and cold meat. He did not usually discuss his work with anyone, but it was the ex-Spymaster who had introduced him to

72

Lord Clarendon, while Leybourn dabbled in espionage himself occasionally, although only for Thurloe. Chaloner trusted them both implicitly. When he had finished, Leybourn's expression was one of unease.

'I do not like the sound of either of these assignments, Tom. The beggar's business must have been important, given that he was willing to risk his life to speak to Williamson, and it will be dangerous to spy on Bristol and his cronies. God alone knows what they get up to once the palace gates are closed – and what they might do to keep their activities secret.'

Thurloe pursed his lips. 'Bristol is an odd contradiction. He feels strongly enough about his religion to declare himself a papist – and the price of that is being banned from holding any lucrative public offices – and yet he is one of the most dissipated, sinful, vice-loving creatures at Court.'

'Lord Clarendon was foolish to oppose that bill that granted indulgences to Roman Catholics,' said Leybourn, off on a tangent, 'because papists like Bristol are now his most bitter enemies.'

'His antipathy towards Catholics is wholly unjustified,' said Chaloner. Having lived abroad much of his adult life, he tended to be more tolerant of the Old Religion than most of his countrymen. 'I cannot imagine why he has taken against them so hotly.'

'Who knows what dark poison fuels any man's bigotry,' said Thurloe, shaking his head sadly.

'I heard Bristol has recruited Sir Richard Temple to help him fight Clarendon now,' said Leybourn. As a bookseller, he was the recipient of a lot of gossip, and was invariably better informed about the Court than Chaloner – and sometimes even than Thurloe.

Chaloner knew the name, although it took a moment to place it: Temple was the man whom Scot did not want to marry his sister. 'I know very little about him.'

'Then you should be ashamed of yourself,' said Thurloe sternly. 'He is Member of Parliament for Buckinghamshire – the county in which you were born, and where your siblings still live.'

Chaloner was irritated by the admonition. 'I would like to learn such things, but *you* sent me from England for more than a decade, and when I came back, the Earl promptly dispatched me to Ireland.'

Thurloe's expression softened. 'True – so I shall en-lighten you. Temple is a vain, shallow man, eager for a government post. However, it is generally agreed that once he is given what he wants, he will almost certainly prove to be corrupt. He is also on the verge of purchasing a slave-worked sugar plantation in Barbados, and *that* makes him abhorrent to any decent person.'

'He is not alone,' said Leybourn. 'Half the members of the Guinea Company are now interested in investing in sugar. A merchant called Johan Behn from the province of Brandenburg is currently based in London, and all he does is wax lyrical about the profits that can be made from such ventures. His predictions of huge fortunes are encouraging others to speculate, too.'

'Behn owns a sugar plantation – and slaves to work it – of his own,' said Thurloe with distaste. 'If I were still Spymaster, I would find an excuse to be rid of him.'

Leybourn regarded him uneasily. 'Rid of him how?'

Thurloe favoured him with one of his unreadable smiles. 'With discretion, of course.'

'Incidentally, Behn is courting your friend Eaffrey, Tom,' said Leybourn, a little disconcerted by the reply.

'And Behn does not know it, but *she* enjoys the odd clandestine meeting with an Irish scholar called Peter Terrell, too.'

Chaloner said nothing. Eaffrey had confessed to loving Behn, and obviously she spent time with 'Terrell' because she and Scot were fellow spies with the same master. When 'Vanders' arrived in White Hall and Eaffrey talked to him, too, wagging tongues would no doubt add a third name to her list of conquests. He was, however, unhappy to learn that Behn's wealth came from sugar – he would not have expected Eaffrey to fall for a man who condoned slavery.

'What about your beggar, Tom?' asked Thurloe, seeing Chaloner was going to make no comment. 'Can we help you establish his identity?'

Although he preferred to work alone, Chaloner did not mind accepting Thurloe's help. The ex-Spymaster was a fount of knowledge about the city and its people, and several of his old spies continued to keep him well supplied with good, reliable information. He also possessed a clever mind, and Chaloner respected his opinions and advice.

'Clarendon thinks May wanted to prevent this so-called beggar from speaking to Williamson. The man was desperate for an interview, so he clearly had something to impart. He confided some of it before he died.'

'Did you tell Williamson what he said?' asked Thurloe, wincing as the cat leapt on to his lap, hauling itself into a comfortable position by liberal use of claws.

Chaloner shook his head. 'It made no sense, so I thought I would make some enquiries first – to set it in context, and be in a position to answer any questions he might have.'

75

Thurloe looked doubtful. 'If I were Williamson, I would want to be told immediately, not left waiting until someone else decided it was time for me to know. And while this beggar's words may mean nothing to you, that does not mean they will be similarly meaningless to Williamson. What did he say exactly? I still know a little White Hall business, and may be able to interpret them for you.'

'He mentioned Terrell and Burne in a way that suggested he thought the names might be aliases, and he wanted Dillon to be saved.'

'He is right about the first part,' said Thurloe promptly, showing he knew more than 'a little' about current affairs. 'Terrell is Scot's present character, and Burne is the name adopted by May in Ireland. I do not know about Dillon – although a spy called Dillon worked for me some years ago.'

'If you are going to save *him*, you will have your task cut out for you,' said Leybourn, sipping the tonic, then setting it aside in distaste. He glanced up to see Chaloner and Thurloe regarding him with puzzled expressions. 'Was your Dillon a tall man, who always wore a large hat to cover his face?'

Thurloe frowned. 'How do you know that?'

'He has been arrested for murder.'

'Murder?' echoed Thurloe, shocked. 'But that is impossible! Dillon is a Quaker, and his religion forbids violence – it was what led me to dismiss him. As Spymaster, I avoided assassination when I could, but sometimes there was no choice. Dillon would not kill under *any* circumstances, and his refusal to eliminate a double agent brought about the deaths of several of my men. One was Henry Manning.'

76

Chaloner stared at him. Manning had been executed in Neuburg – taken into a wood and shot by Royalist soldiers. He could have betrayed other agents when he had been interrogated, but he had not, and Chaloner was still alive to prove it. If Dillon's principles had brought about Manning's capture and death, then he was no friend of Chaloner's.

'Well, he has killed someone now,' said Leybourn. 'He was found guilty and sentenced to hang. The execution is planned for next Saturday.'

Thurloe shot to his feet, and the cat hurtled away in alarm. 'I do not believe it!'

'I am afraid it is true. I attended the trial at the Old Bailey myself – it was quite a case, and I am surprised you did not hear about it. Dillon and another eight men were arrested for the crime, because a letter naming them was sent to the Earl of Bristol by an anonymous witness.'

'Sent to Bristol?' asked Chaloner, bemused. 'Why him?'

'Because he is a decent man who can be trusted to do the right thing,' replied Leybourn wryly. 'According to the letter.'

'And I suppose no one knows the author of this note?' said Thurloe scathingly.

Leybourn shook his head. 'Of course not. But on its basis, soldiers searched the homes of the accused, and a bloody rapier was found in Dillon's. Its tip matched the fatal injury in the victim's chest. The jury was invited to compare wound to weapon, and all agreed that one caused the other.'

'That may well be true,' said Thurloe. 'However, we all know that sort of evidence can be planted.'

'The jury did not think so. Its verdict was unanimous.'

'Who did Dillon kill?' asked Chaloner.

'A merchant called Matthew Webb,' said Leybourn. 'I know nothing about him, other than that he was wealthy. I can find out more, if you like. Some of my customers may know him.'

'That would be appreciated,' said Thurloe, inclining his head. 'What about the other eight who were named in this anonymous missive? Were they sentenced to death too?'

Leybourn rubbed his chin. 'Oddly, no. Only three of the nine turned up at the Old Bailey, and they were the ones convicted. Meanwhile, four had produced official pardons from the King, although no one explained how they came by such things. And the other two "disappeared", but no hue and cry was ever raised to catch them. It was all very strange – and more than a little suspicious.'

'Did no one ask about it at the trial?' asked Chaloner.

Leybourn's eyebrows shot up. 'Of course not! Only a fool would question why a brazenly peculiar verdict was being passed by one of the King's judges.'

'Dillon will certainly be innocent,' said Thurloe, agitated. 'I must do something to help him. I cannot let the poor man die.'

'I will tell you the identity of the beggar when I learn his name,' offered Chaloner. '*He* wanted Dillon saved, so he clearly concurred with your assessment of the verdict.'

'Thank you. I shall make a few enquiries of my own, too. I do not like the smell of this business.'

Chapter 3

Thurloe was unsettled by the notion that one of his former spies was in prison, and decided to visit Dillon in Newgate Gaol immediately; Leybourn went with him. Meanwhile, the day was now sufficiently advanced for Chaloner to head for St Martin's Lane, where the Trulocke brothers had their business, and ask about the beggar's gun. It was drizzling heavily, a sullen, drenching spray that soaked through clothes and turned the streets into rivers of mud. Water splattered from the eaves of houses, black with soot from the smoking, grinding industries that huddled along the banks of the Fleet river.

The streets were a marked contrast to the previous day, and were teeming with life, especially around the elegant piazza known as Covent Garden. In it, an army of beggars appealed for alms, or offered songs or recitations of religious verses in exchange for pennies, and ragged children sold fruit that was almost certainly stolen. They clamoured at passers-by, their voices almost inaudible above the cacophony of hoofs, wheels and feet on stone cobbles. Gulls and kites perched on the chimneys above the square's curiously arcaded houses and on the roof of St Paul's Church, waiting to swoop down on any discarded food, while pigeons waddled and pecked among the filth.

The recently established fruit and vegetable market was in full swing, operating from a collection of ramshackle huts that were supposed to be temporary, but that were beginning to take on an air of permanence – some had elegant awnings, and others displayed the names of their owners in large, gaudily painted letters. The air was ripe with the stench of garlic and stagnant water, and rain had turned the ground into a foetid quagmire of mud, animal dung, human urine and the rotten remains of whatever had been dumped in the past. Splashes of colour were provided by the home-woven baskets that displayed early-cropping apples from Kent, or oranges and lemons from southern France. Traders bellowed about their wares, and a furious altercation was erupting between a barrow-boy and the driver of a carriage, which had collided outside the church. The resulting mess of rolling cabbages, splintered wood and bucking mule was blocking the road, and it was not long before others added their voices to the quarrel and fists started to fly.

Chaloner threaded his way through the melee, leaving the din of traffic behind briefly when he walked down a little-used alley, but emerging into it again when he reached St Martin's Lane. The west side of the street was full of grand mansions, each with its own coach-house, while opposite were shops. Carts rattled and creaked as they went about their business, and there was a tremendous racket from a wagon bearing a cage that was full of stray dogs. The occupants howled, yipped and snarled their distress, and several heartless boys ran behind them, throwing stones to enrage them further. The driver was slumped in his seat with his head on his chest, suggesting he was either asleep, drunk or dead, and his ancient nag plodded along with its ears drooping miserably.

The Trulocke premises stood on the east side of the street, in the shadow of the ornate sixteenth-century Church of St Martin. It was a small, narrow building, with thick shutters and a seedy appearance. A dripping board above the door declared that Edmund, George and William Trulocke, brothers of Westminster, were licensed by the Gunmaker's Company to sell small-arms and muskets. The notice was weather-beaten and its words barely distinguishable, which added to the shop's general aura of neglect and decrepitude.

Chaloner had never had occasion to buy a firearm. When he needed one for his work, he usually resorted to theft, while during the wars, muskets had been provided free of charge to soldiers of the New Model Army. Therefore, he looked around with interest as he made his first foray into a gunsmith's emporium, noting immediately the sharp scent of powder and the more powerful reek of heated metal and hot oil. Displayed on the walls were various types of musket, but Chaloner was surprised to note several handguns, too. Because governments were nervous of handguns – which could be hidden under a cloak, and aimed and fired with one hand, making them ideal for assassins – their sale tended to be restricted, and it was unusual to see so many in one place.

A small but pugnacious dog was tethered just inside the door, and Chaloner was obliged to move smartly to avoid its snapping teeth. A shaven-headed giant with a single yellow tooth jutting from his lower jaw came to see why the animal was barking, and Chaloner could see two more hulking brutes in the workshop behind. He was immediately unsettled: they were not the kind of men he liked to see in charge of weapons stores – it did not take a genius to see they would have them out on the streets at the first sign of civil unrest.

'George Trulocke,' said the man, jabbing a thumb at his own chest. 'You want a pistol, grandfather? To protect you against street felons? We can make you one, but there is a waiting list and you cannot have it for at least a month.'

'Business is good, then?' asked Chaloner, speaking loudly to make himself heard over the dog. The knot on the leash slipped, allowing its dripping fangs to come within a hair of his ankle.

'He will not hurt you,' said Trulocke, sniggering when the spy jumped away.

'No,' agreed Chaloner coolly. 'He will not.'

The man chortled again, and Chaloner realised his Vanders disguise meant people would be inclined to underestimate him. The dog knew better, though, and its barks subsided into a bass growl that saw saliva pooling on the floor.

'Well?' said Trulocke, when he had his mirth under control. 'What do you want? We make a nice wheel-lock dag that would suit a gent your age, but if you want it quicker than a month, it will cost you. However, we might come to an arrangement if you consider ordering several.'

Chaloner masked his surprise at the offer. Handguns were hideously expensive – far more so than muskets – and there could not be many people with the means to purchase 'several'. There was also no need for anyone to want more than a couple – at least, not for legitimate reasons. He recalled that in Ireland, the rebels had been equipped with a unexpectedly large number of them, something he and his fellow spies had discussed at length. Could the insurgents have made an arrangement with an obliging gunsmith like Trulocke? He supposed he should investigate, but for now, he needed to concentrate on the beggar.

'Have you sold a snaphaunce recently?' he asked, referring to the type of firing mechanism he had noted on the vagrant's weapon.

'Why should I tell you that?' asked Trulocke warily.

Chaloner smiled pleasantly. 'Because the Lord Chancellor wants to know.'

Trulocke's wariness increased. 'And you expect me to believe that he asked *you* to find out?'

The dagger from Chaloner's sleeve had been in the palm of his hand ever since he had entered the shop. He took a step back and threw it into the wall behind Trulocke's head. It passed so close to the gunsmith's ear that he raised his hand instinctively, to see if it was still attached. Deftly, Chaloner produced a second blade and held it in a way that made Trulocke know he was ready to use it.

'Are you going to answer, or would you rather we conversed in the Tower?'

Trulocke swallowed, and his eyes slid towards the workshop, where his colleagues were labouring over something that produced a lot of orange sparks. However, he had second thoughts about calling for help when he glanced back at the spy and saw the dangerous expression on his face. The tone of his voice quickly went from belligerent to wheedling. 'Me and my brothers sell snaphaunces all the time. We are gunsmiths, so what do you expect?'

'I expect you to sell mostly muskets,' replied Chaloner, gesturing to the long-barrelled weapons displayed on the walls. 'Shall I be more specific about this particular dag? It has an iron grip, carved with a ornate pattern of winding leaves. And your name is set into the barrel.'

'Fitz-Simons,' said Trulocke with considerable reluctance. 'Richard Fitz-Simons. He bought a snaphaunce from us three months ago, along with a dozen muskets, but we never—'

'Where does Fitz-Simons live?'

Trulocke licked his lips. 'He never told me and I never asked. And I never spoke to *you*, neither. He knows some brutal men, and I am a peaceful sort of fellow who deplores violence.'

Chaloner raised his eyebrows. 'You own a gun shop. That is hardly the activity of a pacifist.'

'I sell firearms for shooting pigeons.'

'You offered me one to use on felons,' Chaloner pointed out. Trulocke opened his mouth to make excuses, then closed it again when nothing plausible came to mind, so Chaloner continued. 'What does Fitz-Simons look like?'

The gunsmith rubbed his bristly chin with an unsteady hand. 'Fat, with a scar in his eyebrow, which is old – probably from the wars. I think he might be a surgeon. Why do you want to know? Is he in trouble? If so, it has nothing to do with us. We run a legal business here.'

'Why do you think he might be a surgeon?'

'Because he owns a bag full of metal implements. I saw them when he opened it to put the dag inside. I broke my leg last year, see, and the barber-surgeon who set it owned equipment like that.'

'Is there anything else? My Lord Chancellor will not like it if I am obliged to come back because you have not been honest. And neither will I.'

Trulocke flinched when Chaloner reached past him to retrieve his dagger. 'No, I swear! However, if *I* wanted to find Fitz-Simons, I would ask for him in Chyrurgeons' Hall on Monkwell Street.'

It was nearing ten o'clock by the time Chaloner reached White Hall, where he learned there was to be a grand ball with music and dancing that day, all part of the festivities commemorating the coronation. He wondered whether His Majesty was aware that only the Court was celebrating, and that outside in busy King Street, people muttered rebelliously as cartload after cartload of food, ale and wine trundled through the palace gates.

Reluctant to use the main entrance when it was being watched by so many hostile eyes, Chaloner headed for a small door that led to Scotland Yard, once a handsome palace for Scottish kings, but now a huddle of sagroofed apartments for minor Court officials. He knocked at the porters' lodge, murmured a password to the soldier on duty, and waited in an anteroom for Colonel Holles to come and admit him.

'Heyden?' Holles asked in an undertone when he arrived, looking around to make sure no one could hear him. 'Your disguises never cease to amaze me. Who are you this time?'

Philip Holles was a professional gentleman—soldier devoted to Lord Clarendon. He had often spirited Chaloner to the Earl's chambers for secret meetings, and sometimes gave him licence to lurk in parts of the palace that were supposed to be off-limits to all except members of the Royal Household. He was a useful ally, and Chaloner had grown to like him. He was tall and burly, with the kind of moustaches no one had worn for years, and everything about him bespoke his military past.

'Kristiaan Vanders from Holland,' replied Chaloner. 'Here to upholster Clarendon's furniture. He thinks Bristol will poach me to decorate *his* house instead, which will allow me to spy on him.'

'Good,' said Holles fervently. 'Someone needs to, because Bristol has been encouraging all manner of unpleasant types to join his side this week – folk such as Lady Castlemaine, Adrian May and Sir Richard Temple. Our poor earl will be destroyed if we do not take steps to protect him.'

'The dispute does seem to be a bitter one,' acknowledged Chaloner.

Holles blew out his cheeks in a sigh. 'That is an understatement – they hate each other! Of course, it was Bristol who started this current quarrel. He went around bragging about being a papist, thus *forcing* Lord Clarendon to remove him from his official posts. He *asked* for what happened to him.'

Knowing Holles would be appalled and bemused by his moderate views on religion, Chaloner declined to comment. He changed the subject slightly. 'Did you say May now supports Bristol, too?'

'Yes, damn him to Hell! I hope this does not mean Spymaster Williamson is about to follow suit. He has remained neutral so far, and it would be a bitter blow if *he* were to declare for Bristol.'

'It is a sorry state of affairs – and petty, too. They should put their energies into something more useful – such as avoiding a war with the Dutch or running the country in a more efficient manner.'

Holles nodded agreement. 'I doubt May will be much of a bonus to Bristol's faction, though. He is a good swordsman by all accounts, but not overly endowed with wits.'

'He is a decent shot,' said Chaloner ruefully. 'He picked off that beggar easily enough.'

Holles grimaced. 'Did the Earl mention that I saw what happened yesterday? I wanted to tell Williamson that the man's death was not your fault, but Clarendon told me to keep my mouth shut.'

'I do not suppose you know a surgeon called Fitz-Simons, do you?' asked Chaloner, wishing the Earl had kept *his* mouth shut. A few words from a respected soldier like Holles would have counter-balanced the poisonous report May was sure to have made.

'Yes, of course – a portly chap with a scar over one eye. He is one of four barber-surgeons who hold royal appointments, so they are often here at Court. Fitz-Simons is conspicuous by his absence today, though, and Surgeon Lisle told me an hour ago that he is worried about him. Why do you ask?'

So, that explained why Lord Clarendon had claimed there was something familiar about the beggar, thought Chaloner, and why Fitz-Simons had inside knowledge about White Hall. 'Did you inspect that beggar's body yesterday?' he asked, ignoring the question.

'No, because May whisked it away too quickly. He brought it here with its head wrapped in a sack, set guards over it, and summoned vergers to cart it off to St Martin's for immediate burial. the Earl demanded to see its face, though, and that Irish scholar – Terrell – contrived to

87

have a quick peek when the guards were looking the other way. Oh, and Surgeon Wiseman marched up and inspected it at length. May threatened to shoot him if he did not leave, and Wiseman pretended not to hear, which was amusing. But May kept everyone else away – including me.'

'What excuse did he give for that?'

'He said putting a corpse on display would be gratuitously ghoulish, although it has never bothered anyone at White Hall before. Do you think he is hiding something?'

Chaloner was surprised he should need to ask. 'You say Surgeon Lisle is worried about—'

Holles suddenly understood the line of questioning. 'You think the beggar and Fitz-Simons are one and the same? It is possible, I suppose – both were plump, although I never saw the dead man's face because of the bag over his head. However, it certainly explains why May was so eager to be rid of the corpse before anyone could identify it.'

'It does?'

Holles nodded. 'He will not want everyone to know he shot a Court surgeon, will he?'

'I imagine that depends on what the Court surgeon was doing. Fitz-Simons was in disguise with a gun, and I wager his motive had nothing to do with medicine.' Chaloner thought aloud. 'But if Fitz-Simons had access to White Hall through his royal appointment, then why would he turn himself into a beggar to pass information to Williamson? Why not just waylay him here?'

'He was only surgeon to the servants,' explained Holles. 'He is not like the other three – Lisle, Wiseman and Johnson – who tend monarchs, dukes and earls.

Fitz-Simons is not allowed to frequent the parts of the palace that Williamson inhabits.'

'I have met Lisle,' said Chaloner, recalling the brown, smiling face of the man who had mixed the potion for the Earl's gout. 'Clarendon told me he is friends with another leech called Johnson.'

'Lisle is a good soul. He volunteers his services at St Thomas's Hospital, because he believes the poor have a right to surgery as well as the rich, and he helps my men when they sustain injuries during training, even though he is not paid for it. He is trying to remain neutral in the Clarendon–Bristol dispute, because he is Master of his Company, and he does not want to annoy half his membership by declaring a preference.'

'And Johnson?'

Holles's moustache dipped in disapproval. 'Bristol helped him get his Court appointment, so he is Bristol's man to the core.'

'What about the last surgeon – Wiseman? Who does he support?'

Holles pointed through the window, to where a man clad in a glorious red robe strutted proudly across the yard. He was unusually large, and cut an impressive figure as he moved, enough to make other people give him the right of way.

'He likes Lord Clarendon. Unfortunately, the fellow has a tongue like a rapier and, because he is on our side, we are obliged to put up with it.'

'Had Fitz-Simons chosen any particular earl to support?'

Holles shrugged. 'He might have done, but he was too lowly for his opinion to matter – as I said, he worked among servants, not courtiers. What do you think he was doing with that gun?'

'What do you know about the Company of Barber-Surgeons?' asked Chaloner, again ignoring the question.

'Just that they have a hall with a dissecting room on Monkwell Street, where they slice up the corpses of hanged felons and give public lectures about them. It all sounds revolting to me, and I would not be seen dead there.' He winced at his choice of words. 'I would rather be in a brothel.'

'I imagine most men feel the same,' said Chaloner, sure the general populace would not be queuing up to witness such a spectacle.

'Then you would be wrong. Dissections are very popular at Court, and you are considered unfashionable if you have not attended one. I just thank God I am a soldier, and so not a slave to such trends – I detest the sight of innards and gore.' Holles shuddered and changed the subject. 'I have discovered a rather splendid bawdy house in Hercules's Pillars Alley. Have you been? If not, I can arrange an introduction. It is very selective about its members, but the lady of the house likes me.'

'She does?' asked Chaloner, somewhat coolly. 'And why is that?'

Holles twirled his moustaches. 'She says I remind her of a soldier in Shakespeare's *Henry the Fourth*, which I am sure is a great compliment. I always tip her girls very handsomely, you see.'

Chaloner suspected it was the tips that made him welcome, and assumed Holles had never seen the play, or he would not have been flattered when Temperance compared him to Falstaff.

The colonel escorted Chaloner inside White Hall, then left him to his own devices. The first person Chaloner saw was Eaffrey, who was far too experienced a spy to ignore the elderly stranger, who indicated that he wanted to speak to her. She slipped away from Lady Castlemaine and her simpering entourage, and went to stand near a fountain in the middle of the cobbled Great Court. The fountain had once spouted clean, bubbling water, but it had not worked since the wars, and what filled its marbled troughs was green, sludge-like and malodorous. Eaffrey tossed a pebble at it, and the stone seemed to hesitate on the surface before sinking out of sight.

'That is an impressive disguise, Tom,' she muttered, glancing at him out of the corner of her eye. 'You will soon be better than William.'

Chaloner sat on a low wall, and pretended to fiddle with the buckle on his shoe. As he did so, he automatically scanned the people who scurried past. 'That large man with the yellow hair seems to be watching you rather closely. Do you know him?'

'That is Johan, my Brandenburg merchant,' said Eaffrey, waving in a way that was distinctly coquettish. The fellow acknowledged with a salute, although he did not return her smile, and Chaloner wondered whether there was something in his disguise that had aroused suspicion. Behn was tall and broad, with a mane of thick blond hair, and his fine clothes indicated he was a man of wealth. 'Is he not handsome?'

'He is all right,' said Chaloner, taking an instant dislike to the bulky Adonis. The physical attraction he had developed for Eaffrey during their passionate interlude in Holland had never completely left him, and he was disgusted when it occurred to him that he might be jealous. Then he recalled what Thurloe had told him – that Behn owned a sugar plantation that used slaves – and felt that alone was reason enough for the man to be the recipient of his antipathy.

She grimaced at his lack of enthusiasm, but did not press the matter. 'Have you come to gather intelligence at the Court ball? If so, then you have badly miscalculated, because you will not be allowed in looking like that. You are far too shabby for such an august occasion.'

'I am supposed to be Kristiaan Vanders, here to spy on Bristol.'

'Vanders died three years ago, of syphilis.' Chaloner started to laugh – he had not known the cause of the old man's demise – but Eaffrey did not join in. 'It is not funny, Tom! You do not need me to tell you that this sort of reckless prank might see you killed. And I doubt you know enough about upholstery to fool all but the totally ignorant.'

'There is nothing I can do about it – Clarendon issued a direct order.'

She gritted her teeth, furious on his behalf. 'That arrogant old fool! Do you need help? I can pass you a little gossip I heard today. A politician called Sir Richard Temple – not the brightest star in the sky, but someone who has declared an allegiance to Bristol – is going to give Clarendon a parrot as a peacemaking gesture. Parrots talk, and the hope is that the bird will repeat something incriminating.'

Chaloner laughed again. 'Truly? Or are you jesting with me?'

'I am perfectly serious: the feathered spy will be presented this afternoon. I heard Temple telling Johan all about it just a few minutes ago. Did I tell you I intend to marry Johan, by the way?'

Chaloner regarded the burly merchant doubtfully, wondering what it was about Behn that had captured her heart. 'Are you sure about this, Eaffrey? I heard he owns a plantation that uses slaves.'

'Yes, but he has promised to do away with it, because he knows how much I disapprove. I would like you two to be friends. Let me introduce you.'

'Wait, I—'

But it was too late to point out that he would be wise to maintain a low profile until he was sure no one at Court had ever met Vanders, because she was already summoning the fair *beau idéal* with a crooked finger. 'Johan, I would like you to meet Mr Vanders, from Holland. He is an upholsterer.'

Chaloner would have had to be blind not to notice the adoring expression on her face when she addressed the merchant, and he supposed she really was in love with the fellow.

'*Kristiaan* Vanders?' asked Behn suspiciously. 'I thought he was dead.'

'There was a rumour to that effect,' replied Eaffrey smoothly. 'But it was premature, and he recovered from his French pox, as you can see. Some men do, if they are touched by God.'

'I am pleased to make your acquaintance,' said Behn in German, a language Chaloner understood, but spoke only poorly. He wondered if Behn knew Vanders was fluent, and was testing him. 'Although I confess I have never been very impressed by your turkeywork sofas – too ornate by half.'

'Each to his own,' replied Chaloner in English. 'We should not use German here, though – people might think we are spies.' Behn opened his mouth to pursue

93

the matter, so Chaloner changed the subject, saying the first thing that came into his head. 'Have you ever had syphilis, Mr Behn?'

Eaffrey shot him an irritable look, and he supposed it was not the sort of conversation she had envisioned for his first meeting with the man of her dreams.

'No,' said Behn, sufficiently startled by the bald query to abandon his interrogation.

'Good,' said Chaloner, before he could resume. 'It is an extremely uncomfortable condition.'

'That was rude,' hissed Eaffrey, when Behn's attention was caught by a flurry of trumpets that heralded the arrival of the Duke of Buckingham. 'Johan is important to me – and you should know how I feel, because you have been in love yourself. With Metje,' she added, lest he needed reminding of the woman he had once intended to marry, but who was now dead.

Chaloner relented, and tried to make himself more amenable when Behn turned to face him again. 'I hear you own a sugar plantation,' he said, determined, however, that the conversation would not be in German or about sofas, either. 'How interesting.'

'There is money to be had in sugar,' said Behn. 'Especially if you use slaves to work your fields.'

'I see,' said Chaloner, taken aback by the blunt admission. Eaffrey seemed to be holding her breath in anticipation of fireworks, but Chaloner could not afford to draw attention to himself with a quarrel. He swallowed his growing dislike for the merchant and smiled in what he hoped was a benign manner.

'Of course, there are those who disapprove,' Behn went on, 'but they usually concede my point when I challenge them to settle the matter with swords. *I* am no weakling, afraid to shed a bit of blood for what I believe – especially if it is someone else's.' He fingered the hilt of his blade meaningfully.

'Johan is a member of the Guinea Company,' gabbled Eaffrey, desperately scrabbling about for a non-contentious topic. 'He expects to be elected Master soon.'

Chaloner sincerely hoped that an august body like the Company of Royal Adventurers Trading to Africa – the Guinea Company, for short – would have more decency than to vote for someone who held such reprehensible convictions. 'They must think very highly of you,' was all he said, although Behn seemed to sense his distaste, even so.

'They do.' The merchant scowled at Chaloner, who supposed the disdain he felt was being reciprocated in full. 'However, their feasts can be dangerous. A member called Webb was stabbed on his way home from one just three weeks ago. Have you noticed how many unnatural deaths there are in London, Vanders?' Behn drew his dagger and inspected it, testing the blade with his thumb.

Chaloner shook his head artlessly, although his thoughts were racing. Eaffrey had mentioned a merchant stabbed after a Guinea Company dinner, although he had not realised then that the victim was Webb – the man Dillon was accused of killing. Scot said he had been there, spying on the man who wanted to marry his sister, and Chaloner was suddenly hopeful that a good and reliable witness might help him unravel what had happened. Meanwhile, Behn was glowering, underlining his threat by wielding his knife in a way that was distinctly provocative.

'I heard three felons are awaiting execution for that crime,' said Chaloner, patting his arm paternally, just hard enough to make him fumble the blade and drop it. Eaffrey shot him an anguished look, which he felt was unjustified – after all, *he* was not the one brandishing weapons. 'So, I doubt there will be any more murders of men walking home from dinner. You need not be frightened.'

Furious, Behn retrieved his dagger. 'It is not *my* safety I am concerned about. I am young and fit, and know how to look after myself. It is the elderly who should be worried.'

'Did you see Webb the night he was killed?' asked Chaloner, treating the threats with the contempt they deserved by pretending he did not understand them. He glanced at Eaffrey and saw her regarding Behn unhappily. It occurred to him that she was seeing her lover in a new and unattractive light, and sincerely hoped she would think very carefully about a future with him.

'That is an odd question,' snapped Behn. 'It sounds as if you think *I* might have killed him.'

'Why would I do that?' asked Chaloner, who had thought nothing of the kind – although Behn's overly defensive comment certainly made him consider the possibility. 'I was just wondering whether he had argued with anyone at this Guinea Company dinner, and the wrong men sit in Newgate Gaol.'

Behn's eyes flicked towards Eaffrey in a way that made it obvious he was hiding something. 'I cannot discuss Company business with outsiders,' he declared. 'The subject is closed.'

'You opened it,' Chaloner pointed out.

'I think Lady Castlemaine wants us, Johan,' said Eaffrey, hastily cutting across the indignant response Behn would have made. 'Look, she is waving.'

'She obviously means to ask you where she left her clothes,' said Chaloner. 'Because she does not appear to be wearing them.'

Behn swivelled around quickly, and his mouth fell open. The lady in question strutted towards the Duke of Buckingham in what appeared to be a shift. The material was outrageously thin, and every detail of her elegant figure could be seen through it. Chaloner glanced around, and saw that at least thirty men were watching her, ranging from the Bishop of London, whose small eyes were transfixed in glittering admiration, to the King, who frowned in a way that suggested he objected to sharing.

'*Gott in Himmel!*' breathed Behn, transfixed. 'What a magnificent pair of onions!'

'Speaking of onions, here is Bristol,' said Eaffrey, placing herself between Behn and the glorious apparition as a black carriage with a scarlet trim rattled into the courtyard. 'I can smell him from here.'

'And *I* can smell Lady Castlemaine's perfume,' said Behn, ducking around her to resume his ogling. 'It makes a man heady with delight.'

Chaloner had wasted enough time on Behn, and was keen to get on with his investigation into the death of Fitz-Simons. 'Can you introduce me to any surgeons, Eaffrey? I understand the Court has several.'

'Suffering from a recurrence of your French pox, are you?' asked Behn with mock sympathy, only turning towards him when Lady Castlemaine had disappeared inside Bristol's carriage.

'Stiff knee,' replied Chaloner, leaning down to rub his left leg. A twinge told him he would have a real one if he was obliged to spend too long hobbling around as the arthritic Dutchman.

97

'Sore joints are a symptom of syphilis,' said Behn in his native tongue. 'The disease fills the bones with pus, which eventually addles the brain. Perhaps that is why you have forgotten your German.'

'Or perhaps I just do not choose to speak it with oafs,' retorted Chaloner, nettled at last. Surely Eaffrey could not expect him to endure insult after insult without making some defence?

'There is Lord Clarendon,' said Eaffrey tiredly. 'You had better go and introduce yourself, Mr Vanders, since you said he is expecting you.'

Chaloner bowed and abandoned the happy couple. He heard Eaffrey asking, in a somewhat strained voice, whether Lady Castlemaine's onions were really all that special, but did not catch the merchant's response. He put Eaffrey out of his mind as he made his way to where Clarendon, clad in a glorious coat of deep pink, was talking to a pale, thin fellow with broken blood vessels in his nose and a shabby, dissipated air. The man was Clarendon's favourite cousin, Sir Alan Brodrick.

Everyone knew Clarendon had great ambitions for Brodrick, but most people also knew the hopes were unlikely to be realised, because of Brodrick himself. He drank too much, attended too many wild soirées and, although he was intelligent enough to hold high office, he was also lazy and careless. the Earl was the only person who thought he owned any virtues, and dismissed the tales of his kinsman's debauchery as spiteful rumour. Chaloner would have despised Brodrick with the rest, were it not for the fact that the man was an accomplished violist. They had enjoyed several evenings of duets and chamber music together – and Chaloner was willing to forgive a great deal where music was concerned.

'My Lord Chancellor,' said Chaloner, effecting the kind of bow favoured by the Dutch. 'I am—'

'Assassins!' screeched the Earl, when he turned to see the squalid fellow bobbing at his side.

Chaloner stood his ground. 'It is me, sir,' he whispered, aware that soldiers were responding to the alarm and hurrying towards him, weapons drawn. Behn was among them. 'Heyden.'

But the Earl was not listening, and flung out a chubby arm to protect himself. Chaloner ducked to avoid being slapped, and was off balance when Behn made a flying tackle that saw them both crash to the ground. In a desperate attempt to preserve his disguise, Chaloner clutched his wig, not wanting his brown hair to spill from underneath it. It meant he landed awkwardly with the full weight of the Brandenburger on top of him, and he felt something twist in his left arm.

'I have him,' yelled Behn, gripping Chaloner by the scruff of his neck and hauling him to his feet. Chaloner's hand was numb and he could not feel whether his dagger had dropped from his sleeve into his palm – although it would have done him scant good if it had, since he could hardly stab Behn in the middle of White Hall. 'I *knew* there was something odd about him. Shall I slit his throat?'

'No!' cried Brodrick, catching on to the situation far more quickly than his bemused kinsman and stepping forward to prevent Behn from following through with his kind offer. 'This is Mr Vanders the upholsterer. Unhand him immediately, sir.'

'Oh,' said Clarendon sheepishly, finally realising what had happened. '*That* Vanders.'

* * *

99

'It was your own fault,' said the Earl accusingly, as he sat with Chaloner and Holles in his White Hall office. 'You should have warned me. And the incident has done neither of us any good, because now people think I bully old men – and I can imagine what Bristol will make of *that*.'

Chaloner drank more of the wine Holles had poured him, and made no reply. He was more angry with himself than with Clarendon, disgusted that he had allowed Behn, of all people, to knock him to the ground. He comforted himself with the knowledge that at least his disguise was still intact. The wig had remained in place, and Behn had not managed to smudge any of his carefully crafted wrinkles.

'Do not worry,' said Holles kindly. 'The surgeon will be here soon, and he will put all to rights.'

Chaloner did not need the services of a *medicus*, but it was too good an opportunity to miss by saying so. He was not sure which of the bone-setters – Lisle, Wiseman or Johnson – would answer the summons, but he intended to make full use of whoever arrived by asking whether they knew why their colleague Fitz-Simons had been so desperate to speak to Spymaster Williamson. His wrist was sore, but it was nothing that would not be better by morning, and he was actually in more discomfort from jarring his lame leg, although he was not going to admit *that* particular weakness to anyone in White Hall.

The door opened to admit Brodrick, who had offered to fetch the surgical help. He was alone, and Chaloner assumed he had allowed himself to become side-tracked by the copious bowls of wine that had been placed in every public corridor. These were to ensure the ball got off to a good start.

'The rumours have started, cousin,' said Brodrick to the Earl, trying to keep the amusement from his voice as he leaned against the wall, goblet in one hand and smoking pipe in the other. '*Everyone* is talking about how you felled an insolent Dutchman with a vicious punch to the nose.'

'I did nothing of the kind!' cried Clarendon, appalled. 'I flung out an arm, but no contact was made. It was Behn who bowled Heyden from his feet. Is it Bristol who is telling these lies?'

Brodrick grinned as he sipped his claret. 'He is certainly making sure they are common knowledge, but the tale actually originated with Surgeon Wiseman. He says he saw it happen.'

'Then he is mistaken!' wailed the Earl. 'I thought Wiseman was on my side. Has he migrated to Bristol's camp, then?'

'Absolutely not,' replied Brodrick. 'And what he has done is rather clever: he has let it be known that you have teeth, and that you are prepared to use them. He has done you a great favour.'

Holles nodded agreement. 'It is true, My Lord. Bristol will be obliged to revise his opinion of you now, and that cannot be a bad thing – it is always good to have one's enemies off balance. He will think twice about insulting you again, lest you wallop *him*, too.'

Brodrick laughed. It was the kind of scenario that suited his sense of the ridiculous. 'And now, if you will excuse me, I am off to spin a few tales of my own. I shall say the Dutch upholsterer lies at death's door, and that those who meddle with the Lord Chancellor do so at their peril.'

'Yes!' said Holles, eyes gleaming. 'And I shall add to the speculation by ordering a coffin.'

'No!' shouted the Earl, horrified. 'I do not want to be considered a ruffian! I shall tell anyone *I* meet the truth: that the Brandenburg merchant was the one who harmed Heyden . . . I mean Vanders.'

Brodrick winked conspiratorially at Chaloner, to let him know that he thought this would only add fuel to the fire. It would be seen as a case of 'he doth protest too much', and would 'prove' Lord Clarendon had indeed indulged in a brief spurt of violence.

'I hope this injury will not affect your playing, Heyden,' said Brodrick, hastily changing the subject when he saw his cousin begin to lose his temper for real. He removed a sheet of paper from his pocket. 'Here is the new piece I commissioned from Locke, and you will see that the bass viol has some challenging solo work. I shall have to invite Greeting if you are unavailable, and he will not be easy to dislodge once he is installed. Can you come tonight?'

'Yes,' said Chaloner firmly, taking one look at the music and deciding wild horses would not prevent him from taking part.

'Good. I tried to summon Lisle to tend you – he is the gentlest of the Court surgeons, and to my mind the best – but a carriage has overturned in King Street and he was the only *medicus* willing to help the victims without waiting to hear whether they have the resources to pay him. So he is unavailable. However, I met your friend Eaffrey, and she is scouring the palace for Wiseman or Johnson.'

'Let us hope it is Wiseman, then,' said Holles, when Brodrick had gone. 'I would not let Johnson near my worst enemy. But I did not know you were a friend of the lovely Eaffrey, Heyden.'

Chaloner glanced sharply at him, and saw from the colonel's glistening eyes that his interest in brothels probably extended to the ladies at Court, too.

'Eaffrey,' said the Earl, his voice dripping disapproval. 'Williamson told me that he sends her to "bestow her charms" on men, which means she offers her body in exchange for their innermost secrets. He says she is very good at it. I hope you do not enjoy *that* sort of relationship with her, Heyden. I would not like *my* innermost secrets blurted across a silken pillow.'

'If she "bestowed her charms" on me, I would let her have her wicked way, then fob her off with rot,' said Holles, saving Chaloner from informing the Earl that he was perfectly capable of enjoying a woman without discussing his work, and it was no one's business who he slept with anyway. And he was about to tell Holles that Eaffrey was used to men thinking like him, and that the colonel would be putty in her hands regardless, when a servant knocked on the door. He announced that Sir Richard Temple was waiting to present a peace-offering, in the fervent hope that relations between him and the Lord Chancellor might be more friendly in the future.

'You see?' said Clarendon miserably. 'Temple is so terrified by my newly violent reputation that he feels obliged to bribe me, to make sure I do not savage *him* with my fists for siding with Bristol. Hide behind the curtains, if you please, Heyden. I do not want him to see you damaged.'

'He is here to provide you with a parrot, sir,' said Chaloner, remembering what Eaffrey had told him. 'It has been trained to repeat conversations, apparently. You should accept it, then teach it some rubbish – to trick him.'

'I most certainly shall not,' said Clarendon haughtily. 'I am Lord Chancellor of England, and such deceptions are beneath my dignity. I shall accept his gift graciously, and demonstrate my moral superiority by rising above sly pranks.'

Chaloner felt like retorting that he would not remain in office long if he refused to meet his enemies on their own ground, but supposed it was the spy in him talking. Perhaps the Earl was right to remain aloof from petty behaviour, and an ethical stance would see him victorious in the end. Obediently, he went to stand behind the heavy drapes in the window.

Temple was not alone when he sidled into the Lord Chancellor's domain, and Chaloner saw the Earl's expression harden when Lady Castlemaine swept in behind him, still wearing her skimpy shift. In deference to the Earl's sensibilities, however, she had thrown a cloak around her shoulders, although the appreciative Holles was still treated to the sight of a pair of shapely calves emerging from under it. Pointedly, Clarendon kept his own eyes fixed on her companion.

Temple was not an attractive man. His complexion was swarthy, and he had more warts than Oliver Cromwell. Although not yet thirty, he had no teeth whatsoever, and when he flashed an insincere smile of greeting at the Earl, he revealed a disconcertingly large array of gums. Studying him through a hole in the curtain, Chaloner could see no earthly reason why Alice Scot should have selected him as a potential husband, and thought there was no accounting for taste. In his hand, Temple carried a cage covered with a dark cloth, which he set carefully on the table.

the Earl sneezed. 'What can I do for you, Temple?'

Lady Castlemaine's catlike eyes narrowed when he declined to acknowledge her presence, and Chaloner thought him unwise to goad such a dangerous enemy for no good reason – even a simple nod would have been enough to satisfy her.

Carefully, Temple removed the cloth to reveal a bright-green bird. Parrots had been unknown in England a century before, but with more of the Americas being discovered every year, they were becoming an increasingly common sight in the menageries of the wealthy. The parrot eyed Clarendon malevolently and flapped its brilliant wings.

'Roundheads!' it squawked piercingly. 'Thousands of 'em.'

Clarendon regarded it balefully. 'Is that for me?'

'I thought you might like it,' said Temple with a smile so obsequious that Chaloner winced. 'I know my association with Bristol means that we have been at logger-heads of late, but I am weary of strife. I would like to be your friend.'

Clarendon regarded him with raised eyebrows. 'Would you indeed? And what does Bristol have to say about this, pray?'

'Bristol!' said Temple, feigning disgust. 'He is a man with no official Court post, whereas you are Lord Chancellor of England. But please do me the honour of accepting this bird as a token of my esteem. I assume you do not have one already?'

'If you do, I am more than happy take this little fellow off your hands,' crooned Lady Castlemaine, closing the distance between her and the Earl like a hungry panther. She placed a slender hand on his arm, and he recoiled, as though he had been burned. A small, mischievous smile crossed her face as she reached out to straighten his wig.

'Desist, madam!' Clarendon cried, backing away in alarm; Holles looked on enviously, clearly wishing she would assist *him* with *his* hair. the Earl reversed frantic-ally until he reached his desk, and when she followed, he scrabbled about until his groping fingers encountered a quill. He brandished it like a sword, and Chaloner struggled not to laugh aloud.

'Lock the doors,' announced the bird. 'And give us a kiss.'

The Lady giggled, obviously taken with the creature, and Chaloner saw an acquisitive light in her eyes that told him she intended to have it, no matter what she had to do. Temple grimaced at her antics.

Clarendon sneezed a second time, transparently relieved when she turned her predatory attentions to the bird. 'It is very kind of you, Temple,' he said weakly. 'Green is my favourite colour.'

'I know,' gushed Temple. 'It is why I chose it.'

'It is mine, too,' said Lady Castlemaine, turning abruptly back to the Earl. He cringed when she walked her fingers up his sleeve towards his shoulder, and shot Holles a look that begged for help. But the soldier was gazing on with a silly smile that said there would be no assistance from that quarter.

'You cannot have it, My Lady,' snapped Temple, becoming angry with her. 'I told you – it is for Lord Clarendon. And why did you come with me anyway? I thought Bristol asked you to stay with him while I completed my business here.'

'I do what I like,' she hissed, a little dangerously. She shrugged out of her cloak, letting the garment fall to the floor. Holles made a strangled sound at the back of his throat, and the Earl squeezed his eyes tightly shut. 'You keep your rooms very well heated, My Lord.'

'Bugger the bishops,' announced the bird casually, performing some intriguing acrobatics on the branch that served as its perch. 'And make way for the Catholics.'

the Earl sneezed a third and a fourth time in quick succession. 'It has very controversial opinions,' he said, opening his eyes, but keeping them on Temple.

'I did not teach it that,' said Temple uneasily. Lady Castlemaine looked smug.

'I heard there is a miasma around foreign birds that can prove dangerous to some men,' she said, brushing imaginary dust from Clarendon's collar. 'They start by sneezing, but finish not being able to breathe. It can be fatal, so I am told.'

the Earl jerked away from her, and ink shot from his quill in a long, dark arc across the pale satin of her shift. 'Oh, dear,' he said hoarsely.

Lady Castlemaine shrugged, to show she did not care. 'The King will buy me another. But you are full of surprises today, My Lord. First you punch an elderly Hollander, and now you hurl filth at His Majesty's favourite companion. Bristol will be intrigued to hear about this particular incident, I am sure. Of course, I shall say nothing, if a parrot comes my way.'

'Take the bird, woman,' said Clarendon, scrambling away from her. He turned to Temple, who was regarding him in dismay. 'The gesture of friendship is deeply appreciated, sir. I shall let it be known what you have done, and perhaps it will help to close this rift between our factions.'

They were obviously dismissed, so Lady Castlemaine

grabbed the cage before he could change his mind. Temple trailed after her, his toothless mouth working helplessly as he tried to think of a way to salvage his plan. When the door had closed behind them, Chaloner heard him berating her in a furious whisper. There was a short silence, then a guffaw of genuine mirth when she saw how she had inadvertently foiled his 'cunning' attempt to undermine the Earl. The parrot joined in, and their joint cackles echoed away down the corridor.

Clarendon dabbed at his nose and sniffed. 'I think she may have been right about that miasma. With any luck, it may adversely affect *ladies*, too.'

Time was passing, but there was still no sign of a surgeon. Chaloner glanced out of the window, and saw Eaffrey strolling arm-in-arm with Behn on the opposite side of the courtyard. He supposed she had not considered Brodrick's request pressing, and was grateful his was not a genuine emergency.

'Did you hear about the murder of a man called Webb?' he asked emerging from his hiding place and going to join Holles and Clarendon at the table. Both had poured themselves large cups of wine after the encounter with Lady Castlemaine, although for completely different reasons.

'I did,' said Holles. He went to retrieve her cloak from the floor, and pressed it to his face like a lovesick youth. Almost immediately, he hurled it away from him. 'Ugh! Onions!'

'What did you hear?' asked Chaloner.

'It is a bad business when a man cannot walk home from his Company dinner without having a rapier plunged into his breast,' said Holles, sitting down again. 'Damned shameful.'

108

the Earl frowned. 'Are you talking about Matthew Webb? The Guinea merchant?'

Holles nodded. 'He was stabbed three weeks ago. You knew him, of course, My Lord. He owned the house next to yours on The Strand, and he invited you to dinner once. You declined when you learned his wife was going to be there, too.'

'The dreadful Silence,' mused Clarendon. 'A more misnamed person does not exist. Have you met her, Heyden? She is a pickle-seller's daughter, and an exceptionally large lady – fatter than me and taller than you – but insists on wearing dresses suitable only for the very slender. And her voice . . . ' He trailed off, waving a plump hand, as words failed him.

'Loud and vulgar,' elaborated Holles. 'And she has no sense of occasion. It was her who made that awful *faux pas* last year at the funeral of Henry Lawes the composer. Everyone talked about it for weeks. Do you remember, Heyden?'

'No,' said Chaloner patiently. 'I was in Holland last year.'

'So you were,' said Holles. 'Well, it was warm for October, and you cannot organise a decent funeral in Westminster Abbey outside a month, so Lawes was . . . well, suffice to say Silence brayed about the stench all through the service. And *then* she complained about the choice of anthems.'

'Unfortunately for her, the music had been specially selected by the King himself,' said Clarendon. 'And His Majesty was none too pleased to hear from a pickle-seller that his artistic tastes were lacking. Why are you interested in this, Heyden?'

'A man called Dillon has been convicted of Webb's

murder,' explained Chaloner. 'And I think Dillon might know the beggar who was shot yesterday.'

He could have told the Earl then that the 'vagrant' was a surgeon called Fitz-Simons, but he wanted more time to explore the connection before sharing his findings with anyone at White Hall – what the Lord Chancellor did not know, he could not inadvertently reveal to the wrong people.

'Dillon will hang next Saturday, I believe,' said Holles. 'He and two others were sentenced to death, although there were actually *nine* names on the anonymous letter of accusation that was sent to Bristol.'

'Bristol!' spat the Earl, unable to help himself. 'He probably devised a list of men he does not like and sent it to himself. Why else would *he* be the recipient of such a missive?'

'It seems to me that the real question is not who *received* it,' said Chaloner, 'but who *sent* it.'

'No one knows who sent it,' said Holles. 'And its authorship was discussed at length at the trial, because Dillon argued – not unreasonably – that he should not be convicted on the word of a man unwilling to reveal himself.'

'You seem to know a lot about this,' said Clarendon. 'It sounds as though you were there.'

'I *was* there. A pretty maid-in-waiting wanted to go, and asked me to accompany her, to protect her from rakes and vagabonds. I remember the three guilty men – Dillon, Fanning and Sarsfeild, all from the parish of St Martin-in-the-Fields – but I forget the names of the other six. Four of them produced King's pardons, though, and I heard the order for their release came from a High Authority.' He pursed his lips.

'Who?' asked Clarendon curiously. 'The King?'

'No,' said Holles, a little impatiently. 'It is how we soldiers refer to matters of intelligence and state security. I mean Spymaster Williamson, My Lord,' he added in a low hiss, when the Earl continued to look blank.

Chaloner groaned. Williamson was unlikely to be pleased with anyone who began poking about in a case in which a politically expedient verdict had been secured. Unfortunately, though, Chaloner had offered to look into the matter for Thurloe, as well as for the Earl, and was committed to obtaining at least some answers. He had no choice but to continue.

'That is a sound I like to hear,' said a massive, red-robed figure from the door. 'It means my services are needed. Groans are music to any surgeon's ears.'

Chapter 4

Lord Clarendon and Holles beat a hasty retreat when Surgeon Wiseman began to unpack his jangling bag of implements. the Earl claimed the ball was about to begin, and there were young ladies to whom he had promised dances – although Chaloner suspected they would not be overly disappointed if more sprightly, fun-loving men stepped in to take his place – and the colonel decided he was in need of an escort. Holles's face turned pale when Wiseman produced a short saw, making Chaloner wonder how he had coped with the gore that was an inevitability in military confrontations.

Chaloner expected the Earl to berate Wiseman for spreading rumours about his allegedly violent behaviour, but Clarendon merely muttered that he had no intention of prolonging an encounter with the surgeon, lest he be obliged to witness something unpleasant. Master Lisle was gentle and conservative with treatments, he said, but Wiseman had another reputation entirely, and no sane man wanted to watch *him* with his victims.

'Send me your bill, Wiseman,' he said as he shot through the door, Holles close on his heels. 'And make sure you tell a servant to clean up the mess before I come back.'

Wiseman watched them leave, an amused smile stamped across his florid features. 'Well, if I am to be paid whatever I decide to charge, then I may as well dispense some expensive therapy. We had better have a glass of claret first, though, to fortify ourselves.'

Chaloner regarded him uneasily. 'I do not think that will be necessary.' He was about to add that nothing was wrong with him, but then there would be no reason for the man to stay and answer questions.

Wiseman poured two cups full to the brim, and handed one to his patient. 'This is my way of demonstrating my perfectly steady hands. See how I do not spill a single drop, even though there is a meniscus over the top? Damn! Do not worry. It will come out if you soak it in cold water.'

The surgeon had flowing locks of a reddish-brown colour, which almost exactly matched his eyes, and there was arrogance in everything about him – from his flamboyant scarlet clothes to the superior gaze he directed around the Earl's offices. His lips curled in a perpetual sneer of condescension, and he regarded Chaloner as though he considered him some half-wit from Bedlam. The spy decided there was only so far he was willing to go for this particular investigation, and he did not like the way the surgeon was laying out rows of sharp implements.

'There is no need for—'

'Yes, yes,' said Wiseman irritably. 'You are suddenly feeling better. All my patients say that when they see me prepare, and it is highly annoying. Your arm is broken and it needs my attention.'

Chaloner was astounded by the diagnosis. 'It is not!'

Wiseman grabbed Chaloner's wrist in a way that hurt. 'Do not tell me it cannot be broken because you can still move your fingers: that is a layman's myth. If I do not apply one of my special splints now, the bone will rot from within, and it would be a pity to see it cut off for want of a little surgery.'

Chaloner regarded him in disbelief; the man was deranged. 'You are mistaken. It is only a—'

'Are *you* qualified to say what will fester?' demanded Wiseman. 'No, you are not, so kindly allow *me* to decide what is best. I am proud of my Court appointment and decline to lose it just because *you* refuse treatment and die. However, you are lucky, because I recently devised a new dressing for this kind of injury – one that I predict will make me very wealthy. Wiseman's Splint will do for me what Goddard's Drops did for Jonathan Goddard. God knows, I could do with the money.'

Chaloner had no idea what he was talking about. 'Goddard's Drops?'

Wiseman regarded him askance. 'Where have you been for the last year? The moon? They are his famous recipe for fainting, and have made him extremely rich. My splint will do the same for me. It is a revolutionary mixture of starch, egg whites, strong glue and chalk. But do not worry – it will only be for a month, and then we shall have it off.'

'Have what off?' asked Chaloner warily.

'The splint, of course. The arm should survive, but only if you follow my orders.'

It was clear that Wiseman had not been joking when he had proposed prescribing an expensive 'cure' in order to charge the Earl an exorbitant fee, and although he disliked being used for such a deception, Chaloner decided not to object if it allowed him to ask questions about Fitz-Simons. Besides, none of the ingredients in the bandage sounded particularly sinister, and he would be able to pull it off as soon as he was away from White Hall. Wiseman seemed to read his thoughts, however.

'You think you will get rid of it the moment I have gone. Well, you can try, but once it is in place, it can only be removed by a professional, such as myself. And do not think I do this for the money, either. The Court never pays its bills, and any treatment I provide will almost certainly go unrecompensed. Why do you think I am so poor? Of course, my colleagues Lisle and Johnson never seem short of funds. Indeed, of late they have both been awash with money. I cannot imagine how.'

'But my viol,' objected Chaloner, beginning to be unsettled. 'I need both hands—'

'It will be as good as new in a month,' said Wiseman, going to a table and starting to mix powders in a bowl. A rank smell began to pervade the room. 'Probably. You can forget about music until then, though. But we were talking about the fact that my colleagues always seem to earn more than me.'

'Perhaps it is something to do with their nicer bedside manners,' said Chaloner pointedly.

Wiseman snorted his disagreement. 'There is nothing wrong with the way I deal with patients. They are nearly all fools, and so should expect to be treated as such. Did you know that Lisle reaped so much money last week that he was in a position to donate *three* bone chisels to St Thomas's Hospital? Meanwhile, Johnson is moving in higher circles at Court than he was before – and socialising with such folk is an expensive business. Perhaps they are growing rich because they both support Bristol over Clarendon. Should I change allegiances, do you think?'

'I doubt that has anything to do with it – Bristol is notoriously short of funds himself, so cannot afford to pay for friendship. And Lisle does not side with Bristol anyway. He is neutral.'

'True,' acknowledged Wiseman, whisking the contents of his bowl with considerable vigour. 'And I would not demean myself by siding with Bristol, anyway. He is too debauched for my liking.'

Chaloner was keen to bring the discussion around to Fitz-Simons. 'You are a member of the Company of Barber-Surgeons?' he asked, watching Wiseman empty a packet of white powder into his concoction. There was a soft fizzing sound, as something reacted with something else.

'Why?' demanded Wiseman archly. 'Do you doubt my credentials?'

'I am making conversation.'

Wiseman carried the bowl to the table. His mixture looked like thick glue. Then he took Chaloner's arm and began to bind it with strips of cloth and thin pieces of metal, pausing every so often to slather on his evil-smelling adhesive. Apart from the stench, it looked harmless enough, and Chaloner let him proceed in the interests of learning what he wanted to know. Regardless of what the surgeon said, the dressing would be off that evening.

'I am the Company's most celebrated member. Have you heard about our Public Anatomies – so called because we invite members of the public to watch the dissections of convicted criminals four times a year? There is one next Saturday, as it happens. Would you like to come?

116

There is always room for a man disguised as an elderly Dutch upholsterer.'

Chaloner glanced sharply at him. 'How did you—'

'The skin on your arm – it no more belongs to a sixty-year-old man than mine does. I suspect you are Heyden, the Lord Chancellor's henchman. He said you were recently back from Ireland, and it seems you have made a dramatic re-entry into Court life. Do not worry,' Wiseman added, before Chaloner could think of a suitable lie or object to the term 'henchman'. 'I will not give you away, especially if you are here to oppose Bristol.'

'Then you can help me do just that by answering some questions,' said Chaloner, seizing the opportunity while he could. 'Do you know a man called Richard Fitz-Simons?'

'Why? Does he owe you money? If so, you are unlikely to be repaid. He does not own a large practice – and never will, as long as he disappears for months on end. In fact, he left a few weeks after Christmas, and only returned ten days ago. We were worried that he would miss the Public Anatomy.'

'He will miss it,' said Chaloner. 'He is dead.'

Wiseman gazed at him. 'Are you sure?' he asked eventually.

Chaloner nodded. 'And since Colonel Holles has already told me that you inspected the body of the man I believe to be Fitz-Simons, this news cannot come as a surprise to you.'

Wiseman frowned, although more in concern than annoyance at being caught out. 'I saw something familiar in the shape of the body that was carried across the court-yard in White Hall, and I defied May by going to look. May does not seem aware that the beggar and Fitz-Simons

117

are one and the same, though. Will you tell him? I hope you do not.'

'Why was Fitz-Simons in disguise in the first place?' asked Chaloner, declining to make promises before he had the whole story.

Wiseman stirred his glue, which was beginning to set in the bowl. His expression was pained, as if he was undergoing some kind of internal debate, and it was some moments before he spoke. When he did, it was hesitantly, and some of his arrogance seemed to have left him.

'I have not mentioned this to anyone else, but you *are* the Earl's spy, and it might do me good to share my burden. Fitz-Simons often vanished, as I said. In February, he claimed he was going to visit his mother in York, but that is untrue, because I know both his parents are dead. And then Johnson saw him board a ship bound for Dublin.'

Chaloner's thoughts began to race. 'Why there?'

'I do not know for certain. However, he had a friend called Dillon – Irish, as is apparent from his name – who is currently accused of murder. Now, it seems strange to me that Dillon and Fitz-Simons left for Dublin before the Castle Plot started, and returned after it failed.'

Chaloner gaped at him. 'You think Fitz-Simons went to join the rebellion?'

'I would have said no – except for one thing.' Absently, Wiseman, smeared more of his glue on the dressing. 'There was a plan of Dublin Castle in his room – I saw it when I went to borrow some ink. It was a detailed diagram, and I have not been able to put it from my mind. Treason is a terrible crime of which to accuse a colleague . . . '

Chaloner was thoughtful. *Had* Fitz-Simons taken part in the uprising? Was that why he had bought a gun from Trulocke – and why Trulocke claimed Fitz-Simons kept company with 'dangerous men'? And was Dillon a rebel, too? If he had worked for Thurloe during the Commonwealth, then it was quite possible that he still hankered after the 'Good Old Cause'. And if that were true, then Thurloe might be accused of treachery himself if he openly tried to secure Dillon's release.

'The plan of the castle was probably Dillon's,' Wiseman went on. 'I saw him myself, walking about with large pieces of paper rolled under his arm. He is distinctive, with the hat that always covers his face.'

'Do you think Dillon was accused of murder because he took part in the Castle Plot, then?'

'It is possible,' replied Wiseman. His relief at having shared his 'burden' was palpable, and his hauteur was returning fast. 'What was Fitz-Simons thinking, to become embroiled in such dark affairs? I hope it does not bring the Company into disrepute.'

'Did you know the man Dillon is said to have killed?' asked Chaloner. 'Webb?'

Wiseman nodded. 'Although it is not an acquaintance of which I am proud. Webb was a vile fellow, who saw nothing wrong in a business that involves the selling of human lives. He owned a ship that transported sugar purchased from slave-driven plantations, you know.'

'So, someone *might* have killed Webb because he was unscrupulous,' mused Chaloner, thinking aloud. 'And if so, then his death may have nothing to do with the Castle Plot. I am told he was stabbed on the way home from a Guinea Company dinner. I did not suppose you were there, were you? I know it is common practice for

119

the city companies to invite auspicious guests to these occasions.'

'Being auspicious, I have attended such feasts in the past,' replied Wiseman without the flicker of a smile. 'But I was not at that one.'

'Did Fitz-Simons know the others who were sentenced with Dillon – Sarsfeild and Fanning?'

'Not as far as I know, although it is possible. Hah! I have finished. What do you think?'

Chaloner's forearm was encased in a rigid shell that carried the odour of boiled horse bones. 'It is not very pretty.'

'Surgery seldom is. Your limb is completely immobilised, which will facilitate clean healing. Come to Chyrurgeons' Hall tomorrow, and I shall check it. You will not be able to remove it, so do not try – I added a secret compound that renders the material resilient to tampering by amateurs. As I said, only a qualified *medicus* – with special compounds and equipment – can do that.'

The moment the door closed behind Wiseman, Chaloner attacked the splint with a knife. He was horrified to discover that it was already rock hard, and all he did was blunt his blade. He tried smashing it on the Earl's marble fireplace, but that hurt him more than the dressing, and he realised he would have to borrow one of his land-lord's saws when he went home. Abandoning his efforts, he began to review what he had learned about Dillon and Fitz-Simons instead.

Both men had been in Ireland at the time of the Castle Plot, and now one was dead and the other awaiting execu-tion. May had killed Fitz-Simons as he had tried to tell Williamson that Dillon was innocent. What did that say about May? Or was the incident just how it had appeared: May had shot a man wielding a knife? And what about the anonymous letter received by the Earl of Bristol, which had incriminated Dillon? Was that someone's way of making sure a rebel was hanged? And if so, then did it mean the two men condemned to die with him – Fanning and Sarsfeild – were also rebels?

Chaloner went to sit in the window, to consider the matter further. Because the Earl's offices were located on the first floor, he found himself with an excellent view of the ball, which was centred around the spacious galleries fringing the Privy Garden below. He realised it was a unique opportunity to observe which courtiers sought out Bristol's company and who preferred Clarendon's. He prised the casement open, too, so he could also catch snippets of conversation as people passed underneath him.

The King's musicians were playing in the Stone Gallery, a long ground-floor corridor that formed the eastern edge of the courtyard, and their sweet sounds wafted upwards. One had a bass viol, and Chaloner gazed at his hand, hoping he would be able to join Brodrick's consort that night. He did not want to lose his place to the status-seeking Greeting, who would never relinquish the opportunity to perform in such lofty company once he was established. The players were bowing a piece by Henry Lawes, which reminded Chaloner of Silence Webb's ill-considered comments at the composer's funeral.

The Webb murder was odd. Nine men had been accused – a suspiciously large number for a crime that tended to be committed by a single perpetrator – but only three had been convicted. *Had* Williamson arranged the four pardons, as Holles contended? And what had happened to the two men who had 'disappeared'? Chaloner did not like the notion that someone could write an anonymous letter, and it would result in men sentenced to death. As Thurloe had said, it was easy to plant a bloody rapier in a man's home.

His mind drifted as the courtiers and their hangers-on began to assemble in small groups. He saw Holles, resplendent in his ceremonial uniform, gazing lasciviously at a trio of pretty ladies-in-waiting. Then Lady Castlemaine appeared, and the colonel's moist eyes remained fixed on her provocatively swinging hips until they turned the corner and were out of sight. When Eaffrey sauntered into view, the bulging orbs swivelled around to leer at her. Chaloner wondered what was wrong with the man, and thought he would do well to find himself a wife, a mistress or both before his indiscriminate ogling landed him in trouble.

Behn was with Eaffrey, and she was listening to what he was saying as though it was the most interesting thing she had ever heard. Chaloner was disgusted, because he had imagined that she had owned more taste – and more self-respect than to throw herself quite so completely at the feet of such a man. She sensed she was being watched, because she suddenly looked up at Chaloner's window. She murmured something in Behn's ear; he bowed, then strode away in the opposite direction. Moments later, the door to Clarendon's office opened, and Eaffrey slipped inside. Scot was with her, still disguised as the Irish scholar. Eaffrey's eyes opened wide with astonishment when she saw Chaloner's bandaged arm, and Scot frowned in concern.

'So, the rumours are true?' asked Scot. 'I thought

Wiseman was just trying to unnerve Bristol with his tales of the Lord Chancellor's sudden penchant for savagery.'

'Or was it Johan, and not the Earl, who harmed you?' asked Eaffrey. Chaloner tried to decide whether she admired or disapproved of her lover's display of manly aggression, but he could not tell. 'He flew to Clarendon's aid like a rampaging bull.'

'This splint is just Wiseman's way of letting the Earl know he is getting his money's worth for my treatment,' said Chaloner, loath to admit that Behn had bested him. He might try it again, and Chaloner did not want to hurt the man Eaffrey intended to marry. 'There is nothing wrong with me, but I cannot get the damned thing off.'

Scot sat next to him, and a dagger appeared in his hand, as if by magic. He began to hack at the dressing. 'I was worried when I heard Wiseman was sequestered in here with you. Had you not emerged by three o'clock, I was going to fabricate an excuse to come to your rescue.'

'Why?' asked Chaloner. 'Do you know something that suggests he might be dangerous?'

Scot was sawing furiously. 'Not really – I just have an uncomfortable feeling about him. His Court appointment means he must be good at his trade, or he would be dismissed. Yet he has very few patients outside White Hall, and even less money. It is oddly inexplicable, and I do not like it. Also, I know for a fact that he is a liar. An example is the Guinea Company dinner. Did I tell you I went there to spy on Temple? Well, *I* did not go exactly – my "scholar", Peter Terrell, did.'

'And Wiseman tried to mislead you in some way?' asked Chaloner.

Scot paused to wipe sweat from his forehead with the back of his hand. 'Yes. A few hours before it was due to start, he and I were in a tavern with a group of fellows from the Royal Society, talking about the plantations in Barbados. I am more interested in the botanical aspects of the business, but Wiseman was rattling on about the slaves. Someone mentioned that Webb – who I have since learned was the man stabbed on his way home from the dinner – owned a ship that transports sugar from Barbados to London, and Wiseman pretended to be surprised.'

'How do you know he was pretending?' asked Chaloner.

'Because I heard him and Webb having a violent set-to about it in the Turk's Head Coffee House around Christmas time. So, Wiseman knows perfectly well how Webb made his fortune, and it was odd that he denied doing so later. Personally, I think Wiseman is fighting a losing battle as far as his objection to slave-produced sugar is concerned. England wants cheap sugar, and the only way to get it is by using forced labour. It is an economic necessity.'

Chaloner disagreed. 'Merchants are resourceful – they will find another way to make their ventures profitable. We live in enlightened age, and owning fellow humans is barbaric.'

Scot regarded him askance. 'You sound like a Quaker, man! And the use of slaves in Barbados is a fact. If you disapprove, then make a stand by refusing to consume sugar. I wager your lofty principles will not last long, because coffee is unpalatable without it.'

Chaloner felt himself growing angry. He accepted the challenge. 'Very well. Any business that involves slavery is objectionable, and I want no part of it.'

'I agree,' said Eaffrey. She eyed Scot defiantly. 'And so would any decent man.'

Scot raised his hands defensively. 'It is the way of the future. I deplore it, too, but there is nothing we can do to stop it. A man who harvests slaves today will be wealthy tomorrow. Ask anyone in the Guinea Company – including Johan Behn. He uses slave labour on *his* plantations, Eaffrey.'

'He is in the process of changing that,' said Eaffrey stiffly. 'He promised.'

Scot made no reply, although it was clear that he doubted Behn would do any such thing. He renewed his assault on the splint.

'Did Wiseman attend the Guinea Company dinner after this altercation in the tavern?' asked Chaloner, also keen to talk about something else. 'He told me he did not.'

Scot shrugged. 'I am afraid *I* cannot prove him a liar on that count, because the hall was very crowded and my attention was divided between talking about plants and watching Temple – my would-be brother-in-law. I have no idea whether Wiseman was there or not. I remember Webb, though – or rather, I remember Silence. She told Bristol he stank of onions.'

'Well, he does,' said Eaffrey. 'I thought I might pass out when he spoke to me just now.'

'There was certainly *one* medical man at the dinner, though,' Scot went on thoughtfully. 'Clarendon's debauched cousin – Brodrick – "accidentally" cracked Temple over the head with a candlestick at one point, and I heard someone say that a Court surgeon had tended the wound. I cannot tell you which of the three – Lisle, Wiseman or Johnson – did the honours, because I was busy discussing orchids at the time.'

'Someone sent Bristol a letter listing nine men who

125

are supposed to have murdered Webb,' said Chaloner. 'Have you heard any rumours about who might have penned it – and why to Bristol?'

'Yes, actually,' said Scot, nodding keenly. 'Ever since Eaffrey and I tumbled to the fact that the Dillon mentioned by your beggar is none other than the Dillon convicted of murdering the Guinea Company man, we have been asking questions on your behalf, gathering information. The letter that saw Dillon indicted has given rise to all manner of speculation in the city, but although there are rumours galore – including one that says Bristol wrote it himself – no one knows for certain who penned it.'

'Why would Bristol write it himself?'

'He would not,' replied Scot, stabbing the dressing as hard as he could in an effort to crack it. 'It is malicious slander, which originated with Brodrick.'

'And *I* heard that Adrian May was the author,' said Eaffrey, 'because the grammar and spelling were poor, and everyone knows he is an uneducated ignoramus.'

There was a sudden snapping sound, and Scot hissed in exasperation. 'I cannot get this damn thing off, and now I have ruined my best dagger. What did Wiseman use to make it? Stone?'

'Let me,' said Eaffrey, elbowing him out of the way. She inspected the bandage and regarded him in astonishment. 'All that huffing and puffing, and you have barely made a dent!'

Scot glared at the broken tip of his knife. 'It was not for want of trying.'

Chaloner took the weapon from him, appalled that Wiseman's splint should be capable of damaging such good-quality steel. 'I am sorry. Take mine.'

Scot shook his head. 'You may need it. I hear Eaffrey's future husband has taken against you.'

'Johan does not go around attacking people,' protested Eaffrey, bending over Chaloner's arm. 'May might, though, while Bristol would not pass up a chance to remove his rival's spy, either. You have more enemies in White Hall than William and I put together, Tom, which is impressive – you have not been home a week.'

Chaloner sighed, thinking he had never been so unpopular in Holland – and that was an enemy state. He thought about Scot's brother. 'Have you heard a date for Thomas's release yet?'

Scot's expression was troubled. 'They keep coming up with legal reasons for the delay, and I do not know enough law to tell whether they are real, or just excuses.'

Chaloner gave him Leybourn's address. 'He sells legal books. Ask him to look it up for you.'

Eaffrey threw up her hands in disgust. 'I cannot break this splint, either. Wiseman is famous for his experiments, and I think he might have just performed one on you. I suspect you are stuck with this thing until he agrees to remove it himself – which may cost a lot, given that he claims he is short of money at the moment. How are your current finances?'

'Not good,' replied Chaloner ruefully. 'Clarendon keeps forgetting to pay me.'

'We have broken into houses, fortresses, offices and halls, and escaped from all kinds of prisons,' said Scot, emptying his purse on the table. He did not seem much better off than Chaloner. He shoved the coins towards his friend, but Chaloner pushed them back, not liking to borrow money when he did not know when he would be able to repay it. 'Yet we are defeated by Wiseman's glue.'

'There is Johan,' said Eaffrey, gazing to where Behn was looking around with two cups of wine in his meaty hands. 'I should go, or he will think I dispensed him on an errand to be rid of him.'

'You did,' said Chaloner.

She pouted prettily. 'Yes, but there is no reason for him to know it.'

Chaloner followed Scot and Eaffrey out of the Lord Chancellor's office, but when he reached the garden, he found his way barred by Behn in one direction and May in another. He did not feel inclined to speak to either, so he retraced his steps and returned to the window seat. This time, he made sure he was concealed by the curtains as he stared down into the grounds.

The casement was still ajar, so he listened to snatches of conversation as people passed below. He saw Brodrick congratulating the musicians, one of which was Greeting, and heard them laughing together. Meanwhile, Temple was also strolling towards the consort, unwittingly following a path that would lead him straight to Brodrick. Chaloner recalled Scot's tale about how Clarendon's cousin had hit Temple with a candlestick, and did not imagine they could have much to say to each other – at least, nothing genteel. Sure enough, the toothless Temple baulked when he saw where his amble would take him, and started to change direction. Unfortunately, the lady accompanying him – an older woman, who wore yellow skirts and a fashionable mask that concealed the top half of her face – was determined to speak to the musicians. She resisted his tug on her arm, and then it was too late.

'Good afternoon, Brodrick,' said Temple stiffly. He raised one hand to his pate and rubbed it, although

128

Chaloner could not be sure whether the gesture was intended to be a deliberate reminder of the incident at the Guinea Company dinner. 'I trust you are well?'

Brodrick forced a smile. 'Yes, thank you. I understand you gave my cousin a parrot. How kind.'

'A green one,' Temple's expression darkened. 'Unfortunately, Lady Castlemaine persuaded him to part with it before it could . . . '

'Could give him a fatal ague?' finished Brodrick sweetly when Temple faltered. 'The Lady told me some men are susceptible to them. However, I am sure that is not what *you* intended.'

'No!' cried Temple, genuinely shocked. 'I had no idea birds could be dangerous, and I sincerely hope Lord Clarendon does not think I harbour murderous intentions towards him. Nothing was further from my mind.'

'I am pleased to hear it,' said Brodrick, beginning to move away. 'Good day to you.'

But Temple grabbed his arm. 'Since you are here and we are alone, there is a small matter I would like to discuss. As treasurer of the Guinea Company, it is my duty to collect subscriptions, and yours is outstanding. Perhaps you might . . . '

'You mention this at a Court ball?" asked Brodrick in distaste. 'That is hardly gentlemanly, sir.'

Temple flushed. 'You are a difficult man to track down at other times, and I cannot waste hours of my valuable time hunting you out. Will you oblige me with thirty pounds now?'

Brodrick bowed curtly. 'Stay where you are and I shall fetch it. Do not move.'

He turned and hurried away, and Chaloner was amazed when Temple did as he was told. Personally, he would no more have expected Brodrick to return loaded with money than see the sun turn blue and drop from the sky. The politician and his lady had been loitering just long enough to know they had been tricked when they were joined by Bristol, who was clad in clothes so outdated that he looked like an actor from a theatre. They exchanged meaningless pleasantries, and a waft of onions drifted upwards. Chaloner wondered what the man did to make them hang so powerfully around him.

Eventually, Chaloner tired of watching courtiers – a complex social dance in which he understood too few of the steps – and decided to fetch his viol in readiness for Brodrick's consort. He was about to leave, when the door opened and the Earl bustled in. He was flustered and unhappy, and waved Chaloner back down when he started to stand.

'Do not disturb yourself, Heyden. Wiseman has been telling everyone how you narrowly escaped death at my hands. I hope you do not die – Thurloe will never forgive me.'

Chaloner made room for him on the seat. 'Wiseman is a loyal friend, sir. He thinks he is helping you fight Bristol with these tales.'

'Well, I wish he would not. I do not want a reputation for being a bully-boy. I—'

the Earl broke off when the door opened a second time. Outraged that someone should dare enter without his permission, he was about to surge to his feet and say so, when Chaloner silenced him with a warning hand on his shoulder. The Lord Chancellor's room was about to be burgled, and the spy was keen to know by whom.

As the uninvited guests set about closing the door and discussing who should do what, Chaloner drew the

130

curtain in a way that concealed the window seat completely. When he was sure the Earl was not going to give them away with an indignant challenge, he moved until he could see what was happening through a moth-hole in the material.

Two men had invaded Clarendon's domain. The first was tall, with an unfashionably bushy beard and a puce coat that was stretched unattractively tight across his ample paunch. The second was an angular courtier, who wore tight yellow breeches and matching hose, which made his long, thin legs look like those of a heron. While the bearded man stood at the door and kept watch, Yellow Legs rifled through the desk. the Earl was outraged by the presumption, and started to stand again. Chaloner stopped him.

'We need to see what they are doing.'

'We *can* see what they are doing,' hissed the Earl, his voice loud enough to make Chaloner glance through the moth-hole in alarm. Fortunately, it coincided with the start of some music in the garden below, and the burglars did not hear. 'That fellow is George Willys, one of Bristol's creatures, and he has his filthy hands in *my* private correspondence.'

Chaloner was grateful the chamber piece wafting through the window was being played with such gusto. 'We should see what they want *specifically.*'

'But Willys will mean me harm – he is Bristol's man to the core. That bearded fellow is Surgeon Johnson, who also supports Bristol. He—'

Chaloner stopped him. The burglars were talking, and he wanted to hear what they said.

'Hurry up,' snapped Johnson. 'We do not have all day. I am not sure Bristol was right when he said Clarendon had gone home early – he may come back to do some work.'

'He will be exhausted after trouncing that Dutchman,' said Willys. 'However, I am afraid there is nothing in his desk, except papers referring to affairs of state.'

'Those are no good,' said Johnson impatiently. 'Bristol wants us to find something that shows he embezzles public money. We need bills or letters from shady merchants – Matthew Webb, for example. He is the greatest villain in London, and no upright man should ever have dealings with *him*.'

'Webb is dead,' said Willys.

A crafty expression crossed Johnson's face. 'Then he is not in a position to say what letters he received, is he? *We* shall send him something from Clarendon. That should satisfy Bristol.'

'Actually, it will not,' came another voice. Chaloner experienced a sickening lurch of shock when he recognised Scot, still dressed as his Irish scholar.

It was Johnson who recovered his wits first. 'What do you mean?' he demanded. 'Of course Bristol will be happy with evidence that implicates his rival in something sordid.'

'I am sure that is true,' said Scot. 'However, he will *not* be pleased when the "evidence" is exposed as a forgery, and *he* is blamed. Now, I suggest you stop whatever it is you are doing and leave. This kind of behaviour is beneath professional men, and you should be ashamed of yourselves.'

'Who are you to lecture us?' demanded Johnson. 'An Irish squire, only interested in flowers!'

'His name is Terrell,' whispered the Earl to Chaloner. 'He is only pretending to be a scholar, and is actually one of Williamson's spies, but I cannot recall his real name. Perhaps I was never told. It was an unfortunate name to choose, though, because there is a dishonest fishmonger called Peter Terrell.'

'Spymaster Williamson sent me here,' said Scot coldly to the two burglars. 'He heard men who should know better were in the process of breaking into the office of a government official, and he ordered me to stop them before they did anything rash. If you do not leave immediately, he will have you charged with treason.'

Johnson did not like the word treason, and neither did Willys. Both were out of the door in a flash. Scot closed the door behind them, and for one awful moment, Chaloner thought he intended to resume the search himself, but he merely closed the drawers Willys had opened, and set all to rights. When he was ready to leave, Chaloner motioned for the Earl to stay where he was and emerged from behind the curtain. Scot jumped in alarm, then grinned his relief.

'You startled me! Did you leave this office open deliberately, to entice that pair to break the law? You certainly succeeded in springing your trap – they were in like moths at a flame.'

'They came of their own volition.'

'Then why are you still here? Are you hoping to prevent Eaffrey from seeing Behn? I would not meddle, if I were you. You will not succeed in parting them, and she will resent the interference.'

'Why did you let Willys and Johnson go? You caught them red-handed.'

Scot nodded. 'Thanks to Wiseman – he told the Spymaster what was afoot. Apparently, he overheard them planning the escapade in a public room, which goes

133

to underline how incompetent they are. However, there is no point in prosecuting them – they will deny all, and Williamson thinks Bristol might use the incident to make similar accusations against Clarendon.'

'They would not be true.'

'I know, but dirt will stick, as it always does. Williamson says it will be better for Clarendon if this distasteful farce is quietly forgotten, and he is almost certainly right.'

'What would you have done if they *had* found something? They were considering fabricating documents, as you must have heard.'

Scot nodded. 'Then I would have marched them to Williamson and let him deal with the mess. God help us, Chaloner! All I want is for my brother to be released so I can take the next ship to Surinam. I am weary of petty politics and incompetents like Johnson and Willys.'

As soon as Scot left, the Earl emerged from behind the curtain. He was deeply unsettled by what he had witnessed, but relieved to know that Williamson and his spies were capable of being objective. He told Brodrick, who had come looking for him, to summon a locksmith first thing in the morning, and wanted a guard posted at his door day and night.

Brodrick had a viol. 'Greeting's,' he explained, when he saw Chaloner looking at it. 'Play me a scale.'

Chaloner took the instrument, running appreciative fingers over the silken wood. He grasped the bow but found, to his horror, that the splint limited the movement of his left hand, and he could not produce the right notes, no matter how hard he tried.

'Wiseman said you would be unable to perform,' said

Brodrick, regarding him unhappily. 'Greeting will be pleased, although I shall be sorry to lose you.'

'This thing will be off within the hour,' Chaloner said hastily. 'My landlord will have some tool that will work. He has implements for everything.'

'Wiseman claims amateur removal is impossible,' said Brodrick. 'It needs some special chemical to dissolve it, apparently, and he says he will not apply it for at least a month – for your own good. I am sorry, Heyden but I need everyone at his best tonight, because the Queen will be listening.'

'Greeting will be difficult to dislodge once he has a foot in the door, cousin,' said the Earl reproachfully. 'Heyden will lose his place permanently if he does not play tonight.'

Brodrick shrugged. 'It cannot be helped. Locke gave the bass viol some important solo work, and Greeting is the only available musician capable of mastering it at short notice. Like most courtiers, I am short of funds, and commissions to play in the houses of wealthy courtiers are fast becoming imperative. I cannot afford to be kind to Heyden, not when the Queen might recommend me to her entourage.'

Disgusted and dismayed, Chaloner watched him stride away. He was suddenly sick of White Hall, and longed for the peace of his own chambers. Unwilling for 'Vanders' to be the centre of any more attention, he washed the paint and false beard from his face, and borrowed a cap and coat from Holles. He plodded along a series of little-used corridors, then cut across the expanse of cobbles known as the Great Court. Like the Privy Garden, it was full of revellers, but there were also servants going about their business, so no one looked twice at him as he walked away from the celebrations. Except one person.

'Thomas Chaloner,' said a masked woman in yellow, speaking in a voice that was far too loud. It was the lady who had been with Temple. Chaloner regarded her in alarm, not liking his real name bawled in such a place. 'What are the palace guards thinking, to let *you* in here?'

'Alice Scot,' said Chaloner, when she removed her mask. It had only been five years since they had last met, but time had not been kind to her. Bitter lines encircled her mouth and eyes, and even a liberal slathering of beauty pastes could not conceal the discontent that was etched into her small, pinched features. She did not return his tentative smile of greeting, and he supposed he was still not forgiven for exposing her first husband as a man with dubious morals. 'I did not know you were in London.'

'I am here because my brother is in the Tower, being drained of secrets regarding the Castle Plot. I intend to rescue him and take him home to Buckinghamshire, where he will be safe.'

'Rescue him how?' asked Chaloner uneasily, hoping she was not planning to embark on some wild scheme that would see her entire family in trouble.

'By offering a large sum of money to anyone who will set him free. I am rich, and can afford it – I just need to find out who to bribe. William thinks *he* can do it by pestering people, but money speaks louder than words, so we shall see who is right. Was it you who suggested Thomas should hand himself over in exchange for a pardon? If so, it was bad advice.'

He was tempted to tell her the truth – that it had been Scot's idea – but friendship stilled his tongue. 'He surrendered willingly when he learned it would save him from hanging. Besides, he knew by then that the rebellion was a foolish venture to have supported, and he was eager to make amends.'

'So, now my poor brother is an idiot, is he?' she asked angrily.

'I understand you want to marry,' he said, to change the subject. As soon as the words were out, he wished he could take them back. Given that he had fought a duel with her last spouse, matrimony was a topic best avoided.

'Richard Temple,' she said, surprising him with a sudden smile. 'I cannot recall ever enjoying a man's company as much as I do his. William refuses to give me his blessing, but what would *he* know about love? Like most men, he is only interested in whores.'

Chaloner considered the pairing of Alice and Temple, and decided that she probably had the better end of the bargain. Temple was physically unattractive and his association with the slave trade made him loathsome, but he was almost certainly better company than Alice.

'May I escort you somewhere?' he forced himself to ask. It was growing dark in a part of the palace that was not particularly secure, and she was Scot's sister, after all.

'Not when you are dressed so shabbily, thank you. What are you doing here, anyway? I thought you were still in Ireland. Or have you forsaken espionage to follow a more respectable profession?'

'Your father and brothers were spies,' he pointed out.

'And look where it has led them. My father hanged, drawn and quartered for regicide, Thomas in the Tower, and William itching to begin a self-imposed exile in

Surinam. In his last letter, William told me he had discovered a fancy for flowers. I wrote back and recommended that he consult a physician.'

'That was unkind. Would you deny him a chance to find contentment?'

'I will acknowledge *his* new-found love of plants when he accepts *my* liking for Richard.'

'What is it about Richard Temple that you admire?' asked Chaloner curiously.

She smiled again. 'His ambition and financial acumen, mostly. When we marry, he will use my money to buy a sugar plantation in Barbados. He says it will make us both richer than ever.'

'I have heard that particular venture is on the brink of collapse,' lied Chaloner. 'Due to bad harvests and falling prices. Anyone who invests is likely to lose everything.'

'Richard says otherwise, and I trust his opinion more than yours,' she said. 'And now you must excuse me. Supper is about to be served, and *I* have been asked to sit next to the Earl of Bristol.'

It was late by the time Chaloner reached home, and his ears rang with the sound of loud music and the yells of people who had drunk too much wine. His landlord was still awake, and they spent a long time plying every tool in his arsenal against the splint, but were forced to concede defeat when all they did was warp it into a shape that was uncomfortable. He retired to bed, but his leg ached from his tumble, and he tossed and turned for hours before he was able to sleep. Then he woke as the bells were chiming five o'clock, feeling as though he had only just dropped off. He forced himself up, knowing he should not waste any of the day.

The first thing he did was to go to his viol, which stood near the shelf where he kept his music. He sat, placed it between his knees, and took the bow in his right hand. But the previous night's tampering had made the splint shift down his arm, so it was impossible to reach the frets, and the tune he produced had his landlord banging on the door to make him stop. He set down the bow with a sigh.

He dressed in some of his better clothes for Chyrurgeons' Hall – there was no point in going as Vanders, since Wiseman had already seen through that disguise. He wore a dark-blue long-coat with front buttons, knee-breeches and a 'vest' – or waistcoat – that was as plain as it could be without being brazenly outmoded. Meanwhile, Temperance's friend Maude had been true to her word, and one of his shirts – now adorned with so much lace that it was four or five times its original weight – had arrived. His hat was a wide-brimmed one, which matched the sash that held his sword; no gentleman ever went out without a sword.

Thurloe always rose early, and was already in Lincoln's Inn garden when Chaloner arrived, strolling among the ancient boles in the grey, misty light of dawn. Here, the sweet scent of wet grass and dew-soaked soil was stronger than the ever-present reek of sewage and coal smoke that pervaded the rest of the city. The only times Chaloner noticed London's noxious stench was when it was not there, when he became aware that there were places where clean air prevailed, although the rapid development of houses in the suburbs meant this happened with decreasing frequency. When he approached Thurloe, the ex-Spymaster had stopped next to a gnarled apple tree, and was touching its bark with outstretched fingers, oblivious to the soft rain that fell soundlessly around him.

'I do not think I shall stay in London after Prynne has destroyed my sanctuary,' he said quietly. 'I shall not find peace in his desert, and the loss of these old companions is too sharp a wound to bear.'

Chaloner regarded him in dismay, thinking what a chasm the departure of his mentor would leave in his own life. 'I could ask the Earl to intervene,' he offered.

'That would mean him trying to circumvent a direct order from the King, and I can imagine what Bristol would make of that. I am afraid I shall have to hope for a small victory in Yates's flower seeds.' Thurloe turned to face him, and his eyes immediately lit on the splint. 'Lord! What happened to you? You must come inside and allow me to prepare you a tonic.'

Chaloner shook his head, having tasted some of Thurloe's tonics on previous occasions. 'Did you see Dillon in Newgate yesterday?'

'We were only granted five minutes, but he assures me he is innocent. He also says he is not worried by his situation, because he expects to be rescued by the man who hires him. However, he declined to tell me the identity of his master, or how the fellow plans to snatch him from the jaws of death.'

'There is a lot that is odd about Webb's murder, so Dillon is probably telling the truth about his innocence. He is a pawn in some larger game, perhaps one designed to damage this secret employer of his.'

Thurloe looked unhappy. 'You are almost certainly right. What have you learned about the affair?'

Chaloner began to recite facts in random order. 'No one knows who sent the anonymous letter to Bristol – the rumours that say it was May or Bristol himself have nothing to support them. The men sentenced to hang with Dillon are called Sarsfeild and Fanning. No one seemed to like Webb very much. The man May shot was a surgeon named Fitz-Simons – I shall visit Chyrurgeons' Hall later, and ask his colleagues about him.'

Thurloe nodded appreciatively. 'You have been busy. Is there anything else?'

'Yes. Please do not communicate with Dillon again: there is some suggestion that he might have been involved in the Castle Plot.'

Thurloe rubbed his eyes. 'I suppose it is possible. He is an Irish Parliamentarian, and his family suffered badly when the Royalists confiscated their lands after the Restoration.'

'Your enemies may use any renewed association with him to harm you. I do not want you arrested on trumped-up charges of treason, so it would be best if you had no more to do with him.'

'I cannot leave a former employee to hang, Tom,' said Thurloe reproachfully. 'All my spies risked their lives when they worked for me, and I owe them my loyalty in return.'

'Is Dillon worthy of it?' asked Chaloner, sure he was not. 'He caused Manning's death, and you were obliged to dismiss him. He does not sound like the sort of man to lose your freedom for.'

'It is not for me to judge him,' said Thurloe stubbornly. 'I leave that to God.'

Chaloner knew there was no point in arguing with Thurloe once God was involved. However, while he admired Thurloe's dogged devotion to his people, he thought it misplaced in Dillon's case. He tried one last time. 'It does not sound as though he needs your help, sir. His new master—'

'We all need help on occasion, Thomas. But I shall

141

refrain from visiting him if *you* agree to go in my stead. I am not sure his faith in this patron is justified, and I would like to know more about the fellow *and* what Dillon himself understands about the crime for which he was convicted.'

Chaloner hated prisons with a passion, and tried to think of an excuse to avoid the commission. 'I doubt the guards will let me in,' was the best he could do on the spur of the moment.

Thurloe raised an eyebrow. 'I do not recommend knocking on the door and asking to be admitted. It will be better to show the wardens a permit from their governor.'

Chaloner regarded him uneasily. 'And how do I obtain one of those?'

Thurloe gave one of his enigmatic smiles. 'I prepared – *forged*, perhaps I should say – a letter last night. The governor will be away until Monday afternoon, so you will have to go before then. early tomorrow would be best, because that is when supplies are delivered and all is chaos. Do you mind?'

Chaloner knew Thurloe would do it for him, if their roles were reversed. 'No,' he lied, hoping he did not sound as unhappy as he felt. 'Not at all.'

Monkwell Street not only boasted the eclectic collection of buildings associated with the Company of Barber-Surgeons, but it was also where Chaloner's friend Will Leybourn lived. It was a narrow road, dominated by Chyrurgeons' Hall to its west, and St Giles without Cripplegate to the north. Leybourn's shop stood on the eastern side, and comprised a chamber full of crooked shelves and chaotically arranged tomes, with a printing–binding room and kitchen behind. The upper floors boasted bedchambers and the tiny garret Leybourn used for writing his own erudite works on mathematics and surveying. Suspecting Leybourn was still asleep, Chaloner picked the lock and let himself in. He was warming ale and toasting bread over the fire when the surveyor crept down the stairs with a poker in his hand.

'I wish you would not do that,' Leybourn grumbled irritably. 'What is wrong with knocking?'

'You need a better lock,' said Chaloner. He did not add that the best ones in London were unlikely to keep *him* out – it was rare to find a building he could not enter, once he put his mind to it.

Leybourn regarded him in concern. 'What happened to you? It was nothing to do with this Dillon business, was it?'

Chaloner shook his head, declining to admit, even to Leybourn, that he had been tackled by the boyfriend of an ex-lover while attempting to hang on to his wig. 'You are good at alchemy. Can you concoct something to dissolve this dressing?'

Leybourn inspected it carefully. 'That is Wiseman's work. I heard he had invented a new method for immobilising damaged limbs, and that he intends to make his fortune from it. I would not tamper, if I were you. Chemical substances often react unpredictably, and we might do real harm if we meddle. It might explode or release poisonous gases.'

'Christ!' muttered Chaloner. 'What sort of surgeon is he?'

'A talented one, by all accounts. Ask him to remove it. It will be safer for all of us.'

'Later today, then,' said Chaloner, determined to be rid of it. It was beginning to chafe, and he was sure it – not anything Behn had done – was the reason his wrist ached. He drank some warmed ale and stared at the fire. 'I am doing something I swore I would never do again: working for two different people.'

'Thurloe and Clarendon,' said Leybourn. 'But at least it is on the same case: Dillon.'

'Yes, but Thurloe is determined to save Dillon, and since it looks as though Dillon was involved in the Castle Plot, they are probably hoping for different outcomes.'

Leybourn was full of questions, so Chaloner told him all he had learned, finding it helpful to voice his thoughts aloud and listen to Leybourn's observations. They discussed Dillon, Webb and the Castle Plot until a jangle of bells told them St Giles's was ready for Sunday service. Chaloner glanced out of the window to see people flocking towards its doors. New laws and a vicious back-lash against non-Anglicans meant those who did not attend were regarded as either nonconformists or Catholic, and thus objects of suspicion. Folk stayed away at their peril.

St Giles's was a large church with a tall, thin tower and chimneys tacked on to its aisles, to keep its congregation warm in winter. The medieval glass had fallen victim to Puritan fanatics who thought bright colours might distract the faithful from God, but most of the memorials had survived their depredations. Tablets still clung to ancient walls and elderly merchants continued to rest in marble eternity under its steeply pitched roof. Some had broken noses and fingers, where the iconoclasts' hammers had tried to cleanse the world of unnecessary art, but the majority of them had outlasted the frenzy.

'The main advantage of St Giles's is that the sermons are short,' said Leybourn, as they entered the nave. 'If we had gone to St Mary Staining, we would be there until noon, and there is a book I want to finish. It is about Martin Frobisher, a man I admire. Did you know he is buried in this very church?'

Chaloner shook his head. 'Who was he? A politician?'

Leybourn pursed his lips. 'I doubt I will ever admire a politician, Tom! Frobisher was an explorer, who searched for a Northwest Passage to the Orient. I am reading about his first voyage, though, which was to Guinea. It is enlightening, because Webb had business interests in that part of Africa – and it was at a Guinea Company dinner that he was murdered.'

'I thought he was murdered on his way home – *after* the feast.'

'His carriage failed to arrive, apparently, and suddenly everyone was too busy to offer him a ride home. He was obliged to walk, and was attacked outside his mansion. It is a long way from African House to The Strand, so his killers had plenty of time to organise themselves.'

'That means it was a premeditated attack – not just robbers who saw a rich man alone at night.'

'Yes, it does, and I am sure that is the case. I recall from the trial that Webb's purse, rings and expensive clothes were still on his corpse the next day. No robber would have abandoned such easy pickings.'

'The killer might have been disturbed before he could strip the body.'

'True, but then the alarm would have been raised sooner. Robbery was not the motive.'

'Do you know *why* Webb was elected a member of the Guinea Company in the first place?' asked Chaloner curiously. 'He was not a man who would have brought them credit. He owned a ship that brought slave-produced sugar to England, and the city guilds are sensitive to negative public opinion, because they do not want their halls targeted for looting when the next riot occurs.'

'Unfortunately, the current outcry against slavery will not last. Soon, Englishmen will visit the coasts of Africa to gather slaves, and our government is keen for them to try, because it means wresting lucrative resources away from the Dutch – and we all know war is brewing with Holland. So, men like Webb will soon be the norm, not a despised minority – and the more progressive members of the Company know it.'

Chaloner sincerely hoped he was wrong. He resumed his analysis. 'So Webb attended a feast, where he was tolerated in the hope that he might make other members wealthy. Then his carriage failed to arrive and he was killed as he walked home. Have you discovered anything else about him?'

'He was born in the gutters, but made a fast fortune, which always attracts dislike – from those who are jealous of his success *and* from those who resent him joining their rank in society. However, in Webb's case, I think the dislike was deserved: no one seems to have a good word to say about him.'

'Clarendon said his wife made offensive remarks at Henry Lawes's funeral,' said Chaloner, as they squeezed into a pew that already contained a baker and his large brood. The church was packed, and a clerk was busily recording names in a ledger.

Leybourn chuckled. 'She complained about the smell, which was crass: corpses do reek, but decent folk pretend not to notice, out of respect for the next of kin. And she

146

took exception to the music the King had chosen. She was lucky everyone was too startled by her opinions to arrest her. Did you say there is some suggestion that Webb's killer – Dillon – was involved in the Castle Plot?'

Chaloner nodded. 'He and Fitz-Simons had charts of Dublin Castle, and they left London on an Ireland-bound ship before the rebellion began. The government knew about the revolt long before it happened, which must mean someone betrayed it.'

'Someone?' echoed Leybourn quizzically. 'You mean a someone like Fitz-Simons or Dillon?'

'It is possible. Or perhaps Webb was the traitor, and *that* is why Dillon killed him.'

'I thought Dillon was innocent. Thurloe says so, and he is not usually wrong about such things.'

Chaloner sighed. 'True.'

Leybourn was thoughtful. 'Webb knew a lot of people, not all of them salubrious. Perhaps he did catch wind of a plot involving Londoners, and tried to curry favour by passing the information to official quarters. You will have to find out if you want to get to the bottom of his murder. So, you have a choice of motives: rebellion or slavery. Neither will be comfortable to explore.'

'Murder is seldom comfortable,' said Chaloner. He did not add that neither was anything else Thurloe and Clarendon asked him to investigate.

Chapter 5

Chyrurgeons' Hall had started modestly, with a simple house raised in the fifteenth century. It had expanded since, and now the Company of Barber-Surgeons owned several buildings. These included the impressive Great Parlour, which boasted a first-floor refectory with an open undercroft beneath it. This was attached to the equally handsome Anatomical Theatre – by means of a cloister at ground level, and a covered corridor above. In addition, there was the Court Room, in which the Company held its meetings, bounded by a number of semi-permanent sheds, a granary and several cottages. The complex was accessed by a gate from Monkwell Street, which was manned by a watchful guard – the Company was wealthy, and often attracted thieves and burglars. The guard told Chaloner that Wiseman was still at church, but that the Company Clerk, Richard Reynell, was willing to entertain his visitor until he returned.

Reynell was a middle-aged man with a foxy face and small, intelligent eyes. His clothes were surprisingly stylish for one whose salary could not have been huge, although the oily hair that hung in lank tendrils down his back detracted from the overall impression of elegance. Surgeon Johnson – the bushy-bearded fellow who had attempted to burgle the Lord Chancellor's office – was with him, dressed in the same puce-coloured, paunch-hugging coat he had worn the previous day. A multitude of stains suggested its owner had enjoyed a good night at the palace. Around his right forefinger was a bandage, and he held the afflicted member high above his head, as if testing the direction of the wind.

'I am draining out poisoned blood,' he explained, seeing Chaloner looking at it. 'It was bitten by a green parrot, you see, and it is well known among the more educated men of my trade that they are the most dangerous kind. No man wants to be savaged by a *green* parrot.'

'If you drain the bad blood by holding your finger aloft, then surely the toxins will flood into your arm,' said Chaloner, puzzled. 'And then into the rest of your body.'

'Yes, but that is what livers are for,' declared Johnson. Even Reynell frowned his surprise at this particular piece of information. 'They attract dirty blood and convert it to pellets that are then expelled in vomit. I shall take a purge later and will be cured tomorrow.'

Chaloner was glad it had not been Johnson who had answered the summons to tend him the day before. 'How did you come to be pecked in the first place?' he asked.

'I was attending a lady, who was racked by a fit of violent sneezing. I immediately ascertained that this was being caused by a crucifix on her wall. As I was removing the offending object, the bird landed on my hat, and I was injured in the ensuing struggle.'

'Do you physic many White Hall courtiers?' Chaloner

asked politely, feeling some sort of response was required, but declining to address Johnson's bizarre diagnosis.

'Dozens,' bragged Johnson. 'I am far more popular than that scoundrel Wiseman, because *I* do not regard patients as subjects for wild experiments.'

'I can see why that would have an appeal,' agreed Chaloner.

'Some people even prefer me to Lisle,' Johnson went on. 'Despite the fact that he is much loved in London. The problem with Lisle is that he is a bit too free with the truth. Who wants to know he is going to die? It is better to tell a man he is going to get better. Also, patients tend to be more generous with the fees when you give them good news, so there is always that to consider, too.'

'the Earl of Clarendon,' said Chaloner innocently. 'Have you ever tended him? In his offices?'

Johnson's eyes narrowed. 'Certainly not! He has set himself against poor Bristol, you know. I like Bristol, because he got me my Court post. He and I are going to invent a revolutionary new chewing machine for men with no teeth. It will make us a good deal of money.'

The clerk looked concerned. 'We are already rich, so should not draw attention to ourselves with odd inventions – we do not want a reputation like Wiseman's. It is better to maintain a low profile.'

'Why?' asked Chaloner, bemused.

Reynell's expression was unreadable. 'Once people know you, they start to pry into matters that are none of their concern. Fame is not a desirable condition.'

'Piffle,' countered Johnson. He turned to the spy. 'We were talking about me and my battle with the Devil's familiar.'

'Clarendon?'

'The parrot,' said Johnson impatiently. Chaloner regarded him coolly. He liked birds, but he had not taken to Johnson; if the surgeon had done anything unsporting, he was ready to extract revenge on the creature's behalf. 'After our tussle, it flew out of the window. The last I heard was that it has made friends with the Bishop of London, and refuses to leave his shoulder. Since it raced to save that crucifix, I can only conclude that the bishop is also of the Roman persuasion, and that the parrot has recognised one of its own – an agent of Satan.'

'Christ!' muttered Chaloner, wondering what it was about religion that turned men into drooling fanatics. He addressed Reynell, keen to change the subject. 'Have you worked here long?'

'Long enough,' replied Reynell cagily. 'Why do you want to know?'

Chaloner did not want to know; he was just making conversation. He tried again, 'I have never been here before, but I understand your Anatomical Theatre was designed by Inigo Jones.'

'Jones was an architect,' announced Johnson, as if he imagined Chaloner was a half-wit. 'He threw up the Banqueting House, and . . . and a few other places, too. We asked him to do us a new Anatomical Theatre because the public kept looking through the windows of the old one, wanting to know what we were up to. So, Jones built us one with windows that are unreachable by nosy ghouls.'

'Would you like to see it?' asked Reynell.

Chaloner was not seized with any particular desire to inspect a place where corpses were dismembered, but he had raised the subject and felt he had no choice but to accept. He followed them towards an oval building, inside of which were four tiers of cedar-wood seats, placed so every spectator would have an unimpeded view of the large dissecting table in the centre of the room. The walls were graced with statues of the Seven Liberal Sciences, and for some inexplicable reason, the signs of the zodiac were painted above them. Dominating all was a painting by Hans Holbein, depicting King Henry VIII handing the barbers and the surgeons the warrant that made them an official city guild.

The spy was disconcerted to see the table occupied by a cadaver, because Wiseman had told him Public Anatomies only took place four times a year. The body was covered by a sheet, but a pair of yellow feet protruded from the bottom. There was a faint pink stain over the area of the heart, and Chaloner was not sure why, but he was suddenly seized by the absolute conviction that the corpse belonged to Fitz-Simons, shot in the chest by May. He moved closer, wanting to know for certain.

'My speciality is pumping wax into a corpse's veins,' announced Johnson, flicking up the sheet to reveal two plump, greyish legs. The major blood vessels in the groin had been exposed, and one partially removed, so it could be attached to a bowl by means of a pipe. Chaloner also noticed grazes on the corpse's knees, as if the man had fallen as he had died. 'For the demonstration of the venous system. It is a skilled business, and you will not be surprised to learn that I am extremely good at it.'

Chaloner nodded. He was not particularly squeamish, but there was something about the cold, dispassionate treatment of the body in Chyrurgeons' Hall that unsettled him. Surreptitiously, he edged towards the sheet, intending to tweak it off 'by accident', then take his leave as soon as he had his answer.

'Stand back,' ordered Johnson. 'Bodies are delicate, not to be pawed by non-members.'

'I will not touch it, I assure you,' said Chaloner fervently, wondering what sort of 'pawing' was enjoyed by the elite who were members.

Johnson raised a cynical eyebrow, apparently of the belief that onlookers would be unable to help themselves.

'Laymen can be very salacious,' explained Reynell. He started to sniff. 'Does this room smell? I have been among the odours of the trade for so long that I can no longer tell.'

Chaloner nodded. The corpse stank and, since he assumed it was being prepared for the Public Anatomy the following Saturday, he was glad he would not be around when the demonstration started; by then, it would be overpowering to the point of noxious. He was surprised Fitz-Simons had grown rank so quickly, and wondered if he had been left in a warm place. 'I doubt surgeons will mind,' he said. 'They must be used to it.'

'We are not concerned about surgeons,' said Johnson. 'This particular anatomy is to be private.'

Chaloner regarded him blankly, but Johnson did not seem to think the statement required further clarification, and turned back to his charge, covering the legs with the sheet and patting it tight around the edges in a macabre parody of tucking someone into bed. It was Reynell who explained.

'We perform two types of anatomy: private and public. The latter are major events, and Company members are permitted to invite guests. Afterwards, because it is a well-known medical fact that watching dissections makes men hungry, we have dinner together with plenty of wine. It is always very jolly.'

'Jolly?' Chaloner was not sure he would feel 'jolly' after enduring such a spectacle.

Reynell nodded keenly. 'There are four *Public* Anatomies a year, and we are assigned executed felons for that express purpose. Of course, it is not always easy to lay claim to them, because sometimes the families get there first. Or the spectators at the scaffold.'

'Witches try to steal the fingers,' elaborated Johnson. 'And the ears, and sometimes the—'

'We also perform *Private* Anatomies,' Reynell went on. 'Often, a surgeon may want to demonstrate some aspect of physiology to students, or perhaps test a novel theory. In addition, we conduct Private Anatomies for interested amateurs, because the founding of the Royal Society has precipitated an insatiable demand for scientific learning. This body is for a Private Anatomy, which will be this afternoon.'

'On a Sunday?' asked Chaloner. 'Is that allowed?'

'We have special dispensation, on the grounds that sometimes corpses cannot wait,' said Reynell darkly. 'However, all these new religious laws may mean a curtailing of our activities in the future. We shall go the way of the Puritans, and all Sabbath-day pleasure will be banned.'

'Dissections come under the definition of "pleasure" do they?' asked Chaloner, amused.

Reynell nodded fervently. 'People enjoy them *very* much. You should tell Wiseman to invite you next Saturday. You will not *believe* the fabulous time you will have. And, as for the dinner afterwards . . . well, suffice to say there are already three bullocks hanging in the kitchens.'

Chaloner thought it astonishing that people would

want to eat after seeing entrails brandished about. Surgeons he could understand, but he was not sure *he* would be ready to devour red meat after watching some hapless villain ruthlessly sliced to pieces.

'Did Surgeon Fitz-Simons ever hold Private Anatomies?' he asked.

A furtive look was exchanged. 'Why do you ask about him?' demanded Johnson curtly.

Chaloner shrugged, and pretended not to notice the hostility. 'I met him once, that is all.'

Johnson ushered him towards the door in a way that was only just polite. 'I have work to do.'

Chaloner was relieved to be outside, despite the fact that he had failed to confirm whether the corpse was Fitz-Simons. He took a deep breath of relatively untainted air, thinking wistfully of the sweet scent of Thurloe's garden. Meanwhile, Johnson and Reynell were engaged in a low-voiced debate, but when Chaloner took a few steps towards them, the clerk grabbed the surgeon's arm and pulled him away. Chaloner was puzzled: Reynell had not been odd before the question about Fitz-Simons.

He was not left alone for long before a familiar figure approached. It was Lisle, his brown, wrinkled face creased into a smile. 'Mr Heyden,' he said pleasantly. 'the Earl of Clarendon's friend.'

Chaloner gestured to Johnson. 'I may not be welcome here if you tell *him* that.'

Lisle laughed. 'Johnson is a man who sees life in extremes – you are either in Bristol's camp or you are an agent of the Devil. Wiseman is much the same in his defence of Clarendon. Personally, I prefer not to become involved in squabbles that are none of my business.'

'Where is African House?' asked Chaloner, deciding to learn whether Lisle was the surgeon Scot said had attended the Guinea Company dinner. 'I have been ordered to represent Lord Clarendon at a function there, but I am a stranger to London, and have no idea how to find it.'

'Behind Throgmorton Street,' replied Lisle promptly. 'As Master of the barber-surgeons, I am often invited to the dinners of other guilds, and those held by the Guinea Company are among the best. They are good men.'

'I was under the impression that some condone slavery. That does not make them "good men".'

'The government would disagree – it has issued charters for the exploration of Africa with a view to expanding trade; this will ultimately include slaves. Wiseman is furious about it, and spends a lot of time lobbying politicians and merchants in an effort to stop it from happening. Personally, I think it is a lost cause, and prefer to donate a day of each week to treating London's poor, because they are people I *can* help.'

'I heard there was an argument at the last Guinea Company dinner, between those who object to slavery and a merchant called Webb.'

'The dear departed Webb,' said Lisle with distaste. 'It is difficult to condemn anyone for arguing with *him*. I seldom meet a man in whom I can see no redeeming qualities, but Webb was one.'

'Did he pick a quarrel with you, too?'

Lisle grimaced. 'He once accused me of overcharging for a treatment. It was untrue, of course.'

'Of course. Were you at the Guinea Company dinner?'

'You mean did I see anyone there who was so offended

by Webb's vile presence that they stuck a rapier into his black heart?' asked Lisle with a wry smile. 'I imagine there were plenty, but I was not among them. I *was* invited to the dinner, but the moment my carriage arrived at African House, I received an urgent summons from a patient. I never got inside.'

'What about your colleagues?' asked Chaloner. 'Johnson or Wiseman. Or Fitz-Simons?'

'Invitations were issued to all, but I cannot tell you who accepted and who declined.' Lisle's gaze strayed to the splint on Chaloner's arm, and his eyes narrowed in sudden anger. 'Damn it! Wiseman has been practising with different glues again – and after I forbade him, too! You will be lucky to regain the use of your hand once this comes off. He has been experimenting with some exceptionally resilient substances recently, ones *I* feel endanger a patient's life.'

'I thought a blacksmith might—'

'No!' cried Lisle. 'His splints set extremely hard, and you may find yourself seriously maimed if you let an amateur at it. It is a task only a surgeon can perform.'

His vehemence was making Chaloner uneasy. 'Wiseman intends to leave it in place for a month, but I shall need two good hands long before that.'

Lisle patted his shoulder. 'I can help you there, but not yet. I have learned from experience that Wiseman's glues begin to dissolve after a few days, which makes them easier for the professional man to remove. Next Saturday would be a good time. Come to me then, but do not tell Wiseman – he will certainly object to me "poaching" a patient.'

'Next Saturday?' asked Chaloner, aghast. 'I cannot wait until then!'

'It is the best I can do, now the adhesive has been applied. Do not be too distressed. Miracles happen every day, and perhaps your hand will recover in time.'

'But there is nothing wrong with it,' cried Chaloner, deciding it was the last time he would ever let a surgeon loose on him, just for an opportunity to ask questions.

'Wiseman misdiagnosed?' Lisle was thoughtful. 'Yes, he might have done. He believes himself infallible, which is a sure way to make mistakes. But we shall put all to rights next week, so do not fret. And in the future, you will know to be more selective about your surgeons. We are not all the same.'

Chaloner was tempted to leave Chyrurgeons' Hall while he was still in one piece, but he was angry, and disliked the notion that Wiseman had conducted an unlicensed experiment on him. He decided to stay and confront him about the matter.

'Lord!' groaned Lisle suddenly, looking towards the Great Parlour. 'Wiseman and Johnson have just started one of their spats. I do wish they would not squabble in public – and that it did not fall to me, as Master, to keep the peace between them.'

He hurried away, and Chaloner watched as he inserted himself between the two men. His intervention was not a moment too soon, because Johnson looked as though he was girding himself up to swing a punch. Lisle spoke softly, trying to calm troubled waters, but his colleagues did not seem inclined to be soothed. Their voices carried, and Chaloner heard it was something to do with the dissection that day: Wiseman disapproved, and Johnson was telling him that was too bad. Eventually, Johnson threw up his hands and stalked towards the Anatomical Theatre. The spy eased forward until he reached a

158

doorway, where he could hear what Lisle was saying to Wiseman, but could not be seen.

'I refuse to have anything to do with it,' Wiseman was snarling. 'It is wrong.'

'But Temple will expect you – our most celebrated theorist – to do the cutting this afternoon,' said Lisle gently. 'If you insult him by refusing, he may not make a donation towards our new library, and our colleagues will call for your dismissal. Think very carefully before you follow this course of action.'

'I am a surgeon, not a performing monkey,' raged Wiseman, although he looked very simian that morning, his hulking frame towering over his Master. 'I do not approve of so many Private Anatomies. Dissections should be for education and research, not for the entertainment of wealthy courtiers.'

'We live in turbulent times,' said Lisle reasonably, 'so we do not have the luxury of such choices. You *can* decline to cater to your Company's requests, but it may see you banned from practising surgery. How else will you make a living?'

'With my splint,' argued Wiseman. 'It will make me so rich that I will not be obliged to practise. And Johnson can go to the Devil, because I shall *never* bow to *his* demands.'

Lisle sighed. 'I suppose I will have to make an excuse for your absence – say you have been summoned to White Hall, or some such thing. You will see matters differently tomorrow when your temper has cooled, and you are almost certain to wish you had acted more prudently.'

He walked away, and Chaloner stepped out of his hiding place to intercept Wiseman before he could disappear. The surgeon peered at him.

'You look thirty years younger without paint and grey hair. Did you hear any of my discussion with Lisle? He is obliged to fabricate tales to cover Johnson's appalling lack of judgement. Johnson is a serious liability for the Company, and he should be dismissed.'

'I see,' said Chaloner, supposing the large surgeon had chosen to interpret the incident in a way that suited his inflated opinion of himself. 'How has Johnson misjudged, exactly?'

'Because he has scheduled yet *another* Private Anatomy in our theatre. He organises far too many of them, and we are reaching the point where science is taking second place to entertainment.'

'I do not understand.'

'I mean people *pay* to attend these sessions, and Johnson and Lisle have a long list of rich folk who are eager to commission one. It is not right, and it goes against all I believe. Dissections should be about furthering knowledge, not amusement.'

'It *is* an odd idea of amusement.'

'The fellow who commissioned this afternoon's spectacle is Sir Richard Temple, and I suspect he will bring a horde of friends with him – a pleasant diversion for a wet Sunday. It will turn public opinion against us eventually. The common man has strong ideas about anatomy.'

'Temple,' mused Chaloner. The toothless politician seemed to be cropping up at every turn, but only two days ago Chaloner had never heard of him.

'He is not a man with whom honourable folk should associate,' declared Wiseman viciously. 'He is planning to purchase a sugar plantation that will be fuelled by slaves. It is disgusting!'

'Who is going to be dissected today?' asked Chaloner. 'Fitz-Simons?'

Wiseman had been about to continue his rant, but Chaloner's question stopped him dead in his tracks. 'Of course not! Whatever gave you that idea? We do not dissect people we know.'

'Who do you dissect, then?'

'Criminals, mostly – hanged felons.'

'That accounts for the four Public Anatomies, but what about the private ones?'

'The same. People die in gaol and no one claims their corpses; beggars and vagrants keel over on the street; and then there is the river. We have the pick of them all. In a city this size, there is no shortage of material, and I assure you, we would never slice up another surgeon.'

Chaloner was unconvinced. The legs that had protruded from under the sheet in the Anatomical Theatre had been those of a plump man, and he doubted they belonged to a felon or a vagrant. Someone at the Company of Barber-Surgeons was not telling him the truth.

Wiseman declined to examine Chaloner's arm in the open, so led him to the old hall, where a number of elegant offices were located. Wiseman's had books lining one wall, and a large map on a table that showed the discovered parts of the Americas. It was held down by what appeared to be human long-bones. Adjoining the room was a smaller chamber, which had a heavy oak bench in the middle, and shelves containing an enormous number of bottles and phials. There was a window, but it had been boarded over in a way that suggested the breakage had been due to some kind of explosion. It reeked, and Chaloner detected the distinctive odour of sulphur.

'Experiments,' explained Wiseman. 'I intend to bring surgery into the seventeenth century. It is time we stopped hiding behind our medieval heritage and embraced new ideas and inventions. Take your splint, for example. Broken bones need to be immobilised for at least four weeks to allow them to knit, but all we do is wrap them in a few bandages and hope for the best. My dressing will keep your arm stiff and unmoving for as long as it remains in place.'

'I could not play my viol today, and—'

Wiseman looked pleased. 'Good! It is working – protecting patients from themselves. Has anyone else examined you? Lisle for example? If he has, and has offered you treatment, I want to know.'

Chaloner would no more have revealed Lisle's offer than he would have allowed Wiseman to splint his other arm. 'Why?'

'Because, despite the fact that he is the Company's Master, he is not a good surgeon – he tells too many people they will die, and I am sure some just give up the struggle because of his brutal honesty.' Wiseman's eyes narrowed angrily when he inspected the dressing. 'Someone has been hacking this with saws and knives. Was it Lisle? God help you, if it was. Still, no real damage has been done.'

'Not to the splint, perhaps,' muttered Chaloner.

'After a month, the glue will decay, and then it can be dissolved with a special compound I have invented. Until then, any attempt to remove it will be futile.'

Chaloner thought about what Lisle had said, and

wondered which man he should trust. Each seemed confident of his own skills – and worryingly scathing of the other's. 'I have already lost my place in Brodrick's consort because of this damned thing, and I object to being used—'

'Viols are outmoded,' interrupted Wiseman. 'And will soon be abandoned in favour of the more versatile violin. You should take this opportunity to learn something else – the trumpet, perhaps.'

Chaloner gaped at him. 'That is like me telling you to become a grocer, if Johnson succeeds in revoking your licence to practise surgery.'

'Rubbish. What *I* do is important. You cannot blame me for what happened, anyway. It is your injury that put you in this position, not the *medicus* who is trying to heal you.'

'How much will it cost to remove the thing now?' asked Chaloner, recalling what Eaffrey had said about Wiseman: that he would charge a princely sum to dismantle his handiwork. He realised he was willing to go to considerable lengths to raise whatever was demanded.

Wiseman was affronted. 'Unlike some I could mention, *my* professional integrity is not for sale. The splint stays for a month, and not a day less. And if anyone says otherwise, then I demand that you tell me about it immediately. Now, is there anything else, or can I get on with the business of transforming the art of surgery into a reputable science?'

Chaloner considered holding a knife to the man's throat and putting his request a second time, but decided he would be safer waiting for Lisle. He stood.

'I asked last night if you wanted to attend Saturday's

163

Public Anatomy,' said Wiseman, sitting back in his chair. 'Have you decided yet?'

Chaloner was startled – he had not imagined the offer to be a serious one. However, watching some poor felon's corpse being anatomised was low on his list of pleasures for a free spring afternoon. 'I am washing my hair on Saturday.'

Wiseman grimaced. 'Do not be flippant, Heyden. These are auspicious occasions, followed by meals fit for a king, and invitations are very difficult to come by – my offer is a great privilege, and you should be flattered. And, since *I* am performing the dissection, and not some blithering imbecile like Johnson, you are sure to learn a great deal.'

'I *am* flattered,' said Chaloner, trying to be gracious. 'But surely you know someone more worthy of this honour?'

'Actually, no. All the other surgeons are awash with guests, but I cannot think of anyone they have not asked already. And I do not want them to think I do not have any friends.'

Chaloner thought that if he was the best Wiseman could muster, then the colleagues might have a point. 'I hear your subject will be a hanged felon. I do not suppose his name is Dillon, is it? He is due to be executed on Saturday.'

Wiseman nodded. 'But we keep their faces covered, so if you know him, you need have no fear. He will not be looking at you.'

It did not make the prospect any more appealing.

Still holding forth about what he promised would be a memorable experience, Wiseman escorted Chaloner to the gate and saw him off the premises. The spy walked along Monkwell Street until he reached a small, unnamed alley that bordered the northern extent of the barber-surgeons' estate, and gazed up at the wall they had built to keep out intruders.

Normally, he could have climbed it with ease, but the splint interfered with his grip, and he was obliged to pick the lock on a neighbouring house instead. Hoping the closed door meant its owners were out, he made his way through the building and into the garden, at the end of which stood the surgeons' fifteenth-century hall. Here the protective wall was lower, although scaling it was still an awkward struggle. Eventually he managed, and walked towards the Anatomical Theatre, taking care not to be seen. Ever cautious, he turned his coat inside out and wore it in the manner of a cape, then changed his hat for a simple black cap, tucking his hair underneath it, so he would look like an impoverished clerk to anyone who happened to spot him.

Johnson was poring over the corpse, doing something unspeakable with red wax, tubes and a pair of bellows, so Chaloner tossed a stone up at one of the windows and waited until the surgeon came out to investigate. While Johnson scratched his head in puzzlement, the spy darted inside and yanked the sheet away from the cadaver. He was startled when the face that gazed at him through half-closed eyes was not Fitz-Simons's, but that of an older man.

The stain on the sheet came from an oddly shaped wound in the chest, which Chaloner recognised as being caused by a rapier – fluid had leaked from the hole during a recent washing. Pale circles around fat fingers suggested rings had been worn, and the well-fed body indicated it had been a man of wealth. Chaloner was almost certain – especially as he could now see the fellow had been dead for weeks rather than days – that he was looking at Webb. He gazed at the corpse in confusion, and wondered whether Temple knew he was about to be treated to the dicing up of a Guinea Company colleague.

There was no more to be learned by staring, and the theatre was no place to linger, so he left. Outside, Johnson was gesticulating at a cracked window, informing Reynell that a bird was responsible. Wryly, the clerk pointed out that it must have been a singularly heavy one. Chaloner could not leave the barber-surgeons' grounds the way he had entered, because Lisle was now standing near the old hall, talking to Wiseman. He decided to leave through the main gate instead, knowing that as long as he moved confidently, no one was likely to stop him – guards tended to monitor who came in, not who went out. However, he was out of luck that day, because Johnson spotted him.

'Hey!' he bawled. 'I do not know you. Come here at once, and give an account of yourself.'

Chaloner considered brazening it out, but it would be difficult to explain why he had changed his hat and cloak – and why he had returned in the first place. Plus there was the fact that the sheet that had covered Webb was now lying on the floor, and Johnson would want to know what he had been doing. All told, it was better to escape without being obliged to answer questions. He looked around, quickly reviewing his options. The guard on the gate had been alerted to the presence of an intruder by Johnson's yell, so he could not go that way, and Lisle and Wiseman had abandoned their discussion and were moving towards him – one was sure to grab him if he tried to run past. So he headed south, to where Chyrurgeons' Hall abutted on to grounds owned by the Company of Silversmiths.

Immediately, Johnson broke into a run. He was fast for someone with so large a paunch, and began to gain on his quarry. Chaloner scrambled over the wall to find himself in a yard full of sheds. An indignant shout told him that the silversmiths' apprentices, who were playing dice around a brazier, did not appreciate trespassers on *their* property either. They came to their feet as one when he scaled a second wall, and he heard a furious commotion behind him when they laid hold of the pursuing Johnson instead. The surgeon's garbled explanation earned Chaloner vital seconds, allowing him to vault across a third barrier, which led to yet another garden. The only way out was across a fourth fence, which he hoped would see him in the churchyard of St Olave's Silver Street.

But another garden followed, and another partition, and he felt himself begin to tire. Each barrier was becoming more difficult to climb with his useless arm, and it occurred to him to give up. He changed his mind when he glanced back and saw the expression on Johnson's face. The man would not be taking prisoners; he intended to exact justice on the 'thief' with his fists and boots.

At last, Chaloner reached the graveyard and crawled into a tangle of undergrowth at the back of the church, breathing hard. Within moments, the first of the apprentices arrived and, as Chaloner had hoped, hared towards the gate that led to the street. Others followed, and the spy's gamble that they would expect him either to claim sanctuary in the chapel or head for the nearest exit seemed to be paying off. Through the foliage, he saw Johnson heave himself over the wall, but instead of following the boys, the surgeon trotted to a shed at the bottom of the cemetery and produced a key. He opened the door, peered inside, then locked it again and waited for the apprentices to return.

'Is he in the charnel house?' asked one of the lads, arriving hot and gasping a few minutes later. He stepped past Johnson and put his shoulder to the door with the obvious intention of breaking it down, but the surgeon shoved him away.

'No, he is not there. I have just checked.'

'Who was he?' asked the youth, hammering on the wood anyway. 'One of your students?'

'A burglar,' said Johnson angrily. 'I imagine he wanted to steal the Grace Cup.'

'You mean that big silver bucket with the bells on?' asked the lad keenly. 'The one you shake when you want it filled with wine? It rings, and the servants come rushing to your aid?'

Johnson nodded. 'We always get it out for the meals we enjoy after our dissections, and there is to be such an event this afternoon. That rogue must have heard about it, so came to try his luck.'

'Did you get a look at his face?'

Johnson gestured to his eyes. 'I do not see well. He had a brown cloak, though. Did *you* see him?'

'He always kept his back to me. Do you want us to scout around for men with brown cloaks? It will cost you a shilling for every hour we are out.'

'Here is sixpence,' said Johnson. 'And a crown is available if you bring him to me – quietly, though. I do not want to bother my colleagues with this.'

The lad tapped his nose, then went to tell his fellows of their good fortune. It was some time before Chaloner felt it was safe to leave his hiding place – and he turned his coat the right way out before he did so. He emerged carefully, then went to the shed and picked the lock, closing the door behind him in case anyone came back. The charnel house, used to store bodies until they were buried, had only one occupant, and Fitz-Simons's name was written in chalk on a piece of slate at the end of a crude table. Chaloner pulled off the sheet, and was confronted with a face that was unfamiliar.

He gazed down at the purple features thoughtfully. Fitz-Simons had disguised himself as a beggar, and the dead man in front of him certainly looked as though *he* had been a vagrant. Could there be two dead men with the same name? Chaloner supposed it was possible. Then he recalled Holles saying that vergers had been summoned from St Martin's Church – not St Olave's – to collect Fitz-Simons's body. Had *Surgeon* Fitz-Simons been buried already, and Beggar Fitz-Simons was completely unrelated to him? Or had someone taken the opportunity to exchange corpses? Chaloner stared for some time before accepting that these were questions he could not answer.

The chase had exhausted Chaloner, and he did not feel like walking all the way home, so he visited Leybourn instead. The surveyor said nothing when he flopped in a chair next to the fire, although his eyes lingered on the grazed hands and the torn, soiled clothes. He poured himself some wine and went back to his reading, commenting occasionally on a particularly interesting passage. Frobisher's descriptions of Guinea made it sound like paradise, and Chaloner wondered how its people survived being torn from their homes and transported to the plantations. He found a copy of *Musaeum Tradescantianum*, and learned a lot about edible plants before Leybourn announced he was going to bed. Chaloner took advantage of the spare room, and did not stir until the clocks chimed six o'clock the next morning.

'Are you in a better mood today?' asked Leybourn, looking up from where he was scraping mould from a piece of bread. 'You were sullen company last night.'

'I cannot play my viol, Will,' said Chaloner in a low voice. The loss of music had been uppermost in his mind when he had woken up, and meant he would probably be 'sullen company' at breakfast, too. 'I tried yesterday, but it was like using someone else's hand.'

Leybourn was sympathetic. 'Your skills will return once a surgeon removes the . . . ' He pointed.

'It is a new invention that will revolutionise surgery, according to Wiseman. Or a dangerous experiment that will maim its victims, according to Lisle.'

'Wiseman is the best surgeon in London, and I doubt either he or Lisle made a mistake over something as basic as a broken arm. I am sure they both know what they are doing.'

'They cannot *both* know,' said Chaloner irritably. 'Their diagnoses are contradictory.'

Leybourn handed him some ale. It was stronger than the brews Chaloner usually drank first thing in the morning, and would make him drunk if he had too much of it, which would not be a good way to interview Dillon. He set it aside and ate some of the mouldy bread instead, then left for Newgate Gaol, hoping Thurloe was right when he claimed the governor would not arrive until later.

170

Newgate was one of London's most notorious prisons. It was a robust structure that exuded a sense of despair and hopelessness, and even its recent refacing did little to render it less forbidding. It was stone-built with a massive front gate and virtually no windows, which Chaloner supposed was not surprising for a house of confinement. He hated such places intensely, having spent time in several when spying missions had not gone according to plan, and did not find it easy to step up to the door and present Thurloe's letter to the guard. When the man spent a long time reading it, he considered abandoning the escapade altogether. Arrest would be inevitable if the document was recognised as a forgery, and the prospect of another spell in a dark, dripping underground pit brought him out in a cold sweat.

'All right,' the soldier said eventually. 'We are expecting the governor a bit earlier than usual today, so with luck, you will see him before you leave. I will tell him you are here.'

It was too late for second thoughts, and Chaloner had no choice but to follow him through a series of dank, echoing corridors that led deep inside the maze of cells. A rank stench enveloped him. It was of sewage, old bedding, inedible food, and unwashed bodies. He put his sleeve across his face, thinking that even the decaying reek in the Anatomical Theatre was preferable to a prison's odour.

Newgate was a noisy place, too. People shouted and moaned as he passed, women as well as men. They clattered chains against the walls, and there always seemed to be a door slamming. A few prisoners had pewter cups or plates, and they clanged them against the bars of their windows – if they were lucky enough to occupy a chamber with real light. Others were crammed into dismal dungeons, their feet squelching in rotten straw as they paced back and forth.

'The governor is stopping off at Smithfield Market for a bucket of bull's blood on his way in,' said Chaloner's guide conversationally as they went. 'His wife makes these puddings, see. I am sure he will not be long, though, and he likes it when friends come to see him.'

'Oh,' said Chaloner weakly, feeling his trepidation mount.

The guide escorted him to an 'interviewing room' and told him to wait. It was a nasty chamber, with a dirty lamp hanging from the ceiling and no furniture but a table and two chairs. The floor had been swept, but there was an ominous stain on one of the flagstones. Chaloner sat and rested his head in his hands, wondering whether he would be able to learn what he needed from Dillon and escape before the governor exposed him as an impostor.

'Now *there* is a pose visitors should be encouraged to avoid,' came a mocking voice from the doorway. Chaloner leapt to his feet, supposing the governor had arrived sooner than expected. 'It is bad for the morale of the inmates.'

'This is Mr Dillon, sir,' said the guide, bowing as he backed out of the room. Chaloner shuddered when he heard a key turn in the door on the other side.

'Why the gloom?' asked Dillon. 'I am supposed to be the one in despair – *you* are free.'

Chaloner only hoped he would remain so. Dillon wore a large hat that shielded the upper half of his face, although it was more affectation than disguise. He was extraordinarily well dressed, and was wiping greasy

172

fingers on a clean piece of linen – Chaloner's arrival had evidently interrupted his morning meal. He looked around the cell in distaste, flicking the chair with his cloth before deigning to lower his elegantly clad rump on to it. Dillon, it seemed, was no ordinary prisoner, but one who was afforded a considerable degree of comfort.

Meanwhile, Chaloner tried to push from his mind the fact that it had been Dillon's refusal to kill an enemy that had brought about his old colleague Manning's death, and he half wished Thurloe had not told him. It was difficult to sit in the same room as a man whose actions had resulted in the execution of a friend. Dillon removed his hat, revealing his face for the first time.

'You!' Chaloner exclaimed in astonishment.

Dillon raised his eyebrows, and spoke in the same laconic drawl Chaloner remembered from Ireland. 'I might be forgiven for saying the same. What are you doing here, Garsfield? The guard said you are a friend of the governor, but I doubt you are anything of the kind.'

'I did not know your name was Dillon,' said Chaloner. 'I thought it was O'Brien, and that you were one of the Dublin rebels who escaped when we rounded up the culprits.'

Dillon glanced towards the door and lowered his voice. 'Not everything is as it seems. People called you Thomas Garsfield in Ireland, but I suspect you are actually Tom Heyden, Thurloe's man. He said he might send you to see me if he could not come himself. However, from our brief acquaintance in Dublin, I was under the impression that *you* worked for the Earl of Clarendon.'

'Not everything is as it seems,' repeated Chaloner. 'How do you come to be in this mess?'

'I am accused of murdering a merchant called Webb, but I assure you I did not. The charge is a ruse, to be rid of me.'

'Because you were involved in the Castle Plot?'

'Very possibly, since one of my companions from that particular incident – Richard Fanning – was sentenced with me. I do not know Sarsfeild, though. However, I suppose he *might* have played a role unknown to me. It was a large revolt, involving hundreds of people, after all.'

'What about the others? I understand nine of you were accused.'

'Nine! As if it would take nine men to dispatch one. What nonsense!'

Chaloner struggled not to jump in alarm when there was a sudden thump on the door. The dagger slipped into his hand, and he wondered whether it would be better to fight his way out or bluff when the governor arrived. But it was only the guide sweeping the floor outside.

'Do you know the others?' he pressed, keen to ask his questions and leave. 'Other than Fanning?'

Dillon shot him an unreadable smile. 'I really cannot recall. Prison has a numbing effect on a man's mind, and I do not blame Fanning for taking matters into his own hands.'

'What do you mean?'

Dillon leaned close to Chaloner and lowered his voice again. 'He will not be in Newgate this time tomorrow, because his friends are going to pull a trick with poisoned wine. *He* says such a rescue is safer than waiting for our master to help us, although I disagree.'

'How do you know what Fanning intends?' asked Chaloner. 'Are you in adjoining cells?'

'Lord, no!' exclaimed Dillon with a fastidious shudder. 'I am a man of means, and do not fester in the kind of pit Fanning can afford. My guards are kind enough to let us exchange missives – for a price – so I am aware of his plans. I told him he is making a mistake: he should wait for our patron to act.' He touched his coat absently, and Chaloner saw a bundle of papers in an inner pocket, at least one of them much fingered.

'Does your master write to you in here?' he asked, looking at it.

Dillon's fingers dropped away from the letters, a movement that looked furtive. 'No. He will not let me down, though, not a man of his eminence. He told me I would come to no harm, and I believe him.'

'Thurloe says you have an aversion to killing,' said Chaloner, changing the subject abruptly.

'I am a Quaker.' Dillon's expression was unreadable again. 'Did you know Manning? Is that why you are hostile now you know my real identity? His death was not my fault, you know; I had already abandoned Thurloe to work for the Royalists when he ordered me to eliminate that double-agent. But I could hardly kill one of my new colleagues, could I?'

'You have a curious history,' said Chaloner, declining to comment. 'First, you work for Thurloe, then you become a Royalist, and now you travel to Ireland to ferment revolt. I saw you with Thomas Scot before he surrendered himself. You were lucky you were not taken with the men he betrayed.'

'That was not luck.' Dillon shot him a nasty grin. 'You are not the only one capable of infiltrating a hopelessly amateur rebellion by pretending to be part of it.'

Chaloner was not sure whether to believe him. He

stood and began to pace, aiming to put himself behind Dillon and grab the papers from his pocket. 'Who sent you there?'

Dillon looked smug. 'I am not at liberty to say, although not everyone wanted the revolt to fail, just as not everyone wanted it to succeed. The politics of our time are very complex.'

'They are when you become involved,' muttered Chaloner. He saw he would have no straight answers about the Castle Plot, so moved back to the murder of Webb. 'Two of the eight accused with you were Fanning and Sarsfeild—'

'Both here, in Newgate,' interjected Dillon. 'Meanwhile, four had the King's pardon and two have disappeared completely – all of which is very revealing.'

'Not to me. Perhaps you would care to explain.'

Dillon sighed. 'The anonymous letter that listed us was a flagrant piece of spite – some cowardly rat attempting to avenge himself on all his enemies in one fell swoop. However, he picked on men who have powerful friends. Four were influential enough to be released the moment their names were known – Willys, Clarke, Fitz-Gerrard and Burne.'

'Burne?' echoed Chaloner, startled. He certainly knew that alias.

'Gregory Burne, more usually known as Adrian May. It is no secret that he is Williamson's spy and proud of it. A dangerous devil, with all his pride and arrogance. Have you met him?' Dillon did not wait for an answer. 'I doubt *he* had anything to do with Webb's death, because he is too slow and stupid for stealthy murder. The two who vanished were Fitz-Simons and Terrell. I *know* you have come across Fitz-Simons, because Thurloe told me.'

Chaloner kept his face impassive, but his stomach churned. It was not the mention of Fitz-Simons that unsettled him, but that of Terrell: his friend William Scot.

There was another thump on the door, and his time Chaloner failed to disguise his agitation. Dillon give his lopsided grin, amused by his visitor's growing unease. Chaloner struggled to pull himself together, resenting the notion that he was a source of entertainment to the leering man opposite. He rubbed his head as he paced back and forth, trying to make some sense of the gloating revelations.

First, there was Terrell. Had Scot's name been included in the letter because someone did not like him, as Dillon believed? All spies had enemies – sometimes very dangerous ones – so it was not impossible that Scot had incurred someone's wrath. And recently, he had been crucial in undermining the Irish rebellion – it might well have succeeded, had Scot not come up with the idea of using his brother to yield vital information. Or was it not Scot's alias that was included in the letter, but the 'dishonest fishmonger' of the same name, whom both Scot himself and Clarendon had mentioned?

Secondly, there was 'Burne'. May had also been in Ireland, and was the kind of man to accrue enemies – and not only from spying. As Dillon had said, May was dangerous and arrogant, and Chaloner was not the only one who disliked him.

Thirdly, there was Willys. A man called Willys had tried to burgle the Earl's offices with Johnson. Of course, it was a common name, and Chaloner knew coincidences were not impossible.

And finally, there was Fitz-Simons, who had disguised

himself as a vagrant in a desperate attempt to talk to Williamson. Did that mean he was Williamson's spy, too? His last words had been about three other men accused of killing Webb – Terrell, Burne and Dillon – so he clearly knew something about the case. Chaloner frowned as he considered the shooting. He had assumed May's shot was fatal, but perhaps he was wrong, and Fitz-Simons was not dead at all – that the 'death' had been a ruse to allow him to disappear for ever. It would explain why May had opened fire unnecessarily – he had been following orders to help the man. And the body in St Olave's charnel house was certainly not the same person Chaloner had seen killed. There had been plenty of blood and a 'hole' in Fitz-Simons, but these could be fabricated with paints, and Chaloner had not bothered to feel for a pulse. Furthermore, May had almost immediately covered the 'beggar's' head with a bag, thus preventing anyone from seeing his face.

Dillon was trying, unsuccessfully, to read his thoughts. 'Fitz-Simons was shot at Westminster last Friday. Thurloe told me you were with him, and that he had asked you to make sure I was safe.'

Chaloner nodded. 'You and Fitz-Simons were friends. You visited him at Chyrurgeons' Hall, where you studied plans of Dublin Castle together. And the two of you boarded a ship for Ireland in February.'

Dillon's smile was condescending. 'You have been busy! We were not friends, though – we just worked together. Perhaps *he* killed Webb, and left me to take the blame.'

But Fitz-Simons had not seemed sufficiently compe-tent for murder – and he had obviously felt some affec-tion towards his colleague, even if it was not reciprocated, because he had insisted twice that Dillon should be saved. 'You say *you* had nothing to do with Webb's stabbing?'

'The murder weapon was found in my house, but it was not mine. I had never seen it before.'

'Who hates you enough to want you hanged?'

'Presumably, the man who really did kill Webb.'

Chaloner stifled his impatience. It was difficult enough to be civil to the man who had been responsible for what had happened to Manning, and Dillon's half-answers were not helping. 'And who might that be?'

'I have no idea.' Dillon leaned back in his chair. 'I see you are eager to apprehend the villain on my behalf, but you need not trouble yourself. My master will do all that is necessary.'

'Who is he?' asked Chaloner. 'Thurloe?'

Dillon's expression was disdainful. 'I have far more influential patrons than a deposed Secretary of State, but please do not press me on this particular question. I shall not reveal his identity, and you will be wasting your time if you ask.'

Chaloner supposed he referred to Williamson, and wondered whether his confidence was justified. Then he thought about Fitz-Simons's 'death', and supposed the same powers might swing into action to secure Dillon's release. He jumped violently as a door slammed nearby. There were voices in the corridor and he braced himself for the governor. Then they faded away, and all was quiet again. But time was passing, and Chaloner was tiring of Dillon. He made a sudden lunge, and had the papers out of the man's pocket before Dillon realised what was happening. Dillon was furious, and tried to snatch them back, but Chaloner ducked away from him.

He found himself holding a bundle of notes, all in

cipher, which he would be able to decode given time, but that certainly made no sense to him as they were. And there was an older, soiled letter, but Dillon ripped it from his hands before he could open it.

'How dare you!'

'You are a fool to keep Fanning's messages,' said Chaloner, making a wild guess at what the notes contained. He relinquished them with some disgust when Dillon did not contradict him. 'That could see his escape plans exposed and his accomplices hanged with him.'

'That is hardly my problem,' snarled Dillon. He brandished the missives. 'When I am out, I shall show these to our master, to prove who trusted him and who did not. I shall be rewarded for my faith, while Fanning can find himself another employer.'

'Have you told anyone else what Fanning intends to do?'

'Only you, so we shall know who to blame, if he is caught.' Dillon was silent for a moment, then spoke in a whisper. 'I do not care who murdered Webb, but I should like to know who sent Bristol that letter. How are your powers of investigation?'

'They depend on honest answers. Do you have any suspicions to share?'

'Not really – and I have thought of little else since I have been in here.'

'Then perhaps the best way to expose him is by finding out who really did kill Webb. Can you tell me *anything* about his death?'

'I am a member of the Guinea Company, although I was not at the feast that fateful night – I was out drinking with a friend. However, I knew Webb, and I can tell you that almost everyone at African House detested the fellow. He regularly argued with Surgeon Wiseman about slavery. He poached Temple's customers from under his nose. He told Sir Alan Brodrick that his chamber music belonged in a tavern.'

'Webb was not cultured, then? Brodrick's playing is always excellent.'

'Webb was a lout. Meanwhile, Bristol owed him money, and he accused Johan Behn of making a pass at his wife – which you will know is ludicrous, if you have ever met Silence. And surgeons Johnson and Lisle were supposed to perform a Private Anatomy for him, but were unable to comply because the theatre roof was leaking; Webb threatened to sue them for false promises.'

'He certainly has one now,' muttered Chaloner, 'although I doubt it is quite what he had in mind.'

Dillon ignored him. 'He called Lady Castlemaine a whore to her face. Clarendon despises Webb's wife for her crass comments at Henry Lawes's funeral. Even spies found Webb abhorrent, and they tend to be more tolerant than most, because they meet so many low people.'

'Which spies?'

Dillon was enjoying himself. 'Let me see. Adrian May quarrelled with him over an unpaid bet. Eaffrey Johnson was pawed by him. John Thurloe took against him for backing the use of slaves. In fact, you will be hard-pressed to find a Londoner with *no* motive to kill him.'

The list went on, naming people Chaloner did not know, and eventually, he stood to leave. He was wasting time on a man he disliked and distrusted. If Dillon believed rescue was going to come from another quarter, then so be it. He only hoped, for Dillon's sake, that his faith was not misplaced.

'I am sure we shall come across each other once I am

free,' said Dillon, stretching languorously. 'Perhaps I shall buy you an ale, and we shall drink to Manning's memory.'

'Has the governor arrived yet?' Chaloner asked, as he and the guide walked along an unlit hall with glistening green walls and a floor that was soft with decomposing straw and maggot-infested sewage.

The guide shook his head and spoke in a whisper. 'Not yet. For a shilling, I will let you see Fanning, too, but you will have to make it quick. I got other duties today.'

Against his better judgement, which screamed at him to leave Newgate before he was caught, Chaloner handed over the coin and was conducted through a series of vault-like chambers set deep in the bowels of the earth, to emerge in a small, filthy yard. Two women were emptying slops into a drain, although their aim was careless and the ground was splattered with excrement. Another was skinning something that appeared to be a donkey. Flies buzzed, and Chaloner flapped them away from his face as his guide led him down a flight of steps to a cellar that stank so badly it made his eyes water.

'Fanning,' said the guide, gesturing to one of several corpses that lay in an untidy line on the sticky floor. 'He died of gaol-fever last night.'

Chaloner was tempted to ask for his shilling back. Looking at a body was not how he had interpreted the invitation to 'see' Fanning, but that would take time, and he had lingered too long already. He stepped forward to inspect Fanning's face, and recognised it: he had been one of the sullen, slovenly fellows who had accompanied Dillon to meetings and secret assignations in Ireland, and was identifiable not only by his very black hair, but by a purple birth-stain on his left hand.

182

'Do not touch him,' warned the guard. 'Not unless you want to catch a sickness.'

But Chaloner knew perfectly well that strangling was not contagious, and it was no fever that had killed the man. He crouched down to examine the lines around the throat more closely, wondering who was sufficiently audacious to kill a man in prison. Was it one of Fanning's friends, who had decided it was easier to dispatch him than supply guards with doctored wine? Was it the mysterious master, who objected to Fanning commissioning his own rescue? Or perhaps it was Dillon, because he did not want Fanning's escape to anger their patron into washing his hands of both of them.

'When was he found?' he asked, as the guide escorted him out of the vile yard.

'At dawn, when we took him his breakfast. He was not as wealthy as Mr Dillon, so we only looked in on him twice a day – Mr Dillon can have us visit him every time he rings his little bell. Poor Fanning. Gaol-fever gets a lot of them in here.'

'Can you explain how he came by those marks on his neck?'

'It happens when the ague stops their breath,' said the guide in a way that suggested he believed it. 'The governor will be sorry to lose him early – the public hate it when hangings are cancelled.'

'I do not suppose Fanning confided in you, did he?' asked Chaloner, clutching at straws. 'Told you about the crime he was supposed to have committed?'

'He never said nothing,' said the guide, opening a door that led to the main entranceway. Chaloner heaved a sigh of relief. Safety and freedom were almost within his grasp. 'He was a sour, angry cove, with a foul tongue.

He was a ship's chandler, though, so no common villain.'

'Can I see Sarsfeild?' asked Chaloner, while every fibre of his being urged him to walk out of the gate and never return. 'He was convicted of the same crime as the other two.'

The guide looked annoyed. 'I wish you could, because it would cost you another shilling, but he was transferred to Ludgate as soon as we heard Fanning was dead. Hah! Here is the governor at last. Come with me, so I can tell him you are here. He likes it when friends visit.'

The heavy front door had been opened to admit a fat gentleman in a tight red coat. Chaloner's guide started to move towards him with a greasy smile, but another guard got there first and started to talk about a consignment of tallow. A porter leaned hard on the massive gate, to begin the process of closing it. Chaloner took a step towards it, then broke into a run. His guide yelled, and Chaloner turned sideways to shoot through the gap, stumbling when his shirt caught on the rough wood. He tore it free. The door started to open again, and Chaloner saw guards massing behind, ready to pour out. He raced towards the nearby market, where he was soon lost among the chaotic jumble of stalls.

Chapter 6

The stench of prison clung to Chaloner as he left Newgate market. He was due to meet Leybourn at a nearby coffee house in an hour – where they would fortify themselves before going to visit Silence Webb – and he considered going home to change first. Temperance's house was closer, though, and he thought a spell in the yeasty warmth of her kitchen might dispel some of the reek that hung about him. He hesitated when he recalled she had gone from Puritan maid to brothel-master in the course of the last three months, but he did not have many friends in London, and was reluctant to lose one because he disapproved of her new occupation. He tapped on her door, and was conducted to the kitchen by a woman whose hair was a mass of purple ringlets. Temperance was sitting at the table, poring over a ledger. She was pleased to see him, but immediately wrinkled her nose.

'That bad?' he asked apologetically.

She nodded. 'What have you done to your arm? Come and sit by the fire while you tell me, and Maude will make us some of her famous coffee.'

Chaloner rarely discussed his work with 'civilians'.

185

Leybourn was different, because he undertook the occasional mission for Thurloe, but Temperance was another matter entirely. He deflected her questions with a combination of abbreviated truths and subject changes, as he had done with acquaintances all his adult life. Temperance was not so easily misled, however, and refused to accept the explanation that he had simply fallen over.

'Colonel Holles claimed you were viciously attacked at the Court ball.'

Chaloner recalled Holles mentioning Temperance's establishment, and saw he would have to be careful, if the soldier was the kind of fellow to gossip. 'He is wrong – it was just an accident.'

Temperance nodded in a way that said she did not believe him. 'And Will Leybourn told me you are investigating the vagrant May shot. He said there are connections between that death, the murder of Webb *and* the Castle Plot, and asked me to listen for any idle chatter among my guests.'

Chaloner was startled and angry. 'Then he should not have done. It may not be safe.'

'There is no danger in listening, then relaying snippets to trusted friends,' objected Temperance. She grinned suddenly. 'I will be like the Bishop of London's new parrot. He is teaching it prayers, and it is rewarded with a nut each time it masters a new one. How will you reward me?'

She was underestimating the risk, and Chaloner did not care what the Bishop of London did with his bird. 'Please do not do this, Temperance. I have lost too many friends to spying already.'

Temperance's smile was mischievous. 'Perhaps you have, but did *they* enjoy the favour of powerful courtiers

186

like Bristol and Lady Castlemaine? I provide a unique service, and no one will risk the Court's anger by meddling with me. You worry too much.'

'Here you are,' said Maude, placing a dish of dark sludge in front of him. It looked as if it might relieve him of teeth if he attempted to swallow any. 'It has extra sugar, on account of your bad arm.'

'I have forsworn sugar,' he said, relieved to have an excuse, 'because of the slave trade.'

'Have you?' asked Maude, puzzled. 'I am not sure my coffee is drinkable without it.'

Chaloner doubted it was drinkable with. 'Pity.'

'Mr Terrell, the Irish scholar, was here last night, asking for you,' said Maude, downing the brew herself and smacking her lips to show he was missing something good.

'Adrian May and Johan Behn were with him,' added Temperance disapprovingly. 'I do not think much of May at all. He leers at my girls and he has an ugly temper. I do not like Behn, either.'

'I do,' said Maude. Her expression became dreamy and, to his utter astonishment, Chaloner saw she was smitten with the bulky Brandenburger. She was old enough to be his mother, so it was not an attraction he would have anticipated. 'I heard that Eaffrey Johnson wants to marry him, but if she does not make an honest man of him soon, then I shall do it for her. Johan will make a perfect husband for any red-blooded woman – rich, handsome, charming and clever.'

'*Behn?*' asked Chaloner in disbelief, wondering if they were talking about the same fellow. The familiar use of the merchant's first name did not escape his notice, either, and he had the sudden suspicion that Maude might know

187

Behn rather better than was decent for a man with an adoring fiancée.

'He may look pretty, but he has the feel of a bully about him,' said Temperance, cutting across Maude's indignant reply. 'And there is something about him I do not trust. If I were Eaffrey, I would look elsewhere for *my* perfect husband.'

Maude sniffed huffily. 'You do not know what you are talking about, and if you cannot see Johan's charms, then there must be something wrong with you. And he is *not* a bully, either – at least, not with ladies.'

'He bullies men, then?' pounced Chaloner. 'Who, exactly?'

Maude poured herself more coffee. 'He quarrelled with Webb once or twice – I heard some of the Guinea Company men talking about it. Webb had accused Johan of seducing his wife, you see, although obviously a comely fellow like Johan would never set his sights on a woman like *Silence*.' She fluffed up her hair in a way that suggested she considered herself a far better catch.

'Do not forget what else the Guinea Company men told you, Maude,' said Temperance coolly. She disapproved of her friend's hankering for the merchant. 'They also said Behn left the most recent dinner early and in a foul temper because of a quarrel with Webb. And it was after *that* that Webb was murdered.'

'You said Terrell was asking for me,' said Chaloner, after several minutes of listening to Maude's spirited defence of the man who had captured her fancy. There was no point in arguing with her – her case was based on supposition and the kind of wishful thinking that was immune to reason – so neither he nor Temperance tried. 'Did he say why?'

'He had been waiting at your house all evening, and was worried when you did not return,' explained Temperance. 'He said he had something urgent to tell you *and* he was afraid Wiseman's surgery might have had some adverse effects. I told him you were adept at looking after yourself, but my assurances did nothing to ease his concern.'

Maude finished her coffee, and to show there were no hard feelings about their difference of opinion regarding Behn, said, 'I heard Temple hatching a plot against your earl, Thomas. Would you like me to tell you about it?'

'No,' replied Chaloner gently. 'Sometimes, information is leaked to a particular person to test whether he or she can be trusted. You may put yourself in danger if you talk to the wrong people.'

'No one will trace this to me, because I happened to be under a bed at the time. Temple was telling Bristol that the best way to attack Clarendon was to damage his reputation for "moral rectitude".'

'I see,' said Chaloner, more interested in why the bulky matron should have been under a bed containing Temple and Bristol than in learning about the toothless politician's latest hare-brained scheme. Unfortunately for his burning curiosity, it was hardly something he felt he could ask.

'Temple has hired an actress called Rosa Lodge,' elaborated Maude. 'And the plan is for her to accuse him of rape. Petticoats will be left in Clarendon's chamber to support her allegation.'

'That is ridiculous! He is not that kind of man, and no one will believe this Rosa Lodge.'

'That is not the point,' said Maude. 'An accusation does not have to be true for it to cause trouble.'

Chaloner regarded her unhappily, aware that she was

right. Temple would fan the flames of rumour and suspicion, and the Earl would be deemed guilty by default.

'That bandage makes you very visible and you once told me a spy should conceal distinguishing features,' said Temperance, when he made no reply. She stood, and fetched a handsome purple coat from a cupboard in the hall. 'This will hide it far better, because it has longer sleeves.'

'The man who owned it has gone to Rome,' added Maude, guessing the reason for his reluctance to accept it. 'So do not worry about it being recognised. Besides, you cannot go about your business smelling like that – you will have half the dogs in London following you. Take your clothes off, and I will air them in the garden.'

'I am not undressing in front of you,' objected Chaloner, the spectre of Temperance's prim mother looming large in his mind.

'You think this is a brothel, and that we intend to seduce you,' said Maude, eyes narrowed. 'Well, I assure you it is not. It is a *gentleman's club*.'

'I cannot imagine what your parents would think, Temperance,' said Chaloner. This was not true – he could imagine *exactly* what the prudish Puritans would have said about their only daughter's enterprise, and it would not have been pleasant.

Temperance's grimace told him she knew, too. 'I have never criticised the life you lead, Thomas, and you should return the courtesy. At least *I* do not visit *you* stinking of corpses.'

Dressed in the purple coat, a clean shirt and breeches that smelled sweetly of lavender, Chaloner felt more human. He walked along The Strand to Covent Garden, where his favourite coffee house was located. Will's was a comfortable, manly place, full of tobacco smoke and the sharp aroma of roasting beans. Coffee houses were the exclusive domain of men, where they went to discuss politics, religion, literature, the increasing trouble with Holland, and any other contentious subject they felt like airing. The government wanted to suppress them before they became centres of sedition, but Spymaster Williamson had argued that it was better to leave them as they were, so he could plant informers to listen to what was being said and who said it. He even operated one or two shops of his own, and hired to run them men with a talent for encouraging dangerous talk.

That day, Will's was quiet, because it was past the time when men gathered for their midday meals. After Newgate, Chaloner did not feel much like eating, but Leybourn had brought a tray of pastries with him, and devoured the lot while talking non-stop about the Arctic travels of Martin Frobisher.

'You were supposed to be reading about Guinea,' said Chaloner, when he managed to interject a comment into the continuous stream of information. 'To help us solve Webb's murder.'

Leybourn waved a dismissive hand. 'Guinea is boring, but the search for a Northwest Passage is an adventure fit to stir the heart of any Englishman. Are you unwell? You are very quiet.'

'I wish you had not recruited Temperance and Maude to eavesdrop on their customers. You should know better.'

Leybourn grimaced. 'I did not "recruit" anyone. I asked, casually, whether they had heard anything about Webb, the Castle Plot or what Bristol plans to do to your earl, and they leapt at the chance to help us. You seem

191

angry. Why? Surely you cultivated sources like these in the past.'

'Not among my friends.'

Leybourn regarded him coolly. 'You regularly ask *me* for information. Am I not a friend, then?'

'That is different. You undertake assignments for Thurloe all the time.'

'Not *all* the time,' said Leybourn huffily. 'In fact, I am only ever obliged to do it when you appear and start meddling in perilous situations. However, if you are afraid for Temperance, I suppose I can ask her to desist, although it will not be easy. She was looking forward to the challenge.'

Chaloner suspected he was right, and that she would eavesdrop with or without their blessing. He said nothing, and watched Leybourn reduce a pie to a pile of crumbs and discarded peas – Leybourn did not like peas and always picked them out. It was an aversion he shared with Scot, and Chaloner found himself thinking about the letter that had seen Dillon sentenced to death. *Was* Scot's current alias one of the nine names on the list? If so, then why had he not mentioned it when they had discussed Webb's murder at the Court ball on Saturday? Or did the letter refer to the disreputable fishmonger of the same name? What had Scot wanted with him the previous night, and why had he been with May and Behn? Chaloner found himself becoming uneasy with all the questions that rattled around in his mind, and began to wish he was back in Ireland, where everything had been so much more simple.

Leybourn made an effort to overcome his sulks and forced a smile. 'So, you visited Temperance's bawdy house again, did you?'

'It is a *gentleman's club*, apparently. I hope it does not land her in trouble. People are fickle, and what is popular today might be the target of hatred tomorrow. I had no idea she would reveal a hitherto unknown talent for brothel-keeping. She does not seem the type.'

'You know enough madams to judge, do you? Come on, Tom – do not be Puritan about this. We had more than enough of that under Cromwell, and I, for one, like a bordello.'

'You do?' asked Chaloner, startled. He had not thought the surveyor a bordello kind of man.

'I have no wife,' said Leybourn, a little soulfully. 'But I would like to be married, and it is not easy to meet ladies in the bookselling business. Bordellos offer a unique opportunity to enjoy female company, and I am ever hopeful of finding the perfect spouse in one.'

'You may find yourself looking a long time,' warned Chaloner.

'I hope not,' said Leybourn wistfully. 'Have you finished the coffee? We had better tackle Silence Webb before our courage fails. I confess I am not looking forward to this. I know Thurloe told me to explore worthy widows with a view to marriage, but I would rather remain single than take Silence.'

As they walked to The Strand, where the grandly named 'Webb Hall' was located, Chaloner told Leybourn what Temperance and Maude had overheard, and summarised his interview with Dillon. Leybourn stopped him once or twice, to make the point that being given such sensitive information might place *him* in danger, just as it might Temperance, but he had a naturally curious mind, and his pique was soon forgotten as he put his own questions and observations.

'I have no idea whether anything Dillon said was true,' concluded Chaloner eventually. 'The only thing I know for certain is that he was part of the Castle Plot, because I saw him there – he said his name was O'Brien. And I know he expects rescue. Six of the nine accused are already free.'

'Yes, but Fitz-Simons's "disappearance" means he was shot.'

'But perhaps not fatally – it was not his body in the charnel house, remember?'

'That means nothing. I know it is an odd coincidence that a beggarly corpse called Fitz-Simons appears just as Surgeon Fitz-Simons is killed, but it may be just that – coincidence. Besides, May arranged for Surgeon Fitz-Simons's body to be buried in St Martin's Church, if you recall.'

Chaloner inclined his head. 'True. Perhaps Beggar Fitz-Simons *is* irrelevant. However, the way Johnson opened the door to the charnel house was furtive, to say the least.'

Leybourn shrugged. 'I imagine the anatomising of corpses is a clandestine sort of business, so you probably should not read too much into the actions of a man who does it for a living. You say Fitz-Simons whispered two other names before he "died" – Terrell and Burne. Perhaps you should ask Scot and May why *they* think their aliases should have been singled out for mention.'

'If Scot *is* that particular Terrell – there is a fishmonger of the same name, do not forget.' Chaloner saw Leybourn look doubtful. 'Scot is a good man, Will. He has saved me from trouble more times than I can remember, and there are few men I trust more. I can quite honestly say that I would not be alive today if it were not for him.'

Leybourn rested a hand on his shoulder. 'I was not suggesting there is anything untoward about Scot. However, *he* is a spy, and so are the others Fitz-Simons mentioned – Dillon and May. It seems unlikely that Fitz-Simons would cite two spies and a fishmonger. But regardless, the whole case is becoming ever more curious. Dillon is probably right when he said whoever wrote Bristol that letter may just have listed men who had crossed him in some way.'

Chaloner watched the chaos surrounding an overturned fruit barrow near an ornately turreted Tudor mansion called Bedford House. Apples bounced everywhere, and were eagerly pounced on by children, beggars, horses and even a pig, despite the fact that they were wizened and soft from having been stored too long. The barrow-boy screeched his dismay and wielded a stick, but he might have well as railed against the tide, because his entire stock had been spirited away in a matter of moments.

'I thought from the start that it was odd *nine* men should be needed to kill one,' said Chaloner. 'And if they were named from malice, then it means Dillon is wrongly convicted. I hope he is right to put his trust in his patron, though, given what has happened to Fanning.'

'Will you visit Sarsfeild in Ludgate? He might tell you this great man's name.'

Chaloner was not enthused by the prospect. 'I hate prisons. Will you go instead? The guards move about between gaols and I am afraid my escape from Newgate attracted too much attention.'

'I would rather not,' said Leybourn. 'I dislike the smell. Do you think Sarsfeild asked to be transferred when he heard Fanning was murdered?'

'He was transferred because the prison authorities want to make sure he does not die before his execution,' said

Chaloner, surprised by the refusal. He had never asked Leybourn for a favour before, and wondered whether their friendship was as solid as he thought. 'Dillon is in decent lodgings, but Fanning was not, and probably neither was Sarsfeild. The public dislike being cheated of their due, and the governor needs the last two alive.'

'Sometimes I am ashamed to be a Londoner,' said Leybourn. He stopped just past the New Exchange, poking the ground with his foot. 'Webb died here. His body was found by tradesmen the following day – honest ones, or his corpse would have been stripped.'

Chaloner looked around him. The New Exchange – no longer so new, given that it was more than fifty years old – boasted a splendid stone façade in the style of a Gothic cathedral, and inside were two tiers of galleries containing exclusive little shops and stalls. Goods of all descriptions could be bought, although only by the very rich, and it was *the* place to be seen by gentlemen and ladies of fashion. A short distance to the west was Clarendon's city residence, Worcester House. Tucked between it and the New Exchange was a smaller building.

'This is Webb's home?' asked Chaloner, peering through the iron gates. The grounds contained far too many pieces of sculpture for the available space; they rubbed shoulders with fountains and gazebos, as if their owner could not decide what he wanted, so had purchased everything available.

Leybourn nodded. 'Tasteful, is it not?'

Webb Hall had once boasted perfect classical proportions and some of the best Tuscan cornices on The Strand. Unfortunately, someone with more money than taste had lavished entirely the wrong kind of attention on the building, changing its windows, adding chimneys that spoiled its symmetry, and refacing it with cheap bricks. The door had been enlarged and a garish porch tacked on to the outside, complete with window hangings of scarlet lace.

'Oh, dear,' said Chaloner, regarding it askance.

'Oh, dear, indeed,' agreed Leybourn, walking up the path and knocking at the door. 'Now *this* looks like a brothel. I am surprised Temperance is not losing customers to it.'

'Perhaps she is,' said Chaloner, glimpsing a furtive movement at the side of the house. It was a man, hurrying to be away from them. 'Is that Johan Behn?'

'I doubt it,' said Leybourn. 'Or he would not be climbing over the wall like a felon.'

The door was opened by a servant who wore a livery of green and orange stripes. He conducted them along a hallway that glittered with gold leaf and opened the door to a drawing room that faced the river. A massive Turkish carpet covered the floor, anchored down by four Grecian urns. Dark Dutch landscapes shared the walls with the paler hues of the Venetian schools, and small tables had been placed in inconvenient places to display unique works of art. Through the window, Chaloner saw a bulky figure with fair hair aiming for the private jetty that would allow him to take a boat.

'There is a word for this,' whispered Leybourn in Chaloner's ear, too overwhelmed by the interior décor to consider looking outside.

'Vulgar?'

'No,' murmured Leybourn. 'That is the word for *her*.'

A large lady reclined on an exquisite French-made couch, eating sugared almonds. She wore a loose black gown, to indicate she was in mourning, and her hair was in elegant disarray. She also sported at least a dozen 'face patches', which Chaloner found disconcerting, because it reminded him of a case of 'black pox' he had once seen in the Dutch Antilles. He stepped forward to bow, noting that Leybourn remained by the door, as if anticipating that a quick escape might be required.

'Forgive the intrusion, ma'am. My name is Thomas Heyden. The Lord Chancellor asked me to convey his personal condolences for your loss.'

Silence's small eyes gleamed with pleasure. 'That is nice – he lives next door, you know.'

She adjusted her ample bosom, winked at Chaloner and patted the seat beside her, wanting him to sit closer than was seemly. He pretended not to notice and took a chair in the window.

Silence sighed irritably. 'Do not perch where I cannot see you. I insist you come over here – but bring me a glass of wine before you come. No, not *half* a measure – fill it, man! You youngsters do not know the meaning of a "glass" of wine. Do you like my necklace? It is made of *real* emeralds.'

'It is very pretty,' said Chaloner, inspecting it politely. When he tried to move away, she grabbed his wrist and hauled him down next to her. From across the room, he heard Leybourn snigger.

'Good, now we can talk properly,' she said, resting her hand on his knee. He started to stand, but she gripped his coat in a way that would have made escape undignified. 'You look familiar. Are you kin to that rascal Thomas Chaloner, the regicide? My Matthew used to clean his ditches in the old days, and he was always very generous with the ale afterwards.'

'Your husband cleared ditches?' asked Chaloner, deftly avoiding the question. 'I thought he was a merchant.'

'He found a purse of gold in one sewer, and wise investments set him on the road to wealth. Eventually, he was able to buy a ship, and his fortunes blossomed ever after. Poor Matthew. I am devastated by his death. What is Lord Clarendon going to do about it?'

'The culprits have already been apprehended,' said Leybourn. 'And three men sentenced to hang.'

'Three out of the nine who were named,' she said with a pout. 'Four were pardoned and two disappeared, never to be seen again. I believe they *did* kill Matthew – he was a strong man, and it *would* have taken nine felons to subdue him – but I also believe they did it on the orders of someone else. And that same someone then stepped forward and got six of them off.'

'Who?' asked Chaloner.

She sniffed and ate an almond. 'Many men were jealous of my husband. Take Sir Richard Temple, for example. He *pretended* to be our friend, but he bitterly resented Matthew stealing his customers. Perhaps Matthew *did* poach them, but competition is the nature of mercantile business, is it not?'

Chaloner was thoughtful. Temple had been on Dillon's list of suspects, too. *Was* the toothless politician involved in something untoward? 'Who else?'

'I do not like to say it, since Lord Clarendon has been kind enough to send me his personal condolences, but his cousin Brodrick took offence at my husband's dislike of music. Then there is the Earl of Bristol – he owed Matthew money, and no man likes being in debt.'

'How much money?' asked Leybourn.

Silence addressed Chaloner. 'Only *common* people talk

about money. The Bishop of London told me so, when I asked him how much he earns. Suffice to say Bristol owed us a thousand pounds.'

'Let's not talk about money, though,' murmured Leybourn. Chaloner fought the urge to laugh.

'But Bristol needed more,' Silence continued. 'Matthew promised him – well, promised his *broker*, since an earl does not ask himself – another three hundred, which would have been paid today. Unfortunately for him, the lawyers have frozen Matthew's accounts until the will is settled. Still, it will all be mine, so *I* am not worried.'

'Webb was willing to lend him more?' asked Chaloner, startled. 'Even though Bristol already owed him a small fortune?'

'Bristol's broker said he was willing to pay a higher rate of interest for a further advance. However, all this was arranged *before* we were introduced to him at the Guinea Company dinner, and I learned what kind of man he is.'

'Webb did not actually know Bristol?' asked Leybourn, confused. 'Yet he lent—'

'All loans are arranged through brokers,' interrupted Silence, still addressing Chaloner. 'At least, that is how it works with us sophisticated types. Matthew had never met Bristol, and was looking forward to making his acquaintance at that dinner – he wanted to lend him more money, to secure his long-term friendship. But before they could talk, Bristol made a rude remark about my face patches. I was angry, I can tell you! I was going to tell Matthew to do no more business with him, but Matthew was brutally slain before I could speak to him about it.'

'Are Temple, Brodrick and Bristol your only suspects?' asked Chaloner encouragingly.

'No. There is also Surgeon Wiseman. He took against Matthew for supporting the use of slaves in the production of sugar. *He* could have plunged a rapier into Matthew's breast. He is a medical man, after all, and would know where to strike – and he *does* own a sword.'

'Every gentleman owns a sword,' said Chaloner.

Silence ran her fingers down his scabbard. 'I know *gentlemen* do. Do you know how to use it?'

'It is for display,' said Chaloner, not wanting her to demand a demonstration. 'Anyone else?'

'Matthew took a dislike to poor Johan Behn, although Johan would never hurt anyone, so he will not be guilty. Then there is that sluttish Lady Castlemaine, who objected to Matthew calling her a whore – despite the fact that she is one. And he quarrelled with others, too, because he spoke the truth. I cannot name them all, because there are so many.'

'Will you tell us what happened the night your husband died? I understand you went home early.'

'I was tired of drunken men pawing me with their hot hands.' Chaloner heard Leybourn snort his disbelief. 'So I summoned the carriage, and Matthew said he would follow later. We have our *own* transport, you see, like all people of worth. The driver saw me inside the door, and he said he would go back for Matthew at midnight, when the dinner was due to finish.'

'The following day, when you realised Matthew was dead, did you ask the driver whether he had done as he had promised?'

'No. It was obvious he had not, or Matthew would not have been walking. I sent him a note – I wrote it myself – and put it on the table in his quarters to tell him he was dismissed. I have not seen him since, and good riddance. His laziness gave wicked men an opportunity to kill my Matthew.'

'When was the funeral?'

'Last Thursday. I do not approve of delays where corpses are concerned – not after smelling Henry Lawes – but three weeks was the quickest we could manage. I wanted it done properly, you see, with invitations issued to all the right people – people of quality.'

'Did they come?' asked Leybourn, a little maliciously.

She glared at him. 'Most had prior engagements – I obviously chose a bad day. Matthew is in St Paul's Cathedral now, with all those saints and bishops. We bought space in the vault when we first got rich, although we did not expect him to be in it quite so soon.'

They talked a while longer, but it was clear she knew nothing of relevance. She was bitter enough to make Chaloner wonder whether *she* had written the message to Bristol containing the nine names, but then he realised her list would have been a good deal longer. He left when her hand began to move up his thigh and Leybourn's amusement became more difficult to control. Before they escaped from the house, he asked a servant where the driver had lived, and was directed to a room above the stable in the yard.

'You heard what Silence said.' Leybourn was puzzled by the diversion. 'He will be long gone – frightened someone will accuse him of deliberately neglecting to fetch Webb so others could kill him.'

Chaloner opened the door and saw Silence's note, unopened on the table. The room reeked, badly enough to make Leybourn back out with his hand over his mouth. There was a cupboard in the thickness of one wall, used for storage. Chaloner broke the lock, stepping back quickly when something large and heavy toppled towards him.

'Stabbed,' he said, kneeling to inspect the corpse. It still wore its orange and green uniform. 'He has probably been dead since Webb's murder. Someone *wanted* Webb to walk home alone, which means his death was no casual robbery, but a planned assassination.'

'Does this mean Dillon is exonerated?'

'It does not exonerate anyone – including Silence herself.'

'She would not kill Webb. He was her husband.'

'And now she is a very wealthy widow.'

Although Chaloner disliked the notion of asking Scot whether it was his name on the list sent to Bristol – however he phrased the question, it would sound like an accusation, and he did not have so many friends that he could afford to lose them over misunderstandings – he knew he had no choice. He walked to the Chequer, a large coaching inn at Charing Cross, where Scot always stayed when he was in London. But Scot's room was empty, and the landlord said he had not seen him since noon. Because it might be hours before Scot returned, and he was loath to waste time waiting, Chaloner went to White Hall, to update the Earl on his progress.

The clouds had thinned since the morning's drizzle, and a glimmering of sunshine raised London's spirits. Traders yelled brazen lies about their wares, masons sang as they repaired a building that had collapsed during recent heavy rains, horses whinnied, wheels rattled, and everywhere was clamour. A blacksmith was making horseshoes, a knife-sharpener keened blades against his whetstone, children yelped and screeched over a hoop, and street preachers were out in full force, warning against the dangers of sin. Two men ran an illicit cock-fight in an alley, accompanied by frenzied cheers, barking dogs and the angry screeches of the birds.

As usual, White Hall thronged with clerks, servants, soldiers and courtiers. In addition, labourers had been drafted in to clean the gardens, which were still a mess of litter, trampled flowers and discarded food after the ball two nights before. Further confusion came from the fact that Lady Castlemaine was moving from the west side of the Privy Garden to more sumptuous accommodation on the east, which put her considerably closer to the King. Her possessions – along with innumerable items looted from people too frightened to stop her – were being transferred to her new domain, while she stood in the midst of the chaos and snapped impractical orders. She swore viciously at one servant for putting a bowl in the wrong place, and kicked another for dropping a box of wigs.

'She is not very patient,' Chaloner remarked to Holles, who had come to walk with him.

'Good body, though,' remarked the colonel, leering appreciatively as they passed. 'Did you see her in her shift the other day? What a treat for sore eyes! She is even better than the whores at Hercules's Pillars Alley – and that is saying something. Do you not agree?'

'Have you heard any rumours about Webb?' asked Chaloner, changing the subject. Temperance's girls had made no impression on him one way or the other. He supposed his lack of interest stemmed from the fact that the woman he had hoped would become his wife had died the previous year, and he had not felt much like looking at anyone else since.

'No, but there have been plenty about your fictional upholsterer. The most common is that he lies at death's door and that it is Lord Clarendon's fault.'

Chaloner gazed across the garden as Lady Castlemaine howled abuse at a groom, battering him about the head and shoulders with a fan. The implement was made of thin wood and paper, but she wielded it with sufficient force to draw blood nonetheless. 'Is her beauty really enough to compel His Majesty to condone that sort of behaviour? It is hardly dignified.'

Holles laughed, drawing the attention of several retainers. Some wore Buckingham's livery while Chaloner had seen the others serving Bristol at the ball. 'She is in a good mood today, because she is getting what she wants – the most desirable lodgings in White Hall.'

'Holles!' shouted one of Bristol's men. 'Who is he, and where are you taking him?'

Chaloner recognised Willys, the thin, yellow-legged fellow who had searched Clarendon's office. He also recalled that a 'Willys' had been on the letter Bristol had been sent. It was a common name, but he wanted to ask the man about it even so – although preferably not when he was surrounded by armed cronies.

'We are on Lord Clarendon's business,' responded Holles tartly. 'And it is none of yours.'

'You are not allowed to bring just anyone into White Hall,' said Willys nastily. 'There are too many villains around these days. You are lucky May was alert over that beggar business, or *you* would have been blamed for the King's murder. His Majesty was under *your* protection and you failed him.'

'Piffle,' said Holles. 'Go and find someone else to bleat your stupid accusations at. I am busy.'

205

Willys's sword started to come out of its scabbard and his companions prepared themselves for a skirmish, but Holles was too experienced a campaigner to be provoked into a fight where he would be so heavily outnumbered. He sneered his disdain at Willys and strode away, leaving the man spluttering in frustrated indignation.

'Willys is Bristol's aide,' said Holles to Chaloner when they were out of earshot. 'Loyal to his master, but deeply stupid. He has been trying to goad me to do battle with him for days now – he probably thinks it will please Bristol to see Clarendon with one fewer supporter.'

'He is right. Clarendon will be less safe without you watching out for him.'

Holles cleared his throat. 'I am sorry I could not protect you from that Brandenburg ape on Saturday. He flew at you like a madman, and you were down before I could draw my pistol. I had no idea such a lumbering brute could move so fast.'

'Neither had I,' said Chaloner with a sigh.

Chaloner took a circuitous route to the Lord Chancellor's chambers, hoping to see Scot on the way, but he was out of luck. He met Brodrick, though, who told him 'Peter Terrell' had been invited to speak to the Royal Society on his botanical theories, and that the lecture and meal that followed were likely to take most of the day. He smiled ruefully at the spy.

'I am afraid Greeting played well last night, especially the Locke, and the Queen professed herself enchanted. She has asked us to perform for the Portuguese ambassador tomorrow, and Greeting has agreed to join us. It is unfortunate, because I prefer your company to his – all *he* wants is a chance to hobnob with high-ranking courtiers – but it cannot be helped.'

'It is only temporary,' said Chaloner, dismayed. 'The splint will be off on Saturday.'

'Perhaps so, but Lisle told me these dressings often cause permanent damage. However, you may be lucky. When you are well again, I shall talk to some friends and see if they have any vacancies. Musical consorts are all the rage these days, so it should not be too difficult to find you something . . . suited to your reduced abilities.'

Chaloner watched him walk away, shocked. He flexed his fingers. Surely, Lisle was wrong? He could not imagine life without his viol – and a trumpet would not be the same at all. Feeling somewhat low in spirits, he accessed Clarendon's suite via a servant's corridor, and tapped softly on a door that was concealed behind a statue. The Lord Chancellor opened it cautiously, and Chaloner saw it had been fitted with bolts and a bar since his last visit.

'I came to tell you what I have learned about the man May shot, sir,' he said, trying to inject some enthusiasm into his voice. The truth was that any investigation paled into insignificance when compared to what the loss of music would mean for his quality of life.

'What man?' the Earl seemed agitated, and Chaloner supposed he was not the only one who had been un-settled by bad news that day. 'Do you mean that beggar? Forget him, and concentrate on Bristol. He is plotting something serious – I can sense it.'

Chaloner recalled what Temperance and Maude had told him. 'Yes – there is a plan afoot to bring your "moral rectitude" into question. Have you met a woman called Rosa Lodge? She is an actress.'

'Certainly not! Such persons are invariably ladies of

ill repute, and I am a happily married man. I leave that sort of thing to Bristol. And, unfortunately, to the King.'

'Have you found any petticoats among your belongings? Ones that do not belong to your wife?'

the Earl's voice dropped to a prudish whisper. 'There *was* some feminine apparel – an item of an intimate nature – under my pillow last night. I assumed Holles had put it there, to cheer me after an unhappy session with the King. However, I do not approve of lewdness, so I threw it on the fire.'

'Temple hired this Rosa Lodge to accuse you of immoral acts. If any ladies request private interviews, you should refuse them.'

'That will not be a problem. I have turned away three today already – I sent them to Colonel Holles. He has a kind heart, and will help them if he can.'

Chaloner was sure he would. 'Some of these actresses are very good, though. And Temple seems very determined.'

'So am I, Heyden – good *and* determined.'

Dusk had fallen by the time Chaloner had finished talking to the Earl, so he joined Holles in escorting him home to Worcester House. Because Clarendon disliked his crumbling Tudor lodgings, he had purchased land on the north side of Piccadilly with a view to building himself something rather better. Chaloner had seen the projected designs, and was astounded by the display of lavish opulence. It would be the finest edifice in the city, far grander than anything owned by the King, and was certain to cause jealousy and resentment. Tentatively, he had advised scaling down the plans, but the Earl had tartly informed him that he did not know what he was talking about.

As he and Holles left Worcester House, Chaloner happened to glance over at the candlelit windows of Webb Hall next door, and saw the unmistakably hulking profile of Johan Behn framed in an upper chamber. He frowned, trying to think of a good reason why the merchant should visit Silence after dark. Did he intend to take up where her husband had left off, and buy a ship to ferry sugar from the plantations? Chaloner wondered whether Eaffrey knew what her lover was doing.

Holles announced a desire to visit Temperance, so Chaloner went with him, curious to know why her establishment was so popular with powerful nobles. It did not take him long to appreciate the difference between a 'gentleman's club' and a bawdy house. Professional musicians played the latest compositions in an ante-chamber – he was startled to see Greeting sawing away – and skilled cooks had been hired to provide guests with good food and fine wines. The girls were pretty and in possession of all their teeth, and Preacher Hill stood outside to prevent undesirables from entering. He would have repelled Chaloner, too, but Temperance intervened.

'Thomas will always be welcome,' she said, laying a hand on Hill's arm. The preacher–doorman smiled, although the grin turned to a glower as soon as her back was turned.

'Just behave,' he snarled, as Chaloner passed. 'If there is any trouble from you, I will . . . '

'Will what?' asked Chaloner mildly.

Hill bristled. 'Just behave,' he repeated, before turning to vet the next customers.

While Holles made a nuisance of himself with a sadly misnamed lady called Modesty, Chaloner listened to the quartet, thinking with satisfaction that Greeting's bowing was well below par. He stared at his bandaged arm, and hoped with all his heart that Lisle would be able to help him on Saturday. Before he became too consumed with self-pity, he went to sit near Maude, who was holding forth about the latest play at the King's House in Drury Lane, and then listened to a portly gentleman describing plans for a new pheasant garden in Hyde Park. It was well past midnight before he left, slipping away quietly when Holles went moustache-down on the table and began to snore.

He lay on his bed in Fetter Lane, watching the stars through the window and thinking about his viol as he listened to the periodic cries of the bellmen. At five o'clock, he rose and spent an hour practising his bowing, muting the strings with his immobile left hand, so the noise would not disturb his landlord. Then he washed, dressed and set off for White Hall to spy on Bristol. He wore his best clothes and a wig of real hair, so he would be able to mingle with the upper echelons of British high society and not look out of place.

The King liked to ride in St James's Park of a morning, and most high-ranking, early-rising members of the Court went with him. They took their retainers, and the palace's many hangers-on went, too, so the monarch's peaceful gallop was often carried out in the presence of hundreds of people. Unfortunately for Chaloner, it meant most courtiers were either riding with His Majesty or still in bed, and he could hardly eavesdrop in an empty palace.

Annoyed with himself for forgetting that there was little point in visiting White Hall before ten o'clock, he turned his attention to the other leads that needed to be explored. First, he wanted to visit St Martin's Church, to ask whether the vergers really had collected

210

a body – Fitz-Simons's – from May. Secondly, he had to talk to Scot. And thirdly, he needed to go to St Paul's Cathedral and ascertain why Webb was not in his vault, but in the Anatomical Theatre at Chyrurgeons' Hall. He recalled Wiseman saying the faces of the dead were kept covered during the operation, and hoped it was true. He could not imagine Temple being very pleased to discover a fellow member of the Guinea Company was being chopped into pieces before his eyes.

St Martin-in-the-Fields was a sturdy building with a strong tower and lofty sixteenth-century windows, although it had been a long time since it had stood in any meadows. He found a verger, who informed him that he and a colleague had indeed been summoned to White Hall to collect a corpse, but when they had arrived, the body was nowhere to be found.

'Someone stole it, probably as a practical joke,' opined the verger. 'And we had a wasted journey. May refused to recompense us for our time, though. Bastard!'

Chaloner took his leave, full of thoughts. Had Fitz-Simons staged a permanent disappearance by only pretending to die at May's hands? Had *he* killed a vagrant to take his place in the charnel house? If so, then Johnson was complicit in the plan, because he held the keys to the shed where the impostor's body was being stored. Did that mean Johnson would deny access to any surgeon who wished to pay his last respects and view the corpse? Or was the entire Company aware of what was happening, but was rallying to defend one of its own? The city companies were fiercely loyal to their members, and might well try to help Fitz-Simons out of trouble.

Scot was still not in his room at the Chequer, so Chaloner went to St Paul's. It was a long walk from St Martin's Lane to London's mighty cathedral, and he was tired from his late night, so he took a carriage. The driver, keen to deposit him and collect another fare as soon as possible, flew along Fleet Street at a pace that was dangerous. Chaloner gripped the window frame as he was hurled from side to side, certain all four wheels were never on the ground at the same time. All the while, the hackney-man cursed and swore – at his pony, at other coachmen, at people on foot, at men on horses, at stray dogs and at the world in general. Everyone was a fool, he informed Chaloner cheerfully at the end of the journey, and he himself was the only man fit to take a cart along a road.

St Paul's was in a sorry state. A hundred years earlier, lightning had deprived it of its steeple, and the architect Inigo Jones had been invited to remodel its exterior. He had obliged with a façade that looked nothing like the rest of the church, and a classical portico that stood out like a sore thumb. During the Commonwealth, the chancel had been used by a huge congregation of Independents, who could not have cared less about the welfare of the building and only wanted a place large enough to rant in; the nave had been designated as a barracks for cavalry. Soldiers and iconoclasts had smashed its statues, melted down its plate, and punched out its medieval stained glass. Then they had turned their attention to the lead on the roof and in the windows, so that holes now allowed birds, bats and rain inside. Pigeons nested in the ceiling, adding their own mess to the ordure on the once-fine flagstones, and sparrows twittered shrilly above.

When the King had returned from exile, he had been shocked by the sorry state of his capital's cathedral, and invited the nation's most innovative architects to submit plans for its rebuilding. The leading contender was

Christopher Wren, who had in mind a central dome with chunky square aisles. The King was keen to see the work begin as soon as possible, and tiles, marble and wood had already been purchased. However, while His Majesty might have been satisfied with Wren's design, it was not received with equal enthusiasm by the Church, and the project was bogged down in an endless cycle of arguments and opposition. While they wrangled, the old building slid ever deeper into decay.

Chaloner prowled the nave, hunting for a verger who might be willing to let him see the register of burials, to ascertain whether Webb had made it as far as his pre-paid vault. He was in luck. The first man he asked was named John Allen, once a gardener at Lincoln's Inn. A bad back had forced him to retire, and Thurloe had helped him to secure work at the cathedral. Allen was more than happy to help one of Thurloe's friends; he fetched the register from an office, and scanned the list of entries.

'Webb,' he said, jabbing with his finger. There were several names beneath Webb's, suggesting that funerals in St Paul's were distressingly frequent. 'He was supposed to go in the chancel crypt, but that is full at the moment. His wife – a fat, fierce woman – said she paid for an inside spot, and insisted we keep our end of the bargain, so we put him in with Bishop Stratford, whose top is loose.'

'I am not sure what you mean,' said Chaloner uneasily. 'Whose top?'

'The lid of Stratford's sarcophagus.' Allen led the way to one of the transepts. Against the wall was a medieval tomb, all stone pillars and canopies. Prayerful angels had once watched over the dead prelate, although the Puritans had ensured that they now did so without their heads.

Allen grabbed the lid of the tomb with both hands, to show how easily it could be moved.

'Webb is in there?'

'Well, we had to dispense with his coffin.' Allen lowered his voice conspiratorially. 'You are a man of the world – you know that a good, second-hand casket fetches a decent price, if you have the right contacts. For a shilling, I will show you his corpse.'

Chaloner handed over the coin, expecting to have it back when it was revealed that Webb's final resting place was not where everyone assumed. To prove he was getting his money's worth, Allen made a great show of puffing and groaning as he hefted the slab to one side, eventually revealing that Webb was not the only one to enjoy the bishop's company. It was crowded in the sarcophagus, and Chaloner backed away with his sleeve over his mouth.

'That is Cromwell's hat-maker,' said Allen helpfully, pointing to the oldest resident. The prelate's mortal remains were, presumably, the dust at the very bottom. 'He has been here for about five years. Then there were two sisters – they came about eighteen months ago, although they are reaching the point where we can squash them down to make room for someone else. The fellow on top is Webb.'

'This is what burial in St Paul's entails?' asked Chaloner, appalled. 'After a few weeks, the remains are shoved to one side so the next corpse can be rammed in?'

'We leave it a bit longer than that,' said Allen indignantly. 'And space is tight in here, although we have lots of room in the graveyard.'

'That is not Webb,' said Chaloner, pointing to the most recent addition.

Allen regarded him askance. 'It most certainly is! I put him in here myself.'

214

'Webb was a wealthy merchant – well fed and healthy enough to walk from African House to The Strand – but this fellow is severely emaciated. Also, Webb was stabbed, but this man died because his skull has been smashed. It cannot be the same person. Did Silence see the body removed from the coffin?'

'Of course not! We do not let the next-of-kin see that sort of thing. What kind of men do you think we are? We open the caskets and perform the interment after everyone has gone home. But if you are right, then where is Webb? And more to the point, who do we have here?'

'I have no idea, but I recommend you close the tomb and do not open it for anyone else. There is something very odd going on, and you would be wise to have nothing to do with it.'

Allen regarded him soberly. 'If it is *that* odd, then it will be dangerous, too. So, I give you the same advice – have nothing to do with it.'

Chaloner was beginning to wish he could.

The monarch and his Court were still exercising in St James's Park by the time Chaloner returned to White Hall, so he walked to the trees that stood along the wall separating the Privy Garden from King Street beyond, and found a venerable yew with thick, leafy branches. He insinuated himself inside its thick canopy, well hidden from anyone who might glance in his direction, and prepared to wait. He was not particularly interested in watching Lady Castlemaine's possessions being carted this way and that, but there was nothing else to do, and a certain degree of entertainment was to be had from the confusion. She was becoming exasperated, and swore in a way that Chaloner had not heard outside the army

215

– and even then she could have taught his rough old comrades a few choice expressions.

After a while Bristol appeared, wearing a long gown and a soft linen hat that suggested he had only just prised himself from his bed. He stretched, yawned and began to stroll around the garden, but the best place to be was near the trees, where he was safely distant from clumsy servants with heavy pieces of furniture. The spot also put him well away from Lady Castlemaine's sharp tongue, and allowed him to ignore any appeals for help.

He lit a pipe, and the scent of tobacco wafted upwards, almost masking the odour of onions. He was not left alone for long, because Adrian May approached with a letter in his hand. That morning, the spy's bald pate was covered with a dashing red hat that sported the largest feather Chaloner had ever seen – he could not imagine what sort of bird might once have owned it, and only knew he would not like to meet one. With May was the obsequious Temple, exposing his toothless gums in a grin of greeting. Temple wore a gold-brown periwig with curls that flowed so far down his back they covered his rump. Chaloner suspected it had been designed for someone considerably taller.

'Good morning, My Lord,' gushed Temple. 'I bring interesting news from Lincoln's Inn.'

'Is it about the garden?' asked Bristol. 'I already know that twisted old lawyer – Prynne – intends to take a rather pleasant wilderness and spoil it with some nasty design of his own.'

'Oh,' said Temple, crestfallen. He thrust his fingers under his wig and scratched. 'Have you heard about Thurloe, too? How he is so dismayed by the proposed changes that he swallows all manner of tonics to calm himself?'

Bristol shrugged. 'So what? How is such information supposed to benefit me? I know Thurloe has taken Clarendon's side in our dispute, but no one cares what he does any more. His day is past.'

Temple's eyes gleamed. 'But think about it, My Lord. Thurloe is upset by what Prynne is doing, and Prynne has the King's ear. If we can encourage Clarendon to intervene on Thurloe's behalf, it will pit him directly against His Majesty, who will be irked.'

Bristol rubbed his chin, then smiled. 'I like it, Temple. It will deepen the growing rift between the King and his Lord Chancellor without any risk to ourselves. I shall make sure Clarendon hears about Thurloe's distress, and recommend he acts before the poor man pines away from sorrow.'

May stepped forward and handed over the missive he carried. 'This is from Surgeon Johnson, sir. It has just arrived, so I decided to bring it to you at once. I thought it might be important.'

Bristol broke the seal. 'It is about the Private Anatomy he offered to arrange for me – I am obliged to wait a few days, it seems. Johnson! The man is a buffoon. Do you know what he did on Saturday? I made some idle quip – drunken quip, if you want the truth – about breaking into Clarendon's office to look for evidence that he had been embezzling public funds, and would you believe he actually went off and did it? I was appalled – supposing he had been caught, and everyone assumed *I* had put him up to it! How would that have looked?'

'Not good,' agreed Temple. 'Did he find anything?'

'Nothing – except a letter from Thurloe recommending Goddard's Drops as a cure for fainting.'

'Goddard's Drops,' mused Temple, scratching again.

'It might be code – Thurloe *was* a Spymaster, after all. We may be able to . . . can you smell onions?' He looked round him.

'Not really,' said Bristol, sniffing the air. 'And I like onions.'

'I think the Court surgeons might have had a hand in the disappearance of that beggar's body,' said May. He shoved a fingernail under his hat and wiggled it back and forth. 'My sources tell me that a number of people bribed the guards to see the corpse, and that Wiseman was among them.'

'I was among them, too,' said Temple. 'Cost me a shilling, which was a waste, because someone had tied a bag around its head, so I could not see the face. *I* did not make off with the corpse, though, and I imagine Wiseman is far too wrapped up in himself to play pranks on others.'

'Temple is right, May,' agreed Bristol. 'I imagine *Clarendon* stole your dead beggar – you have taken my side against him, so he probably wants to discredit you. You did look like a complete ass when Spymaster Williamson came to view the thing, and you were forced to admit that you had lost it.'

May's expression was dangerous. 'Heyden probably did it, then, on Clarendon's orders. I swear on my mother's grave that I will see that man hanged! So, since they have attacked me, I shall attack them back: *I* will raid Clarendon's offices for you, My Lord, and I will find all the evidence you need to bring them *both* down. I am a spy, after all, and experienced in such matters.'

Bristol shook his head. 'No – Williamson might find out, and I need you in his camp. You provide me with a good deal of very useful information, and I cannot jeopardise *that* without good cause.'

218

'Then I have another suggestion.' May was disappointed with the decision, and Chaloner wondered why he had elected to throw in his lot with Bristol when his master, Williamson, struggled to remain neutral. 'The King will not keep his current bedchamber for long – there are plans afoot to place him in new apartments overlooking the river, which means Lady Castlemaine's chambers will not be as close to him as she imagines. Her move will have been for nothing and when she finds out she will be livid.'

Temple removed his wig and used both hands to rake his scalp. 'Really? Are you saying the King's relocation is Clarendon's idea?'

'Actually, it is the King's,' replied May, rubbing his own head. 'He wants to use the old rooms as a laboratory. However, there is no reason why Lady Castlemaine should know that. You should tell her this is Clarendon's latest attempt to keep her away from her royal lover.'

'That is an excellent idea!' exclaimed Bristol, fingernails clawing under his night-cap. 'Lord, will it put the cat among the pigeons!'

'And quite a cat, too,' said Temple approvingly.

'I shall ask Buckingham to tell her,' said Bristol, taking off his cap and scratching vigorously at the sparse hair underneath. In his tree, Chaloner began to feel itchy, but resisted the urge to move lest he gave himself away. 'She believes anything he says. I had better catch him before he gets at the wine, though. I need him at least half sober when I confide, or he will forget what he is supposed to do.'

All three moved away, scratching in unison. Chaloner waited a while longer, then abandoned his hiding place when he saw Eaffrey and Behn, who had come to see if they could help Lady Castlemaine with her furniture. He was pleased to see Eaffrey looking happy, although less pleased to note that Behn seemed to be the cause. Behn greeted him cautiously when she introduced him as Heyden – and Chaloner was relieved when Behn did not appear to associate him with the elderly upholsterer.

'I understand you are a member of the Guinea Company,' said Chaloner affably, determined to be more courteous to the surly Brandenburger than he had been in his last disguise, out of respect for Eaffrey. 'And you knew the subscriber who was murdered last month.'

'Matthew Webb,' said Behn, nodding. 'He was a very dear friend.'

'Really?' asked Chaloner, his good intentions slipping a little. 'I heard you quarrelled, and that you left the gathering early because of it.'

Eaffrey glared at him, but Behn waved a powerful hand to indicate that he had taken no offence. 'Webb and I were going to let people *believe* we argued, but it was actually a ruse – to weaken our rivals. It was Webb's idea. He was a clever man, and I miss his company.'

Chaloner stared into the bright-blue eyes and had no idea whether to believe him. 'Is that why you spend so much time with his wife?' Eaffrey glanced sharply at him. 'You miss *his* company?'

'The grieving widow,' said Behn, with an expression that was unreadable. 'I have made it my duty to visit and offer condolences. It was a vicious attack, and I shall delight in watching the killers hang.'

When Behn was distracted by a screech of rage from Lady Castlemaine, who objected to a servant informing her that her new chambers were now too full to hold any more looted furniture, Eaffrey glowered at Chaloner.

She had been irritated by his remark about Silence Webb, and the accusation of infidelity that was implicit in it. 'Let us talk about something else,' she said shortly.

'Very well,' said Behn, turning back to Chaloner. 'Eaffrey has told me about the adventures she shared with friends – such as you – in Holland. However, it is wrong to put women in danger.'

'It was my choice to go,' said Eaffrey, before Chaloner could respond. 'It was nothing to do with Thomas. He would never presume to tell me what to do.'

'*I* shall, though,' said Behn coolly. 'It will be my right, once we are wed.'

Eaffrey stared at him. 'That is an archaic attitude to take, Johan. As far as I am concerned, marriage is a partnership in which *both* sides are free to do as they please.'

'Is that so?' asked Behn, raising his eyebrows. 'It is an unusual interpretation of matrimony.'

'Eaffrey is an unusual lady,' said Chaloner.

Behn opened his mouth to say something else, but just then Temple approached, all smiles as he raked his fingernails across his scalp, hard enough to leave red marks.

'Ah, Behn,' he said. 'I intend to nominate you as the next Master of the Guinea Company. I like your progressive attitude to trade, and wish more of our members were like you.'

Behn inclined his head. 'Of course you do, but we can oust the squeamish ones once I am elected. Together, we shall lead your country to untold wealth and mercantile power.'

'In Africa,' agreed Temple, nodding vigorously. 'And in Barbados.'

'You mean by promoting slavery?' said Chaloner. 'That will make our country great, will it?'

'Of course,' said Behn. 'And anyone who does not see it is a fool.'

'You promised you would have no more to do with that sort of venture, Johan,' said Eaffrey quietly. 'I told you I disapproved, and you—'

'I said I would consider your request,' said Behn, testily. 'However, you are a woman, so you cannot possibly understand the complexity of the finances involved. Please excuse me now.'

He took Temple by the arm, leading him away for a private discussion. Almost immediately, he began to scratch his head.

Eaffrey's face fell at the curt dismissal. She turned to Chaloner with tears in her eyes. 'Johan and I have been growing closer for weeks now, and within moments, *you* manage to initiate two topics of conversation that see us voicing opposing and irreconcilable views.'

'He is not worthy of you,' said Chaloner simply.

'That is for me to decide. You had better stay away from both of us in the future. You seem incapable of being civil, and I do not want to lose him over some petty quarrel instigated by you.'

She turned on her heel and stalked away, leaving Chaloner startled and unhappy.

Chapter 7

It was some time before the King and his entourage returned from St James's Park, but when they did, all White Hall knew they were back. Dogs burst yapping into the Palace Yard, with horses clattering behind them. Armies of grooms, kennel-men and stable-boys surged forward to reclaim the animals, while courtiers milled around in a colourful, noisy gaggle. Scot was among the throng, deep in conversation with Brodrick and two lords Chaloner did not recognise.

The brightest and loudest of the throng was Buckingham, and Chaloner watched Bristol sidle up to him and indicate that he wanted to talk. Buckingham waved him away with an impatient flick of his hand, then slipped his arm around the waist of one of the Queen's ladies-in-waiting. She was a pretty young woman, who was unashamedly delighted by the attention. The Queen watched with unhappy eyes, then turned to walk inside the Great Hall. She passed close to where Chaloner was waiting to waylay Scot, and gave him a brief smile as she went.

Scot broke off his conversation the moment he spotted

his friend. Brodrick followed him, although the two nobles hurried to join the clot of drooling men who hung around Lady Castlemaine. She was giving her opinion about her new living quarters, delivering the verdict while wearing a gown so low-cut that nothing was left to the imagination.

'We had some dashed good music last night, Heyden,' said Clarendon's cousin. His face was pale and puffy, and there was a curiously chemical scent on his breath that suggested he had not long stopped drinking. The whites of his eyes were yellow, and he rubbed his stomach as if it hurt. 'I am tempted to offer my consort's services to the Guinea Company, for their feast of Corpus Christi later this month. At the annual dinner, the playing was dismal, because the entertainment was arranged by Webb, who preferred tavern jigs to chamber music.'

'Did you know Webb well?' asked Chaloner, thinking that perhaps it was just as well he had lost his place to Greeting. He played for personal enjoyment, not to entertain audiences and, as a spy, he tried to avoid doing anything that would thrust him into a position where he would be noticed.

Brodrick shuddered. 'God, no! Our paths crossed at the Guinea Company, but that was all – he hated music, you see. And not only was he vulgar, but he was argumentative, too. On the evening he died, I personally saw him squabbling with Temple, Buckingham, Lord Lauderdale, the Bishop of London, that yellow-legged creature of Bristol's . . . '

'Willys?' suggested Scot.

Brodrick snapped his fingers. 'Willys! That is the fellow! Webb was a loathsome specimen. Do you not agree,

Terrell? He was not someone you would have wanted in your Royal Society, eh?'

'Indeed not,' agreed Scot. He did not look at Chaloner. 'After my lecture on grasses yesterday, I spent the evening with the scientist Robert Hooke, and *he* told me that Webb had also quarrelled with two of the men accused of stabbing him. He said it happened before everyone sat down to eat.'

'Yes, their names were Fanning and Dillon,' said Brodrick. 'They were later arrested and convicted of the crime. Dillon is a Company member, and he brought Fanning as his guest – our current Master lets anyone join these days. Thank God he is due to step down, and we can appoint someone else. I shall vote for Johan Behn, I think – it is time we had a leader who is young and vigorous.'

'Did either of you actually *see* Webb arguing with Dillon and Fanning?' asked Chaloner.

Scot shook his head. 'As I told you before, I was engrossed in a botanical discussion. I did not see Webb at all – quarrelling with Dillon, Fanning or anyone else. I am only repeating what Hooke said.'

'I saw them at the festivities, but did not witness the row,' said Brodrick. 'I do not think Dillon and his guest stayed long – I remember them at the beginning of the evening, but not at the end. Perhaps they sneaked off to lie in wait for him. Or perhaps they went to a tavern in an attempt to blot the row with Webb from their minds. Who knows?'

Chaloner recalled that Dillon had denied being at the dinner, and was not sure what to think. Why had he lied? Was it because admitting to fighting with Webb that fateful night would have been incriminating? Or were

225

there people at African House who were spreading tales about Dillon because they wanted him to be *seen* as guilty, perhaps to shield the real killer?

'Do you know an actress called Rosa Lodge?' he asked, turning his thoughts to his other duties – protecting Lord Clarendon from scandal.

Brodrick pointed at the woman the Duke was mauling. 'Temple inveigled her an appointment to the Queen's bedchamber. However, if you are hoping for a private performance, you will be waiting a long time – Buckingham is there first, and he is unlikely to relinquish her until she is all used up. What is so funny, Heyden?'

'Bristol. Can you see his face?'

'It is as black as thunder. Do you know why?'

'Rosa Lodge was hired to seduce your cousin, and Buckingham has unwittingly ruined the plan – if she accuses Clarendon of raping her now, no one will believe her, because everyone can see she is wanton. Bristol will have to move on to his next plot, which entails telling Lady Castlemaine that it is Clarendon's idea to move the King's bedchamber away from her new quarters.'

'Lord!' exclaimed Brodrick, appalled. 'Now that *is* potentially dangerous. I must warn him immediately. The Lady will be furious, and he needs to be prepared.'

When Brodrick had gone, Scot gripped Chaloner's shoulder and hauled him into a small room that was used to store harnesses for the royal carriage. He slammed the door shut, and Chaloner was astonished to see the anger in his face.

'Where have you been these last two days? You have not been home, and I was assailed with a terrible fear that May or Behn had dispatched you. I consigned myself to a dreadful evening in their company, desperately trying to catch one of them out in some inadvertent admission.'

Chaloner was startled to learn Scot should have been concerned, especially over something as ephemeral as a bad feeling. 'I looked for you, too, at the Chequer Inn.'

'The landlord did not mention it.' Scot sounded tired. 'Well, I am relieved to see you safe. The faces of friends lost to spying keep haunting me, and I was afraid yours was about to join them.'

'Why would you think that?'

Scot scrubbed at his eyes, hard enough to disturb his disguise. It was unlike him to be careless, and Chaloner saw he was deeply unsettled. 'Because White Hall is a dangerous place and you have chosen the wrong side – Clarendon's overbearing pomposity makes him deeply unpopular, whereas Bristol is generally liked. And I was horrified when Behn bested you in that tussle. If you cannot defend yourself against him, then how will you fare against May?'

Chaloner thought he was overreacting. 'Behn did not "best" me, I lost my balance.'

Scot glared out of the window, then forced a smile. 'I am fussing like I did when you were a green youth on his first assignment. You must forgive me.'

'Is something wrong? Has something happened to make you more than usually uneasy?'

'Temperance and Maude, for a start. They are both worthy ladies, I am sure, but Maude is apt to be indiscreet. Has she repeated her clients' chatter to you? Yes? Then how do you know she is not repeating *yours* to someone else? I am not saying there is malice in her, but betrayal is betrayal, nonetheless. Then there is your friend

Leybourn. Did you know he and May were acquainted well enough to enjoy a drink in a tavern together?'

Chaloner shook his head uneasily. 'But he owns a bookshop – he deals with a lot of people.'

'Yes, you are no doubt right.' Scot sounded relieved – it was never easy to warn colleagues that those they considered friends might be nothing of the kind, and it was clear he was glad it was over without an awkward confrontation. 'Bear it in mind for the future, though.'

'I will. Thank you.'

'I heard you were you looking for me on Sunday night.' Chaloner had his own questions to ask about the truthfulness of friends. 'I do not suppose it had anything to do with the name Peter Terrell being on a list of men accused of murdering Webb, did it?'

Scot's smile turned wry. 'That was one subject I wanted to air, yes. I am afraid I misled you. My alias *was* on Bristol's letter, and I neglected to tell you so when you raised the subject at the ball.'

Chaloner was taken aback by the blunt admission. 'Why?'

'It is second nature for men like us to keep secrets, so when you started to talk about the letter, I followed my instincts to procrastinate without conscious thought. Barely an hour had passed before I realised there was no need to be furtive with you – and that withholding information might even put you in danger – so I rushed to your rooms to make amends. But you are never there; you do not even *sleep* there, it seems. I waited for hours – on Saturday night *and* Sunday.'

'What were you going to tell me, exactly?'

'That my alias *was* on that poisonous document, but that although I knew *of* Webb, I had never spoken to the

228

man – I was astonished when soldiers came and demanded that I accompany them to Newgate for questioning about his death. Fortunately, I was able to escape, and Eaffrey sent word to Williamson, who made my name "disappear" from the legal proceedings.'

'Not very effectively – a number of people know about you.'

'Yes and no. Williamson fabricated another Peter Terrell, and most people think a dishonest fishmonger is involved in the Webb case, not my Irish scholar. It means I am stuck with this disguise for a while, though, because to vanish now *will* arouse suspicion.'

'What about the four who were pardoned – Clarke, Fitz-Gerrard, Burne, Willys? Do you know them?'

'Yes – they are all intelligence agents. Clarke and Fitz-Gerrard were not even in England when Webb was murdered, so God alone knows why their names were picked for this wretched list. You know Burne, because that is May's alias. And Willys is Bristol's creature.'

'Was Fitz-Simons a spy, too? He and you were the two who "disappeared".'

'He is what we call an "occasional informer", which means he is basically Williamson's eyes and ears at the Company of Barber-Surgeons. He happened to be out when the soldiers called at his house, and he went on the run. I have no idea where he is now.'

'Dead – he is the beggar May killed at Westminster Abbey.'

Scot stared at him in horror. 'Are you sure? May had a bag wrapped around the head when I tried to inspect the corpse. Now I see why! That damned lunatic did not want anyone to see he had shot one of his colleagues. Does Williamson know?'

'I have no idea. Did you ever meet Fitz-Simons in Ireland? He was seen boarding a Dublin-bound ship in February, and he had detailed plans of the castle.'

'No, and I would be surprised if Williamson had used him there – he was an *informer*, not a spy, and he lacked the requisite skills for deep-cover work. However, that said, the Castle Plot was a serious attempt to destabilise the government, so perhaps Williamson *did* employ every resource at his fingertips to ensure it failed, even men at the very bottom of his command.'

'Do you think Fitz-Simons's shooting had anything to do with the Castle Plot?' asked Chaloner, deciding not to mention his suspicions about the surgeon's 'demise' until he was more certain.

'Of course it might, if you say he was in Ireland! Poor Fitz-Simons was sadly inept, so perhaps inexperience led him to reveal himself to the wrong person when he was at his Dublin duties.'

'His name was on Bristol's list, so someone thought he was worth exposing, incompetent or not.'

'True. However, do not overlook the possibility that one of his colleagues objected to him reporting Company secrets to the government. It might have been a barber-surgeon who added his name to the letter.'

'Which one? Wiseman? Johnson? Master Lisle?'

'I do not trust Wiseman,' said Scot. 'It would not surprise me at all to learn *he* has a murderous streak in him. But to return to the letter, five of the nine named were Williamson's men, and one was Bristol's. The selection was odd, though; we six did not work together, and no one should have been able to link us. I can only assume it was an attempt to undermine the entire intelligence network.'

'How?'

'Because applying for pardons made these men visible. Now it will be difficult for them to become anonymous again, which will reduce their value.'

'What about the remaining three – Dillon, Fanning and Sarsfeild?'

'Williamson *says* they are nothing to do with him, but there is no way to know for certain. I have certainly never met any of them.'

'You have – Dillon is the man we called O'Brien, from Dublin.'

Scot gaped at him. 'Really? Then he *is* a spy, but I have no idea whose.'

'Someone he trusts – he thinks he will be rescued from the scaffold. It is too late for Fanning, though, because he has been strangled, although the official cause of death is gaol-fever. It happened on the eve of a planned escape, which may or may not be significant. That leaves Sarsfeild.'

'Sarsfeild,' mused Scot. 'It is similar to the name you used in Ireland: Garsfield.'

Chaloner regarded him askance. 'I am not sufficiently important to be included in any plot, and few people in London know me anyway. Besides, Sarsfeild has been caught and sits in Ludgate.'

'Or perhaps a slip of the pen means that entirely the wrong man is locked in a prison cell. Do not look dismissive, Chaloner – Bristol and his minions will do anything to harm Lord Clarendon, including striking at his people. But why was the letter sent to Bristol, do you think? And why did he pass it to the legal authorities, when his own henchman – Willys – might have been hanged?'

'Perhaps he thought it was a secret test of his integrity,

231

and was too frightened to do anything else. Have you given any more thought to who might have written it?'

'Far too much, and it is beginning to interfere with my other duties – not that my thinking is doing me much good. I am still none the wiser, which bothers me; I dislike not knowing my enemies. Do *you* have any suspects?'

'Adrian May,' said Chaloner, voicing something that had been in his mind ever since he had heard the bald spy urging his services on Bristol.

Scot was thoughtful. 'Eaffrey would agree with you – she heard a rumour to that effect. However, the man most inconvenienced by the missive was May's master: Williamson. His best spies have been exposed, including May himself.'

'Cover,' replied Chaloner immediately. 'It would have looked suspicious for an agent of May's prominence to be omitted from the list, and he is not entirely stupid.'

'Perhaps. The master of Dillon, Fanning and Sarsfeild, whoever he is, has been incapacitated by this letter, too. I suppose, we shall know him when he steps forward to rescue them from the gallows.'

'If he bothers. Fanning is already dead, and Dillon may be counting his chickens before they are hatched. I wish you had told me all this sooner.'

Scot grimaced. 'So do I – although, in my defence, I *have* spent hours looking for you over the last three days. If you were not so damned elusive, you would have known everything ages ago.'

Chaloner sighed and rubbed his head. 'Even with your information, I still do not understand what is going on – not with Webb, Fitz-Simons, Bristol's letter or their links to the Castle Plot. I am better at spying on the

Dutch than on my fellow countrymen. I understand foreigners better, I think.'

'Then come to Surinam with me, That is overrun with Hollanders, and we can do a lot for England there. I shall leave as soon as my brother is free. Of course, that assumes I *can* get him released – his interrogators want to know about weapons now, but Thomas has no idea where the rebels got them.'

Chaloner had his suspicions. 'Try asking the Trulocke brothers, gunsmiths on St Martin's Lane.'

Scot gazed at him, hope burning in his pale eyes. 'You have good reason to suggest this?'

'Good enough to recommend you investigate them.'

Scot took his hand, and Chaloner saw a sparkle of tears. 'This may be enough to see Thomas out.'

'Your sister thinks she is going to take him home to Buckinghamshire when he is released. She will be surprised when she learns you have other plans for him.'

'Not as surprised as when she hears she is coming, too. I cannot leave her here – prey for money-seeking scoundrels like Temple. We shall *all* go to Surinam, although I shall tell her so only at the very last minute. She might marry Temple in an attempt to stay here with him otherwise.'

'Christ!' muttered Chaloner, appalled. 'Please tell me well in advance when you intend to abduct her, so I can make sure I am as far away as possible. She will be furious.'

'Better furious than married to Temple.'

Chaloner was unsettled by the knowledge that the likes of Temple were prepared to employ increasingly shabby tactics to harm Lord Clarendon, and supposed he would have to increase his efforts to monitor them. He was not overly concerned for his own safety, because he had been in far more dangerous situations in the past, and did not feel particularly at risk. He also thought Scot was wrong to think *his* name had been on Bristol's list, because he was simply not important enough to warrant such attention.

He spent the rest of the day in White Hall, moving silently among courtiers and servants, asking the occasional question, but mostly just listening. The palace was not known for its discretion, but even so, he was astonished at how readily people yielded their secrets. No one was safe from wagging tongues, and he was startled to learn that even his fictitious Dutch upholsterer – Vanders – was said to be enjoying a rambunctious affair with one of Lady Castlemaine's maiden aunts.

Tucked in a corner of the spacious Great Court was an awkwardly shaped chamber with a sagging roof known jokingly as the Spares Gallery. It was chiefly a repository for any paintings the King did not like, and included portraits of a few historical black sheep, as well as artwork by famous artists that was not quite up to par. It had been taken over by high-ranking retainers, who used it as a common room. When Chaloner ran out of people to quiz, he repaired to the Spares Gallery, where there was always ale warming over a fire, and usually bread and cheese set out on a table, too.

The hall was crowded, which suited him – it was easier to be invisible in a full room than in one that was half empty. He drank a cup of ale, then spotted Willys slouching morosely in a window seat. He went to sit next to the aide, ready to leave if there was any residual antagonism from the altercation with Holles earlier. Willys, however, seemed to have forgotten the incident, and

Chaloner's sympathetic manner soon had him confiding all manner of intimate details about Bristol.

It did not take long for Chaloner to realise Willys was not very bright. Even the dimmest of retainers knew never to chatter about his master's sleeping habits, dietary preferences – most of which involved onions – and mistresses. Willys, however, was flattered by the fact that someone was ready to listen to him, and once he started, he was difficult to stop. Chaloner tried several times to steer the discussion around to the fact that the aide's name was on an incriminating letter, but Willys declined to be diverted. By the end of an hour, Chaloner's head was spinning, and he knew far more about Bristol's private life than he ever would about his own earl's.

It was not easy to escape from the garrulous aide, and it was dusk by the time Chaloner managed it. Because he felt he had lost his way among the jumble of information he had accumulated, he decided to visit Thurloe – to tell him all he had learned in the hope that the ex-Spymaster might see some order in it. When he arrived at Lincoln's Inn, Thurloe was pacing in agitation.

'I hoped you would come,' said the ex-Spymaster without preamble. 'I went to see Dillon—'

Chaloner was dismayed. 'You promised you would not visit Newgate again.'

Thurloe grimaced. 'I donned a disguise, Thomas; credit me with some intelligence, please. Dillon's execution will be on Saturday, but I have exhausted all I can do to help him. You are his only hope now.'

'That is not true. He is in the pay of a more powerful master than you, and expects to be reprieved.'

Thurloe frowned. 'I know you do not like him because of what happened to Manning – he said you were hostile when you visited – but I am sure you will not allow your personal feelings to interfere with your sense of justice. He says he did not kill Webb, and I believe he is telling the truth.'

'You are probably right. Of the nine names in Bristol's letter, five are government intelligencers and one is Bristol's aide – his spy, in essence. Scot thinks someone cited them as an act of spite – or perhaps revenge – against the secret services. And of the remaining three, Dillon and Fanning are also spies; I saw them in Ireland myself, although I have no idea whose side they were on.'

'It is possible that they were sent by the government, too – unbeknown to the rest of you. However, as I have said, Dillon is Irish, and his family lost lands in the Royalists' reorganisation, so it is equally possible that he was part of the revolt. I asked him about it, but his answers were slyly vague. The only thing I know for certain is that he thinks his master is more powerful than Williamson. What about the last man – Sarsfeild? Is he in the pay of this mysterious patron?'

'Dillon says not, but who knows? Sarsfeild was transferred to Ludgate after Fanning was murdered, so perhaps his patron arranged for him to be in a safer place until he can arrange a release.'

'You must speak to Dillon again. The governor knows the letter you used last time was a forgery, so you will have to devise another way to gain access. And then you must go to Ludgate and interview Sarsfeild. Perhaps *he* will be more forthcoming.'

'Why are you so determined to save Dillon? He betrayed you, and Manning paid the price.' Chaloner thought, but did not say, that Dillon did not want

Thurloe's assistance, and that the ex-Spymaster was wasting his time and energy by attempting to interfere.

Thurloe sighed. 'Because injustice troubles me, Thomas. It always has. I know you are busy trying to save Clarendon from Bristol, but I am sure you can spare a few moments to prevent an innocent man from hanging – because that is what will happen on Saturday, no matter what Dillon thinks.'

'I am not sure visiting him is the best way to a solution.' Chaloner was ready to go to extreme lengths to avoid spending more time inside Newgate. 'It would be better to find Webb's real killer.'

'How? Do you have any clues?'

'Some. Silence took the family carriage when she left the Guinea Company dinner, and the coachman was stabbed to prevent him from returning to collect Webb. Webb was forced to walk home from African House, and the killer or killers dispatched him with a single wound to the chest. It was premeditated murder, not a chance killing. The weapon was later placed in Dillon's room to implicate him.' Chaloner was thoughtful. 'Why Dillon? Why not May, Fitz-Simons or one of the others? Is it a blow aimed at Dillon's patron, to make him reveal himself as a man who hires spies?'

'Or as a man who has dealings with Irish rebels,' suggested Thurloe.

'It seems to me that the answers to some of these questions lie in Bristol's letter. If we learn who wrote it, we may better understand what is happening.'

'How do you propose we do that?'

'By looking at the original. We have only been *told* about these names – we have not seen the document itself. It is possible that it contains more information, or even clues that may identify its sender. Do you know anyone in Bristol's entourage who may be able to tell you where it is now?'

Thurloe nodded. 'And then you can read it *in situ*. Do not steal it – we do not want anyone to know what we are doing.'

'All right,' agreed Chaloner. 'As long as it does not involve climbing any walls.'

It was too late for visiting prisons that night, although Thurloe immediately set off to question his contacts about the whereabouts of Bristol's letter. Chaloner was tired after his restlessness the night before, so went home, stopping at a cookshop on the way to purchase a meat pie, wine and boiled fruit. When he arrived, Scot was waiting, hiding in the cupboard outside his door. Chaloner supposed they had been spies for so long that they resorted to cloak-and-dagger tactics even when visiting friends. He mentioned it and Scot laughed, seeing humour in the way they had been conditioned. They shared the food – after Scot had ascertained it was free of peas – then discussed their futures.

'I shall resign from the intelligence services the moment I secure my brother's release,' said Scot through a mouthful of pie. 'And my whole family will be in Surinam four months later.'

'You will be back within a year, complaining that life on the edge of the world is dull.'

Scot shook his head. 'I am serious about this. I *will* give up spying. Encroaching age has taught me that I am not immortal, and there are things I would like to do before I die.'

'Such as what?'

Scot's expression was shy, as if he was afraid of being ridiculed. 'I really *do* intend to devote my life to botanicals. There are trees and plants in Surinam that have never been seen, let alone described in the scientific literature. I cannot imagine anything more pleasant than a day in the jungle, surrounded by foliage, writing learned dispatches for the Royal Society.'

Chaloner saw he was sincere. 'Then I wish you success of it.'

'You feel the same about music,' persisted Scot, not sure he was truly understood. He tapped Chaloner's splinted arm. 'These things heal, you will regain your skill.'

'That is not what Lisle says. I was sure there was nothing wrong with me, but he is beginning to make me wonder whether I was mistaken.'

'Surgeons are irredeemably gloomy. They do it to frighten their patients into paying them more than they should. Your leg healed well enough, did it not? You barely limp these days.'

'I do if I am obliged to run hard. If my arm becomes like my leg, then I *will* go to Surinam with you, because I will be useless for anything else. Will you have another go at hacking off the splint?'

Scot did his best, and ruined Chaloner's favourite dagger and a metal rasp in the process, but it was to no avail. Chaloner was both disgusted and disheartened.

Scot poured more wine. 'Are you still a creditable forger?'

'Why?' Chaloner was beginning to feel drunk, because although there was plenty of wine, there had not been much food once it had been divided in half and his stomach was still empty.

'Because you may be able to translate your talent for

239

reproducing documents to drawing my specimens. Decent scientific illustrators are worth their weight in gold, and if you are any good at it, you will make a fortune. In fact, you might find yourself in demand for many reasons in Surinam – women like a man with artistic talents, too.'

'They do not flock to my door when they hear my viol.'

'Then perhaps you are not as good a player as you think you are.'

'I do not want Eaffrey to wed Behn,' said Chaloner. His voice was slurred, and he was aware that he was drinking far too much. He poured himself another cup. 'He will crush her spirit.'

'She is more likely to crush his. Do not underestimate her – she knows what she is doing.'

'He is wooing Silence Webb. Secretly.'

Scot stared at him, then burst out laughing. 'Really, Chaloner! I know you do not like the man, but there is no need to malign him quite so badly. No fellow in his right senses would carry on with *her*.'

'I saw him,' persisted Chaloner. 'Twice.'

'How?' Scot raised his hand. 'No, do not tell me. I would rather not know. However, you should remember that Behn did business with Webb, and it is possible that he is paying court to Silence to make sure she does not sign his interests away to another party.'

'What about Alice?' asked Chaloner, seeing Scot would not be convinced, so changing the subject in the random way of the intoxicated. 'Have you devised a way to abduct her before she marries the odious Temple? You should not leave it too long, because she really does love him.'

'Perhaps I should kill him,' said Scot. 'No, that will

not work, because she will know it was me, and I do not want her in one of her tempers. Your duel with her first husband was years ago, but she still bears you a grudge. I could not bear her treating *me* so coldly – not my own sister.'

'Plants,' suggested Chaloner drunkenly. 'You must have read about plants that reduce people to a state of torpor in your *Musaeum Tradescantianum*. Feed her some of those.'

Scot looked shocked. 'I want to save her, not kill her! Besides, Thomas might be stuck in the Tower for weeks, and I cannot drug her indefinitely. The best solution would be if *you* married her. I would not mind you as a brother-in-law.'

'She would have her sharpest dagger in my heart on our wedding night.'

Scot guffawed, and refilled their cups. 'Alice could do a good deal worse, and it is a great pity you do not like each other. Perhaps you will fall in love en route to Surinam.'

Chaloner had no idea how late he and Scot stayed up, but he woke to find himself slumped uncomfortably across the table with his head on his arms, while Scot snored on the bed. It was still dark outside, but dawn was not far off, and he supposed it was the rumble of the day's first cart that had disturbed his sleep. He lurched to the window and opened it for some fresh air. Scot did not stir, not even when Chaloner tripped over an upturned chair, suggesting the older man had imbibed even more than he had. His head pounded viciously as he washed his face and changed clothes that were stiff with spilled claret. Before he left, he placed a blanket over the slumbering Scot.

'You reek of strong drink,' said Thurloe accusingly

when he arrived at Lincoln's Inn. 'And you look as though you have been up all night, carousing – red eyes, pale face, wincing because you think my voice is loud. Anyone would think you were a courtier.'

Chaloner flopped into Thurloe's fireside chair. 'I expected you to be walking in the garden.'

'I could not bring myself to go. Prynne showed me the plans for his dovecote yesterday – the only feature in this barren wilderness he dares to call an arbour. It is ugly in the extreme, and I cannot see any self-respecting bird deigning to take up residence in it.'

'*Cave fanaticum*,' murmured Chaloner, trying to remember how much wine he and Scot had actually swallowed the previous night. He suspected it was the best part of a gallon jug.

'Beware the fanatic,' translated Thurloe. 'I am surprised you remember any Latin, given the state you are in. Speaking of Latin, did I tell you Prynne gave me a copy of his *Histriomastix* in an attempt to ingratiate himself? I have never read such vitriol! Even *my* deeply held Puritan convictions do not lead me to rant against bay windows, holly bushes and New Year gifts.'

'Bay windows?' echoed Chaloner, wondering why religion led people to rage against such peculiar things.

'I am ashamed to call him a fellow bencher. And his diatribes against Jews defy decency, logic and sanity.' Thurloe turned when there was a tap at the door. 'Yates? Is that my morning bread?'

The wall-eyed porter bustled in with a tray, the Inn's tabby cat stalking at his heels. Yates kept one eye on the cat and the other on Thurloe, as he began to inform the ex-Spymaster, in unnecessary detail, about the state of his usual servant, who had gone to his sister to recover

242

from a bout of the bloody flux. Chaloner wondered how Yates had prised such intimate details from a man who, as far as everyone knew, was mute. He tried to tune out the chatter, which was far too graphic to be heard so early in the morning. Eventually, Yates finished his gruesome monologue and left. Thurloe sat at the table and selected a sliver of barley bread, while the cat jumped into his lap.

'You should try this. It is said to be good for the digestive health.'

Chaloner felt his gorge rise at the prospect of food, as it always did the morning after too much wine. 'I came to ask whether you had discovered the whereabouts of Bristol's letter.'

'It is in his house on Great Queen Street. We are almost neighbours – I can see his roof from here.'

'I thought he lodged at White Hall.' Chaloner recalled him wandering around the Privy Gardens in his nightclothes the previous morning.

'Only when he is too drunk to go home. There is a rear-facing office on the upper floor of his mansion, in which there is a large China-painted chest. The letter will be in that.'

'Do you know anything about the lock?'

'Three separate keys are required to open it. I took the liberty of acquiring two – do not ask how; suffice to say I need them back as soon as possible – but you will have to pick the last. However, I do not recommend going now. It is too near dawn and Bristol might be awake.'

'He sleeps late, so now will be the perfect time,' countered Chaloner, thinking about what Willys had told him. Bristol seldom rose before nine o'clock, no matter where he slept, which his married mistresses found inconvenient.

'If you will not eat anything, then drink this.' Thurloe handed Chaloner one of his infamous potions. 'I made it myself, and it contains Venice Treacle among other things, which is an excellent remedy for overindulgence. You cannot burgle a house while you are still half drunk.'

Chaloner swallowed what was in the cup without thinking. Then, for the next few minutes, he fought a violent urge to be sick, and sat with his hands pressed hard against his face. Eventually the nausea receded, and he opened his eyes to see Thurloe looking pleased.

'The most efficacious medicines are always the most unpleasant, and judging from your reaction, I suspect this one has done you much good. The barber-surgeons say Venice Treacle is a quack remedy, but I beg to differ. They are clever fellows, but they do not know everything about health.'

'Do you know a medic called Wiseman?'

Thurloe nodded. 'He deplores the Court's excesses, and supports your earl's efforts to curb them.'

'What do you think of him as a man?'

'Arrogant and cynical – but if I were obliged to rummage in people's innards, I might be arrogant and cynical, too. He is probably decent, at heart. You are lucky to have him as your surgeon.'

Chaloner was not so sure, preferring to take his chances with Lisle. He pulled uncomfortably at the splint, looking forward to Saturday, when it would come off. 'What about Lisle and Johnson?'

'Wiseman thinks they are mediocre practitioners, but both have royal appointments, so he is almost certainly wrong. I like Lisle, who provides his services free of charge to the poor. Why do you ask?'

'Dillon listed all three as possible culprits for killing Webb.'

Thurloe was thoughtful. 'Wiseman *did* despise Webb, mostly because of his involvement with the slave plantations, but there was also an incident just after the Restoration in which Webb accused Wiseman of revealing personal secrets. I do not know if it was true, but it damaged Wiseman's practice – no one wants a *medicus* who gossips about embarrassing symptoms.'

'So, he has a powerful reason for wanting Webb dead?'

'He is not the only one. Lisle had a dispute with Webb, too – Webb claimed he overcharged for a phlebotomy, and the matter went to the law-courts. Webb won, but there was evidence that money changed hands to secure the verdict he wanted. Then Webb commissioned a Private Anatomy at Chyrurgeons' Hall, but Lisle and Johnson were obliged to cancel at the last minute – something about a leaking roof – and Webb threatened to sue again.'

'Dillon also included Temple and Brodrick among his suspects.'

Thurloe considered the accusation, nodding slowly. 'Temple lost customers to Webb, and Webb insulted Brodrick's music – something very dear to him.'

'And then there is Silence. If Webb was as awful as everyone says, then perhaps she is better off without him. She is not very grief-stricken. She did not bury him in the place he bought for himself, either, but let him be shoved him in someone else's tomb – not that the corpse was his, anyway.'

'How do you know all this?' asked Thurloe uneasily. 'I hope you have not been opening graves.'

'I wanted to know whether the surgeons will deposit him in his own vault when they have finished with him. Perhaps they intend to, but have not yet had the chance – he was only dissected on Sunday, after all. But then what happens to the body already there – the emaciated fellow?'

'I do not see how this is relevant to Dillon, and time is passing,' said Thurloe. He frowned as he pushed the cat from his lap. 'I still believe this is no time to burgle Bristol. Perhaps I should come with you. I may be out of practice, but I have not forgotten all the skills I once taught you.'

'No,' said Chaloner hastily. He would hang for certain if he was caught burgling Bristol in company with Cromwell's old Spymaster. He stood, feeling his stomach pitch at the movement, and heartily wished he had declined the tonic.

Dawn was beginning to paint the eastern sky, although the streets were still in deep shadow. Chaloner walked briskly, hoping exercise might make him feel better, taking deep breaths of comparatively fresh air as he went. Great Queen Street lay to the west of Lincoln's Inn Fields, and had a rural feel about it. Trees whispered in the breeze, birds sang and the wind blew from the west, so brought with it the sweet scent of new crops. He found the lane that ran around the back of the houses and located Bristol's garden, which was almost entirely laid down to onions. A maid was in it, hanging washing on a clothes line. He waited until she had gone, then slipped quietly through the gate, moving through the burgeoning crops to reach a paved yard fringed by sculleries and pantries.

Apart from the maid, there was no activity, and he

supposed the staff had adapted themselves to their master's erratic hours – Bristol probably disliked being woken early by clattering pots, but demanded attention late at night. Chaloner let himself in through the rear door and slunk stealthily up a silent corridor to the main rooms at the front. He could hear someone snoring, and opened a door to a handsome parlour to see Bristol himself, reclining comfortably in a cushion-filled chair. A cup dangled from one hand, while the other rested on his paunch; his head was back and he breathed wetly. Around him was the debris of a good night. Empty decanters littered a card-strewn table, and the air was still thick with tobacco smoke. Chaloner felt his stomach pitch at the powerful scent of wine, and held his breath until the feeling passed.

Voices emanated from the room opposite, so he tiptoed towards it and peered through a crack in the door. A dozen people had gathered there, picking at the bread and biscuits that had been laid out under cloths on a sideboard. Chaloner recognised three of them. Temple worked his toothless jaws, as if sleep had rendered them stiff. Alice Scot looked bright and alert, and was chattering gaily about Lady Castlemaine's new diamond ring. And the whites of Surgeon Johnson's eyes were deep red, to match the wine that had spilled down his coat during the revelries of the night before.

'I like Lady Castlemaine,' Johnson announced, loudly enough to make several of his companions – and Chaloner – wince. He lowered his voice, putting a hand to his own head. 'I am told she is probably a papist, but I am ready to ignore that, because she has such fine thighs.'

'A good reason for tolerance,' said Alice facetiously.

247

'And what about Lord Bristol, who is also Roman Catholic? Will you forgive him, too, on the basis of his fine thighs?'

'I doubt his rival Lady Castlemaine's,' said Johnson, evidently unequal to irony at such an early hour. 'He puts on a good card game, though, so I am willing to overlook the matter of his religion.'

'Most noble,' growled a man Chaloner thought was a bishop. 'His God must have been watching over him last night, though, because he carried all before him. What do you say to a game tonight, Johnson?'

'I am afraid not. I have another Private Anatomy to perform.'

'Another?' asked Temple with sudden eagerness. He took Alice's hand. 'Can we come? We enjoyed the last one you arranged. It was highly entertaining.'

'I had no idea Webb contained so many entrails,' agreed Alice. 'Of course, he was a very slippery fellow, so I suppose it should come as no surprise that he owned more than most.'

Chaloner was startled, because Wiseman had said the face of the subject remained covered during the cutting – so Alice and Temple should not have known whose innards they were being shown.

'He had three times as many as the average man,' declared Johnson authoritatively. 'And they were twice as oily. But I am afraid you cannot come to the dissection this evening, because it is a *very* private affair. However, I can arrange another, if you found the last one edifying. It will cost, but . . . '

'It will not be Webb, though,' said Temple with deep regret.

Chaloner gaped at him. Was this the motive for Webb's

murder? He was killed to provide Temple's entertainment? Or had the surgeons merely taken advantage of an opportunity presented?

Johnson grinned, and raised his cup. 'No, but I promise you will not be disappointed, even so.'

Servants were beginning to stir, aware that while Bristol might still be sleeping, his guests nevertheless required attention. Chaloner did not have much time – and certainly should not be spending it pondering the question of how Webb had ended up at Chyrurgeons' Hall. He climbed the stairs, thinking about what Thurloe had told him about the location of Bristol's letter. He saw a 'China-painted' chest in the second room he explored, and moved quickly towards it, first closing the door behind him. Thurloe's two keys worked perfectly, although it took him longer than he expected to undo the last lock. It was old and worn, which made it difficult to pick, and the smell of tobacco and old wine had turned his stomach to the point where he was feeling sick again. He took a deep breath and tried to force away the nausea. He did not have time for it.

Cheery greetings suggested Bristol was awake and had joined his visitors. The clatter of plates and cups followed, and then the scent of cooking meat wafted up the stairs. Chaloner put his hand over his nose so as not to inhale it. The last lock finally snapped open and he wrenched up the lid with more force than he had intended, so it cracked sharply against the wall. The voices downstairs immediately went silent. Chaloner began to rummage through the haphazard papers within, then stopped when he heard footsteps on the stairs. Someone was coming.

He rifled more urgently, hearing a second set of feet

join the first. Bristol's voice drifted upwards, asking a servant whether he had left a window open. Stopping, the servant declared he had not, because everyone knew that night air was poisonous to sleeping men. The footsteps continued up the stairs and started along the corridor. Now there were more than two sets, and Chaloner supposed other retainers had joined their master. He knew that if he was caught, there would be no excuse for what he was doing and he would be hanged, especially when Bristol learned he was in Clarendon's pay. There came the sounds of doors being opened.

Then he found what he was looking for. There was no time to read the letter and replace it, as Thurloe had recommended, so he shoved it in his pocket and ran to the window. He tried to unlatch it, but it was painted shut. He raced to another one, aware that Bristol was in the next room. He wrenched desperately at the catch, and it opened with a screech. The ground was a long way below, and a scullion was right beneath him, sitting on a stool as he enjoyed an early-morning pipe. Then the office door was flung open, and he heard Bristol give a furious yell as the intruder was spotted.

Chaloner did not look around, because he did not want Bristol to see his face. Taking a deep breath, he scrambled on to the sill, then launched himself into the ivy that covered the wall, aiming to climb down it. It was not as strong as it looked, and began to tear away from its moorings. With a tremendous hissing and scraping, the entire mass peeled away, bearing him with it. He braced himself, expecting to land hard – probably hard enough to damage his lame leg and prevent him from escaping. But the plant was reluctant to yield its hold on the wall, and did so slowly, so he was carried down at a perfectly comfortable pace to land gently on both feet without the slightest jar. The pipe-smoking scullion fared less happily, and disappeared under the billowing foliage with a cry of alarm.

Chaloner fought his way free of the leaves and started to run through the garden, but a sudden, gripping wave of dizziness made it difficult for him to see where he was going. Bristol leaned through the window and yelled orders at his servants, and soon several were in pursuit. Temple, abandoning his breakfast, panted along behind them. Chaloner reached the end of the garden and wrenched open the gate. Then, instead of haring through it into the lane, he ducked back inside and hid behind a rack that was used for drying onions. He knew he could not outrun fleet-footed pursuers while he was sick and reeling, and that concealing himself was his only hope of escape. He leaned against a wall and took a deep, shuddering breath, closing his eyes as he did so. The servants and Temple thundered past, followed by Bristol, who was yelling at the top of his voice. Alice Scot walked sedately after them.

Alice hailed from a family of spies, and knew perfectly well that tearing blindly after an invisible target was a waste of time. She studied the ground as she went, then stopped to inspect a broken twig. Chaloner watched in horror as she looked directly towards his onion rack. She stepped off the path and bent to touch the soil. She had surmised that the culprit had not fled into the lane, but was still in the garden. He swallowed hard, thinking how delighted she would be when she discovered the identity of the thief. He tried to push himself upright, but his knees would not support him.

'Alice,' came a familiar voice, just as Chaloner was

251

bracing himself for capture – even a woman would have no trouble securing him when he could barely stand. 'What on Earth are you doing?'

'William!' she cried in delight. 'I did not expect to see you here.'

Scot did not return her friendly greeting. 'Obviously not.'

Her face fell when she saw what he was thinking. 'It is nothing untoward, brother – just a card game that lasted until dawn.'

'I assume Temple was there, too.' Scot's voice was cold.

Alice sighed. 'Yes, although we were sitting at different tables for most of the night. And you? Are you on an assignment for Williamson? Is that why you appear so unexpectedly in the Earl of Bristol's vegetable garden in the hour after dawn?'

Scot rubbed his eyes, and Chaloner saw he did not feel particularly healthy, either. 'I am sure our father was never obliged to do this sort of thing. Espionage is not what it used to be, Alice.'

'Then why do it? You promised to finish with spying after Dublin. You said it was too dangerous.'

'Believe me, I shall – the moment Thomas is free.'

'Have *you* had any luck? I still have not found the right man to bribe, but I am working on it.'

'Keep your money, because Thomas's situation took a great leap forward yesterday – Chaloner told me about a crooked gunsmith, which allowed me to expose some illegal arms dealing. Williamson is delighted, and I sense it will not be long before he persuades his masters to let Thomas go.'

Alice smiled. 'At last.'

Scot pointed back towards the open office window, and

showed her a goblet. 'Williamson asked me to acquire a gold cup that holds a certain significance for His Majesty – something to do with a mistress. Obviously, I must have made too much noise, because I was almost caught. Will you help me escape? Go back inside, and when he returns, tell Bristol that you saw a large, red-headed thief jump over the wall into the garden next door. Hurry, though! I can hear them coming back already.'

She kissed his cheek and strode away. Moments later, Scot joined Chaloner behind the onions. 'That was close,' he said with a grin. 'She almost had you.'

Scot put his finger to his lips as Bristol and Temple stamped back through the garden, muttering venomously that the felon was too fast for them, and declaring that the servants had better have more luck or there would be trouble. Eventually, they went inside and Scot helped Chaloner to his feet.

'How did you know I was here?' asked Chaloner, feeling his stomach roll as he stood.

'You had gone when I woke, and there is only one man you visit at such an ungodly hour.' Scot held Chaloner's ornamental 'town' sword in his hand. 'I set out after you when I thought you might have forgotten this – no sane spy goes unarmed these days.'

Chaloner indicated the military-style weapon he carried at his side. 'I prefer something a little more robust when I burgle the houses of powerful courtiers. You taught me that. Did you see Thurloe?'

Scot nodded. 'For the first time since I became a Royalist. He is not a man to bear grudges, but I was uneasy nonetheless. I have never been able to read him, to know what he is really thinking.'

Chaloner was not surprised that Thurloe declined to be open with a man who had defected at a critical moment in the Commonwealth's painful collapse. 'He is not an easy man to understand.'

'As it happened, my apprehension was unnecessary. When I arrived, I found him preoccupied with another matter. His cat had swallowed some of his morning tonic, and had immediately become ill. He suspects poison, and is beside himself with worry, because he said you had taken some, too.'

'Prynne,' said Chaloner, holding his stomach. 'Because Thurloe opposes his garden plans.'

Scot shook his head wonderingly. 'Hell hath no fury like a lawyer crossed. Anyway, it would have been sheer folly for Thurloe to rescue you himself – I imagine he is horribly out of practice – so I persuaded him to let me do it instead. He is waiting nearby, in a carriage.'

'His damned tonics!' muttered Chaloner venomously. 'My wits were too befuddled from last night's wine to refuse it.'

Scot brandished the cup. 'Fortunately, mine were not. I took this to cover up whatever you were doing in there – now they will assume it was a simple theft when they look to see what is missing. We should not talk here, though. Put your arm around my shoulder. We shall pretend we are drunk, as we did in France when you saved me from that vengeful cardinal. We both reek of wine, so our ploy—'

He stepped smartly out of the way when the mention of wine was more than Chaloner's stomach could bear. The spy felt far better once the tonic had been added to the onions, and he wondered whether they would die as a result. Leaning heavily on Scot, he staggered out of the garden.

'Turn right,' ordered Scot, closing the gate behind them.

'We will run into Bristol's servants if we go that way.'

'I know what I am doing,' said Scot impatiently. 'And you are not well enough to—'

Chaloner did not feel like arguing. He took his own route, and was proven right, because moments later, a pack of retainers converged on the gate. They were hot, cross and disappointed, and would certainly have challenged two 'drunks' so close to their master's home.

Scot shot him an apologetic grin. 'It seems the apprentice has surpassed the master – either that, or I am losing my touch. Christ, my head aches! That will teach me to drink with a man who cannot afford a decent vintage.'

Thurloe was waiting in a carriage, which was cunningly concealed behind some trees in the expanse of open land known as Lincoln's Inn Fields. The ex-Spymaster closed his eyes in relief when he saw Chaloner. Scot turned to leave, claiming he had pressing business, although Chaloner knew he was discreetly allowing him to report to Thurloe alone. He caught his friend's arm.

'You took a risk in coming to my aid.'

Scot was dismissive. 'Hardly! And it was nothing compared to your rescue of me in Holland last year.' He brandished the cup he had stolen. 'Do you want this, or shall I toss it in the river?'

'Send it anonymously to Lady Castlemaine. That should confuse everyone.'

Scot laughed, liking the notion of causing mischief. Then he saluted Thurloe and walked back towards the city.

'I am sorry, Tom,' said Thurloe, opening the door to the carriage and helping Chaloner inside. He peered anxiously into his face. 'I would have come to save you myself, but Scot said he would be better at it – and he was right, of course. He is his father's son for daring escapades.'

'Who tried to poison you?' asked Chaloner. 'Prynne?'

'Prynne?' Thurloe was shocked. 'He is a bigot, not a killer! I thought my elixirs were safe from meddlers, as I keep them locked in the pantry upstairs, but the tonic is definitely the culprit, because it is the only thing the cat managed to steal. The poor thing is terribly ill. Shall I take you to a surgeon?'

'No, thank you!' said Chaloner hastily. He handed over the letter he had retrieved from Bristol's chest. It was written on the kind of cheap paper that was available to everyone, although the ink was an unusual shade of blue.

To my Ld Bristoll, by Ye grace of God:

This verye nyght I did Witnesse an act of Grayte Evill, that is Ye Murder of Mathew Webbe by Nine Persons of Wycked Violence. These Persons naymed are Willm Dyllon, Thos. Sarsfeild, Rich. Fanyng, Waltr. Fitz-Gerrard, Lowence Clarke, Geo. Wyllys, Greg^y Burn, Rich. Fissymons and Petr. Terel. Ye Murder was Donne as a Revengge becaws Ye said Webbe was Parte of Ye Layte Busness in Ireland, and was a Rebell. Then he betrayd his Comraydes, becaws his Conscience called Hym. I am marvel-lously praepared to leave all my Apprehenshons to wyser men, for it is God Almightie and Hys Instrumentes who will delivere alle evill spyes and intel-ligencers to the Gallowes, for Hee shalle not suffere them to live. I knowe Youe are a decent Mann, who wille see Right Donne in God's Goode Nayme.

'Look at the way he wrote Sarsfeild,' said Thurloe thoughtfully. 'His S may be a G, which would make it Thomas Garsfield – the alias you used in Ireland. I hope this was not aimed at you.'

Chaloner did not think so for a moment. 'I am not sufficiently important.'

'You hail from an old and distinguished family, and your forebears were eminent politicians and intellectuals. You are not as invisible as you seem to believe. Perhaps *Sarsfeld* had nothing to do with Webb's murder, and an innocent man sits in Ludgate Gaol.'

'We could ask him – check his alibi for the time of the murder, if he has one.' Chaloner did not feel like making an assault on a prison that morning, but it would have to be done soon, because it was already Wednesday, and the executions were scheduled for three days' time.

Thurloe tapped the letter with his forefinger. 'Still, at least we know why Bristol was chosen as the recipient, and not Williamson. The writer dislikes spies – and Williamson hires them.'

'Bristol has a spy called Willys, though,' Chaloner pointed out. 'And Willys is one of the men cited in the letter.'

Thurloe shrugged. 'Perhaps the writer did not know that – perhaps he thinks Willys is a servant and no more. What do you think of the Earl's cousin, Brodrick – *other* than his musical abilities?'

Chaloner was taken aback by the abrupt change of subject. 'Other than those, not much. He does not *do* anything, except attend parties. I do not know why Clarendon places such faith in his abilities, when he never sees them used.'

'That is probably what people say about you, but all the while you are working very hard at gathering intelligence and listening to idle chatter.'

Chaloner tried to understand what he was saying. 'You think Brodrick is a spy?'

257

'It is possible. Have you shared any sensitive information with him?'

'I told him about a plan to have Clarendon blamed for the location of the King's new bedchamber.'

'Then you must question Clarendon immediately. If Brodrick *has* shared this information with him, then perhaps he is loyal. If he has not, then you might want to ask yourself why.' Thurloe turned to the letter again. 'Now we have yet another motive for Webb's murder; this claims he was involved in the Castle Plot, but betrayed it to the government.'

'Well, someone did,' said Chaloner. 'We had weeks to infiltrate the rebels and foil their plans.'

A second visit to Newgate could be postponed no longer, even though all Chaloner wanted to do was to lie down until his stomach stopped pitching. He did not think he had felt so unwell since he had been injured by an exploding cannon at the Battle of Naseby – and then he had been expected to die.

'You have not forged another pass for me, have you?' he asked weakly.

'There are many ways to gain access to prisons, and counterfeit letters is just one of them,' replied Thurloe evenly. He handed Chaloner a very heavy purse. 'Another is bribery.'

Leaving Thurloe outside, Chaloner used the ex-Spymaster's money to secure an interview, although even the princely sums on offer bought him no more than five minutes in the condemned man's company. He had borrowed Thurloe's hat and coat, and smothered his face with a chalky powder the ex-Spymaster had thought to bring with him. A black eye-patch completed the disguise,

258

which was crude by Chaloner's standards, but hopefully good enough to ensure none of the guards would associate him with the man who had deceived them two days before.

'You again,' said Dillon, as Chaloner entered the visitors' room. The prisoner sported his trademark hat, so his eyes and upper face were hidden. He looked sleek and contented, and his clothes were different to the ones he had worn last time. 'Nice patch. Is it a disguise, or have you been fighting?'

'Do you know Thomas Sarsfeild?' asked Chaloner.

'I have already told you no,' said Dillon. He stood. 'Is that all? I am reading John Spencer's book on the end of the world in the year sixty-six, and I want to how what to avoid when the time comes.'

'Thurloe said you refused to tell him anything that might allow him to save you,' said Chaloner, thinking Dillon was very certain about his longevity. He was not sure *he* would have been so complacent, had he been in the condemned man's situation.

'His interference is unnecessary and unwelcome. My master will save me when the time is right.'

'Four men named in Bristol's letter have already been pardoned and two allowed to disappear. If you were going to join their ranks, surely something would have happened by now?'

'Why should you care what happens to me?'

'I don't,' said Chaloner, thinking of Manning. 'But Thurloe does, and I have agreed to help him. Who wrote this?' He handed Dillon the letter he had stolen. 'Do you recognise the writing?'

'Ah – the famous accusation! I saw it at my trial, although I cannot imagine how you come to have it.

259

However, I *still* do not know who wrote it, and I *still* do not recognise the writing. Next question.'

'Was Webb involved in the Castle Plot? Did you kill him because he betrayed you, and so was the cause of the rebellion's failure? I know you argued with him the day he died.'

Dillon raised his eyebrows. 'You have been assiduous in your researches! Next question.'

'You have not answered the ones I have already asked.'

'And nor shall I. Leave this business alone, Heyden. I will not hang. My master has a sense of the dramatic, and I do not anticipate that the crowds at my execution will be disappointed.'

'You expect to be rescued at the scaffold?' asked Chaloner doubtfully.

Dillon winked, then demanded to be returned to his cell. Chaloner did not linger once he had gone, eager to be away from the reeking gaol. He climbed wearily into Thurloe's carriage, feeling his heartbeat slow to a more normal level – the guard had taken rather too long to open the last gate.

'What is the matter?' asked Thurloe in alarm. 'Is Dillon unwell? Dead, like Fanning?'

'He is perfectly happy. I just hate prisons.'

'Because of that business in France four years ago? Perhaps *I* should visit Sarsfeild in Ludgate.'

'No,' said Chaloner, although he was tempted. 'It is too dangerous for you. I will do it.'

Ludgate was one of the portals that had once formed part of the city's defensive walls. It had been rebuilt eighty years before, and its upper chambers had always been used as a prison for petty criminals and debtors. It was a long, functional building that lacked the formidable security associated with Newgate, and Chaloner was relieved to note it lacked Newgate's stench, too. Inside, a second purse disappeared into the pockets of guards as Chaloner bought his way towards a convicted felon.

'Newgate's governor did not want to lose a second convict to gaol-fever before he can be strung up,' chattered one particularly helpful – and impecunious warden – as they walked to Sarsfeild's cell together. 'The event has already been advertised, see, and folk are disappointed when they do not get what they are promised. Dillon is different, because he has money to buy a clean, safe cell, but Sarsfeild is poor and was at risk from infection.'

'Have you heard any rumours about Fanning's death?'

The warden held out his hand for another of Thurloe's coins. 'One guard said there was a cord around his neck when the body was found, but he is given to strong drink, and no one believed him. Unfortunately, he died the following night, so you cannot ask him yourself.'

'He died?' asked Chaloner uneasily. 'How?'

'Hit by a cart when he left his favourite tavern. Strong drink, see. Never touch it myself. There was a whisper that Fanning was going to escape by plying us guards with poisoned wine, but we have not been fooled by that sort of thing since the Middle Ages. We *are* professionals, after all.'

Chaloner was conducted down a narrow corridor, which smelled of boiled cabbage, to a cell at the far end. It was a dismal hole, but at least it had a window that allowed relatively fresh air to blow in. Sarsfeild was a small man whose clothes had once been respectable. Now he was filthy, unshaven and frightened. When he came towards Chaloner, his face was streaked, as though he had been crying.

'I will tell you anything,' he said, tears flowing. 'I will *say* anything, only please let me go. I did not kill Matthew Webb, or even know him. I am a confectioner – I deal in sugar and sweetmeats. I have no reason to stab anyone. There has been a terrible mistake.'

'Sugar?' asked Chaloner. 'Where does it come from?'

'Barbados, I believe.'

'I mean which merchant sells you the raw materials for your trade?'

Sarsfeild's face was a mask of despair. 'All right, I admit I met Webb once or twice, because he sold the cheapest sugar, but I did not murder—'

'Where do you live?'

'The Strand; I have a shop in the New Exchange. I know how this looks – I bought sugar from Webb, and we are almost neighbours – but that is where our association ends. I did *not* kill him!'

Chaloner thought about Scot's theory, reiterated by Thurloe: that a mistake had been made, and that the letter's author had intended Chaloner's name to be on the list. And so 'Garsfield', who had been active in thwarting the Castle Plot, was overlooked in favour of Sarsfeild the confectioner, because the man was an associate of Webb's and lived nearby. Could it be true? The man in Ludgate had none of Dillon's dash and swagger, and certainly was not expecting rescue.

'The King himself has tasted my wares,' Sarsfeild continued, when Chaloner made no comment. 'If you tell His Majesty about my predicament, and ask for a royal pardon, I will keep you in sweetmeats for the rest of your life.'

'I do not have that sort of authority, I am afraid. Where were you the night Webb was murdered?'

Sarsfeild looked relieved. 'I keep telling people, but no one will listen: I went to see a play called *The Humorous Lieutenant*, then I went home with an actress called Beck Marshall who lives in Drury Lane. Please go to see her. She will tell you I was with her all night, so cannot have murdered Webb.'

'I will do what I can. Did you hear what happened to Fanning?'

Sarsfeild gave a bitter smile. 'Gaol-fever – it was why I was moved. The governor does not want the public to be cheated of their entertainment on Saturday.'

Chapter 8

At the western end of the great expanse that was St Paul's churchyard was a coffee house with a sign above it that identified it as the Turk's Head. There were several places of refreshment in the city with that name, but the one in St Paul's was famous because it was used by local booksellers to strike deals with their customers. Besides coffee, the Turk's Head offered sherbets flavoured with roses or lemons, chocolate – a dark, bitter beverage endured only by truly dedicated followers of fashion – and stationery. For six shillings, a pound of East India 'berries' could be purchased, along with free instructions on how to produce the perfect dish of coffee. Thurloe bought some when he learned the East India type was said to be good for 'griping pains in divers regions'.

'Are you sure you do not want any sugar?' asked the ex-Spymaster, as they took seats in a room so warm that its patrons' clothes – wet from the morning's drizzle – steamed furiously. 'Coffee does not taste very nice without it. It does not taste very nice *with* it, either, but at least it is an improvement.'

'Sarsfeild bought sugar from Webb,' said Chaloner,

thinking about what he had learned. 'And they lived close to each other, although I imagine Sarsfeild's home is rather less grand than Webb Hall. These two connections may have been enough to see him accused of a crime he did not commit. Alternatively, they may mean he had a motive to stab Webb, since most people seem to have been seized with the desire to stick a rapier in the fellow once they had made his acquaintance.'

'Which do you think is true?' asked Thurloe, sipping his coffee and wincing at the flavour.

'I have no idea. The disparity between the two convicted men is puzzling. Dillon has everything he wants, and is convinced he will be saved in a dramatic gesture by his patron. Sarsfeild has no money to pay for his keep, and is certain he is going to die.' Chaloner rubbed his head. He still felt sick, and the unsweetened coffee was not helping. 'They do not seem like the kind of men to work together.'

'So, you think the letter might have meant to accuse "Garsfield" after all?'

'No – I only used that alias once, and that was in Dublin. Most of the rebels I met are either dead or in prison, and my fellow spies either know me as Heyden or by my real name.'

'Let us review this logically. How many agents were involved in thwarting this rebellion?'

'About two dozen that I know of. Some are still in Ireland, some have been sent to new assignments overseas, and the only ones currently in London are May, Eaffrey and Scot.'

'But these three know you by more familiar names, so would not have used Garsfield anyway. What about *Thomas* Scot? Was he aware of your real identity?'

265

'We have known each other since we were children, so yes, he knew.'

'You were part of a covert operation that resulted in his imprisonment, the failure of his revolt, and the death or incarceration of his co-conspirators. Perhaps he wants revenge on you, and used your Garsfield identity to ensure the letter was not traced back to him.'

'But his brother's alias is in the letter, too,' argued Chaloner. 'And Thomas would never hurt his family. They have grown closer since their father's execution, and he would never put Scot at risk.'

Thurloe was quiet for a long time, making patterns in the sludge at the bottom of his bowl with a pewter spoon. 'I think you are right,' he said eventually. 'This letter did not refer to you. That leaves two possibilities. First, Sarsfeild's name was included for spite – perhaps his confectionery made someone's teeth fall out—'

'Temple!' exclaimed Chaloner.

Thurloe inclined his head. 'And secondly, Sarsfeild *is* guilty of the murder, but is ready to say or do anything to escape the inevitable.'

They continued to discuss the letter, but found they could not agree on its meaning. Thurloe thought it proved that Webb had been part of the Castle Plot – had betrayed his co-conspirators and been killed for it – but refused to believe that Dillon had struck the fatal blow. Chaloner was unwilling to dismiss the possibility that linking Webb to the Castle Plot might just be someone's way of trying to make sure the letter was taken seriously.

'I should do as Sarsfeild suggested,' said Chaloner, changing the subject when they started to go around in circles. 'Speak to the actress Beck Marshall of Drury Lane, to see if he has a credible alibi.'

'I could go with you,' said Thurloe reluctantly, 'although it is distasteful. I dislike the theatre and all it has come to represent: immorality, hedonism and vice.'

'Prynne would be pleased to hear you say that. It is what he thinks.'

Thurloe smiled bleakly. 'Yes, but, unlike him, I do not itch to burn them all to the ground with players and audience still inside.'

Beck Marshall was in bed when they knocked on the door of the house she shared with her sister. A servant went to rouse her, but it was a long time before she sauntered, semi-naked, into her front parlour. Her face bore the ravages of a wild evening, and her fashionable patches were sadly smudged, giving her a striped appearance. She reeked of wine, and Chaloner wondered whether *he* had looked as dissipated when he had arrived at Thurloe's rooms that morning.

'Sarsfeild,' Beck mused. 'Yes, I entertained him on the night *The Humorous Lieutenant* opened, because he brought me a box of sugared almonds. I still have some left. Would you like one?'

'No, thank you,' said Thurloe coolly. 'Did Sarsfeild leave you at all that night, or did he stay with you the whole time?'

She shot him a leering smile that made him recoil in revulsion. 'I cannot remember one man from another, to be frank, although you might prove to be the exception. Shall we find out?'

'We shall not, madam,' said Thurloe icily. 'Now, please try to remember Sarsfeild, because his life may depend on it.'

'Why is everything so *desperately* important these days?' Beck asked in a bored voice. 'I thought we were done with all that when the King ousted those miserable Puritans. All I want is some fun—'

'Sarsfeild,' prompted Thurloe curtly. 'Did he stay all night with you?'

Beck pouted. 'He probably did, because he will have wanted his money's worth for the almonds, but I cannot recall for certain. Do you have any sweetmeats on offer, Mr Heyden? You look like a man who knows how to enjoy himself, even if your prudish friend—'

'No, he does not,' snapped Thurloe. 'And you should wash your face, girl. You look like a tiger.'

Chaloner was laughing as they took their leave of Beck Marshall. Thurloe's reaction to her had taken his mind of his roiling stomach, for which he was grateful, because he was beginning to feel better. The ex-Spymaster glared at him.

'You were tempted by her,' he said accusingly. 'I could see you were seriously considering providing her with a gift in exchange for an hour of her company.'

Chaloner regarded him in amusement. 'I have never paid a prostitute in my life.'

Thurloe was unimpressed. 'That is an ambiguous answer, because it suggests you inveigle their services free of charge. But discussing your sinful past will take us nowhere. What did you think of Sarsfeild's alibi? Can we believe he spent the night with that flighty child or not?'

'Her testimony is inconclusive. Miss Marshall would say anything for the right price, but she honestly does not remember how long Sarsfeild stayed with her. Also, we cannot discount the possibility that she might have passed out from wine at some point, and awoke to find him next to her in the morning. Unfortunately for Sarsfeild, he chose the wrong woman to speak for him.'

268

'I imagine he will be more careful next time.'

'If there is a next time,' said Chaloner soberly.

Thurloe insisted on taking Chaloner to White Hall in his carriage after they had left Drury Lane, even though it was in the opposite direction from Lincoln's Inn.

'Take my coat again,' he said, handing it over. 'Bristol might be there, and although you say he did not see your face, he certainly saw your clothes and that purple is distinctive. I am sure you have a spare cap. You usually do. And wipe that powder from your face. It makes you look like a Court debauchee – although perhaps it is not the chalk that is responsible. Even Brodrick would have been shocked by your rakish appearance this morning.'

'Perhaps, but at least *he* would not have given me poison to drink,' retorted Chaloner.

Thurloe winced. 'I have said I am sorry – several times. Are you sure you are feeling better? Your temper does not seem to have improved. Perhaps you should go home.'

'I would like to, but you told me to warn Lord Clarendon about Lady Castlemaine and the King's new rooms, because you fear Brodrick cannot be trusted.'

'Well, that is what he is paying you for,' remarked Thurloe, a little acidly. 'Meanwhile, I shall take Bristol's letter to a handwriting expert I know, and see what he can tell me about it.'

Chaloner made his way towards White Hall's main gate, stopping to state his business in the guard room, where he was immediately hauled into a private chamber by Colonel Holles.

'Good God!' exclaimed the soldier, peering into Chaloner's face. 'What happened to you?'

'I drank something that disagreed with me. I am sure

I would feel better if I could remove this damned splint, though. You would not believe how much it itches. Wiseman is a quack.'

Holles kicked his foot and looked oddly furtive. 'He is not a quack,' he said in a loud, artificial voice. 'He is a good, honest fellow. A veritable Hypocrites.'

Chaloner snorted his disdain. 'Lisle does not think so. I have tried at least three times to hack this thing off, but it has set like a rock. Wiseman must have used too much glue.'

'The amount of glue I used was precisely what that was needed,' came Wiseman's haughty voice from the adjoining chamber, where he had been binding a soldier's bruised ankle. He looked larger than ever that day, because the room was small and his bulk took up more than his share of it. Holles gave him an embarrassed grin before shooting out on the pretext of interviewing a band of acrobats.

'Then why is it so hard?' demanded Chaloner, not intimidated by the surgeon's vast red presence.

'Because I *made* it hard,' replied Wiseman. 'What has Lisle been saying about me?'

Chaloner was sure Wiseman would not approve of his colleague's intentions for Saturday, and was not going to risk a confrontation between the two surgeons that would result in neither removing the splint. He procrastinated. 'He said you have a reputation for innovation.'

Wiseman knew he was being fobbed off with an answer that meant nothing. He grabbed Chaloner's hand and his jaw dropped when he inspected his handiwork. 'God in heaven! What have you been doing? Climbing trees?'

Chaloner hoped the surgeon would not associate him with the 'thief' who had escaped Chyrurgeons' Hall by

270

scaling its protective walls. 'Nothing I would not normally have done,' he replied coolly.

'Well, what you "normally do" does not seem to suit your humours,' said Wiseman caustically. 'Have you been drinking?'

Chaloner objected to the man's accusatory tone. 'Yes – a tonic containing Venice Treacle.'

Wiseman frowned. 'Venice Treacle should not have harmed you. However, I know the lingering effects of wine when I see them. My advice to you is to drink plenty of watered ale, to wash them out.'

'I would feel better without this splint. It is hot and it rubs. It is time you removed it, and—'

Wiseman sighed impatiently. 'It is *not* time. Look, I know what I am doing, Heyden, because I am the best surgeon in London. In fact,' he said as he walked away, '*I* am a genius.'

Chaloner was tempted to see whether he would feel quite so full of hubris with a splint cracked across his pate. He was not usually given to violent urges, but it had not been a good morning, and although he felt better than when he had been burgling Bristol's home, the combined effects of too much wine and whatever Thurloe had fed him lingered on. He was stalking across the Pebble Court when someone tried to collide with him. Even preoccupied with the state of his health, his instincts did not let him down. He jigged automatically to one side, and May staggered into thin air.

'Watch where you are going!' May snarled, trying to regain his balance. His latest hairpiece – a pale-ginger periwig – slipped to one side, then tumbled to the ground, revealing his shiny head.

'I was,' retorted Chaloner tartly. 'Fortunately for you.'

'Are you threatening me?' demanded May, hand dropping to the hilt of his sword.

'Threatening you with what?' asked Chaloner, all the frustrations of the morning suddenly boiling up in a spurt of hot temper. The dagger dropped from his sleeve into the palm of his hand. 'Ridicule, for losing the body of the man you shot?'

May glowered at him. 'If I find out you were responsible for that, I *will* kill you.'

'You can try,' said Chaloner contemptuously. 'Of course, mislaying corpses is not the only stupid thing you have done recently. The letter you sent Bristol, which might see innocent men hanged, *will* be investigated and I shall see its culprit brought to justice.'

May gazed at him, anger forgotten in the face of his astonishment. 'You think *I* wrote that? But my alias – Burne – was among the accused. If I had been the author, I would have left it off.'

'You included yourself deliberately, to allay suspicion.'

May stepped back. 'You are clearly unwell or you would not be making such wild accusations. I do not fight sick men, and you look terrible.'

'Then *talk* to me instead.' As quickly as it had flared, Chaloner's rage subsided, and he knew he was lucky May had declined to react to his inflammatory remarks. The King had forbidden brawling among courtiers, and while a Groom of the King's Privy Chamber might escape with a reprimand, matters would be a lot more serious for an ex-Cromwellian spy. He replaced the knife surreptitiously, masking what he was doing by leaning down to retrieve May's wig. 'Who sent the note?'

'I have no idea. It saw me accused of murder, too, but I spent no more than an hour in Newgate before my

272

pardon arrived. Williamson does not allow his best men to rot in prisons.' When May reached out to snatch the hairpiece away from Chaloner, his fingers brushed the splint, and he grabbed it before the spy could stop him. 'I *knew* there was something wrong with you. What happened?'

Chaloner chose not to answer. 'I do not suppose it was you who was going to rescue Fanning by sending his Newgate guards a barrel of poisoned wine, was it?' He had no reason for asking, other than that it had been an idiotic notion and May was an idiotic man.

May's expression was haughty. 'Hardly "poisoned" – just treated with a soporific. How do you know? Fanning swore he would tell no one but Dillon – to ask whether he wanted saving, too.'

'And did he?'

May shook his head as he replaced his wig. 'He said he preferred to wait for his patron to do it. Still, my efforts were not needed in the end, because Fanning died of gaol-fever before I could act.'

'Why were you willing to help him escape? Was he one of Williamson's men?'

May's expression was disdainful. 'Your wits *are* slow today, Heyden. Of course he was not one of Williamson's men – if he had been, he would have been pardoned with the rest of us. However, he once helped me in an embarrassing matter pertaining to a lady, and I wanted to pay a debt due.'

Chaloner wondered whether Fanning might still be alive, were it not for May's ill-conceived and not-very-secret rescue. 'Apparently, guards have not been fooled by drugged wine for centuries.'

'So they say, but it has never failed me yet, and the

best tricks are always the old ones. Remember that, Heyden. It may save your life some day – if you live that long. Incidentally, I heard your earl hid his whore's petticoats under his pillow the other day, then tried to burn the evidence.'

Chaloner laughed, genuinely amused. 'Anyone with even the smallest smattering of intelligence will know that he would never betray his marriage vows. You will have to do better than that, if you want to drag him into the mire with you.'

May regarded him with dislike. 'I shall see that as a challenge issued.'

The Stone Gallery was a long chamber with portraits of venerable old Royalists lining one wall, and windows that flooded them with light on the other. Nobles and government ministers gathered there, and it was said that more state decisions were made in the Stone Gallery than in meetings of the privy council. The Lord Chancellor grabbed Chaloner's arm and led the way to his offices; the hallway was also a place for eavesdropping and gossip, and not somewhere to receive briefings from spies.

He was bemused when Chaloner told him about Bristol's plan to see him in trouble with Lady Castlemaine, because Brodrick had already given him the details, and they had discussed the matter at length. Lord Clarendon had then raised the matter with the King, who was highly entertained by the situation, but promised to inform 'the Lady' that the idea to move apartments had been his own idea, and nothing to do with his Lord Chancellor. The crisis had already been averted.

The Earl was so absolutely certain of Brodrick's loyalty

that Chaloner wondered whether Thurloe was right to question him, especially when the man in question arrived with yet more information about Bristol's schemes, and had obviously spent the morning working on his kinsman's behalf. He had learned that the remnants of the incinerated petticoats had been interpreted as firm evidence that Clarendon kept a mistress, and rumours were already rife as to her identity.

'But it is all false!' cried the Earl, appalled. 'How could Bristol say such things about me? I much prefer the company of dogs to loose women.'

Brodrick struggled not to smirk. 'You had better not tell him that, cousin, or he will be telling everyone to lock up their spaniels as well as their daughters.' He cocked his head at a knock on the door. 'That will be Lisle. I asked him to come and see me about a Private Anatomy, which are all the rage these days. I am tempted to ask my consort to play a little chamber music to accompany the dissection. What do you think, Heyden?'

'The sound of saws ripping through entrails might drown out the quieter movements,' said Chaloner, thinking such a perverted notion could only have come from a man with too much time on his hands and too great a devotion to increasingly bizarre forms of recreation. He started to withdraw, intending to go home and drink watered ale, but was stopped by Lisle, who peered at him in concern.

'You look unwell,' he said. 'It must be the toxic compounds percolating through the skin of your arm from Wiseman's glue.'

'An excess of wine can make a man feel seedy, too,' said Brodrick wryly, clearly speaking from experience.

'Actually, it was poison,' said Chaloner, declining to

admit to drunkenness in front of the Lord Chancellor. 'It was intended for someone else and I took it by mistake.'

'Poison?' echoed Clarendon, horrified. 'It was not meant for me, was it?'

'What kind of poison?' asked Lisle. 'I hope it was nothing containing Goddard's Drops. They are the latest tonic of choice among the fashionable, but Wiseman has learned that you only have to double the recommended dose for them to be fatal.'

'How did he discover that?' asked Chaloner uneasily.

'He has patients,' said Lisle darkly. 'Did this potion taste of silk? Volatile oil of silk is just one of the dangerous ingredients included in Goddard's Drops. I wish he had made his fortune by marketing a more benign compound, personally.'

'Bristol is next to that statue of Mars with a bucket of paint,' said Brodrick, bored with the discussion, so looking out of the window into the garden below. He started to laugh. 'He is giving him a blond wig like . . . ah.' He stopped sniggering and looked uncomfortably at his cousin's fair curls.

Clarendon shot from the room, Brodrick at his heels, so Chaloner and Lisle left the Lord Chancellor's offices, and began to walk across the Palace Court towards the gate. It was busy, because the King was showing off one of his new chronometers; Chaloner noticed Surgeon Wiseman among the throng that had gathered to make polite comments about it.

'You *must* come to see me on Saturday,' said Lisle urgently, glancing around to make sure no one else could hear. 'I could not mention it in front of your earl, because he and Wiseman are friends, and I do not want trouble. In fact, I would appreciate it if you said nothing to anyone about our appointment – keep it between the two of us.'

'Why?' asked Chaloner curiously.

'Because it would be seen as "patient poaching", which could see me expelled from my Company. However, I dislike seeing people suffer, which is why I work among the poor each Friday. Wiseman has made a terrible mistake with his splint, and I feel duty-bound to rectify it.'

'Then take it off now,' said Chaloner. 'There must be suitable tools somewhere in White Hall.'

Lisle smiled kindly. 'It is a little more complicated than plying a saw, and I have already told you it needs time to degrade before we can tamper. Do not be too hopeful about the outcome, though – and be warned that you may have to take up something that requires less manual dexterity than the viol. Singing, perhaps. Damn! Wiseman is coming to talk to us, so we shall say no more about our private arrangement. Agreed?'

Chaloner nodded. 'Thank you.'

'Ground snails with a minced earthworm is something I always recommend for fevers,' said Lisle as Wiseman approached, speaking as though they were in the middle of an in-depth conversation. 'It is quite palatable when sweetened with sugar.'

'I decline to recommend sugar to *my* patients,' said Wiseman immediately, making Chaloner itch to point out that invading other people's discussions without invitation was unmannerly. 'It is the commodity that makes slavery a necessity, and slavery is an abomination in the eyes of God.'

'Webb made his fortune transporting sugar from the slave plantations,' said Chaloner innocently.

Wiseman's expression was cold. 'Exactly. He had his

just deserts when he was cut down in the gutters of The Strand like an animal. Crime begets crime, and his was unforgivable.'

'How long had you known him?' asked Chaloner guilelessly.

Wiseman looked mystified. 'Why?'

'Because you puzzled a friend of mine. He heard you arguing with Webb in a coffee house around Christmas time, but when you joined his group of learned companions in a tavern last month – a few hours before the Guinea Company dinner – you denied knowing the man.'

Wiseman sighed, aware that Lisle was regarding him with an expression of dismay. 'All right, I admit I may have been less than honest. But Robert Hooke was among that particular gathering, and he is vehemently opposed to slavery. As I would like to be elected to the Royal Society, and Hooke is its Curator, I decided to disclaim any prior dealing with Webb. Webb damaged me enough with his spiteful allegations, and I did not want him ruining my chances of joining the Royal Society, too.'

'Did you go to the dinner, Wiseman?' asked Lisle. 'I know we were all invited, but I cannot recall who said he was going. No, wait! I saw you dressed in your best scarlet robes before I left Chyrurgeons' Hall – I offered you a ride in my carriage, if you recall.'

'And I declined, because I had business at the hospital to attend,' replied Wiseman smoothly. 'It transpired to be more complex than I thought, and I was obliged to miss the feast. I believe I told you as much the following day.'

'So you did,' said Lisle. 'Meanwhile, I had no more reached the doors of African House before I was called away to tend the Lord Chancellor's gout. We were both prevented from enjoying ourselves.'

278

However, Chaloner knew that at least one surgeon had been present, because an expert had tended Temple's broken pate. He believed Lisle, because he had told the same story before, but there was something about Wiseman's reply that set alarm bells ringing. The man had lied about knowing Webb, so what was to say he was telling the truth about missing the Guinea Company dinner? Had he objected so strongly to Webb's slave investments that he had been driven to dispatch the man? The rapier *had* entered Webb's heart, after all, and an anatomist might well strike with such neat precision.

Or had it been Johnson who had physicked Temple? Chaloner might have assumed so, were it not for the incident with the surgeon's parrot-savaged finger. Johnson had odd ideas about healing, and Chaloner could not shake the conviction that if *he* had done the honours, then he would have devised a treatment so bizarre that it would have been gossiped about afterwards. Of course, there was always the possibility that he was wrong, and that Johnson had been in an orthodox frame of mind that night.

'Webb was unpopular with everyone,' elaborated Lisle hastily, seeming to sense that Wiseman's answers were leading Chaloner to consider him a suspect for foul play. 'He accused me of overcharging for a phlebotomy, then he bribed the courts to secure himself a favourable verdict. *And* he was threatening to sue the Company for postponing the Private Anatomy he had commissioned.'

'You were at White Hall when Webb was murdered, Master Lisle?' asked Chaloner, eager to eliminate at least one man from his lengthy list of potential culprits. 'You came here to tend the Earl?'

Lisle shook his head. 'I was at Worcester House – his

home. I arrived at six o'clock, and remained with him most of the night. He slept eventually, but I did not want to leave until I was sure the attack had passed. Gout is very painful.'

Chaloner nodded, disappointed. If the Earl had been asleep, then it meant he could not vouch for his surgeon, and Worcester House was next door to the place where Webb had been killed. Thus none of Chaloner's suspects from Chyrurgeons' Hall could be eliminated. However, some of their names could be underscored. After all, why would anyone lie, unless to mask guilt?

On his way home, Chaloner stopped off at the Golden Lion, and swallowed as much watered ale as he could manage. He was tired after two nights of poor sleep, and when he reached his rooms, he lay on his bed with the intention of dozing for ten minutes before returning to White Hall in a new disguise. He woke only when the bells were chiming six o'clock.

He felt better than he had done in days, and supposed Wiseman had known what he was talking about with regard to the poison. He was just shaving with his sharpest dagger when a messenger arrived with an invitation to dine with Eaffrey and Behn in an hour. It was an odd time to eat – most people did it in the middle of the day – but Eaffrey had never allowed herself to be constrained by convention. He was tempted to decline, because an evening with the belligerent Brandenburger held scant appeal, but he supposed it was Eaffrey's way of making peace after their quarrel, and he did not want to reject the hand of friendship. He donned his best clothes and set out for Behn's home.

Leather Lane, part of the rapidly expanding area

known as Hatton Garden, lay near the edge of the sprawling metropolis, north of Holborn. It was a pleasantly affluent part of the city, with spacious houses and well-tended gardens, and was named after Hatton House, a rambling Elizabethan ruin that was fighting a losing battle with nettles and ground-alder. The Fleet river lay not far away, but the wind was from the west, so blew away the fumes from the slaughterhouses, tanneries and sundry other reeking industries that plied their trades along its foetid banks.

Chaloner knocked at Behn's door, and was admitted by a liveried servant. When he was shown into the dining room, the merchant greeted him coolly, suggesting the invitation had not been his idea. Chaloner was bracing himself for a trying evening when a Frenchman wearing an outrageous outfit of orange silk burst in, all fluttering fans and heavily accented English. It took a moment for Chaloner to recognise Scot's pale eyes under all the make-up, but he was pleased: the gathering would not be tedious at all if Scot was in one of his flamboyant moods.

The table was set for nine people: Eaffrey and Behn sat at either end, and between were their guests. In the seat of honour was Brodrick. Next to him was a pair of giggling adolescent girls. Chaloner had been listening to Scot furtively whispering his latest discovery – that Fanning was suspected of smuggling guns to the Irish rebels – and had missed Eaffrey's introduction, but it did not matter, since neither child said a word to him all evening, and each time he tried to talk to them, their response was to dissolve into paroxysms of helpless laughter.

'Is there something wrong with them?' he asked Scot in an undertone.

'They were invited so Eaffrey would not be surrounded by too many men. Personally, I think she is being overly prudish. She should dispense with the wool-heads and invite a couple of fellows from the Royal Society instead. *They* know how to entertain a man after dinner.'

'Who are the last two guests?' Just then, the door opened and they were ushered in. 'Oh, no!'

It was Alice, clinging proprietarily to the arm of Richard Temple. She wore the yellow skirts she had donned for the ball, and he was resplendent in a suit of blue satin, complemented by a highly laced pink shirt. Alice's expression darkened when she spotted Chaloner.

'Lord!' groaned Scot. 'Eaffrey should have warned me. Now you two will squabble all night, and when I am not trying to keep the peace, I shall be forced to smile and nod at the snake who wants my sister for her money. Eaffrey will be cross if I spoil her party by being rude to the fellow.'

'I would not have accepted this invitation had I known *you* were going to be here,' said Alice, coming to speak to Chaloner when Temple and Brodrick began a barbed conversation in which there was no room for anyone else – the spy and Scot's prickly sister were not the only ones at the party who disliked each other.

'Please, Alice,' said Scot quietly. 'He is my friend.'

'William!' cried Alice in delight when she recognised her brother. She coloured furiously at the careless slip and lowered her voice. 'Your disguise certainly fooled me! Who are you meant to be?'

'A Parisian perfume-maker. It is a ruse to insinuate myself into Brodrick's company – he has the ears of powerful men, and I want to talk to him about Thomas's release. That is mostly why Eaffrey arranged this little gathering, along with the fact that she wants to give Chaloner another chance to befriend Behn. I suppose Behn must have insisted on asking Temple – to prove *he* has friends, too.'

'Richard plans to nominate him as the next Master of the Guinea Company,' explained Alice. 'They are becoming firm allies, and will probably discuss business all night. Lord! I hope that does not leave *me* talking to Chaloner.'

'Please do not argue this evening,' begged Scot of them both. 'I cannot work on Brodrick if he is more interested in listening to you two snipe at each other. And I would be grateful if you did not betray Chaloner, either, Alice. No one here knows his real name, and I want it to stay that way.'

'Why?' demanded Alice. 'Is he ashamed of his Parliamentarian connections, then?'

'Because he is going to ask Lord Clarendon to help Thomas,' replied Scot, knowing her weak spot. 'If you expose him, you deprive our brother of a possible means of escape.'

'I suppose it is only for a few hours,' said Alice begrudgingly. 'And he *did* tell you about the Trulocke guns.'

Scot nodded. 'Williamson now knows Thomas is innocent of buying illegal firearms, and if *he* is convinced, he will persuade others, too. Thomas's situation is looking decidedly more promising.'

'What are you three muttering about?' asked Temple. Eaffrey had provided sweetmeats to hone the appetite before the meal, and they contained nuts, which Temple's gums could not accommodate. He spat them politely into his handkerchief, then shook the linen out so they pattered to the floor.

'*Mon Dieu!*' exclaimed Scot, fluttering his fan. He flicked Temple's collar with it. 'I see you have trouble with the laundry, too. They *will* wash the red with the white, and we shall all wear pink if they cannot be taught otherwise.'

Temple's eyes narrowed. 'It is supposed to be this colour. It is the fashion.'

Scot winked at him. 'Of course, monsieur. That is what I shall say, too. We shall not allow these laundresses to defeat us, *n'est-ce pas*? I hear you are kin to Sir John Temple of the privy council. You are honoured to have such a man in your family. I have long admired his horses.'

Temple nodded keenly, insults forgotten. 'I like horses myself. If you come to Hyde Park tomorrow, I shall introduce you to John, and you shall see the best of his collection.'

'Good,' murmured Alice in Scot's ear. 'John Temple is a powerful voice on the privy council, and may be able to help secure our brother's release. I should have thought of it myself.'

'Yes, you should,' Scot muttered back, a little unpleasantly.

Temple was ready to embark on a detailed discussion about horses, but Brodrick had picked up a candelabra, and was casually admiring it. Instinctively, Temple's hand went to the pate that had been dented when Clarendon's cousin had last laid hold of such an implement.

'I understand you were obliged to call on the services of a surgeon at the Guinea Company dinner, Temple,' said Chaloner, immediately seeing a way to further his investigation.

Brodrick laughed derisively. 'He remembers nothing about it – although the wine was responsible for that, not the candlestick. A surgeon *was* summoned, although none of us recall which one.'

Temple glared. 'And if the fellow was as drunk as *you* were that night, then I am lucky he did not saw off my head.'

The company was about to sit down to eat when the door opened yet again, and everyone was startled when Silence Webb glided in. She was clad in a black gown to which had been attached a chaos of white ostrich feathers; Chaloner's immediate thought was that they made her look like an oversized magpie. Her plump fingers were encrusted with rings, and there were so many necklaces under her chins that she glittered as she breathed.

'Mrs Webb,' stammered Behn. 'We were not expecting you.'

'I heard you were planning a soirée,' said Silence with a leer. 'And when you came to console me for the death of my Matthew, you were kind enough to say that I could visit you at *any* time. I am sure you have room for a little one at your dinner table.'

'Of course you must join us,' said Eaffrey graciously, moving forward to take Silence's arm. It took a lot more than an uninvited guest to disconcert her. 'Please come and sit down. We shall make space for you between this handsome French perfumer and—'

'No, thank you!' said Silence, regarding Scot with deep suspicion. 'I do not like the look of him at all. I shall sit between Mr Behn and Lord Clarendon's aide. Mr Heyden and I are old friends. I knew his kinsman, old Thomas Chaloner, you see.'

'Chaloner?' pounced Behn. 'You mean the regicide? Heyden is kin to him?'

285

'He is not,' said Eaffrey firmly. 'Although Silence is not the first to notice the uncanny resemblance. Mr Heyden is a mercantile clerk from Manchester, in London to make his fortune by working in White Hall.'

Silence sighed, disappointed. 'Pity. Old Chaloner was such an amusing man. He was always playing jokes and could put away more wine than my Matthew, which is saying something! But I shall still sit next to Mr Heyden, anyway. He will welcome the opportunity to get to know me better.'

'Will he?' asked Eaffrey, while Chaloner tried, by covert signals and desperate glances, to tell her he would not. 'Then I shall arrange for your place to be set at his side.'

'Well, come on, then,' said Silence, plumping herself down and producing a large spoon from the front of her robe. 'Grab a seat and let us be at the food before it gets cold. I could eat a horse.'

'I am sure she could,' murmured Scot to Chaloner, as they took their designated seats. 'So make sure she does not eat you, too.'

Silence's rearrangements meant Chaloner was sandwiched between her and Alice, and he resigned himself to a long evening. In proper London fashion, the meal was served in two courses. The first consisted of roasted beef, boiled carp, venison and a dish of sweet potatoes that no one ate. The second comprised pork, tench served with lemons, steamed chicken and two fruit pies. Following the French way, knives and two-pronged forks were provided, although a finger-bowl was required for Silence, who had not been taught how to manipulate a fork, and so was obliged to use her hands.

She rested a hot, heavy palm on Chaloner's knee, which

attracted a scowl from Behn, who sat on her other side. 'Has Lord Clarendon said anything else about my husband's murder?' she asked.

'I am afraid not, ma'am,' said Chaloner, moving his chair away from her. He bumped into Alice, who pushed him back more forcefully than was necessary or polite. He glanced at Scot, expecting him to say something, but the older man was talking to Brodrick, clearly intent on making his brother's case before the courtier became too inebriated for sensible conversation.

'Mr Behn tells me Dillon is certainly the man who struck the fatal blow,' Silence continued in a whisper. 'Him *and* the other two – except that one has escaped justice by dying of fever. I still believe they were under orders from someone else, although I shall enjoy seeing them die anyway. Will you attend the hangings, Mr Heyden?'

'No,' said Chaloner shortly, trying to make himself as small as possible, so he could maintain his distance from Silence without invading the space claimed by Alice.

'I enjoy hangings, as long as the weather is fine,' Silence went on. 'Will you accompany me on Saturday? I would appreciate an escort, and you cannot refuse a recent widow.'

'*I* will accompany you,' said Behn, taking her hand and raising it to his lips. Chaloner glanced at Eaffrey, but her attention was occupied by the chortling teenagers. 'I am always ready to be of service.'

Silence shot the merchant a smouldering look. 'You are a true gentleman, sir.'

'I am not surprised *you* want to make sure the villains are hanged, Behn,' said Temple conversationally. 'You did a lot of business with their victim, I understand.'

'Yes, Webb was a dear friend,' agreed Behn.

'Oh, silly!' said Silence, thumping him playfully. 'You know he was not! In fact, he would not approve of me sitting here with you at all, but he is dead, and so not in a position to do much about it.'

Behn looked decidedly shifty. 'We were close companions, Sil— Mrs Webb. You know we were. We occasionally pretended to be enemies, but that was just to flush out common foes.'

'You challenged him to a duel,' countered Silence. Her expression became disconcertingly simpering. 'I believe it was over me, because he thought you entertained a fancy for his little Silence. Of course, he made sure he was out of London on the relevant morning, and sent you a letter—'

Behn laughed uneasily. 'A joke, Mrs Webb. Just two merchants amusing themselves.'

Chaloner regarded him thoughtfully, recalling the discussion Temperance had overheard: Behn and Webb had quarrelled, and Behn had left the Guinea Company dinner early. Was Behn the killer? He watched with interest as, desperate to deflect attention from himself, Behn turned on the startled Temple.

'*You* were not Webb's friend, though – you signed a deed at the Guinea Company dinner that would have ruined you. I heard him tell you so after you had put pen to paper – when it was too late to withdraw from the agreement.'

'I am not a novice in business,' objected Temple indignantly. 'I knew what I was doing, and he was mistaken about the outcome of that particular arrangement. It *would* have made me wealthy, and I was deeply sorry that his death rendered our contract null and void.'

288

'Well, there you are, Chaloner,' murmured Scot a little later, when people were taking the opportunity to stretch their legs by walking around the table. 'Two more suspects for Webb's murder: Behn, whose "friendship" may not have been all he declared, and Temple, who had been beguiled into signing something that might have seen him destitute.'

'You were at that Guinea Company dinner, William,' said Eaffrey, pausing for a moment with a sniggering girl on either side of her. 'Did *you* see Temple almost sign away his fortune? I thought he had more sense than to put his name to deeds without considering their repercussions, and you must ask yourself whether you want him managing Alice's money.'

'I did see Webb and Temple together, but I slipped away too early to see how their discussion concluded. Webb must have produced these writs later, when Temple was befuddled with wine.'

'You left early?' asked Chaloner, when Eaffrey had gone. 'I thought you said you spent the evening holding forth about plants.'

'I did not say I left early – I said I slipped away *too early* to know what happened,' corrected Scot pedantically. 'I *was* enjoying my botanical debate, but even trees could not distract me from the lice in Terrell's hairpiece, and after a while, I simply had to go. I should have returned it to the wig-maker, but Williamson wanted me in place quickly and there was no time. I cannot tell you how much I am looking forward to throwing this whole business to the wind and never adopting a disguise again.'

'Not even when Peter Terrell presents his botanical researches to the Royal Society?'

Scot smiled. 'I will be in Surinam. Someone will *read* my dissertations to the learned gathering.'

'I visited your husband's tomb in St Paul's,' said Chaloner to Silence, when everyone had reclaimed his seat, and the footmen were concluding the meal by serving a syllabub – a dish popular at Court, because the King claimed it refreshed the mouth after riding and love-making. 'Clarendon sent me.'

'How kind,' said Silence, leaning across him to claim more dessert. 'They could not fit him in the crypt, so they slipped him in with a bishop instead. He would not have minded; he liked bishops.'

'He did not,' stated Brodrick, overhearing and so preventing Chaloner from probing Silence to see if she was aware that Webb was not interred at all. 'He detested the lot of them. I can see why: they are worse than Puritans for prim morals.'

'I like a little fun myself,' said Temple amiably, taking more wine. 'And the latest fashionable way to do it is to purchase a Private Anatomy from the barber-surgeons. Has anyone— Ouch!'

He gaped at Alice, who had apparently kicked him under the table. Then gradually, it dawned on him that the one *he* had commissioned had involved the husband of the woman who sat opposite him. He had the grace to look disconcerted, although Silence did not appear to notice what was going on.

'I have never attended such an event,' she said. 'Matthew tried to buy one, but the barber-surgeons fobbed him off with some tale about a leaking roof. Can you specify which corpse you want? I would be very interested in seeing inside a Dutchman, because their innards are made of cheese.'

'We shall be at war with Holland soon,' remarked Eaffrey, trying to raise the discussion to a more intelligent level. 'Especially if the Guinea Company tries to poach its slaving monopoly.'

'Good,' said Temple, rubbing his hands. 'We shall show the cheese-eaters a thing or two,'

'War with the Dutch should be avoided at all costs,' argued Chaloner. 'They have bigger and better ships, a navy in which its sailors are paid, and their weaponry is superior to ours. We would be foolish to take them on in open battle.'

'That is an unpatriotic statement,' declared Alice. 'Are you a traitor, then, who believes England is inferior to other nations?'

'In some respects we are,' said Chaloner, aware of Scot glaring at her across the table. 'And to claim otherwise would be to do Britain a disservice. We cannot win against the Dutch at sea.'

'Speaking of Dutch matters, did you hear that upholsterer is mortally ill?' asked Temple. 'If he dies, Bristol says it will be murder, because Clarendon struck the old fellow when he was defenceless.'

Brodrick made a disgusted sound. 'Vanders is not dying. I saw him today, in perfect health.'

'Pity,' said Temple. 'I would like to see Clarendon swing for murder. He is a tedious bore, and—'

'He is my kinsman, sir,' interrupted Brodrick icily. 'And I suffer no man to insult him.'

'I am sure no harm was meant,' said Eaffrey quickly. 'And we should not let the quarrel between Bristol and Clarendon spoil our evening. Let us talk about something more pleasant.'

Behn accepted the challenge. 'Would you like to invest

in my new ship, Temple? It will carry some very valuable cargoes, and you look like a man who is not afraid to be bold in the mercantile world.'

'New ship?' asked Chaloner.

'It was Matthew's,' explained Silence. 'It was doing no one any good sitting in a harbour with its holds empty, so Mr Behn and I made an agreement.'

'And what will this vessel carry?' asked Chaloner coldly. 'Sugar again?'

'Slaves,' replied Behn, startling the spy with his bald honesty. 'That is why anyone who invests with me will be rich. There is a good market for slaves in Barbados and Jamaica, and there is plenty of money for those willing to take a few risks. Do *you* have any spare income you want to invest?'

'Not for that purpose,' said Chaloner quietly. 'And nor does any decent man.'

'This is not suitable dinner conversation, either, *messieurs*,' said Scot, seeing Eaffrey look stricken. 'Have I told you about Bristol's *oignon* gardens? He has acres devoted to the plants, and walks among them, savouring their scent.'

'That is a lie – one put about by Clarendon,' said Temple immediately. He cut across Brodrick's indignant response and addressed the Brandenburger. 'You can put me down for a few hundred, Behn. I never let a good business opportunity slip past.'

'Blood money,' said Chaloner, disgusted. He saw the hurt expression on Eaffrey's face and saw he should keep quiet if he did not want to spoil her party.

'Brodrick?' asked Behn, fetching ink, pen and paper from a nearby cabinet. 'How about you? Do you have womanish principles, or are you a man?'

'I am not sure—' began Brodrick uneasily. It was common knowledge that he had no money of his own, which was why he clung so firmly to his cousin's coat-tails.

'*I* shall invest with you, Mr Behn,' said Alice, shooting Chaloner a spiteful glance. 'I am not afraid to speculate in the world of commerce, and my Richard tells me it pays to be bold.'

The evening wore on. Silence held forth about music in a way that told Chaloner she was entirely ignorant on the subject, and he found the best thing to do was nod and smile but not listen. He caught Scot's eye and the bleak expression on his old friend's face told him he was not having much success with furthering brother Thomas's cause, either. The meal came to a merciful end when Silence went face-down in her finger bowl. Chaloner rescued her from an ignominious death, although Brodrick suggested leaving her to drown. The spy struggled to lift her enormous weight, but Behn was the only one who bothered to help him.

'Is her carriage outside?' Chaloner asked, adding without enthusiasm, 'I will escort her home.'

'So you can seduce her, I imagine,' said Alice unpleasantly.

'Yes, I doubt I will be able to resist,' he replied acidly. 'So *you* had better take her instead.'

Her expression was murderous when she saw she had been outmanoeuvred, and she continued to glare as Chaloner and Behn levered Silence into her coach. Temple declined to accompany them on the basis that it would be improper for him to witness a woman's indignity, and Brodrick was on his horse and out of Behn's stable with a haste that was only just decent. Chaloner stepped into the shadows with a sigh of relief, grateful the evening was over, and determined to stay out of sight until everyone had gone – when he would emerge and lie to Eaffrey about how pleasant it had been.

While he waited for the teenagers – drowsy with the lateness of the hour and the wine they had consumed – to be packed into a cart and dispatched home, he breathed in deeply of the blossom-scented air. The stars were very bright, and, as he gazed up at them, he was reminded of the velvety darkness of a summer night at his family's manor in Buckinghamshire. He experienced a sharp desire to see his brothers and sisters again, to walk in their woods and meadows, and supposed tiredness was making him maudlin.

Scot, Eaffrey and Behn lingered in the yard after the girls had gone, also enjoying the freshness of the evening. When Scot bowed to his hosts and took his leave, Chaloner decided it might be better to write his thanks to Eaffrey the following day, instead of waiting to give them in person. He did not want another encounter with Behn. Then Eaffrey kissed her lover's cheek, whispering something that made him laugh. Behn tugged her hand in a way that suggested he was ready for bed, but she pulled away, indicating she wanted more time to clear her head. Before Chaloner could emerge from the shadows to speak to her alone, someone else approached. It was Scot.

'What happened to Chaloner?' he asked, peering into the house to make sure the Brandenburger had gone. 'It is unlike him to leave without saying goodbye.'

'I do not blame him. Sitting between Alice and Silence all night cannot have been pleasant. I know she is your sister, William, but even you must admit that Alice is not an easy lady. I wish he had not disappeared quite so soon, though. There is something I need to tell him about Webb.' Eaffrey chuckled. 'Silence has such gall that I am filled with admiration for her. Even *I* would have baulked at inflicting myself on such a gathering – and I am paid to do that kind of thing.'

'Your company would never be a burden, though,' said Scot tenderly. 'Unlike hers.'

Chaloner was half out of his hiding place, to share their amusement about the evening and its ups and very considerable downs – and to find out what she had to tell him about Webb – when Eaffrey and Scot flew together for a very passionate kiss.

The bells of St Andrew's Holborn were chiming eleven o'clock as Chaloner left Leather Lane, but he did not feel like going home. He had just consigned himself to sitting alone in a tavern, when he recalled Temperance's club. He walked briskly down Fetter Lane, hand on the hilt of his sword, because few men had honest business at such an hour and anyone he met was unlikely to be friendly, crossed Fleet Street and aimed for Hercules's Pillars Alley. The tavern of that name was doing a roaring trade, and noisy patrons spilled out on to the street. The air nearby stank of spilled beer, pipe smoke, vomit and urine. By contrast, only the faintest tinkle of music could be heard from Temperance's house. Chaloner slipped past Preacher Hill, who was saying goodnight to one of the city's most prominent judges, and padded along the hall to the kitchen. It was not many moments before Temperance arrived, come to fetch nuts for the Earl of Sandwich.

'Thomas!' she cried in delight. 'Will you join the revels

in the main parlour? The Duke of Buckingham has brought Lady Castlemaine again, and there is a lot of laughter and japes.'

Chaloner was not in the mood for foolery. He saw he had made a mistake in coming and stood to leave, loath to keep her from the fun. 'I do not know why I am here. Your company, I suppose.'

Temperance waved him back down, handing the nuts to one of her girls before sitting opposite him. 'There is no need to sound begrudging about it. There are occasions when only friends will do, and I am glad you felt you could come here. I am also relieved, because there is something you should know – Maude told me today that Dillon will be the subject of a dramatic rescue, just as the noose is put around his neck. All London is expecting some fine entertainment.'

'So is Dillon himself.'

'She also heard that Dillon is innocent of murder, and is going to the gallows because he is an Irish rebel – fabricating charges of murder is the government's way of ridding itself of such people.'

'That is false. Why do you think most countries have a secret service? It is so knives can be slipped into the backs of awkward subjects without the need for public trials and executions.'

Temperance regarded him with distaste. 'Is that what you do?'

'There is nearly always another solution.'

She was silent for a while. 'I asked a few of my guests about your surgeons – Wiseman, Lisle and Johnson. Lisle is a good man who spends one day a week working for the poor, and is well liked. Wiseman is unpopular, because he is condescending to his patients, and no one likes being treated like a fool. And Johnson *is* a fool, but knows enough of his trade to be a menace.'

'So Johnson and Wiseman are bad; Lisle is good?'

'In essence. I also heard that you accused Adrian May of sending the letter that saw Dillon and the others arrested. Did you?'

He regarded her askance. 'Christ, Temperance! Does *anything* happen in that damned palace that is not immediately brayed around the whole city?'

'This is *not* general knowledge; Colonel Holles told me. He came to see me this morning, to apologise for manhandling Modesty the other night – although she does not remember what it is he is supposed to have done. While he was here, he asked me to warn you against antagonising May.'

'Why would he do that?'

'Perhaps he likes you, Tom. There are not many left who are faithful to Lord Clarendon, after all. *Did* May did send that letter?'

Chaloner nodded. 'The more I think about it, the more it seems likely. He is jealous of his influence over Williamson, and that missive allowed him to be rid of the main competition. He included his own name, so it would not be conspicuous by its absence.'

'Does that mean *he* was involved in the killing of Webb, too? He committed the murder himself, and let Dillon, Fanning and Sarsfeild take the blame?'

Chaloner rubbed his eyes tiredly. 'I do not have the faintest idea.'

Chapter 9

Chaloner woke early the following day, and sat in his window, making use of the gathering daylight to compose letters to Thurloe, Clarendon and Eaffrey. He used cipher without conscious thought, a different code for each recipient. Thurloe would read his immediately, without resorting to a crib. Clarendon would ask one of his clerks to translate, so Chaloner seldom confided too much in his written messages to his employer. Eaffrey's was one they had used for years, and could be broken by anyone who knew them. He thanked her for her hospitality and wrote some polite observations about her silver forks, tactfully saying nothing about the company or the level of conversation.

In the Earl's note, he announced his intention of resurrecting the Dutch upholsterer, in the hope that 'Vanders' might provide new opportunities for spying on Bristol. He would not normally have revealed such plans in advance, but he had learned his lesson about surprising Clarendon with disguises, and did not want a recurrence of what had happened the last time. His message to Thurloe contained the information he had gathered about Webb the previous evening.

When he had finished, he went to the Golden Lion – a tavern that never closed, so the landlord had no trouble locating a boy to deliver the notes. Then he found a quiet spot near a fire, and ordered ale and bread. He rubbed his eyes as he waited for them to arrive, wondering how long Eaffrey and Scot had been lovers. Did that mean she still intended to wed Behn, and their marriage would be based on deceit? Or had she lied about her love for the merchant? Chaloner could tell from the way she and Scot had fallen into each other's arms that it was not the first time it had happened. Of course, Behn was enjoying an illicit affair with Silence, and perhaps Eaffrey knew it. Or was Behn's dalliance just a calculated attempt to get his hands on Webb's idle ship? If so, then it appeared to have worked.

All told, Chaloner was happier to think of Eaffrey with Scot than with the Brandenburger. Scot lived a dangerous life, like Chaloner himself, and might not be there to protect her when she needed him, but he was a good man who would not suffocate her in a restrictive marriage. And nor would he oblige her to live on riches earned from sugar and slaves. Chaloner hoped she knew what she was doing, and that Behn would not find out and avenge himself on Scot. Chaloner knew from personal experience that the merchant had a strong arm.

At six o'clock, he returned to his room and found the clothes he needed to become Vanders again. He was even more meticulous with his disguise than he had been the previous Saturday, knowing people would pay him greater attention if rumours had been spread about his poor health, and he took special care to conceal the splint with his lacy cuffs. The last time he had played Vanders, he had dispensed with his sword in the interests of authenticity, but White Hall no longer felt safe to him, and he had no intention of going without the means to defend himself. It was an hour before he was satisfied with his appearance, during which time he hoped his note to Clarendon would have been delivered, and the Earl would be ready to play his part in the charade.

He reached White Hall without incident, although he felt eyes on him as he began his hunt for Clarendon. It did not take him long to identify them: it was Bristol's man, Willys. He had exchanged his yellow stockings for black ones, which hung loose on his long, thin legs and made them look more spindly than ever. Willys watched Chaloner for a moment, then hurried away. The spy eventually located the Earl outside the Stone Gallery, waiting for a carriage to take him to the site of his new Piccadilly mansion. Clarendon narrowed his eyes and regarded 'Vanders' intently.

'It *is* you, Heyden,' he muttered. 'You never know when someone might be an assassin these days, and I am ever wary. I had your letter half an hour ago. I am glad you decided to try the upholsterer business again, because now people will see the rumours about me hitting you are unfounded. And the vultures are gathering already, because here is Bristol and his entourage, come to inspect you. Do not forget what you promised to do – infiltrate his household with a view to spying for me.'

Chaloner did not dignify the reminder with a response. Why else did the Earl imagine he was dressed up in such a ridiculous fashion?

'Vanders?' asked Bristol. His clothes were rumpled, he stank of old wine, and he looked as though he had yet to retire to bed. 'I am told you excel at turkeywork sofas, and I am in the market for such an object. Do you have any for sale?'

'I might,' said Chaloner cagily, hoping he would not want details. He was not entirely sure what 'turkeywork' meant, and it would not take many minutes before he was exposed as a fraud.

'I shall leave you to discuss it, then,' said the Earl, a little too readily. 'Here is my carriage, come to take me to Piccadilly. Clarendon House will be the talk of all London once it is built, and I have already secured some excellent black marble for its stairs. The King will want to visit me there, away from the shallow vices – and people – of Court.'

'It would not be the black marble intended for the repair of St Paul's Cathedral, would it?' pounced Bristol. 'That is a House of God, and your immortal soul will be stained if you take that for yourself.'

'Papist claptrap,' muttered Clarendon, waddling away on his short, fat legs.

The dark expression on Bristol's face told Chaloner that the Earl had made a serious tactical error by attacking his rival's religion. Bristol had sacrificed the chance to hold lucrative public office by professing his Catholicism, proving that his beliefs were important to him; mocking them was unwise. Then Lady Castlemaine arrived in a flurry of yapping dogs and jabbering voices. Bristol immediately turned to join her, but he grabbed Willys's arm and whispered something first. Willys nodded, and approached Chaloner.

'There is a private hall where senior retainers often gather of a morning, Mr Vanders,' Willys said politely. 'Will you take a cup of ale there with me?'

Chaloner accepted the invitation, thinking it might be a good opportunity to quiz him about his name being included in Bristol's letter. He followed the aide to the

Spares Gallery, recalling with wry amusement that it had been Willys who had kept him company the last time he was there.

Because it was early, the Spares Gallery was relatively empty. Three musicians were restringing a violin at the far end, Wiseman's massive bulk was crammed into a chair near the fire, and an elderly equerry in a blue coat dozed in the sunshine that flooded through the windows. Wiseman raised a hand in greeting, but was more interested in reading his book than in talking; he did not wait for Willys to wave back before his attention was riveted on the pages again.

'You see that surgeon?' whispered Willys, as they took seats at a table. 'He was summoned at two o'clock this morning, because the King complained of a blockage. His Majesty went to bed at four – still constipated – and is unlikely to rise before noon, but Wiseman is obliged to wait until he does, lest another royal summons is issued. It serves him right for taking against Bristol! I caught him searching our carriage last night, although he claims he was only looking for a bat that flew into it. Well, there was a bat, as it happened, but I think it just provided him with an excuse to rummage.'

'Rummage for what?'

'Evidence that my master was involved in the Castle Plot, probably. That took place in Ireland, which is full of Catholics. And since Bristol is Catholic, Lord Clarendon might say *he* instigated it.'

'Did he?' asked Chaloner.

Willys regarded him as though he was insane. 'Of course not! He sent *me* to Dublin to help thwart it – and I was instrumental in seizing a vital shipment of rebel guns. Just because a man is a papist, does not mean he is desperate to overthrow a monarchy. But let us talk of other business.

302

I have been authorised to make you an offer: My Lord Bristol wants *his* furniture upholstered, and says he will pay twice what Clarendon has offered you.'

'That is very generous,' said Chaloner, smothering a smile. Everyone knew Bristol had no money, and could never afford to double an asking price. The spy could only assume the impecunious noble intended to default on payment, just as he probably did with his other creditors.

'Yes, it is. However, there is something he would like you to do in the meantime: while you work in Clarendon's domain, keep your eyes and ears open, and report any unusual happenings to me.'

'You mean spy?' asked Chaloner, managing to inject considerable distaste into the word.

Willys nodded, oblivious to the disapproval. 'I do it myself, all the time. In fact, I had a look in Clarendon's rooms on the day of the ball, although I did not find anything useful. Do not worry about being caught, though. If that happens, powerful men will . . . make arrangements.'

'How can I be sure of that?'

'Because I was in an awkward position myself recently, and I was saved the very same day.'

'Really?' Chaloner pretended to be impressed. 'How?'

Willys leaned closer, and his voice dropped to a confidential whisper. 'My name was included in a letter that accused me of murder. I was innocent, of course, as were the eight men listed with me, and we have all been pardoned or allowed to disappear. As I said, great men look after their own.'

'I heard about that case, but I was told three of the nine have been sentenced to death.'

'True, but they have not been hanged yet. There is

303

still plenty of time for rescue – although one of them has died of gaol-fever, which is unfortunate for him.'

'I should say! How do you know none of those three are guilty?'

'Because Dillon is a Quaker, and they abhor violence. Besides, I was with him in the Dolphin tavern – the one over by the Tower – the night Webb died. That is a long way from The Strand, where the crime took place. Dillon had been at the Guinea Company dinner with a friend called Fanning, but he escaped early because he said it was dull, and we both got roaring drunk together.'

'Dillon was with you *all* that night?' Chaloner recalled Dillon claiming he was drinking with a friend when Webb was killed. However, he also recalled Dillon claiming that he had been nowhere near the Guinea Company dinner, and Willys was now the third person – after Scot and Brodrick – to say that was not the case. Why had Dillon lied about the dinner? Because he did not want anything made of the fact? And why had he not mentioned his 'alibi' to the judge who had tried him? Chaloner could only suppose it was because Willys was also on the list of the accused. Or was Willys just trying to protect a comrade by spinning yarns now?

'I passed out at some point,' Willys admitted sheepishly. 'Yet I will swear on my mother's grave that Dillon was in no state to dash across the city, stab a man and be with me when I woke a couple of hours later.'

'What about Fanning? Did he stay at the dinner after Dillon had left?'

'I have no idea. All I can say is that he was not with Dillon and me in the Dolphin. Ah! Here is May, come to find out whether you have agreed to spy on Clarendon for My Lord Bristol.'

304

Chaloner stood to leave as May swaggered towards them. His disguise was good, but there was no point in taking risks by conversing with men who knew him well. May was dressed for riding that day, with leather boots, a cloak and spurs. His shaven head was covered by a functional grey wig that fitted him like a cap. A sturdy fighting sword was at his waist, and thrust into his belt was a snaphaunce gun that looked suspiciously similar to the one owned by Fitz-Simons. Chaloner mumbled something about buying curtain hooks from Covent Garden, but May grabbed his arm to stop him from leaving. It was not a hostile gesture, but as soon as May's fingers closed around the splint, the game was up.

'Heyden!' he yelled, hauling out his dag. It discharged with an ear-splitting bang, and Chaloner was astonished that he should have missed at such close range. May was furious. He hurled the firearm away and drew his sword. 'Now I have you!'

'This is Vanders,' said Willys, looking from one to the other in bewilderment. 'I have just recruited him to work for Bristol.'

'Fool,' snarled May, as Chaloner backed away. 'He is Clarendon's creature.'

Chaloner was trapped, and there was nothing he could do or say to extricate himself from his predicament, so he made no effort to try. 'Put up your sword, May,' he said quietly. 'I do not want to fight you – not in White Hall. Brawling is forbidden here, and we will both be arrested.'

'*I* will not be brawling,' said May, advancing with his weapon held in a way that showed he meant business. '*I* have just unmasked a traitor. Are you going to defend yourself, or do I just kill you?'

* * *

'You would stab me here?' asked Chaloner softly, while Willys gaped, appalled at how he had been duped. 'In front of witnesses? My Earl will not stand by when his people are killed in cold blood, and Spymaster Williamson will not want a murderer on his staff.'

May lunged, and the tip of his sword went through Chaloner's sleeve – and would have pierced his arm had the splint not been there. Reluctantly, the spy drew his own weapon to parry the next blow, but still made no move to attack. The elderly equerry and Wiseman clamoured at them to sheath their blades before the palace guard arrived, and Chaloner saw the musicians had already dashed off to fetch them. He did not feel himself to be in any particular danger, because he had seen May fight in Ireland and knew he was no swordsman. All he needed to do was stay out of blade-range until May either came to his senses or someone disarmed him. However, he revised his strategy smartly when Willys drew a wicked-looking rapier with a furious expression on his face. Two opponents were an entirely different matter.

'May cannot kill you, because you are *mine* to skewer,' Willys declared, becoming angrier by the moment as the enormity of what had happened dawned on him. He was not a clever man, but even he could see his 'recruitment' had given Clarendon some powerful ammunition against his master.

Chaloner blocked another blow from May, then struggled to protect himself as Willys advanced with a series of determined swipes. May started to move behind him, dividing his attention, and he saw it would only be a matter of time before one of them scored a lucky hit.

'Stop this at once,' barked Wiseman, although he was

careful to stay well away from the flashing steel. 'You should be ashamed of yourselves.'

'You are behaving like Dutchmen,' added the equerry in disgust. Recklessly, he tried to lay hold of May's flailing weapon; Chaloner ran forward to deflect the impatient swipe that would have seen the old man injured. 'Desist immediately, you silly young goats.'

'Stay away, grandfather,' warned Willys, lunging while Chaloner was preoccupied with May. Chaloner twisted to avoid the blow and stumbled over a bench. His leg gave a protesting twinge, and he only just managed to jerk away from Willys's next swipe. 'Or there will be an accident.'

'There will be no accidents,' came a voice from the door. It was Holles and the palace guard, all carrying cocked handguns. 'You know this is illegal. Put up your swords before I shoot you.'

Seething, May did as he was told, glowering as a soldier hurried forward to snatch the weapon from his hand. But Willys was too enraged to see reason, and advanced on Chaloner with murder in his eyes. Chaloner raised his sword to deflect the first blow, then ducked in surprise when a ball smacked into the wall near his head.

'Next time, I will do more than make a hole in the plaster,' snarled Holles. 'This is your last chance – both of you.'

Since he looked as though he meant it, Chaloner let his sword clatter to the floor. Immediately, Willys raced forward. Chaloner leapt away, and felt the man's blade pass so close to his face that it sliced through the brim of his hat. Willys staggered from the force of his attack, so Chaloner shoved him hard enough to make him stumble to his knees. The weapon flew from his hand, and three soldiers hastened to secure him while he was down. Meanwhile, Holles grabbed Chaloner, searching him for more weapons. The colonel removed the knives from his belt and sleeve, but did not find the one in his boot.

'I shall charge the lot of you with unbecoming conduct,' he snapped, furious with them. 'And it will be up to your respective masters how they will deal with you.'

Willys tried to free himself, but the guards held him too tightly, so he settled for sneering instead. 'When Bristol hears how you deceived me, he will dispatch you himself, Heyden.'

'It *is* Heyden,' said one of the soldiers, hauling off the wig that hid the spy's brown hair. 'Look!'

Holles regarded Chaloner with unfriendly eyes. 'I did not imagine *you* were the type to brawl in the King's palace. I thought you knew how to behave.'

'It was not his fault,' objected the equerry, while Wiseman nodded earnest agreement. 'He ordered May and Willys to desist, and drew his weapon only to protect himself.'

'It takes two sides to make a quarrel,' replied Holles coldly. He turned to his prisoners. 'You will be taken to the guardhouse, where you will remain until your masters come to claim you. And my dag is reloaded, so do not try my patience by persisting with this spat.'

Chaloner did not think he had ever seen the colonel so angry. He said nothing as he was escorted to the palace gaol, where he and the others were given separate cells in which to wait. The doors were not locked, but there was no point in trying to escape, even so.

Spymaster Williamson arrived almost immediately, but neither he nor May spoke until they were well away. Through the bars in his window, Chaloner watched the two men stride across the yard, May speaking and

Williamson nodding. Then all was quiet, because either Clarendon and Bristol could not be found, or they declined to release their recalcitrant retainers until a more convenient time.

A while later, there was a furious commotion in the yard outside, as a horse, saddled and ready for riding, bucked and cavorted like a wild thing. Soldiers rushed towards it, making it even more agitated, and there were shouts of horror when a flailing hoof caught one man on the temple with a sickening thud. In the next room, Chaloner heard Willys snigger at the spectacle, although the laughter stopped abruptly when Wiseman hurried to help the fallen man, then stepped back shaking his head. Blood began to pool on the cobbles, and Chaloner went to sit on the bench again, not wanting to see more.

Not long after, he heard murmuring in Willys's room and supposed Bristol had arrived. There was a thump, followed by footsteps moving across floorboards that creaked like a rusty hinge, then peace again. Eventually, there were more voices as a crowd of people clattered into the prison. They burst into Willys's room, and there was a short silence, followed by an ear-splitting howl of outrage. Then the door to Chaloner's room was hurled open and Bristol stood there, quaking in fury.

'You killed him!' he yelled. 'You murdered Willys!'

Chaloner regarded Bristol in astonishment, wondering whether the man had been drinking. Behind him, other courtiers were pushing their way forward, and among them was May. The odour of sweat, onions, horse and French perfume wafted into the small chamber as more and more people crammed themselves inside, eager to miss nothing of the brewing confrontation.

'Willys is dead,' said May, fingering the dagger he carried in his belt. 'Stabbed. You and he were alone in this part of the building, so you had better start explaining yourself.'

'Someone came to release him,' said Chaloner, keeping his voice steady so as not to reveal his growing alarm. 'I heard them talking together.'

But he had also heard a thump and retreating footsteps, and if it had not been Bristol coming to retrieve his aide, then it had been Willys's murderer. But why would anyone want to kill Willys? With a sinking feeling, Chaloner saw the man with the obvious motive was himself – he and Willys had quarrelled publicly, and then they had been left alone in adjoining rooms while the horse had distracted the guards. To the dispassionate observer, it would look as though Chaloner had seized an opportunity to dispatch his enemy.

'Liar!' fumed Bristol. He drew his sword and began to advance. 'You slipped into his room when he was watching the escapade with the nag, and you stabbed him in the back.'

'Wait, My Lord!' cried Holles, stepping between Chaloner and the enraged noble. 'If Heyden has committed a crime, we shall go through the proper procedures. We do not dispense justice ourselves.'

'Why not?' demanded May. 'Heyden is the only one who *could* have killed Willys, and his guilt is obvious. Besides, you were willing to shoot him earlier.'

'That was when he was armed,' argued Holles. 'He is not armed now, and we do not want folk thinking we go around skewering people whenever we feel like it. Put up your sword, My Lord. It is for the best.'

May was disgusted. 'I am just grateful Williamson

310

rescued *me* straight away, or Heyden would have slaughtered me, too. The horse's antics were just what he needed – they lured the guards outside, and let him get Willys alone.'

'My men did go to help with the horse,' admitted Holles, regarding Chaloner uneasily. An expression of relief crossed his face as something occurred to him. 'But Heyden cannot be the killer. We disarmed him – we disarmed all of you. He had nothing to use on Willys.'

'In Ireland, he carried additional weapons in his sleeve and boot,' said May. He grinned in triumph when Holles's second search revealed the knife he had missed the first time, and turned to Bristol. 'You should kill him while you can, My Lord, or Clarendon will find a way to inveigle him a pardon.'

Bristol stared at Chaloner for a long time before sheathing his sword. May gaped at him in dismay.

'No,' said Bristol quietly, his temper now under control. 'I do not want the Lord Chancellor complaining that we killed his henchman in cold blood. It is better to drag Heyden through the public courts – and Clarendon will be mired with him.'

'I have just inspected Willys, My Lord,' announced Wiseman, pushing his way through the assembled courtiers like a stately galleon through a flotilla of barges. 'As a surgeon, I have seen more cadavers than you could dream about. Come, and I shall show you something important.'

Bristol baulked at being issued an order, but his curiosity and Wiseman's brash confidence prompted him to do as he was told. Willys was lying near the window, blood seeping from a wound in his back. When everyone,

311

including Chaloner, had entered the cell, the medic began to hold forth.

'The fact that Willys received a blade between his shoulders means he knew his killer,' he declared, speaking as though his conclusions were fact, not opinion. 'And he trusted him. Willys was not a complete imbecile, and would never have turned his back on Heyden, given what had happened earlier today. *Ergo*, Heyden is not the killer.'

'Rubbish!' shouted May, appalled to see Chaloner exonerated with such ease. 'He sneaked in when Willys was preoccupied with watching the horse, and took him unawares.'

'I had not finished what I was going to say,' said Wiseman haughtily. 'However, I shall interrupt my erudite analysis to refute your asinine theory, if that is what you want. These floorboards creak, as you can see for yourself, and Willys would have heard Heyden coming – even above the racket emanating from the yard. So, your assertion, Mr May, is both erroneous and foolish.'

'How dare you—' began May, but Bristol held up his hand and nodded for Wiseman to continue.

'My next conclusion pertains to the wound.' The surgeon pulled the clothes away from the injury and took from Holles the dagger that had been in Chaloner's boot. 'Even the most ignorant of us' – here he looked pointedly at May – 'will see that this broad-bladed weapon cannot possibly have made this tiny round hole.'

'Heyden is a skilled intelligence officer,' said May tightly. 'Of course he knows how to jab a blade into his victims with the minimum of damage.'

'Then show me the blood,' ordered Wiseman, handing him the knife. 'If that is the murder weapon, it will be

312

stained with gore, as will the killer himself. Can you see even the smallest speck of red on it – or on him?'

'He cleaned it,' argued May, not ready to concede defeat. 'He had plenty of time.'

'Cleaned it with what?' pressed Wiseman. 'There is no water here, and you cannot wipe blood off clothes anyway. It leaves indelible marks – and believe me, I know.'

May was sullen. 'Your "evidence" is circumstantial. It proves nothing.'

'On the contrary,' said Wiseman. 'It makes a powerful case for Heyden's innocence. And there is more. If he did kill Willys, then why did he return to his own cell – to sit and wait for the alarm to be raised? Why did he not take the opportunity to escape? The guards had gone, so there was no one to stop him.'

'He wanted to confuse us,' claimed May. 'He—'

'Oh, you are certainly confused,' agreed Wiseman, drawing an amused titter from the watching courtiers. He looked away, as if he could not be bothered to waste time on the likes of May. 'Finally, there is the angle at which the blade penetrated Willys.'

There were exclamations of revulsion as he inserted a thin piece of metal into the hole, to demonstrate the path the murder weapon had taken through the body. It ran from left to right, and was obvious enough that Chaloner wondered whether someone had made sure it had looked that way on purpose. He glanced at May and saw satisfaction stamped on his face, as if he had hoped someone would notice.

Bristol knelt by the corpse to assess the evidence for himself. He stood, and regarded the surgeon thoughtfully. 'This means Willys was struck by a man who held a dagger in his *left* hand.'

313

'Precisely,' drawled Wiseman.

'Heyden can use his left arm as well as his right,' said May immediately. 'I saw him in France once, fighting double-handed to fend off traitors.'

'But he cannot do it at the moment,' said Wiseman. He took Chaloner's hand and demonstrated how the splint prevented him from holding the knife. 'It is physically impossible for him to grip a blade with sufficient strength to deliver a killing blow, so he would have resorted to his right. Lord Bristol has already established the killer was left-handed, so Heyden cannot be the culprit.'

It was Bristol who asked the question that was uppermost in Chaloner's mind. 'Then who is?'

It was not every day the Court was treated to the spectacle of a murder and a man who knew how to interpret clues, and the guardhouse was quickly packed with people, all clamouring questions. Chaloner saw several familiar faces among the many he did not know. At the very back of the crowd were Johnson and Lisle. Lisle was beaming, delighted by his colleague's clever performance, while Johnson glared sulkily, jealous of the adulation that was being heaped on his rival.

Next to the surgeons, Brodrick and Temple stood in a way that suggested they had arrived together. Chaloner wondered why, when they clearly detested each other, and hoped they had not been plotting. Lady Castlemaine stood near the front, but when she learned Bristol was not going to run anyone through, she pulled a face that registered disappointment, and shouldered her way outside again.

Eaffrey and Behn were there, too. Behn asked, in a loud voice intended to carry, whether Heyden could have *hired* a left-handed killer. Before Eaffrey could think of a response, the elderly equerry remarked that Behn was a silly young goat to make such a stupid statement. People started to laugh, and the question was forgotten. With a start of surprise, Chaloner recognised Scot's pale eyes among the equerry's maze of wrinkles, and smiled when his friend winked at him.

Meanwhile, Bristol and his party were still quizzing Wiseman about his deductions; the surgeon answered with a patronising haughtiness that was only just short of insolence. Bristol was quietly angry – not that he had been deprived of a suspect, but because he had been manoeuvred into accusing the wrong man and made to look rash and volatile. And May was livid because Chaloner had been exonerated.

Chaloner listened to people's comments, questions and observations, carefully analysing them in the light of what he had heard and seen himself. It was clear someone had either *taken advantage* of the incident with the horse, or had *engineered* it to provide a diversion. If the latter was true, then it had worked brilliantly: all the guards had raced outside, leaving ample opportunity for the killer to do his work. Chaloner had heard voices, which told him Willys had conversed with his killer, and Wiseman's evidence indicated that Willys clearly had not thought he was in danger, or he would not have allowed himself to have been stabbed from behind. The thump had been Willys's body falling to the floor, and then the murderer had calmly walked away, leaving Chaloner sitting in the cell next door as the prime suspect for the crime.

So, who had knifed Willys and, perhaps more importantly, why? Was it someone who wanted Clarendon's faction accused of murder, to bring the Earl himself into

315

disrepute? It was certainly the kind of ill-conceived strata-gem Temple liked to concoct. Then there was May, delighted with Chaloner's predicament, and deeply dis-appointed when Wiseman had exculpated him. Could May have returned to the guardhouse after he had been released? And finally, there was Holles, who always claimed to be the Earl's man, but who nevertheless had been oddly willing to believe Chaloner's guilt. It was also Holles who had overlooked the dagger in Chaloner's boot, which had then later been produced as evidence against him. Had the colonel intended that to happen? Chaloner had considered him an ally, but in the shifting sands of White Hall allegiances, he suddenly found he was not so sure.

Clarendon arrived at last, breathless and elbowing his way through the courtiers to reach his spy. 'I have only just been told what has happened. Holles swears he sent a servant with a message, but it never arrived and now the fellow is nowhere to be found.'

'Is that so,' said Chaloner flatly.

'You should not have challenged Willys and May to a fight,' chided the Earl. 'Thurloe will blame *me* if you die, and you were reckless to endanger yourself. *Did* you kill Willys, by the way? I shall not be angry if you did. He was an odious fellow, always trying to damage me.'

'No, I did not,' said Chaloner firmly, determined to quash any lingering doubts along those lines. 'I did not even know he was in danger.'

'You will have to unveil the culprit, Heyden, or May will avenge Willys by sliding a sly dagger into *your* ribs. Do you think you can solve the mystery?'

'I will try,' said Chaloner unhappily. He did not see how he would succeed – although he understood *how* the killer had claimed his victim, learning his identity was another matter altogether.

He washed the paint and powder from his face – there was no point in maintaining the disguise now – and left the guardhouse. Outside, folk still milled about. Alice and Temple were with Johnson, and their serious faces suggested business was being transacted. When Chaloner eased closer, to hear what they were saying, Alice hauled the two men away, but she was not quite quick enough to prevent him from learning that Johnson had placed a hundred pounds at Temple's disposal. It was to be invested with the new owner of Webb's ship. Chaloner looked around, and saw Behn standing nearby. The Brandenburger's smile of satisfaction indicated that Temple was operating on his behalf, and Chaloner found himself hoping with all his heart that the ship would flounder before it could reap its grim cargo – and that they would both lose every penny they had ploughed into the filthy venture.

'These accusations were only levelled because you are Lord Clarendon's man,' said Lisle, stretching out a brown hand to waylay the spy as he zig-zagged through the crowd. 'This spat between him and Bristol is becoming increasingly bitter, and the likes of you and Willys are nothing but pawns.'

'Then virtually everyone here is in danger, too,' said Chaloner, gesturing around him. 'Most have declared a preference for one side or the other.'

Lisle grimaced. 'The follies of men never fail to amaze me. There is war brewing with the Dutch, outbreaks of a deadly plague in Venice, and distressing levels of poverty in our great capital. Yet all the Court cares about is this ridiculous squabble. I am just thankful that I have managed to resist the attempts of both sides to recruit me – there are far more productive things to occupy my time, such as my charitable work in the city's hospitals. Do you still plan to visit me on Saturday?'

Wild horses would not have kept Chaloner from keeping the appointment. He nodded.

'It will be a busy day for me, so come between Dillon's hanging and the Public Anatomy – I shall be hosting Company guests after that.'

'What are you two whispering about?' demanded Wiseman, coming to join them. He seemed larger than ever, swelled as he was with the accolades of his success. 'My astute detection work?'

Lisle beamed at him, to hide his own discomfort. 'You were a credit to our Company today, and we shall make sure all our colleagues know it. Eh, Johnson?'

Johnson's face was a mask of pure envy as he approached. 'You need not bother, Master Lisle. I am sure he is quite capable of informing them of his cleverness himself.'

Hastily, Lisle escorted him away before there was a scene.

'Thank you for your help,' said Chaloner. 'When you began your analysis, Bristol had sheathed his sword but May was still armed. I am not sure if Holles would have been able to prevent him from stabbing me if you had not intervened.'

'Would he have tried?' Wiseman's expression was sombre. 'Holles, I mean. Have you asked yourself *why* he left you alone with Willys? And *why* May was rescued so long before you?'

Chaloner regarded him uneasily. 'Holles means me no harm. We are on the same side.'

318

'Are you sure about that? I am not saying Holles *did* put you in a dangerous situation deliberately, only that you should not dismiss the possibility.'

'I shall bear it in mind,' said Chaloner tiredly, thinking Surinam was looking increasingly attractive.

'You were lucky I was to hand, actually: I had *just* received news that the King's blockage has cleared without the need for surgical intervention and was about to leave. I am performing a Private Anatomy this afternoon, you see.'

'There seem to be rather a lot of those these days.'

Wiseman grimaced. 'Yes, but *mine* will show students how the bladder is connected to the kidneys, which is something they need to know for when they perform the operation you laymen call "cutting for the stone". The one Johnson performed yesterday, however, was to amuse rich patrons.'

'Which rich patrons?'

'Buckingham and his entourage. Holles was there, too, incidentally. I glanced in on my way home, and saw him looking very green around the gills. Not everyone has the stomach for dissection.'

'Who was the subject?'

Wiseman was startled by the question. 'You mean the corpse? I have no idea. He would have been some felon, donated by the prisons, as usual. What an extraordinary thing to ask!'

'Not so extraordinary. Do you know who was dissected for Temple's edification? Webb, murdered while walking home from the Guinea Company dinner. *He* was no felon.'

'You are mistaken,' said Wiseman, regarding him in astonishment. Then his face resumed its customary

arrogance. 'Of course, cadavers change their appearance after death and laymen are easily confused.
Johnson probably *told* Temple it was Webb, but it will
have been a joke, although not one in particularly good
taste.'

'I have seen my share of corpses, too, and Webb
was—'

Wiseman's eyes narrowed suddenly and he snapped
his fingers. 'Hah! *I* understand why you think he was
anatomised – it was *you* Johnson saw sneaking around
the other day. I thought I had seen you off the premises, but you obviously came back. There was no
need – if you had told me you were experiencing a
desire to drool over corpses, I would have arranged a
private viewing.'

'You are too kind. But Webb *was* the corpse. And I
also know for a fact that he is not in his tomb in St Paul's
Cathedral. So, how did he end up in your Anatomical
Theatre?'

Wiseman shrugged. 'If you *are* right – and I do not
believe it for a moment – then there will have been a
silly mistake. Gravediggers and vergers can be shockingly
careless – it makes one yearn for immortality.' He saw
Chaloner's scepticism. 'Come with me now, and I shall
show you our procedures. There is nothing untoward, I
assure you.'

It was not an appealing invitation, but Chaloner
accepted anyway. He had no idea whether Willys's murder
was connected to the Webb case, but it was as good a
place as any to start an investigation.

The ride to Chyrurgeons' Hall was an uncomfortable
one for Chaloner. He was daunted by the prospect of

unravelling the twists and turns associated with the various murders he had been charged to solve, and disturbed by his growing conviction that Holles could not be trusted. He was used to working under the assumption that everyone was an enemy, but was disappointed in the colonel nonetheless. Wiseman sang all the way, pleased with himself and his performance at the guardhouse, and Chaloner might have enjoyed his rich bass, had the surgeon not chosen to warble a ballad by the composer–lutenist John Dowland, in which a bitter man contemplated different ways to dispatch his rivals.

When they arrived, students were already beginning to flock to the Anatomical Theatre. Wiseman muttered venomously that they were an hour early, although Chaloner sensed he was flattered; their enthusiasm was testament to the veneration in which he was held. All wore the uniform gowns and hats that marked them as Company apprentices, and there was an atmosphere of scholarly anticipation as they walked in twos and threes towards the door. Wiseman stopped humming abruptly when he saw Johnson arrive in another carriage, accompanied by Lisle. The pair were immediately waylaid by Clerk Reynell, who was gesticulating in an agitated manner. Johnson's face darkened as he listened, then he turned and made a beeline for Wiseman.

'Reynell says you plan to use *four* corpses for your demonstration today,' he shouted furiously. 'The fresh one that came this morning, *plus* three old ones from last month. What are you thinking of? The stench of rotting entrails will linger in the theatre for days, and it will spoil our guests' appetites for the dinner after the Public Anatomy on Saturday.'

'If they cannot stomach a little odour, then they do

not deserve to eat,' retorted Wiseman. His expression was malicious – he was delighted to be causing problems. 'I need four cadavers for comparative purposes, or our students will go away thinking all people's innards are the same.'

Johnson regarded him with dislike. 'Important men will be present on Saturday, ones who make donations. If you destroy our hopes in that direction, I shall invite them all to another dissection the following week: yours.'

Wiseman sneered. 'Then I hope they will not come with the hope of learning anything – not if you are to do the honours.'

Chaloner stepped back, anticipating fireworks, but Johnson displayed admirable restraint. 'Just try not to make too much of a mess. We do not want Reynell scrubbing all day tomorrow, when he should be polishing the ceremonial silver. Incidentally, I have invited an acquaintance to watch you this afternoon. In return, he will give us a pair of silver spoons.'

'You have done what?' exploded Wiseman. 'You invited laymen to *my* dissection? How dare you! It is for students and colleagues only.'

Johnson pointed at Chaloner. '*He* is not a student or a colleague, but you have invited *him*. And our records show that he has not yet settled his account for the treatment you gave him last Saturday, so obviously *he* is not going to give us any silver spoons. Or did you pay *him*, for letting you experiment on his limbs? Lisle says he will never regain the use of his fingers.'

Lisle heard his name brayed, and hurried forward to pour oil on troubled waters. Reynell was with him, and Chaloner was again struck by the clerk's handsome clothes. Close up, however, he saw they had been marred by some very unpleasant stains, and supposed it was impractical, if not impossible, to maintain an air of sartorial elegance while working for the barber-surgeons.

'Gentlemen, please!' said Lisle wearily. 'Not in front of the apprentices.'

'Did you say I botched Heyden's treatment?' demanded Wiseman dangerously. 'And have you offered to rectify it for him?'

'Of course not,' said Lisle soothingly, not looking at Chaloner. 'Although I *would* offer to make amends, if I thought a member of my Company was guilty of malpractice. However, this is neither the time nor the place for such a discussion. Let Johnson's friend watch you today, Wiseman. He may learn something, and silver spoons will not go amiss. Meanwhile, perhaps Johnson would be kind enough to test the syllabub for Saturday. We all know he is an expert on such matters.'

'True,' agreed Wiseman contemptuously. 'God has given every man a unique skill with which to walk the Earth. Mine is surgery and his is scoffing syllabubs.'

'I think it needs to be stored in a cooler place,' said Lisle, before Johnson could respond. 'In fact, I want you to inspect it *now*. I shall come with you.'

'And afterwards, you had better supervise Wiseman,' snapped Johnson, trying unsuccessfully to resist as Lisle pulled him away. 'The last time he performed, he could not locate the gall bladder.'

'Because it was withered with disease,' bellowed Wiseman after him. He lowered his voice to a more moderate level, although it was still loud enough to be heard by passing students. 'Pompous ass! *He* would not know a gall bladder if it came up and introduced itself to him.'

'You should go inside now,' said Reynell to Chaloner. 'The theatre is almost full already, and if you leave it too long, you will not get a seat.'

'He is not here for that,' said Wiseman. 'He has convinced himself that Webb was anatomised here, so I offered to show him our procedure for collecting bodies. Then he will see for himself that such a notion is preposterous.'

The clerk regarded Chaloner in astonishment. 'How in God's name did you reach that conclusion? Webb hated the medical profession, and wanted nothing to do with our Company – he ruined Wiseman with slanderous accusations, he took Lisle to court over the cost of a phlebotomy, and he threatened to sue the lot of us for postponing the Private Anatomy he had commissioned.'

Chaloner resisted the temptation to state the obvious – that Webb would hardly be in a position to prevent his corpse from being misused once he was dead. 'If Webb disliked surgeons so much, then why did he want to come here and watch a dissection?' he asked instead.

'Because it is the current fashion at Court to do so,' explained Wiseman disapprovingly. 'The King expressed an interest in the workings of the human body, so now everyone is fascinated by the subject. Webb was a shallow fellow, who thought buying a performance would prove he had good taste. I, for one, am grateful he died before he could use our profession in a shabby attempt to advance himself.'

'Lisle *did* want to refuse Webb,' added Reynell, 'but Johnson was afraid he might make trouble if we did. Webb was spiteful and vindictive, and I am sure Johnson was right.'

A clock struck the hour and Wiseman took a breath.

'I must go and prepare for my lecture. I always read my notes before I start, lest I omit something important. Not that I make mistakes, you understand. *My* demonstrations are always perfect.'

'Of course,' said Reynell, when the surgeon paused for him to agree.

'Then you will not mind showing Heyden how we prepare cadavers for teaching and research. It is a job for a clerk, after all, not a busy and important surgeon.'

Reynell sighed his resignation as Wiseman strode away. 'I am afraid we shall have to be quick, Mr Heyden. I am very busy with preparations for Saturday. What do you want to know?'

'Start from the beginning,' suggested Chaloner, unable to think of a question that would move the discussion directly to Webb.

Reynell flapped a vague hand towards the north of the barber-surgeons' domain. 'The bodies arrive from the prisons by cart, and we receive them through that little door at the end of our garden. We do not use the main gate, obviously, because it might look ghoulish to passers-by.'

'Right,' said Chaloner, suspecting it looked worse to sneak them in through the back. He followed the clerk to the Anatomical Theatre, which had a small, discreet entrance at the side. It was locked, but Reynell opened it to reveal a flight of steps that was dark, damp and covered in ominous stains.

'The theatre has a special basement,' Reynell explained, lighting a lamp. 'So, when bodies arrive, we take them down there for preparation. Watch your footing. Those spillages can be very slippery.'

Reluctantly – he did not like the look of the stairs or the sound of the vault – Chaloner descended, wrinkling his nose at the eye-watering stench of decay and mould. The cellar was a low-ceilinged chamber, lit by several hanging lanterns that sent eerie shadows around thick supporting pillars. There were no windows, and the only door was the one through which they had entered. The walls were bare brick, and the dank space was used to keep samples as well as corpses, because rows of jars contained all manner of objects. Chaloner saw a tiny human foetus in one, and looked away before he could identify anything else.

'How many of these dissections do you perform?' he asked. Five sheeted figures lay on crude wooden benches, and he realised it was quite an industry.

'Four public ones annually, and a variable number of private,' replied Reynell. His voice was defensive, as if he had detected distaste in the question. 'We are due to receive a freshly hanged felon for the event on Saturday – we cannot use anything but a new cadaver for that, or our guests will not fancy their dinner afterwards.'

'Who are these others?' asked Chaloner, gesturing around.

'The ones we have finished with – or *should* have finished with. By rights, they should be in their graves by now, but Wiseman wants to use them to illustrate anatomical variation in bladders. I shall have to dispose of them before Saturday, though, because Johnson will complain if their reek wafts upstairs. That is the agreement, you see – we get the corpses, and in return, we pay for their burial in St Olave's churchyard.'

'Can I see them?' asked Chaloner. 'Their faces, I mean.'

Reynell regarded him oddly. 'What for? I assure you

326

Webb is not here. I was told he was interred with great pomp in St Paul's Cathedral.'

'Then you will not mind humouring me,' said Chaloner, indicating the nearest body.

The clerk shrugged. 'I suppose it is all right, although it is not a very nice thing to ask.'

He lifted the cover, and Chaloner was hard-pressed to prevent himself from recoiling. The face had not been immune from the anatomists' knives, and had been peeled away to reveal the skull underneath. The torso had been crudely stitched back together, but the single rapier hole in the skin of the chest was still identifiable, and so were the grazes on the knees. Webb was still above ground, and Reynell was wrong in declaring otherwise.

'Do you have a name for this man?' Chaloner asked.

Reynell consulted a ledger. 'Martin Webster from Ludgate Gaol – brained by a fellow inmate while awaiting trial for burglary. You can check with the warden, if you do not believe me.'

Martin Webster, Matthew Webb. Chaloner supposed a clerical error might have seen the wrong man delivered to Chyrurgeons' Hall. Webb would have been kept in his house from his death to his burial, so the hiccup must have occurred *after* the funeral: the vergers had allowed the mourners to leave before tipping Webb from his casket and squashing him inside the bishop's sarcophagus. Ludgate was close to St Paul's, so it was possible that Martin Webster had been granted a religious ceremony in the cathedral before being shipped off to the surgeons – and the bodies had been confused at that point. But surely the vergers could tell the difference between a plump merchant and an emaciated prisoner? Or had they just thought that Webster would be an easier fit in a small space, and had made a decision based on the fact that no one was ever likely to know?

Reynell covered the body. 'You see? Just a felon.'

'Yes,' said Chaloner, keeping his conclusions to himself. He lifted the sheet from the next corpse – because Reynell did not know he had already identified Webb, he was obliged to inspect the rest for appearance's sake – but the subject had been dissected so thoroughly that there was nothing left but bones and a mess of pale organs. The same was true of the next two, but when Chaloner moved towards the last one, the clerk turned away.

It was Fitz-Simons, complete with a hole in his chest that had been made by the ball from a gun. Chaloner glanced him over briefly, but could see no other marks, and he knew from the wars that such a large wound so near the heart would have been instantly fatal. So, Fitz-Simons had not disappeared after all, but had died when May had shot him.

'Richard Fitz-Simons was a good friend,' said Reynell softly. 'And a member of the Company.'

'How does he come to be here?'

Reynell's face was a mask of anguish. 'Because Wiseman managed to inspect the body of the "beggar" everyone was calling an assassin, and recognised it as Fitz-Simons's. We were terrified that someone would identify him, and that his actions – whatever they were – would reflect badly on the whole Company. So we spirited him away without anyone knowing. Will you tell May?'

Chaloner shook his head. 'Why is he not buried? Surely it is safer to put him in the ground?'

'Because his last will and testament specified that his cadaver was to be used for education.' Reynell's voice cracked; he grieved for the man. 'We plan to hold a

328

special dissection next week. Lisle will give a new lecture on the lungs, Wiseman will expound on the bladder, and Johnson will take the musculature. They have vowed to lay their differences aside and do justice to Fitz-Simons's generous spirit. We shall revere his memory, and our apprentices will never forget him.'

Chaloner was sure he was right. 'Wiseman told me surgeons do not dissect their colleagues.'

Reynell gave a humourless smile. 'What would you expect him to say? That any dead *medicus* who wills us his corpse is eagerly received? We would lose our royal charter!'

It all sounded very gruesome to Chaloner. He walked back up the stairs and into the daylight with considerable relief, Reynell following. 'Did you ever meet Webb?'

Reynell nodded. 'Several times, all when he was threatening members of the Company with legal action. He was an odious man. Wiseman in particular despised him, and they had a blazing row on the night Webb was killed.'

'Did they?' asked Chaloner encouragingly. He wondered whether there was anyone in London who had *not* argued with the merchant that fateful night.

Reynell nodded again. 'At the Guinea Company dinner. I was invited because my brother is a member, and Webb and Wiseman had some sort of disagreement over the morality of slavery.'

'Wiseman was at the dinner? He told me he was not.'

Reynell became flustered. 'Did he? Perhaps I am mistaken, then. Yes! It must have been another evening, and not the day Webb died. I am always getting confused. Please ignore what I just said, and put it down to fatigue. I have been working my fingers to the bone in readiness for Saturday. You do believe, me, don't you?'

'Yes,' hedged Chaloner, supposing he had better tackle Wiseman himself, although it would not be a comfortable discussion – the surgeon would not take kindly to being called a liar.

The Anatomical Theatre was almost full, and the dissection was about to begin. The body to be anatomised lay naked except for a cloth across its face, and Reynell was telling porters where to put the ones that were to be used for comparative purposes. Wiseman was already looming over a podium, while Lisle stood ready to begin cutting on his command. Chaloner loitered in the doorway, watching the surgeons and their audience. He was startled to recognise Behn in the front row, sitting next to Johnson, who looked as though he was giving the merchant a lecture on the theatre's architecture. Behn looked bored, and handed him something from a bag, clearly as a way to stem the tide of unwanted information. It was a pair of silver spoons.

Wiseman cleared his throat, and an expectant hush fell over the gathering. 'Today, I shall share with you the mysteries of the bladder,' he declared. 'Master Lisle will make the first incision, revealing the distinct layers of the abdominal cavity.'

Chaloner winced as Lisle began to wield a sharp knife, making clean, practised cuts to reveal a layer of pale-yellow fat below the white skin. A film of connective tissue proved difficult to incise, and Lisle was obliged to exert more force. As he did so, the cloth fell away from the corpse's face and Chaloner gazed in shock when he recognised the small, pinched features of Thomas Sarsfeild the confectioner. There was a red ring around his neck. Like Fanning, he had been strangled.

Chapter 10

There was something about the cool precision with which the surgeons treated the hapless Sarsfeild that disconcerted Chaloner. He had seen wounds and deaths aplenty, but it was not the same as watching a corpse methodically stripped of skin, muscles and whatever lay beneath, and he found he did not like it at all. He left abruptly, and when Reynell reminded him that he was expected at the Public Anatomy in two days' time, Chaloner only just resisted the urge to tell him to go to Hell.

It was a long way from Chyrurgeons' Hall to Lincoln's Inn, and by the time he reached Thurloe's chambers, having taken a tortuous route to ensure he was not followed, the spy was tired, hot and thirsty. There was no reason to suppose anyone was watching him, but it had been a difficult few days – he had been knocked to the ground, poisoned, attacked with swords, subjected to improper surgical procedures and shot at – and his instincts warned him to take more than his usual care. He tapped softly on Thurloe's door, which was opened by Leybourn.

'I was expecting Yates,' said the surveyor, disappointed. 'We sent for some food. Ah – here he is.'

The porter staggered along the hallway with a tray that contained an inordinate amount of bread, cheese and cold meat. Leybourn's eyes gleamed, and Chaloner supposed he was hungry. Yates placed the victuals on the table but, before he left, insisted on sampling everything, to ensure it was poison-free. Thurloe only dismissed him when the surveyor commented unhappily on the rapidly dwindling portions.

Leybourn closed the door behind the jovial porter and turned to the table, rubbing his hands eagerly. 'I am ravenous. Do you want anything, Tom?'

Remembering what had happened the last time he had swallowed something in the ex-Spymaster's chamber, Chaloner declined. Thurloe claimed he had no appetite either, and for a while, the only sounds in the room were Leybourn's knife clacking on the pewter plate, and a rhythmic hammering sound from outside. Chaloner looked questioningly at Thurloe.

'The orchard,' replied Thurloe quietly. 'The felling began today.'

'Already?' Chaloner was stunned. 'I thought you might delay it for a few weeks at least. You are a lawyer, after all, skilled in postponement.'

'I did my best, but Prynne's is a powerful voice, and he invariably has what he wants. Close the window, Thomas. I cannot bear to listen.'

Chaloner obliged, then, to take Thurloe's mind off the destruction, began to tell him all that had happened since their last meeting. The ex-Spymaster was thoughtful.

'Willys's murder does not sound like a carefully laid plan to me. Someone may just have snatched the opportunity presented by the bucking horse – and the fact that you and he were left unguarded. Of course, we cannot discount the possibility that the killer might have wanted you dead, too.'

'Why?' asked Leybourn, appalled by the tale. 'What could anyone gain by dispatching Tom and Willys? They do not work for the same faction. Willys was on the list naming Webb's murderers and Tom was not. Tom has connections with the Castle Plot and Willys did not—'

'He did,' interrupted Chaloner. 'He was used to hinder the delivery of a shipment of arms.'

Leybourn continued as though he had not spoken. 'There is no reason for anyone to strike at both. And perhaps there *was* no intention to have Tom accused of murder – he just happened to be in the cell next door. It was an unfortunate coincidence, which May seized upon with alacrity.'

'May,' mused Chaloner. 'Scot told me you and he went to a tavern together recently. Now why would a decent, law-abiding fellow like you deign to associate with someone like that?'

Leybourn looked pleased with himself. 'He heard you had training as a law-clerk, and was asking which of the Inns you attended – he is obviously hoping to unearth some youthful scandal to use against you. However, when he declined to tell me why he wanted to know, I suggested he should to talk to Prynne.'

'Prynne will not remember me – or my youthful scandals,' said Chaloner, surprised. 'And he is hardly conducive company. If May does go to see him, he will be in for a deeply unpleasant time.'

Leybourn feigned innocence. 'Really? What a pity for him.'

'Let us consider this murder rationally,' said Thurloe, declining to waste time discussing pranks. 'Who might want Willys dead? It will not be Bristol, because Willys was a devious sort of man and such fellows are useful. It will not be Temple either, because he would not deprive Bristol of an aide. What about someone loyal to Lord Clarendon? He would never order a death himself, but his supporters are more practical about such matters.'

'Brodrick?' suggested Leybourn. 'I confess Clarendon's debauched kinsman mystifies me.'

'And I do not like the way these surgeons appear every time there is some dramatic incident, either,' said Chaloner. 'Especially Wiseman.'

'Are you saying that because his splint means you cannot play your viol?' asked Leybourn.

'No,' replied Chaloner shortly. 'I am saying it because he lied about being at the Guinea Company dinner. He swore he did not attend, but Reynell let slip with the truth. Not only that, but Wiseman argued with Webb about slavery on the night of the murder – another detail he neglected to mention.'

'Webb,' mused Thurloe. 'You still have not identified his killer, although you have followed the contorted travels of his corpse. And Dillon will be hanged the day after tomorrow.'

'Dillon does not think so,' said Chaloner.

Thurloe was unhappy. 'I have rescued men from similar situations in the past, and I can tell you that it is unwise to leave it to the last minute. The nearer one comes to an execution, the more paperwork stands between prisoner and reprieve. His master is making a grave mistake by dawdling.'

'I am under the impression the man does not intend

334

to operate through official channels,' said Leybourn. 'Half of London is expecting an audacious rescue just as the noose tightens around Dillon's neck. There is also a rumour that Webb's murder and the subsequent conviction of those three men is connected to the Castle Plot. If that is true, then Dillon's escape may herald the beginning of something dangerous.'

'What do you mean?' asked Chaloner.

'Rebellion,' elaborated Leybourn darkly. 'A rerun of the one that failed in Dublin – only this time, there will be no men hired by Williamson to make it flounder. I predict violence when Dillon reaches the scaffold, and I shall close my shop and make sure the windows are barred.'

'But who *is* this patron with a flair for the dramatic?' asked Thurloe, becoming frustrated.

'It is someone influential, or Dillon would not be so confident,' said Leybourn. 'It cannot be Williamson, because he arranged releases for *his* people within hours of their arrests. Is it Bristol?'

'Because he is Catholic?' asked Thurloe. 'And Catholics feature large in Irish rebellions? If that is what you mean, then I urge you to rethink. Being a papist does not go hand in hand with sedition, although God knows we have given them cause with all this insane Bill of Uniformity.'

'What about Clarendon, then?' asked Leybourn.

An image of the portly Lord Chancellor hurtling forward on a prancing horse to snatch Dillon from the scaffold formed in Chaloner's mind, and he smiled. 'He is not a man for flamboyant gestures. Besides, he is too preoccupied with Bristol to stage last-ditch reprieves for petty villains.'

'Buckingham?' suggested Leybourn, running out of

ideas. 'He is a rash, ostentatious fellow. Or perhaps Lady Castlemaine intends to *seduce* His Majesty into signing a pardon. I have heard she is not choosy about lovers, so maybe Dillon is one of her conquests.'

'We are looking at this the wrong way,' said Thurloe, pursing his lips at the vulgarity. 'We cannot identify Dillon's master unless we know who killed Webb. Webb was murdered for a reason, and we will only unravel this mess when we know what that is. What are your theories, Tom?'

Chaloner raised his hands in a shrug. 'Silence has emerged rather nicely from the tragedy, and so has Behn. Wiseman's practice was destroyed by Webb's accusations. Lisle fell foul of him, too, and so did Johnson. Meanwhile, Webb insulted Brodrick's music, Bristol owed him money, and Temple had discovered the hard way that he was unscrupulous in business.'

'*Dillon* did not quarrel with Webb, though,' said Thurloe with satisfaction. 'And neither did the other eight men named on the letter sent to Bristol.'

'Actually, Dillon did,' said Chaloner. 'He and Fanning were seen arguing with Webb on the night of the murder. As a result, they left the Guinea Company dinner early, and Willys said he and Dillon then got drunk in a tavern together. However, the more I think about *Sarsfeild*, the more I think he had nothing to do with it. There was something pathetically honest about his alibi.'

'I thought we had agreed that Beck Marshall's testimony was inconclusive.'

'I have reconsidered. If Sarsfeild did murder Webb, intending to use Beck to prove his innocence, he would have done something to make her remember him – left her a valuable gift, been sick in her bed, refused to pay.

Yet he did nothing memorable, which makes me think he had no idea she might later be important. There must be another Sarsfeild, and this is a case of mistaken identity.'

'Then perhaps we should try to save him, as well as Dillon,' suggested Leybourn.

'It is too late. He was strangled, and his body is being anatomised as we speak.'

Thurloe closed his eyes, appalled by the mounting carnage. 'What about Fanning? Was his a case of mistaken identity, too?'

'He was murdered before I could interview him, but *he* did not share Dillon's trust of their master – he sent notes in cipher to Dillon, detailing his plans for escape.'

Thurloe was disheartened. 'I had hoped Bristol's letter might yield clues, but it is worthless. I took it to an expert in such matters, but he said the handwriting is too heavily disguised for any conclusions to be drawn. He did say the ink was an unusual blue – possibly foreign – but that was all.'

'You are overlooking the obvious,' said Leybourn. 'It means the sender knew how to change his writing – a spy or a devious businessman, perhaps. Maybe Williamson sent it.'

'Why would he do that?' asked Thurloe. 'It exposed his own people.'

'And he immediately saved them,' said Leybourn, 'thus earning their undying gratitude. Men work better for someone they know they can trust. Perhaps it was all a trick, designed to secure greater loyalty. Or perhaps it is not the ones who were *pardoned* that we should be looking at, but the ones who were *convicted*. It is possible that Dillon, Sarsfeild and Fanning have outlived their usefulness, and this is a good way of dispatching them without too much trouble.'

'I think May sent it,' said Chaloner. 'He is keen to be indispensable to Williamson, but his skills do not match his ambition. He wrote the missive to discredit rivals who are better than him. And he included his own name to allay suspicion, knowing Williamson would arrange a pardon for him – but no doubt hoping he might neglect to do the same for the others.'

'You are allowing personal dislike to blind you,' said Leybourn. 'And I am not sure you are right about Sarsfeild, either. If he was just a hapless bystander, then how did he – of all the men who die daily in London's gaols – end up as a candidate for anatomy?'

'None of this makes sense,' groaned Chaloner. He wondered when he had last felt so hopelessly confounded. 'Perhaps I *should* go to Surinam with Scot – the courts of Holland, Portugal and France did not prepare me for the intrigue and devilry of London. My countrymen have me defeated.'

'Your melancholy is the lingering effects of that poison,' said Thurloe. 'These things take their toll on a body. However, I have concocted a tonic that will—'

'I think he should resist swallowing any more remedies for a while,' said Leybourn briskly. 'Have you learned who tried to poison you yet? Was it Prynne?'

'I thought not, but Yates says his rooms contain a large number of flasks full of unidentified substances. I cannot believe he would harm me, but it seems he certainly has the means.'

When Chaloner returned home that evening, Scot was waiting, sitting on the stairs and reading *Musaeum*

338

Tradescantianum by the light of a single candle. So absorbed was he that he did not hear Chaloner's soft-footed approach and leapt violently when the spy spoke to him. It was the kind of mistake that saw men in their profession killed, and Chaloner wondered whether his friend's sudden desire to reside in Surinam was because he was losing his touch.

'This is the most amazing book ever written,' Scot declared, running appreciative fingers across its pages. 'I have just reached the part where the great gardener and traveller John Tradescan lists all the exotics he and his father collected on their travels to Virginia. Have you read that section?'

Chaloner shook his head. 'Remiss though it may seem.'

Scot smiled ruefully. 'This new science of botanicals is so exciting that it is difficult for me to understand why everyone is not equally smitten. I cannot wait to board a ship for Surinam and dedicate my life to unveiling its arboreal mysteries.'

Chaloner unlocked the door and lit the lamp in his room. 'You are serious about this? You really want to devote your life to plants?'

Scot's expression was quietly earnest. 'I have never been more sincere about anything in my life, Chaloner – not *anything*. The moment my brother is released, I shall take him and Alice – and you, if you will come – to a new life, where we will never again worry about the politics of dangerous men. I am weary of Roundheads and Cavaliers, of bearing the stigma of a regicide father, and of sly assassins in the night. And there was Manning.'

Chaloner had a sudden, sharp vision of the spy who had been shot because of Dillon's betrayal. 'What does he have to do with it?'

'I saw him taken off into that wood, and I knew what was going to happen, but I was powerless to do anything about it. The whole horrible business hit me hard – so hard that I should have resigned, but it was a momentous decision and I kept putting it off. When it became obvious that the Commonwealth was lost, it was partly fear that prompted me to change sides – which is not something I am proud to admit.'

'We were all afraid then,' said Chaloner quietly.

Scot sighed. 'Well, I shall be glad to leave spying behind, and I find myself resenting every day I am obliged to don paints and powder to work for Williamson.'

'It cannot be for much longer. Have you heard any fresh news about your brother's release?'

Scot nodded. 'I have unearthed several documents that prove the Trulocke brothers sold guns to men associated with the Castle Plot, and Williamson is so pleased that he says Thomas might be free in a matter of days. I have you to thank for that – and my way of reciprocating is to take you from this life while you are still in one piece.'

'How would I earn my keep?'

Scot handed him a bundle of scientific sketches. 'If you can draw some of equal quality, we shall make our fortune in Surinam. Try copying a few, to catch the feel of them. You are one of the best forgers I know, and the techniques cannot be so different – an attention to detail, an eye for colour. I have a feeling you will manage very well.'

It was difficult not to become infected by Scot's enthusiasm, so Chaloner did as he was told, and was astonished when he discovered how easy it was to reproduce a respectable copy of the diagram, even using a cheap pen and ink that clotted.

'You *do* have an aptitude for this,' said Scot with immense satisfaction as he inspected the results. 'I knew it! You can sell your viola de gamba, invest in paints and decent brushes, and your name shall stand with mine when we send our work to the Royal Society.'

Chaloner stared at his viol, feeling some of his good humour evaporate. He seriously doubted that drawing flowers would ever replace the joy of making music. 'I am going to see Lisle on Saturday. He has promised to remove the splint and see what damage Wiseman might have done.'

'Then let us drink to Lisle's success,' said Scot, producing a flask of wine from under his coat. 'God knows, I would like to see him score a victory over that treacherous Wiseman – a fellow I would not trust were he the last man on Earth. Why did you leave Eaffrey's house so quickly yesterday, by the way? I know it was a grim evening, but it was unlike you to rush off without thanking your hosts.'

'There was something I needed to do for the Webb investigation,' Chaloner replied vaguely.

'Webb,' mused Scot. 'I listened to Silence wax lyrical about her husband last night. Did you know he bought land cheaply in Ireland after the civil wars – land that had been confiscated from Royalists?'

Chaloner stared at him. 'When the monarchy was restored, most of those estates were returned to their original owners, and the people who had bought them were ousted.'

'Quite. So Webb had a good reason for hoping the Castle Plot would succeed. It would have meant the return of his farms.'

'So he may have taken part, after all.' Chaloner frowned.

'But this makes no sense. Bristol's letter stated that Webb had *betrayed* the Castle Plot, and Dillon and the others killed him for doing it. Why would Webb betray something that would have seen his lands given back to him?'

'Perhaps Webb did nothing of the kind,' suggested Scot. 'Are you *sure* Dillon was a rebel? No, you are not. All you know is that he was in Ireland at the salient time, and that he said his name was O'Brien. Perhaps Webb *did* want the revolt to succeed, and Dillon killed *him* for a traitor. You do not know who Dillon works for, so you cannot know what side he was on in Ireland. Oh, and Eaffrey asked me to tell you that she saw Dillon go into Clarendon's house once, at midnight.'

Chaloner was bemused. '*Clarendon* is the mysterious master who will snatch Dillon from the jaws of death? If so, then Dillon is going to be disappointed: my Earl is not a dramatic sort of man, and if he wanted Dillon pardoned, he would have done it by now. How long has Eaffrey known about this?'

'Ever since a recent drive past Worcester House prompted a half-forgotten memory of a man in an odd hat silhouetted in an upstairs window. She planned to tell you yesterday, but there was no time.'

'She found time to tell you, though,' observed Chaloner.

Scot glanced sharply at him, then smiled. 'I conclude from that ambiguous remark that you saw us together. You did not slink off the moment an escape route presented itself, but lingered, waiting for everyone else to leave. I should have known you were not far away.'

'Have you been lovers for long?' It was none of Chaloner's business, but they were friends, and he was curious by nature and training.

342

'More than a year. We wanted to tell you, but it is difficult to find a quiet moment these days. She is going to have my child.'

'Behn will be surprised. I imagine he is under the impression that she wants to marry *him*, given the looks of simmering adoration she throws in his direction. Does she intend to have you both, then?'

Scot laughed. 'Marriage and love are hardly the same thing. Yes, she will marry Behn, but it is not a partnership that will last. He is already unfaithful, and makes regular visits to Silence Webb, among others. We hope Eaffrey will be a wealthy woman once she offers to leave him in return for a settlement.'

'You are encouraging her to marry Behn with the express purpose of acquiring an alimony? That is sordid!'

Scot was unrepentant. 'The government confiscated my father's estates after his execution, and I do not want our child to grow up poor. Do you really disapprove? I thought you disliked slavery – and the victim of our "deception" is one of its greatest proponents.'

'Could you not just sabotage his new ship instead?'

'God, no!' exclaimed Scot with a shudder. 'I shall have to travel to Surinam by boat, and I am superstitious about that kind of thing. However, Behn is a wicked villain behind that courtly veneer—'

'What courtly veneer?'

Scot was lost in a world of his own. 'I had a good look around his private office yesterday, when I was waiting for him to tire of Eaffrey and go to Silence. He has documents written in cipher. Now why would a merchant use cipher?'

'To protect himself against men like you, presumably. Could you decode them?'

'I could not – not in the time I had. I tell you, Chaloner, the man is no angel. These messages are probably reports from criminals, telling him dirty secrets about his rivals. I know for a fact that he consorts with low types, because I have seen him with them – in particular a thickset fellow with a scarred neck, who always visits after dark. Do you really object to us defrauding a man like that?'

Chaloner shrugged. 'It is none of my affair.'

Scot regarded him thoughtfully. 'Do you remember the letter sent anonymously to Bristol – the one that saw me placed in an awkward position and Dillon convicted of Webb's murder? Well, it occurs to me that Behn might have sent it.'

'Why? He has nothing to do with—'

'He receives *coded* letters,' snapped Scot. 'So do not tell me he is innocent in the world of spying. I imagine he would love our intelligence services to be thrown into disarray, because it would allow him greater freedom to do whatever it is he does.' He sighed impatiently. 'You do not believe me.'

'It is easier to cheat a man you despise than one you like – you are trying to convince *yourself* that he is unsavoury, not me. How can you bear him to touch Eaffrey, if she is your wife in all but name?'

Scot was surprised by the question. 'My previous wife slept with all manner of men to provide me with the secrets necessary for my work. If you were married, your woman would do the same.'

'No,' said Chaloner firmly. 'She would not.'

'When you are my age, you may think differently.'

'The Guinea Company feast,' said Chaloner suddenly. 'You left early – or "too early to know what happened" in the discussion between Temple and Webb, to quote

344

your own words. You said it was because the lice in Terrell's wig were bothering you. Was it really to see Eaffrey?'

Scot grinned ruefully. 'It was a perfect opportunity. Behn is an influential member of the Guinea Company – there is a move afoot to make him Master – so we knew he would be there all night. I stayed at African House long enough to be noticed, then spent the rest of the night in Eaffrey's arms, content in the knowledge that Behn had promised to use the other bedroom when he finally returned, so as not to wake her. Such occasions are rare, so must be seized with alacrity when they arise.'

'I imagine his visits to Silence might provide you with a few.'

Scot's smile widened. 'But not as many as we would like.'

Friday dawned warm and clear. The sky was veiled with a thin gauze of cloud that soon burned away, and the sun shone on the chaos of spires and chimneys that was London. Chaloner walked to Ludgate, acutely aware that time was running out for Dillon. He cut through several alleys, emerging near the scruffy patch of land designated as the graveyard to St Bride's Church, then picked his way along a path that ran parallel to the foetid sludge of the Fleet river. Kites and hawks pecked through the flotsam that had cast up upon its stinking banks, and rats scavenged in the deeper shadows. The stench of urine was powerful enough to sear the back of Chaloner's throat, and it made his eyes water.

He crossed the bridge and headed for the prison, noting how it stood in the shadow of mighty St Paul's – the racket from the shops and stalls in the cathedral's churchyard could be heard even above the rumble of iron cartwheels on the cobbles of Ludgate Hill. He loitered in the porch of little St Martin's, opposite the gatehouse, until he spotted the warden who had taken him to see Sarsfeild. He left his hiding place and handed the man a shilling.

'Sarsfeild,' mused the warden, pocketing the coin. 'Due to be executed tomorrow, but he beat us to it. The governor is furious, because it means we lost two of the three men due to die on Saturday. Sarsfeild was found dead in his cell – hanged with the laces from his own shirt. He done it himself.'

'I was under the impression he wanted to live,' said Chaloner. 'He hoped someone would save him, because he said he was innocent.'

'They are all innocent in there,' said the warden wearily, jerking his thumb towards the prison walls. 'But perhaps his priest convinced him that the time for lies was over. Vicars often have that effect on condemned men: they talk about Jesus and wicked hearts break. I seen it dozens of times.'

'What vicar?' asked Chaloner.

'The Rector of St Dunstan-in-the-West.' The warden screwed up his face as he fought to remember a name. 'Willys – George Willys.'

'What did he look like?'

'Like a priest – shabby black coat, broad-brimmed hat, shoes with holes. He wore a sword, I remember, which is unusual for a religious cove. It was hid under his cloak but I saw the tip.'

'Was Sarsfeild alive after this vicar had left?'

'I expect so, or he would have said something. Priests

do not like it when prisoners die in the middle of evangelical sessions. It makes them feel they have wasted their time, because dead men cannot ponder redemption and that kind of thing.'

In other words, he did not know, surmised Chaloner. 'What time did this visit take place?'

The warden scratched his oily pate. 'Now you are asking. It was after three o'clock, because that was when we finished giving all the inmates their dinner.'

'George Willys was dead himself by then. The man you admitted was an impostor.'

'Well, he *looked* like a vicar,' said the warden defensively. 'He had a Bible and everything. I thought it was odd that the Rector of St Dunstan's should come, when Sarsfeild hailed from the parish of St Martin-in-the-Fields, but it is not for me to question clerics.'

'What happened to Sarsfeild's body?'

'The barber-surgeons had it. They needed one urgent, and they were lucky we had one going spare. It is not every day we have suicides. *We* are not Newgate.'

'Why did they need it urgently?'

'Apparently, a rich patron paid Mr Johnson a lot of money for a Private Anatomy, but Mr Johnson did not have a corpse, so he used one that had been set aside for another surgeon called Wiseman. Wiseman was furious, and told Mr Johnson that if he did not procure a body immediately, he would end up on the cutting table himself. So we let Mr Johnson have Sarsfeild.'

Thoughts teeming, Chaloner was about to visit Newgate, to see whether he could shake any more details from the aggravating Dillon – there was nothing like looming execution to concentrate the mind – when he met Holles. The colonel was striding purposefully along

347

the spacious avenue called Old Bailey, and Chaloner greeted him warily, uncertain of the man and the status of their alliance.

'May is still telling everyone that *you* started that fight in the Spares Gallery yesterday,' said Holles without preamble.

'Do you believe him?' asked Chaloner.

Holles grimaced. 'It is getting harder to tell friend from foe these days, and you have never liked May, so it is possible that you provoked a struggle. And then there was Wiseman – *he* took your side, and *that* is what really turned me against you. You see, not long before your spat with May, Wiseman told me a filthy lie. So, my instinct was to distrust him a second time, too.'

'What "filthy lie" did he tell you?'

Holles looked pained. 'I am fond of Maude from Hercules's Pillars Alley, and Wiseman told me that Johan Behn took her to the New Exchange and bought her a brooch. It cannot be true, because Behn is courting Eaffrey Johnson. So, Wiseman was making up tales, just to upset me.'

'Why would he do that?' asked Chaloner, wondering whether Behn had some perverse fascination with portly, middle-aged ladies, given that he seemed to appreciate Silence's company, too.

'He probably cannot help it – they are all liars in the medical profession. Johnson spouts untruths each time he opens his mouth – on Monday, he told me he fought with Prince Rupert at the Battle of Naseby, when I know for a fact that he spent his war apprenticed to a barber in Paternoster Row.'

'What about Lisle? Does he lie, too?'

'Not as far as I know. He is the only decent one among

348

the lot of them. Incidentally, I examined the horse that killed my man yesterday. When it escaped, all the grooms were being lectured by Brodrick on the correct way to dress a mane, so none of *them* can be responsible for what I found.'

'And what was that?' asked Chaloner, when Holles paused for dramatic effect.

'Someone had put a nail in its saddle, which cut it and made it buck.'

Chaloner was not particularly surprised. 'So, that means Willys's murder was premeditated. Someone deliberately arranged a diversion, so no one would notice when he was stabbed.'

'*A* murder was premeditated,' corrected Holles. '*You* may have been the target, and the wrong man was killed. Or perhaps the killer intended to dispatch both of you, but ran out of time.'

Chaloner would have done virtually anything to avoid setting foot inside Newgate Gaol again. Unfortunately, there was no one to go in his stead. Scot was due to meet Williamson, to discuss his brother's release, and although he offered to visit Dillon as soon as he had finished, Chaloner felt the matter could not wait. Meanwhile, Thurloe had taken Leybourn off on some errand of his own, and no one at Lincoln's Inn knew where they had gone.

With a sigh of resignation, the spy turned his attention to the task in hand. He had no forged letter to the governor and no heavy purse, so this time he was obliged to rely on his wits. He purchased an old black coat and a 'sugar-loaf' hat from a rag-picker – men who collected old clothes and sold them to the desperate – and borrowed a Bible from nearby Christchurch.

349

'I am the Reverend May,' he announced to the porter on duty at Newgate's entrance, trying to quell the uneasy fluttering in his stomach. 'From St Martin-in-the-Fields.' He was not about to make the same mistake as the impostor who had killed Sarsfeild, by claiming the wrong parish. 'I have come to speak privately to Mr Dillon.'

'What about?' demanded the guard.

'His immortal soul,' replied Chaloner loftily. He clasped his hands together, and raised his eyes to the heavens. 'For, as it is written in the Holy Bible—'

'All right,' interrupted the guard. 'I see your point. Follow me, but make it quick, because it is not right to waste too much of a man's last day on religious clap-trap, and he is trying to finish a book.'

'He has accepted the inevitability of his death, then?' asked Chaloner. 'His soul will be—'

'He thinks he is going to be saved,' corrected the guard. 'The reason he wants to finish the book is so he can return it to its owner before he heads to Ireland on Sunday. The governor is worried about tomorrow, and extra soldiers have been drafted in, ready to deal with any trouble from the crowd.'

'Will the execution not take place, then?'

The guard shrugged. 'Dillon says not, and I have told my mother not to bother going. She hates it when she waits for hours and a hanging is cancelled. Dillon is a decent gent – generous with what he gives us – so do not squander too much of his time. Let him finish his reading.'

Instead of being shown into the bleak interview room, Chaloner was conducted to Dillon's cell, where the condemned man was not studying, but playing with a roll of silk. The chamber was larger than the rooms Chaloner rented in Fetter Lane, and the remains of the meal on the table was fit for a king. Dillon looked up as he entered, hat shading his face.

'I am a gentleman, so entitled to be hanged with a silken rope,' he explained with a chuckle. 'Hemp, which is used for the common criminal, tends to stick, but silk slides easily, and I am assured it will strangle me all the sooner. The guards were kind enough to let me twist the noose myself.'

'What about the book?' asked the warden conversationally. 'Finished it yet?'

'No, but I am not in the mood for words. This vicar will make sure it goes back to the man who lent it to me, and I shall purchase my own copy before I sail for Ireland.'

'If you are so sure of rescue, then why bother with the noose?' asked Chaloner, when the guard had gone.

'It gives me something to do, and I was never one for sitting idle. Fitz-Simons told me hanging is painless, because the rope pinches the nerves in the neck and deprives the victim of all feeling.'

'It does not look painless to me.' Chaloner disliked the spectacle afforded by public executions, but he had been unable to avoid them all. It was not a way he wanted to die himself.

'You are trying to unnerve me, because of your friend Manning. You blame me for his death.'

'You may learn about betrayal yourself tomorrow, when you find your salvation does not materialise, and that Fitz-Simons was mistaken when he said hanging does not hurt.'

Dillon regarded him with dislike. 'I have nothing to say to you.'

'Sarsfeild is dead,' said Chaloner harshly. 'Fanning is dead.'

Dillon grimaced. 'I know – and both were strangled. But they were different from me.'

Chaloner sighed. 'I have spent the last week trying to learn what really happened to Webb, but I am no further forward, despite my best efforts. And whatever you may think, I do not want to see an innocent man choke. Have you considered the possibility that your master *cannot* help you – that he has tried to secure your pardon but has been unsuccessful?'

'No,' said Dillon. 'I trust him with my life.'

'If it is Lord Clarendon, you will be disappointed. He would have worked through the law to release you, not promised some dramatic reprieve on a white charger. Thurloe may still be able to help, but he needs information – information only you can provide. Surely you can see it is sensible to devise a second plan to save yourself, lest the first one fails?'

Dillon regarded him impassively. 'What makes you think I am in Clarendon's pay?'

'You were seen in Worcester House with him, very late one night.'

'I visit the homes of many powerful men, but that does not mean I work for them.'

Chaloner was losing patience. Newgate made his hands shake, his heart pound and his stomach churn, and if Dillon did not want his help, then he did not see why he should subject himself to more of it. He tried one last time. 'I need the answers to two questions if Thurloe is to earn your acquittal.'

'Thurloe,' said Dillon meditatively. 'I betrayed him when I changed sides during the Commonwealth, yet he refuses to abandon me now. Why?'

'Because he is a good man. His principles baulk at seeing someone hang for a crime he did not commit, and he cares for all his people, even the treacherous ones.'

'Yes,' mused Dillon softly. 'He always was the best of us. Very well. Ask your two questions.'

'Who killed Webb? And was his murder anything to do with the Castle Plot?'

Dillon was silent for so long that Chaloner stood to leave.

'I did not stab Webb,' said Dillon softly, glancing at the door to make sure he would not be overheard, 'but I was there when it happened. I distracted him while Fanning delivered the fatal blow. I was following orders.'

Now Chaloner was not sure whether to believe him. 'Willys said you and he were roaring drunk in the Dolphin tavern on the night of the murder, and incapable of killing anyone. And Thurloe said you were a Quaker, vehemently opposed to violence. As Manning can attest.'

'It was Willys who was drunk. He was face-down on the table when the message came. It offered me a respectable sum for sullying my hands with Webb's blood – hence my comfort here in Newgate – but I would have dispatched the man for no payment at all.'

'Why?'

'You think me shallow, with no conscience, but you are wrong. I *am* a Quaker, although perhaps not a very good one, and I deplore slavery. It was a pleasure to play a role in murdering that monster – a man who made himself rich on the proceeds of forced labour.'

'You were seen at the Guinea Company dinner, although you said you were not there—'

'Fanning and I left early, because I could not bear to be in the same room as Webb. When Webb tried to stop us, I told him what I thought of his ship and its cargo, and we argued. Then I went to meet Willys at the Dolphin and the note arrived. I left Willys slumbering, sent word to Fanning to meet me, dispensed with Webb, and returned to the Dolphin to put Willys to bed.'

'You are housed in luxury here, but Fanning was not. Why? Did your master pay him less?'

'Our master did not pay him at all – I did. I could not kill Webb on my own, so I enlisted the help of a trusted friend. So, now you have an answer to one of your two questions.'

Chaloner did not think so. 'You and Fanning may have been the means by which Webb was killed, but you have not told me who ordered his death.'

'You will find out at my "hanging" tomorrow, when my master shows his hand. And in reply to your second query, the answer is no: Webb's murder was nothing to do with the Castle Plot.'

'Was Sarsfeild involved?'

'You said *two* questions, but I feel like talking, so you are in luck. Sarsfeild had nothing to do with killing Webb – I have no idea who he was. He said he was a confectioner, so God knows how he came to be on Bristol's list. Fanning and I killed Webb; Sarsfeild is unjustly convicted.'

'Was Sarsfeild part of the Castle Plot?'

'I answered that query when you came the first time; if he was, then I never met him.'

'You had already answered my questions about Webb, too, but now you have changed your mind.'

Dillon clapped his hands in delight. 'You do not know whether to believe me! So, I shall have to *prove* to you that I was instrumental in ending Webb's miserable life. Have you seen his body? If so, you will have noticed deep grazes on his knees. They came when Fanning stabbed him and he stumbled forward. I could not know about such wounds, if I had not been there, could I?'

There had been scratches, Chaloner recalled, and Dillon was right: it was a detail only the killers would know. He glanced at the door, seeing shadows move under the crack at the bottom. Had the guard reported the presence of an unknown vicar, and he and his colleagues were massing for an arrest? He turned back to the gloating face in front of him, hurrying to finish and be gone before he ended up in some filthy hole, to be strangled like Fanning and Sarsfeild.

'Did you kill Webb's coachman, too, and hide his body in his own room?'

Dillon grinned in a way that made Chaloner wonder whether he was entirely sane. 'Fanning did. We needed Webb on foot if we were to kill him on The Strand. It was all a bit of a rush, but we managed. However, Fanning's nerves have since proved weak, and my master left him to stew a little too long – long enough that he asked May to stage a rescue with poisoned wine. I told him my master had the matter in hand, but he did not share my faith. *And* he was ready to bleat about what we had done. I imagine that was why he was killed.'

'And you think the same may happen to you, if you start revealing secrets,' surmised Chaloner. For the first time, he saw a crack in Dillon's armour: he was afraid of the man he expected to save him. 'Then why are you

355

talking to me, when you need your master's help more urgently than ever?'

'Because I admire Thurloe's constancy. He deserves answers.'

'Then give me just one more: who sent you to Ireland?'

Dillon's smile faded. Again, he glanced at the door, to ensure no one was listening, and lowered his voice. 'No one. I went of my own volition, taking Fitz-Simons, Fanning and others with me. I do not approve of what is happening there – families deprived of land they won or bought honestly. I believed in the rebellion, but had the sense to abandon it once I saw it had been infiltrated by spies like you.'

Chaloner raised his eyebrows. 'You confess to treachery? Here, of all places?'

Dillon shrugged. 'Who heard me? You will say nothing, because your family has been victimised by greedy Royalists, too. Your heart was never in thwarting the Castle Plot – I could see it in your eyes.'

Chaloner sincerely hoped no one else had. 'You are lucky to be alive. The other rebels were rounded up, and most are either hanged or in prison.'

Dillon laughed as he gestured around him. 'And my situation is different how, exactly? Will you come to see the fun tomorrow morning? You will not be disappointed.'

Chaloner did not leave Newgate as quickly as he would have liked, because inmates saw his clerical garb and asked for his prayers. He obliged, because he had no choice if he wanted to maintain his disguise, but it was a distasteful deception, and when he was finally out into the fresh air, he thought he might be sick. He ripped off the dark clothes and hurled them at the first beggar he

356

saw, ignoring the man's startled gratitude in his desperation to be away from the prison and its environs. His legs shook horribly, so he hired a carriage to take him to Tower Street.

The Dolphin was a rambling inn, which tended to be frequented by officials of the Navy Office. Chaloner saw one called Samuel Pepys, whom he had met briefly a few months before. A spark of recognition flashed in the clerk's eyes, but Chaloner was obviously not considered sufficiently important – or useful – to warrant an exchange of civilities, and was pointedly ignored.

The Dolphin's landlord remembered Willys and Dillon on the night of Webb's murder, because Willys had been a belligerent drunk who had broken a window. He also recalled Dillon receiving a note and disappearing for several hours – the incident had stuck in his mind because he had been afraid Willys would wake up and cause chaos when his companion was not there to calm him. Chaloner listened to the innkeeper and his regulars for a long time, learning a great deal not only about the night in question, but their views on the certainty of Dillon's rescue, Lady Castlemaine's latest pregnancy, and the Bishop of London's distress over a lost parrot. More pieces of the mystery slotted together, and he finally began to see the answers to at least some of his questions.

'There is one other thing,' said the landlord, catching his arm as he was about to leave. 'Dillon's message was delivered by a slovenly, grubby fellow – the kind who always happens to be to hand when someone wants something shady done. Then a second man came, also wanting to speak urgently to Dillon, but Dillon had already left.'

'What did the second man look like?'

'Better dressed than the first, but it was busy that night,

357

and my memory is . . . oh, yes, sir. Another shilling *might* help me remember. He was big, I know that, and he had thick fair hair. And he was a foreigner, judging by the way he spoke.'

Chaloner left as the sun was setting in a great orange ball, and travelled by water from Botolph's Wharf to Whitefriars Stairs. At that time of day, when the streets were clogged with the carts of traders, all flooding home from their stalls, shops and markets, it was always quicker to go by boat. The sun danced across the filthy water, turning it to a sheet of shimmering gold, and it was almost peaceful, with commerce stopped and the city's clamour quietened by approaching night. Gulls glided above his head, and the sky was full of red and purple clouds. He smiled when he disembarked and saw a familiar face in the crowd that was out enjoying the warmth of the evening. It was Temperance's Maude, a basket of brown onions over her arm.

'Bristol is coming tonight,' she explained, accepting Chaloner's offer to carry it for her.

'That is a fine brooch you are wearing,' he said, thinking it sat oddly with her functional workaday clothes. It would look more at home with the brothel-master's costume she would probably don later.

She fingered it, but without pleasure. 'Johan Behn gave it to me, but he was only after my body.'

Chaloner raised his eyebrows. 'Eaffrey and Silence are not enough for him?'

'Eaffrey! A slip of a girl with no meat on her bones. Johan likes his women with a decent pair of hips, although I think Silence has the edge over me there. She can keep him, though.'

'I thought you liked him.'

358

'I did – when I thought he considered me something special. Then I learned he is carrying on with Silence *and* several others. Like all men, he is just out for what he can get, and his whispered endearments were a sham. Still, at least our affair was one where he gave me gifts, not the other way around. Silence parted with her husband's ship as a token of *her* affection.' She spat in disgust, narrowly missing the onions.

'I am surprised he has time for all this courting. He is a busy merchant.'

'Men can always spare an hour for their pleasure. But I have been thinking about Johan since I was made aware of his loose morals. He says he grieves for Webb, but I know for a fact that he does not. The morning after the murder, I heard him tell an associate that it was good riddance.'

'Which associate? Temple?'

'No, a low, villainous fellow with black hair and a strange purple birth-stain on his left arm. I would recognise him if I saw him again.'

'Fanning,' said Chaloner immediately. 'He had black hair and a mark on his hand.'

'You mean one of the men who was convicted of murdering Webb? How odd! Well, anyway, after this Fanning had left, Johan pulled his pipe from his pocket, and a bundle of letters dropped to the floor. I picked them up for him – I thought they might be love letters, as they were penned in pretty blue ink, and I wanted to catch him out if they were – but they were in a strange language.'

'German,' said Chaloner. 'His native tongue.'

'Does German use numbers for letters, then?' asked Maude curiously. 'I had no idea.'

'Numbers?' asked Chaloner sharply. He rummaged in an inner pocket for a cipher code Lord Clarendon had once given him. 'Do you mean like this?'

She grinned. '*Exactly* like that. German, is it? Well, I never!'

When Chaloner reached home, he half expected Scot to be waiting, but the stairs were deserted. A smattering of crumbs told him someone had lingered there, though, and had fortified himself while he did so. Chaloner bent to inspect the mess. He had eaten enough cookshop wares to know three things. First, these crumbs came from a lamb pie. Secondly, lamb pies always contained a generous helping of peas. And thirdly, both Scot and Leybourn hated peas, so would never have bought one.

So, who had lurked on the stairs in the darkness, waiting for him to return? Chaloner sensed it was no one who wished him well, and spent the rest of the night wide awake, waiting for an attack that never came.

In the faint light of pre-dawn, Chaloner went to Lincoln's Inn, where he found Thurloe standing forlornly among his felled trees – almost half gone already. Leybourn was with him, a comforting hand on his shoulder. The mighty oaks had been carted off to the shipyards, while the fruit trees lay on their sides, waiting to be chopped into logs for the winter. The garden had an oddly lopsided feel to it, and the absence of vegetation along one wall showed it to be in urgent need of repair. Prynne had evidently been unaware that not only had the ancient roots and branches concealed unsightly masonry, but they been critical in shoring up some of the more unstable sections, too.

'Thank you for the note you sent last night, Thomas,'

said Thurloe. He looked miserable. 'But I am afraid all your efforts to help Dillon have been in vain. I was up until the small hours, trying to think of a way to save him, but I failed. He will have to rely on his new master for salvation after all.'

Chaloner had not imagined for a moment that Thurloe would succeed in rescuing his former spy, but he admired him for trying. Prudently, Chaloner's note had neglected to include the fact that Dillon had actually confessed to the crime – it was not the sort of thing that should be entrusted to paper. He had planned to tell Thurloe that morning, but the ex-Spymaster seemed so disconsolate about the destruction of his beloved sanctuary that Chaloner could not bring himself to do it.

'That will be expensive to mend,' he remarked instead, nodding towards the wall. 'And it cannot be left as it is, because it looks as though it is in imminent danger of collapse. Prynne may find he has no money left to destroy the rest of the orchard, once funds have been diverted to make good this mess.'

Thurloe gazed at him, then turned to study the walls. Slowly, a smile lit his unhappy face. A plan was beginning to take shape. 'Do you own any skill with gunpowder, Thomas?'

Chaloner knew exactly what he had in mind. 'A little. Do you know where I might find some?'

'It is not the sort of thing an ex-Spymaster keeps in his chambers, for obvious reasons. However, Prynne used some to clear the well a few days ago. I suspect he has a bit left. It will be in his room.'

Leybourn looked from one to the other uneasily. 'You are going to blow up Lincoln's Inn?'

'Only enough to ensure Prynne will have to pay for

some urgent repairs,' said Thurloe. His face was uncharacteristically vengeful. 'Then he may not have enough money left to hire men with axes.'

Chaloner and Leybourn followed him to the building – already called the Garden Court in anticipation of the splendid views it would enjoy once the trees had gone – where Prynne lived. Leybourn was appalled by their plan, and tried to make them reconsider. They would be caught, he hissed, and made to pay for the damage themselves – or worse. Thurloe informed him curtly that he had no intention of being caught.

Prynne was at dawn prayers, and the Garden Court was deserted as Thurloe led the way to his colleague's quarters and cautiously picked the lock. Then Chaloner searched for gunpowder, while Thurloe kept guard and Leybourn prowled. The surveyor stopped at a desk covered with documents, all filled with Prynne's tiny, crabbed writing. He snorted with disgust as he picked one up and read it.

'I wish we could put a fuse to *this* inflammatory rubbish, too. I did not know men still existed who wrote about matters of which they are entirely ignorant, not in these enlightened times.'

'Why would you think that?' asked Chaloner, opening a chest. 'You publish government pamphlets, for God's sake. Ah, here is the powder. We had better not take too much. There is no point in adding insult to injury by leaving evidence to show we used his own explosives to thwart him.'

While Chaloner scooped the odorous black substance into his hat – it was the only receptacle available to him – Leybourn busied himself among the flasks, decanters and bottles on Prynne's shelves. Chaloner recalled Yates mentioning that there were an inordinate number of them, and Prynne was their prime suspect for trying to poison Thurloe. He heard the clink of glass as stoppers were removed, and sharp intakes of breath as Leybourn sniffed the contents. He concentrated on what he was doing, ladling faster when he thought he heard footsteps in the courtyard below.

Eventually, he had enough to accomplish what he needed to do, but Prynne's supply was too obviously depleted. Swearing under his breath, he replaced what he had taken with soot from the chimney. But then he saw that the dust was a different colour from the explosive, so he was obliged to mix it in. Stirring gunpowder was not something that could be rushed, and he was acutely aware that the whole operation was taking far too long. After what felt an age, he finished, and looked up to see Leybourn in the process of drinking something dark red.

'What are you doing?' he exclaimed, aghast. 'You know he keeps poisons here.'

'None of *these* are poisonous,' said Leybourn, grinning in a way that indicated he had taken his experiment rather too far. 'They are all wine. Most labels say otherwise, but I know a decent claret when I taste it. Prynne is a secret drinker, with a palate for vintages that would impress a king.'

He upended a decanter and drained it before Chaloner could stop him. Horrified, the spy grabbed his arm and pulled him outside. Leybourn staggered, and it was not easy to drag him in the direction they needed to go. He began to warble, a tuneless, reedy tenor that reminded Chaloner why he always fabricated an excuse for not accompanying him on the viol.

'What is wrong with him?' asked Thurloe, as they hurried away from the Garden Court.

'He has discovered that your colleague's collection of liquids is nothing more dangerous than wine. Prynne is innocent of attempting to poison you, it seems.'

'Yates told me—' began Thurloe. He stopped, and his eyes narrowed. 'I had a letter yesterday from my old manservant, begging me to take him back. He is under the impression that I dismissed him, while *I* was told he had left because he was ill. Someone is causing mischief.'

'It must be Yates,' said Chaloner. 'There he is – you can ask him.'

Leybourn reeled drunkenly, and Chaloner was hard-pressed to hold him upright and keep the contents of his hat from spilling at the same time. He cursed the splint that made him clumsy, and decided the dressing *would* come off that day, no matter what else happened. And if Lisle could not do it, then he would borrow Thurloe's gun and hold it to Wiseman's head until the surgeon had removed every last shred of the damned thing.

'Mr Thurloe,' said Yates with an uneasy smile as the ex-Spymaster bore down on him. Thurloe's blue eyes were hard and cold, an expression that had set more than one Royalist spy trembling in his boots during the Commonwealth. 'Can I fetch you anything from the kitchen?'

'Who hired you?' demanded Thurloe. He grabbed Yates by the collar when the porter tried to make a run for it, displaying surprising speed and strength for a man who so seldom engaged in any kind of physical activity.

Yates licked dry lips, one frightened eye on Thurloe and the other one on Chaloner. 'I do not know what you are talking about.'

'Oh, I think you do,' said Thurloe in a low, sibilant voice that was distinctly sinister. Yates paled. 'You have been spying on me ever since you arrived, and I know it was you who sent my servant away under false pretences. Now, are you going to be cooperative, or shall we do this another way?'

Yates struggled, but the ex-Spymaster's grip was powerful, and it was not long before he abandoned himself to his fate. 'I have done nothing wrong. I only did what I was told.'

'By Temple,' said Chaloner to Thurloe. 'He knows you are taking more tonics than usual at the moment – I heard him tell Bristol about it. And Temple knows because Yates briefed him.'

'There is nothing wrong in reporting that,' bleated Yates. 'It is hardly a state secret.'

'No,' agreed Thurloe in the same soft whisper. It was making Chaloner uncomfortable, so he did not like to imagine how Yates felt. 'But that is not all you did. You doctored my tonics – it must have been you, because you are the only person who has had access to them since my own servant left. I might have died, had not the cat stolen some first. It is still poorly, and I am fond of that animal.'

'And you almost killed Tom,' slurred Leybourn. He began to sing again, crooning the words to a popular tavern ballad with no heed to the tune that usually went with them.

Yates shook his head vehemently. 'That was not me! I had nothing to do with it, I swear on my mother's grave! Temple accused me of it too, and said he wanted information, not murder. But it must have been one of your other enemies – God knows, you have enough of them.'

Chaloner almost believed him, but Thurloe did not. He summoned a pair of porters with orders to escort Yates to Temple with the message that he could have this would-be assassin back alive, but that the next one would not be so lucky. When they had gone, he turned to Chaloner.

'You must tell Lord Clarendon immediately. If Temple and Bristol are hiring spies to watch men who are only peripherally associated with him, his close friends will be far more closely monitored – and Brodrick is apt to be indiscreet when he is drunk. And speaking of being drunk, can you not stop William from caterwauling? He is drawing attention to us.'

'Good,' said Chaloner, thinking fast. 'Go and stand in the middle of Dial Court, where everyone can see you, and expect fireworks within a quarter of an hour. I will meet you at Tyburn at nine o'clock, for Dillon's . . . I assume you will be there, to see him rescued?'

Thurloe smiled grimly, immediately understanding Chaloner's plan to provide him with an alibi for the incident that was about to unfold. He handed him a tinderbox. 'Yes, I will. Be careful with that powder; Prynne said the batch he bought for the well was unusually potent.'

Chaloner jogged back to the orchard, and spent several minutes enlarging holes in the walls for his charges – for the explosion to have an impact, the powder needed to be in a confined space, so it would destabilise the structure when it expanded on ignition. He fiddled until he was satisfied, then laid a thin trail of the black substance, so it could be lit from a safe distance. He did not have much left, so the 'fuse' was not as long as he would have liked, but he knelt and set Thurloe's

366

tinderbox to it before someone could come along and ask what he was doing.

'Roundheads!' creaked an avian voice from above his head. 'Thousands of 'em!'

Chaloner glanced up at the parrot in alarm, and waved his arms in a desperate attempt to frighten it away. The bird stepped from side to side, but did not seem inclined to fly off. The powder began to splutter. Chaloner lobbed a handful of soil at the parrot, before turning and running as hard as he could, to take cover behind one of the remaining oaks. He reached it just as the first of his charges blew with a dull thump. Fragments of masonry shot into the air, then rained down all around him. He covered his head with his hands, smelling the powder in his hat as he did so. The second blast was smaller and deeper, but did more damage, because a huge part of the wall toppled inwards in a billow of dust. The third and final boom served to smash some of the foundation stones into pieces too small for reuse, thus ensuring the repairs would cost Prynne especially dearly.

Chaloner moved away from the tree and gazed into its branches, but there was not so much as an emerald feather to be seen. He sighed. He liked birds, and was sorry to have been the cause of one's demise.

'Bugger the bishops,' came a voice from behind him. He turned to see a beady eye regaling him balefully. 'And make way for the Catholics.'

Chaloner smiled, then clapped his hands to shoo it away. It was not a good idea to have mysterious voices chanting pro-Roman sentiments at the scenes of explosions. The bird flapped towards the chapel roof, and the spy trusted it would not come back. He stepped behind the tree again as people began to converge on the devastation he had wreaked, yelling and shouting their alarm. Prynne was among them and so was Thurloe, Leybourn clutching drunkenly to his arm. The surveyor lurched forward, and appeared to be genuinely puzzled by the wreckage. Chaloner held his breath, hoping he would not say anything incriminatory. Thurloe tried to pull him back, but Leybourn freed his hand impatiently, almost falling as he did so.

'Lightning,' he slurred. 'I heard the crack as it struck the wall.'

'Lightning?' asked Prynne suspiciously. 'It is not the right weather for lightning.'

'God does not care about weather when He produces divine bolts,' declared Leybourn, grabbing Prynne around the neck to hold himself up. 'Did you not hear the rumble of His wrath?'

'I heard a rumble, right enough,' said Prynne dryly, 'but it was an exploding rumble, not thunder.'

'Obviously, you have not read John Spencer's book on prodigies and prophecies,' said Leybourn waving a finger in the lawyer's face. 'If you had, you would know what this means.'

'Oh?' asked Prynne, trying, without success, to free himself. 'And what is that?'

'That God does not like His trees knocked down and sold as firewood,' said Leybourn. 'And He will send great balls of fire to destroy the walls of those who do. Just like He did at Jericho.'

Chaloner's regicide uncle had taught him about the combined power of superstition and rumour, and he saw a good example of it at Lincoln's Inn that day. Thurloe stood back, arms folded in satisfaction, as servants and benchers began to agree that Leybourn might have a point. Even Prynne looked uncertain. As a fervently – some might say violently – religious man, Prynne was sensitive to what God might or might not like. It looked as though the plot had worked better than Chaloner could have hoped, because there was no suggestion from anyone that gunpowder might have been the culprit.

He left Lincoln's Inn and went to White Hall, where he told Lord Clarendon how Temple had hired Yates to spy. the Earl was appalled, and ordered Brodrick to visit all his friends and warn them, lest they make indiscreet remarks in front of loyal servants who were nothing of the kind.

'May has been spreading tales about you,' said Brodrick, walking with Chaloner to the gate. 'He says *you* murdered the real Vanders, and the Dutch government has offered a reward for your head. Some greedy fool will decide to have the fabulous sum he says is available, which means you are in serious danger – he knew what he was doing when he concocted such a tale.'

'This *must* mean I am right about him being the author of Bristol's letter,' Chaloner said, more to himself than Brodrick. 'I am close to the truth, and he is desperate to silence me before it is too late.'

'Actually, I think he just dislikes you,' said Brodrick. 'If I were you, I would tackle him about it before it is too late. He is in the Spares Gallery.'

Reluctantly – he resented wasting time combating the bald spy's spiteful antics – Chaloner walked to the hall where 'Vanders' had been unmasked, May and Willys had tried to run him through, and Holles had come close to shooting him. It was unusually busy that morning, because people had risen early to attend the public hangings at Tyburn. May was there, muttering to Behn.

'Played any good tunes recently, Heyden?' May asked, when Chaloner approached. He leaned against a wall and grinned with calculated malice. 'If you cannot hold a dagger, then I imagine you cannot hold a viol, either, and I know how important music is to you.'

'I would not mind buying a viol,' said Behn, chuckling nastily. 'I hear they make good firewood. Do you have one cluttering up your house that you want rid of?'

Chaloner smiled, unwilling to let them see how much their remarks rankled. 'I hear you are making up stories, May, hoping to stop me from uncovering evidence that proves you wrote Bristol that letter. But why name those particular nine men? Was your intention to strip Williamson of all his best agents, so only you would be left?'

'How many more times?' snarled May. 'I had nothing to do with that damned missive! But you are right about one thing: I *have* made it known that the Dutch government is offering a thousand pounds for Vanders's killer. And it will be only a matter of time before someone dusts off his dag in order to lay claim to the reward. Your days are numbered.'

Chapter 11

The bells were chiming eight o'clock by the time Chaloner left White Hall, and he supposed it was time to make his way to Tyburn. He took a carriage, which travelled up St Martin's Lane to St Giles-in-the-Fields, a large, handsome church that was only forty years old. Unfortunately, it had attracted the attention of Puritan iconoclasts, and there was not a single statue that owned a head, hands or feet, and the once-fine chancel screen had been wrecked by axes. The 'fields' around St Giles were long gone, too, although there was a rural echo in its leafy churchyard.

Past St Giles's, the driver turned along the Oxford road, where people sat or stood, waiting for the cart carrying the condemned men to pass – the governor had decided that Fanning and Sarsfeild should be replaced, to ensure the crowd had its money's worth, so Dillon's final journey would be made in company with a robber and a mother who had smothered her baby. Some spectators had brought food and ale, and shared it with others as they lounged in the sun. The atmosphere was festive, accompanied by an air of eager anticipation, and Chaloner saw that people were looking forward to witnessing Dillon's fate, whatever it might be. Among the spectators were soldiers, pale and uneasy, and Chaloner was under the impression that they might decide to make themselves scarce if a well-orchestrated plot to release the prisoner did swing into action.

Thousands had gathered in the area of desolate scrub known as Tyburn. To accommodate their needs, traders sold ale, oranges, tobacco, pies and gingerbread from carts and barrows. Wooden stools could be rented for a penny, to ease legs that did not want to stand for hours; cushions cost extra. Pickpockets roamed, looking for victims, and prostitutes offered their services for now – bales of hay and a hedge were available – or later. Already, people were drunk. Some sprawled snoring in the grass, while others reeled and weaved, knocking into the sober and yelling songs or insults.

The first person Chaloner recognised was Wiseman, who was striding away from Tyburn and back towards the city. The surgeon wore his distinctive scarlet robes, and when one undersized fellow sidled up to him and tried to grab his purse, he responded with a careless flick of his wrist that saw the would-be thief cartwheel into an apple-seller. Wiseman stopped when he saw Chaloner.

'You are interested in these events, Heyden? I expected better of you.'

'Then why are you here?'

'I came to ensure Lisle has help for when he claims the corpse. He is a gentle soul, and might be overwhelmed by the mob – there are those who would snatch the body that is ours by rights, and sell parts of it for quack cures. Did you know some folk still believe that placing the hand of a hanged man on the neck will cure scrofula? It is ridiculous, when we all know the only sure remedy for that is the touch of the King. The common man is very gullible, and has no idea what is best for him.'

'Like wearing your splints, I suppose,' said Chaloner caustically.

Wiseman inclined his head. 'Yes, just like that. People are fools, and they are lucky there are men like me to save them from themselves.'

'So, are you not staying to help Lisle?' asked Chaloner, declining to argue with him. It was not worth the aggravation.

'Johnson, Reynell and a dozen apprentices are with him, so my services are not required. I am glad. There are more profitable ways to spend a morning than witnessing this sort of thing.'

'You lied to me about the Guinea Company dinner,' said Chaloner, seizing the opportunity to question the man. 'You said you were not there the night Webb died, but that was false.'

Wiseman sighed irritably. 'I suppose you wormed the truth out of Reynell, did you? How tiresome. I should have anticipated that would happen, and told him to keep his mouth shut. Very well, I admit I was at the dinner. And I also admit that Webb and I quarrelled when I told him what I think of men who condone slavery. So, what are *you* going to do about it? Reprimand me?'

'Ask why you felt it was necessary to prevaricate.'

Wiseman grimaced. 'All right. Since you are being gentlemanly about the matter, I shall confide. I lied because I did not want my enemies at the Company of Barber-Surgeons – Johnson, in essence – to make an issue of the spat. He will do anything to harm Lord Clarendon, and linking me – the Earl's most prestigious supporter – to a murder was an opportunity he would have seized with delight. However, although Webb and I argued, *I* did not kill the fellow.'

'Was it you who tended Temple's head, after the incident with the candlestick?'

'Yes – it was the only remotely interesting thing that happened all evening, although Temple was too drunk to appreciate my skills.' He glared at someone who jostled him, and brandished a meaty fist. 'It is becoming too rough here for me. Good morning to you.'

He strode away up Tyburn Lane, scattering people before him like a hot knife through butter. He shouted for a sedan chair to take him to Chyrurgeons' Hall, but the chair-bearers hastily made themselves scarce. His bulk would not make for an easy fare, and they preferred to wait for a lighter customer. When he had gone, Chaloner turned towards the field of execution.

At the centre was the triangular gallows, built so nine felons could be dispatched simultaneously. There was an ancient oak on a slight hill to the west of the gibbet, and Chaloner knew he would find Thurloe there. He eased his way through the hordes, pausing to watch a small bear dance to the laboured notes of a cracked flute; the animal was an odd shape, and he suspected a boy or an undersized man was inside its skin.

Prostitutes clawed at him as he walked, offering treats for a penny, and street preachers were using the opportunity to proselytise. Temperance's doorman Hill was among them, and Chaloner saw spittle fly from the man's mouth as he spouted his poison. He had an audience of avid admirers, who were quite happy to believe that God did not like Catholics, taverns, Dutchmen, dancing or large windows, and that 'decent Christians' would be perfectly justified in going out and attacking a few in His name.

Eventually, Chaloner reached the rise and looked around for Thurloe. The ex-Spymaster was standing in the shade, his silent servant lurking protectively at his shoulder. The fellow smiled shyly when he saw Chaloner, and Thurloe said he had appeared after the 'lightning strike' that morning.

Thurloe was not so rash as to go to a public place without a disguise, partly because he still had enemies who wanted him dead, but also because crowds had a habit of turning into mobs, and once-powerful Parliamentarian spymasters made for tempting targets. He wore the drab uniform of a chancery clerk, and his face was half hidden by the kind of bandage worn by those who had toothache. A wide-brimmed hat pulled down over his eyes meant very little of him could be seen.

'How is Will?' asked Chaloner, hoping the surveyor had been left in a safe place.

'Prynne and I carried him to my quarters after the explosion. He is currently sound asleep.'

'You will not try to cure him with one of your remedies, will you?' asked Chaloner uneasily. Leybourn might awake too befuddled to refuse, and he did not want him made worse. He saw Thurloe was offended that he was perceived as a menace to helpless drunks so added, 'Who knows what Yates might have done to them?'

'The first thing my servant did when he returned was pour them all down the drain. Temple will be disappointed if he thinks his creature might still succeed in harming me.'

'Does Prynne believe the destruction of his wall was due to heavenly fury?' Chaloner asked to change the subject. He hoped he had not done so much damage that the old lawyer was suspicious.

'He says he cannot be sure, but the other benchers

say they know a Divine Sign when they see one, and they are more willing to oppose him – and the King – now they think God is on their side.'

'Will it save your trees?'

Thurloe smiled. 'I believe it might. We cannot leave a gaping hole in our defences, and Prynne has already been forced to hire masons to begin repairs. He is dismayed by the additional expense, and I think he can be persuaded to work the remaining trees into his grand design. I have lost a portion of my orchard, and he will have a reduced expanse of grass, but we can both live with that.'

'I dislike these occasions,' said Chaloner, reacting sharply when he felt a hand slip into his pocket. The thief reeled away clutching a bleeding arm, and Chaloner returned the dagger to his sleeve. 'There must be ten thousand spectators here, enough for a riot of enormous proportion.'

'I would sooner be at home, too, but I want to know the identity of Dillon's master, and I do not trust anyone but myself to deduce the right answer from what occurs. Come with me. I have hired a cartwheel for us to stand on – we will not see a thing otherwise. There are simply too many people.'

A great cheer went up from the distant city, and Chaloner supposed the cart carrying the convicts had started its journey from Newgate. He followed Thurloe to a place where a number of semi-permanent structures had been rented to spectators over the years. There were several large wheels, all with spokes arranged like ladders, along with a stand of crudely stepped planks, where people could sit but still be high enough to enjoy the view. These cost a good deal of money, so only the wealthy could afford them – especially for an occasion like the execution of a

376

man who thought he was going to be rescued. Chaloner was not surprised to see Temple perched on the highest tier, his mouth almost disappearing under his nose as he devoured something with his toothless jaws. And nor was he surprised to see Alice, thinking uncharitably that a hanging was exactly the kind of entertainment that would appeal to her bitter soul.

He *was* surprised to see Eaffrey however, because he thought she had more taste. She was with Behn, who looked as though he was thoroughly enjoying himself. He had bought oranges from a fruit-seller, and was sharing them with Temple and Alice. Eaffrey declined, and Chaloner thought she looked pale. He waited until the seat-vendor was looking the other way, then slipped past him to join the chattering party on the top rung. Behn grimaced in annoyance when Chaloner insinuated himself between him and Eaffrey, and Alice pointedly looked the other way.

'I expected Silence Webb to invite me to join her party,' said Temple, as if to explain why he had not secured himself a better place. 'She has been allocated a spot at the front, because Dillon is the rogue who killed her husband. Unfortunately, the surgeons got there first. Damned vultures! You can see them with her now – but only because they want to make sure they get the body.'

Chaloner looked towards the gallows, and saw a number of barber-surgeons forming a solicitous circle around Silence. Lisle had a fatherly hand on her shoulder, although she did not seem particularly distressed by the occasion. On the contrary, she was revelling in the attention; her eyes sparkled, and so did the jewels at her throat. Johnson and Reynell stood next to a coffin. Both carried unsheathed swords, and Reynell appeared to be terrified. With them

377

was a gaggle of apprentices, blades flashing as they kept the crowd at bay. Chaloner could hear Johnson's braying voice informing anyone who happened to be listening that oranges rotted the bladder, because they were caustic.

'Silence may have neglected you, but she invited *me*,' said Behn to Temple. Then he shot Eaffrey a false and wholly unconvincing smile. 'I declined, because I prefer to be with my sweet lady.'

'Johan and I have quarrelled,' said Eaffrey in a low, sad voice to Chaloner, when Behn and Temple began to discuss the pros and cons of standing too near the scaffold when a man was hanged. 'He thinks you and I are lovers, and he finds himself jealous.'

'Good,' said Chaloner. 'It might make him appreciate you more, and forgo the pleasures offered by Silence and Maude.'

'And Adrian May's mother,' added Eaffrey with a rueful smile. 'Johan seems to like crones, so perhaps he will leave me alone once we are married. I will not complain. He is a bit of an ape.'

'An ape with deep pockets.'

She smiled wanly. 'I sincerely hope so. I understand William told you our plan? Do not be too harsh on us, Tom. It is not as if Johan is kind or decent.'

Suddenly, Behn lurched violently to one side, rocking the structure hard with the obvious intention of making Chaloner lose his balance and fall. Unfortunately for him, it was not the spy who took a tumble off the back, but Temple. Alice gave a shriek of horror and tried to clamber towards her beau, but her skirts snagged in the rough wood, and the more she struggled, the more firmly she became ensnared. Behn's fumbling attempts to free her made matters worse, and so did Temple's increasingly

378

agitated demands for help; he had landed in a morass of rotten fruit peelings left from previous executions, and the midden was too slippery for an escape under his own power.

'Have you seen William, Tom?' asked Eaffrey, studiously ignoring the melee. 'He was supposed to visit last night, but he failed to arrive. It is unlike him to miss an assignation without sending word, and I have looked *everywhere* for him. I even visited Thurloe, and since relations between those two have been strained since William changed sides during the collapse of the Commonwealth, you can tell how desperate I am.'

'I have not seen him since Thursday – two days ago – but he knows how to look after himself.'

'I found a body yesterday,' she whispered. Chaloner glanced at her in shock, and saw the deep unhappiness in her eyes. 'In Johan's office. I think he killed the man.'

Chaloner was alarmed. 'Then you cannot go home with Behn today, and if Scot was here, he would say the same thing. Stay with me – or I will take you to Scot's rooms in the Chequer.'

She smiled wanly. 'No, I shall foist myself on Alice. William told her that he and I are close, so she will not refuse me sanctuary. Johan might try to kill you or Scot for taking me away from him, but he would never harm her, because she is a woman.'

'Whose body did you find?' asked Chaloner, hoping her assessment was right. He disliked Alice, but she was Scot's sister, and he did not want to see her in danger.

'A man who has visited him before – an ugly, squat fellow with a scar on his neck. He was knifed in the back, probably early in the evening, when I was out at White Hall. The corpse was gone by this morning.'

379

'Gone where?'

She shook her head. 'Perhaps Johan dropped it in the river under cover of darkness.' She fought back tears. 'I want *William*, Tom! And I want him *now*!'

'I will look for him this afternoon,' he said soothingly, wishing he could take her in his arms and give her the comfort of a hug. 'Do not worry – he will not have gone far.'

'I love him,' she whispered. 'And I cannot imagine life without him. I know you considered him as a suspect for Webb's murder, because he left the Guinea Company dinner early and declined to explain himself. But you know why now: he came to see me.'

He smiled at the notion. 'He was never a suspect! I was bemused by the inconsistencies in his story, but he is not the kind of man to kill and let others hang for the crime. I do not understand why he declined to confide in me, though. We have shared far more sensitive secrets in the past.'

'He did not understand it, either, which has made him worry all the more about the way our occupation has begun to warp his judgement. He trusts you with his life, but lied instinctively when you asked questions. It taught him something about himself that he did not like.'

'It will not be for much longer,' said Chaloner. 'The Lord Chancellor told me today that Thomas will be released in a few days. This time next week, you will all be on a ship sailing for Surinam. A big, happy family – you and Scot, Behn, Alice and Thomas. And perhaps even Temple, too.'

Eaffrey lowered her voice further, choosing to ignore the mockery in his voice. 'William was going to tell Alice he was taking her to Surinam last night – without

Temple. She is a strong lady, and I am afraid she might have . . . '

'Alice would never harm him. It is a fiercely close family, no matter who wants to marry whom.'

'Temple, then. He will not want to lose his wealthy widow. And then there is Johan, who courts his fat ladies, but hates the thought of me seeing anyone else.'

'I assume you are having second thoughts about marrying him now?'

'William is, but I do not know how else we can secure a future for our child. However, the more I come to know Johan, the less I understand him. I am used to clandestine dealings – for obvious reasons – but he has far more than a merchant should. He writes letters in a complicated cipher that I cannot break, and there is an air of controlled violence about him. He would never hurt a woman, but I fear for the men who cross him, including you. And I am afraid that he might have done something to William.'

'Behn is a lumbering brute,' said Chaloner confidently. 'He could never best Scot.'

Eaffrey's face was a mask of unhappiness. 'Spymaster Williamson asked me yesterday whether I thought Johan might have murdered Webb – or hired louts to do it for him.'

'Williamson is interested in Behn? That is enlightening.'

'Johan is not a spy, Tom,' said Eaffrey, seeing the road his thoughts had taken. 'That is what *I* was charged to learn. How else do you think we met?'

Chaloner had guessed the relationship had owed its origins to Eaffrey's work for the intelligence services. 'So, when did you decide to relieve Behn of his fortune by marrying him? Before or after Williamson charged you to seduce him for his secrets?'

'After – when I learned how rich he is.'

'How can you be sure he is not a spy for Brandenburg?'

'Lord, Tom! You are like the inquisition today! Because all the evidence points to ugly mercantile dealings, not treachery. Believe me, I investigated this very carefully before I decided to marry him. Given my own occupation, I can hardly wed an enemy intelligencer, can I?' She winced when a great cheer went up from the crowd. 'Dillon has arrived.'

Chaloner left Eaffrey when Behn abandoned his attempts to extricate Alice from the splinters and devoted his attention to the condemned man instead. He was one of those who liked to play an active role in public executions, and began to howl abuse at Dillon. Such behaviour was common among apprentices or drunken labourers, but merchants, on the whole, tended to be more genteel. Alice screeched at him to come back and help her, but Behn was oblivious to all except the scaffold. Eaffrey winced at his coarse manners, and went to assist Alice. Chaloner was about to do the same for Temple, but a pair of thickset louts beat him to it. They hauled the politician to his feet, then relieved him of his purse while they were dusting him down.

The spy returned to Thurloe, and climbed two of the wheel's rungs, enough to see Dillon's head and shoulders among the mass of people by the gibbet. Dillon wore his distinctive hat, which he doffed to the crowd, earning himself cheers of admiration. The robber and the baby-killer had already been turned off their ladders, and their bodies twisted and turned as they swung in the breeze.

'I hope to God they were guilty,' said Thurloe. 'Not innocent, like Dillon.'

It was time to reveal what had been omitted from the letter written the previous night. Chaloner took a deep breath and began, sorry for the pain he knew he was about to cause his friend. 'Dillon described yesterday how he distracted Webb while Fanning stabbed him. He claimed he acted on his master's orders, but that he would willingly have helped to kill Webb anyway, because he despises slavery. His master sent him a note, which he received in the Dolphin tavern after he had left the Guinea Company dinner. He had abandoned the event early, because he had quarrelled with Webb.'

Thurloe regarded him with a stunned expression, then shook his head. 'He was not telling the truth. Perhaps this so-called confession is part of this complex game he is playing – he and his master.'

'Not so, sir,' said Chaloner gently. 'I went to the Dolphin tavern afterwards, where I found a pot-boy who admitted to following Dillon to The Strand on the evening of the murder. The lad is a thief, and I imagine he intended to rob Dillon, which is why he has kept his story to himself until now.'

'Yet he told you?' asked Thurloe sceptically. 'After all these weeks?'

'I had a dagger at his throat, and he was far too terrified to tell me anything but the truth. He said he saw Dillon reach Webb's house and hide in the shadows. Eventually, Dillon was joined by a second man whose description matches Fanning's. At that point, the boy became uneasy and ran away.'

Thurloe shook his head stubbornly. 'This unsavoury lad's tale does not mean—'

'Dillon told me Webb fell to his knees when he died, injuring them. I saw Webb's body, and there *were* grazes on his legs. Only his killers would know such a detail.'

Thurloe gazed at him, shocked and hurt. 'So, the conviction was sound? I have been working to free a guilty man? The bloody rapier was not planted by spiteful hands, but was his – or Fanning's?'

Chaloner nodded. 'It would seem so.'

'Then it explains why Dillon is so certain he will be saved today,' said Thurloe tiredly. 'He did his master's bidding, and he has a right to expect his master's protection. So, whoever wrote Bristol's letter was telling the truth. Does this mean the other seven men were guilty, too?'

'Dillon said it was just him and Fanning. I wonder how May – the author of the letter – came to know Dillon and Fanning were the culprits. I suppose I shall have to ask him.'

'I will tell my expert to compare May's handwriting with that on Bristol's note. It may prove conclusive. Did I tell you Eaffrey came to see me after you left this morning? She is worried, because Scot is missing, and she thought I might know his whereabouts. I showed her Bristol's letter and, after studying it with my enlarging glass, she demonstrated how Garsfield had been changed to Sarsfeild.'

Chaloner was dismissive. 'I do not think—'

'She made a convincing case. I could not see it until she copied the letters in a larger hand and showed me what had happened. I believe she is right: the writer changed his mind after writing your alias, and altered the letters to spell a slightly different name.'

'Why would May do that? He would rather have me accused than all the others put together.'

'Perhaps it was because you were in Ireland when Webb was murdered – like the spies Clarke and Fitz-Gerrard – and he knew that if there were too many who could not possibly have committed the crime, it would lead to the whole letter being brought into question.'

Chaloner did not believe him, so Thurloe handed him the note and the glass. 'I can see the ink is blurred in places,' he said after several minutes of careful study, 'but the changes are barely visible.'

'You have ruined your eyes by studying music at night, and I have spoiled mine with too much reading. But I am sure Eaffrey is right. When she realised you might be in danger, she begged me to send you on an errand out of London, to keep you safe. She is a good friend to you, Thomas.'

The crowd went quiet when Dillon began to hold forth, using the condemned man's prerogative to say whatever he liked during his last moments on Earth. He sounded smug and confident, an attitude that was appreciated by the people, who cheered at the jests he made. Next to him, the executioner showed signs of impatience. Dillon ignored him, but after an hour the mob became restless, too; they liked a speech, but they liked a hanging more. At the front, someone yelled that he had a business to run. Would Dillon mind hurrying up? The horde laughed and Dillon's smile slipped a little.

Chaloner jumped down from the wheel, not wanting to see what happened next. Dillon continued to orate, giving his rescuers every opportunity to come, but eventually he fell silent. There was a smattering of applause as the ladder on which he stood was turned, and he was left kicking in the air.

'Is anyone coming to save him?' asked Chaloner.

'No,' said Thurloe, looking away.

When the hangman announced in a ringing voice that Dillon was dead, the crowd surged forward, following an ancient superstition that touching a hanged man would work all manner of charms, ranging from curing warts to ending an unwanted pregnancy. Chaloner imagined the surgeons would be struggling to prevent sly knives from making off with parts of the body, and thought he could hear Johnson bawling threats.

'His last expression was one of utter bewilderment,' said Thurloe bleakly. 'He really did believe he was going to be reprieved, and was astonished to learn his faith was misplaced.'

'Perhaps there were too many people,' suggested Chaloner. 'And his rescuers could not find a way through them. The press is very tight around the scaffold itself.'

'Shame!' hollered Temple. He was standing on his seat, waving his fist in the air. His clothes were covered in slimy smears from his tumble, and he was besieged by interested flies. 'What happened to the rescue?'

'I prefer a hanging,' countered Behn, equally loud. 'That is why we came, and I would have been disappointed had the occasion not ended with a death. Dillon murdered a Guinea Company colleague, and it is only right that his neck has been stretched.'

'That is boring,' argued Temple. 'You can see executions any time. *I* wanted a rescue.'

Chaloner regarded them thoughtfully, noting how most people sided with Temple. There was a growing rumble of resentment that they had been cheated of what they had been promised, and someone yelled that it was Dillon's

386

fault. Immediately, the mob pressed forward a second time, and the barber-surgeons' weapons flailed as they used steel to keep the horde away from their cadaver.

'Where are you going?' asked Thurloe, when Chaloner started to walk away. The spy had had enough of the day's 'entertainment', and did not want to linger when the situation looked set to turn violent. Leybourn had been right: Dillon's hanging might well precipitate something dangerous.

'Monkwell Street. Lisle is going to remove my splint, thank God. And you should not linger here, either. People feel defrauded, and who knows where they may direct their disappointment.'

Escape was easier said than done, however. Afraid that Dillon's master might attempt to snatch the corpse – perhaps in the hope of reviving it – soldiers prevented anyone from leaving until the surgeons and their prize had fought their way free of the chaos and were in a cart heading towards the city. Then there was a fierce bottleneck, and Chaloner and Thurloe held back, trying to avoid the scuffles that broke out as people pushed and shoved in a futile attempt to hurry it along. The sun beat down on bare heads, and the ale that was needed to cool parched throats was doing nothing to calm the situation.

Eventually, the soldiers managed to assert control, and captains on horseback used their mounts to drive the multitude in the direction they wanted it to go. Chaloner saw Thurloe safely into a sedan chair, with his manservant running at his side, and set off towards Chyrurgeons' Hall, hoping Lisle would be able to find the time to help him.

It was a long way from Tyburn to the barber-surgeons' domain, but there were no hackneys available, because there had been a scramble for them when the hanging was over. Then Chaloner saw Temple and Alice climbing into the politician's personal carriage. Both looked worse for wear: Alice's skirts were torn, while Temple's beautiful silk coat would never be the same again. Eaffrey was with them, white-faced and unhappy, but there was no sign of Behn.

Chaloner knew Temple lived near Moorgate, and would pass Monkwell Street on his way home, so he waited until the driver flicked his whip at the horses, then jumped on the back, standing on the platform designed for a footman. The driver did not notice, Eaffrey, Temple and Alice could not see him, and it was a lot faster than walking. He leapt off when they reached Wood Street, almost taking a tumble when his foot skidded in fresh manure. A group of leatherworkers cheered his acrobatics, causing Alice to glance out of her window. Her face hardened when she saw Chaloner, and he bowed insolently. He shot up the nearest lane when she screeched at the coachman to stop, unwilling to miss his appointment with Lisle by letting himself become embroiled in an altercation.

When he knocked on the door to Chyrurgeons' Hall, he found everyone engaged in fevered preparations for the Public Anatomy. Apprentices were sweeping paths and scrubbing windows with long-handled brooms, and an army of servants scurried around the kitchen block, obeying the frenzied shrieks of the French chef. Delicious smells wafted across the yard, making Chaloner think that he might attend the exhibition after all, even if only to avail himself of the feast afterwards. Reynell spotted him and offered to conduct him to the Anatomical Theatre, where Lisle was waiting.

'He is going to remove my bandage in that dissecting room?' asked Chaloner uneasily.

'In the basement,' explained Reynell. 'He is desperately busy, mixing coloured waxes and making sure all his implements are in order, and does not have time to traipse back to his rooms to deal with patients. It makes no difference: a hacksaw can be wielded anywhere, and he said you would not mind where he performed the operation, just as long as Wiseman's splint comes off.'

'Did you manage to secure Dillon's corpse? I saw you leave Tyburn with a coffin, but it was impossible to tell what was in it.'

'There were some problems.' Reynell did not elaborate, and Chaloner did not really want to be regaled with a grisly story, so they walked to the theatre in silence. Reynell glanced around a little furtively as they reached the stairs, as if he did not want to be seen.

'What is the matter?' asked Chaloner, immediately wary.

'We cannot let Wiseman know what we are doing. This is not the first time Lisle has been obliged to rectify his mistakes, and he is apt to be nasty about it. Lisle cannot afford a confrontation – not today, of all days – but no one is looking, so we are all right.'

Chaloner followed him down the stairs to the gloomy vault. This time, only four bodies were present. One did not have a sheet, and Chaloner recognised the thin, wan features of Sarsfield. Shirt laces still bit into the confectioner's throat, because Wiseman's dissection had focused on the abdomen, and the head and neck had so far been left alone.

'There you are, Heyden,' said Lisle, smiling genially. 'Come in, come in. I hope you do not mind me tending you in here, but I am terribly busy today, and this will save time.'

Chaloner was about to sit in the chair Lisle indicated, when the hairs on the back of his neck rose, and all his instincts warned him that he was being watched. He hesitated, and the covert glance passed between Lisle and his clerk confirmed that something was amiss. He began to back away, aiming for the door. He did not get far before Reynell produced the gun he had kept hidden under his coat, pointing it at Chaloner with a hand that was far from steady. Then came the sound of the door being closed, and Chaloner glanced around to see Johnson. He carried a sword, and the fact that its blade was stained red with blood suggested it was not the first time he had used it that day.

'Oh, dear,' said Lisle unhappily. 'I was hoping there would be no need for histrionics. Please sit down, Heyden. We will make this as fast and painless as possible.'

Johnson gripped his rapier in both hands, muttering something about the unruly mob he had been obliged to fend off at Tyburn. Meanwhile, Lisle held an implement that might have had a surgical application, but that he brandished like a cudgel, and Reynell cocked his weapon; it trembled in a way that was dangerous. Deftly, Lisle removed the sword and daggers from Chaloner's belt. He found the one in his sleeve, too, while the one from his boot had been confiscated at White Hall. Chaloner was weaponless, although not, he hoped, defenceless.

'There is no point in yelling for help,' said Lisle, smiling again. 'No one will hear you. The theatre will not be occupied for at least another two hours, and the walls to this basement are very thick. They were built that way to keep it cool for specimens, but they also serve to dampen sounds.'

390

Chaloner had no intention of wasting energy with howls for assistance. He assessed his chances of dodging around Johnson and reaching the door, and decided they were fair; the man did not look agile, although he was probably strong. The problem lay with Reynell and his shaking dag.

'What do you want?' he asked, speaking to give himself time to consider his options.

'You,' said Lisle simply. 'We want you.'

Chaloner was mystified, but then he understood. 'For your Private Anatomies?'

Lisle nodded, and suddenly his grin did not seem so genial. 'There is a great demand for them these days. The prisons cannot supply our needs, because we require *decent* corpses, not ones that are emaciated and covered in scabs. So, we are obliged to go elsewhere for material. You will be perfect.'

'*And* we shall have the reward from the Dutch,' added Johnson. 'You murdered an upholsterer, and the Netherlanders have offered a thousand pounds for your head.'

'Is this why you wanted me to come today and not earlier?' asked Chaloner. 'You need me fresh?'

'Yes,' replied Lisle. 'I hope you did as I asked, and told no one else about our appointment.'

'I mentioned it to several friends,' countered Chaloner immediately. 'Men who are used to unravelling mysteries. They will certainly learn what you have done.'

Lisle shrugged. 'You would say that, but it is immaterial anyway. Johnson and Reynell will support me in saying that you went home after I removed the splint. I have also taken the precaution of giving you reason to despair – by telling everyone that your hand will never mend and that your viol-playing days are over. I will swear you left in low spirits, and you will not be the first to hurl yourself in the river, never to be seen again.'

Johnson addressed Lisle. 'You do realise that my friend will not be very pleased about his death? It will spoil his plans, and Reynell and I went to some trouble with . . . well, you know.'

'With what?' demanded Chaloner.

Lisle ignored him. 'What he wants is irrelevant. He asked for the favour to which you have just alluded, and he wanted documents signed and sealed. We have done all that, so our obligations to him are complete.'

'True, but he is in an excellent position to procure us corpses,' argued Johnson. 'I do not want to incur his displeasure when he might prove useful to us in the future. I dislike being forced to kill people, just because we are short of a good body, and he might provide us with an alternative source of material.'

Chaloner regarded him in distaste. 'You just go out and pick someone when you need a corpse?'

'We have no choice,' snapped Johnson. 'We tried using those of our patients who died from natural causes, but their families kept declining to let us have them, even when we offered to pay. We cannot disappoint powerful courtiers, so we have no alternative but to hasten the end of a few nobodies.'

Lisle rolled his eyes. 'We can hardly oblige your friend by letting Heyden live now you have told him all that, Johnson! Hurry up and make an end of this – there is a lot to do before the dissection this afternoon, and we cannot afford to waste time.'

Chaloner's mind was working fast. 'Did you arrange for Fitz-Simons to be killed, because you wanted his body?'

'Of course not!' cried Reynell, shocked. 'What do you think we are? He was a friend – a barber-surgeon.'

'Then why is there a different body in your charnel house, marked with his name?'

'We have already told you,' replied Reynell impatiently. 'Wiseman realised Fitz-Simons was the so-called "assassin" shot by May, and we could not allow his misguided actions to bring our Company into disrepute, so we were obliged to snatch him from White Hall before anyone could identify him.'

'I put another corpse in the charnel house, to deflect any awkward enquiries,' added Johnson, pleased with himself for considering all eventualities. 'But my precautions were unnecessary, because no one has come. And, before you ask, he really *did* bequeath us his corpse, to be used for the edification of our apprentices.'

'And what about Webb? Was he murdered to provide you with a specimen?'

'Certainly not,' said Johnson indignantly. 'I have just told you we only take nobodies.'

'You exchanged his fat body for a waif from the prisons, though,' surmised Chaloner, not sure whether to believe him. 'I imagine you made the swap in St Paul's, while Webb was waiting to be jammed into the tiny space allotted to him.'

'The vergers we bribed were relieved when we offered a solution to their predicament,' gloated Johnson. 'Little Martin Webster slipped into Bishop Stratford's tomb a lot more easily than the portly Webb would have done. Everyone was a winner in that bargain.'

'Except Webb. Does Silence know?'

'Goodness me, no!' exclaimed Lisle. 'She would be furious – and might even demand a share of our profits.

You *will* die today, Heyden, so you may as well go quietly. Come and sit down, and let Johnson bring an end to this unsavoury business. He is a surgeon and knows how to do it quickly. There will be very little pain, I promise.'

Chaloner made a sudden lunge for Reynell's gun. The clerk shrieked in alarm, and the weapon discharged, making everyone duck. Chaloner emerged the victor, but the dag had been fired, so was useless until it could be reloaded. He lobbed it hard at Lisle, but the man flinched away, and it cracked harmlessly into the wall behind him. Johnson advanced with his sword, but Reynell, desperate to arm himself, got in his way as he dived towards Lisle's tray of surgical implements. Their momentary tangle allowed Chaloner to grab a broom.

Lisle sighed. 'There is no point bucking against the inevitable, so just let us do our business. You will not be missed. You have no family in the city, and when you disappear, your colleagues will assume you could not bear the thought of a life without music. So be reasonable, Heyden. Do not make this harder for all of us.'

'How many people have you killed?' asked Chaloner, backing away quickly when Reynell laid hold of a long knife. He managed to reach the tables on which the bodies lay, using them as a barrier between him and the relentless advance of his three assailants.

'Do not tell him,' advised Reynell, feeling his knife's blade and wincing when he cut himself. 'It is none of his business, and he is only trying to distract us.'

But Johnson was of a mind to be garrulous, presumably because it was not often that he had the opportunity to brag about his achievements. 'I cannot recall, precisely. It has been about six months since we started, but we avoid slaughter when we can. I have put it about that we receive corpses with no questions asked, and people have been very obliging.'

'We anatomise them, then give them a decent burial in St Olave's Church,' elaborated Lisle. 'It is only right that the subject gets something out of the arrangement.'

'Very noble,' said Chaloner. 'Then tell me how many people you have killed this week, if you cannot recall all the poor souls you have dispatched over the last half year.'

'You will be our fourth,' said Johnson. He glanced up at the ceiling, counting on his fingers. 'Yes, just three others this week.'

'Fanning and Sarsfeild,' said Chaloner in disgust. 'Men in prison, unable to defend themselves.'

'Fanning, yes, Sarsfeild no,' said Johnson. 'May let slip that he was going to help Fanning escape from Newgate, you see. We could not afford to lose such a good, strong specimen, so I bribed a warden to let me at him first. Then I bribed him a second time to record a verdict of gaol-fever.'

'Was it the same warden who later had an "accident"? He was hit by a cart?'

Johnson was defensive. 'He took our money, then started telling everyone that Fanning had a cord around his neck. He could not be trusted, so I dispatched him. We would have added *him* to our collection, too, but he was too badly mangled.'

'So, Fanning and the warden are two,' said Chaloner. 'Who is your third victim?'

'We plan to dissect him this afternoon,' said Lisle comfortably. 'For the Public Anatomy.'

'I thought Dillon was—'

'Dillon is too fresh, and will bleed,' said Lisle impatiently.

'Our guests do not want to see that sort of thing, so we procured another fellow yesterday.'

Chaloner ripped the sheet from one of the cadavers, evading a wild blow from Johnson's sword at the same time. A squat man lay there, with an old scar on his neck. Blood had pooled on the table beneath him; the fatal injury had been to his back. Chaloner's thoughts tumbled in confusion. He matched the description of the man Scot had seen visiting Behn after dark, and whose corpse Eaffrey had discovered in Behn's office. Now Chaloner knew what had happened to it. The surgeons had evidently been pleased to get it, because the limbs had already been detached, probably for students.

Chaloner jerked away from Johnson's blade a second time, and tore the cover from the next subject. Willys's waxen face stared at him. 'How did you get—?'

'Holles was kind enough to ask *me* to deliver him to his own parish,' said Johnson, pleased with himself. 'A scrofulous beggar is now in Willys's grave, and we have a fine, disease-free subject to dissect for Brodrick, although we shall have to keep his face covered, as they knew each other.'

Chaloner dragged the sheet away from the last body, expecting to see Dillon, but what he saw made his stomach lurch in horror. William Scot lay there, peaceful and relaxed in death. Chaloner felt the walls closing in around him, and for a moment was aware of nothing but the pounding of his own heart.

'Dear God, no!' he whispered.

'It is the scientific gentleman from Ireland,' explained Lisle. 'Peter Terrell. For some inexplicable reason, he came here last night, so Johnson dispatched him with a blow to the head. It is a good way to kill, because it does not damage anything we need for our dissections.'

Shock had allowed Chaloner's guard to slip, and Johnson managed to grab his arm before he came to his senses and repelled him with a punch to the jaw. The surgeon reeled away, while Chaloner's numbed mind worked feverishly to analyse the information. He had told Scot that Lisle planned to remove his splint, and somehow Scot had learned Lisle was not the kindly healer he appeared to be and had come to investigate. They had killed him, and intended to use him for their grotesque dissection that afternoon. Chaloner gazed at his friend's still face, and made up his mind that it would not happen, no matter what the cost.

'Is your entire Company complicit in this monstrous plot?' he demanded, stepping briskly around the table to avoid Reynell's knife. His wits were suddenly sharp and clear, as they always were in desperate situations. He removed his hat – the one he had used to steal Prynne's gunpowder – and hurled it, ostensibly at Lisle, but it landed on the lamp. Flames licked towards it. 'Or just you three?'

'The "entire Company" does not bear the responsibility of securing its future,' replied Lisle tartly. 'Arrogant fellows like Wiseman sit back and enjoy the benefits of belonging to a licensed guild, but it does not run on air. It is my duty, as Master, to ensure we are solvent. These Private Anatomies are an excellent way to achieve our aim, and I salute Reynell's ingenuity in devising such a plan.'

'You keep some of the profit for yourselves, though,' said Chaloner. 'Wiseman has noticed your sudden upturns in fortune – your generosity in donating implements to the hospitals, Johnson moving in expensive Court circles, and Reynell's suspiciously fine clothes.'

Reynell was becoming unsettled by the amount of time that was passing. 'We should hurry. I keep thinking Wiseman might come, wanting to know whether this afternoon's corpse is ready.'

'He will not stop us,' said Lisle. 'He is poor, because Webb's scurrilous lies have destroyed his medical practice – his silence can be bought.'

'And if he proves awkward, then there are always uses for a large cadaver like this,' added Johnson, a little longingly.

'Where is Dillon?' asked Chaloner. Smoke was curling from his hat. 'Did he escape after all?'

'Do not answer – just dispatch him,' begged Reynell. 'People will start to arrive for the Public Anatomy soon – they always come early, to get good seats – and it would be awkward if someone came down here by mistake and saw us chatting to a future subject.'

'We shall dissect *you* for Lady Castlemaine,' said Lisle with his pleasant smile. 'It will be the first time a woman has requisitioned a performance, and you are sure to please her.'

'Then she is going to be disappointed,' said Chaloner, launching himself forward and bowling Reynell from his feet. When the clerk tried to stand, Chaloner hit him under the chin with his knee, forcing his head back against a wooden table with a dull thump.

Johnson clutched his sword in both hands and came at Chaloner with a howl of fury, so the spy was obliged to jump hastily behind the table. At that moment, the flame reached the remnants of the gunpowder in his hat, and it puffed like a firework. It was not much of a display, but it made Johnson spin around in alarm, allowing Chaloner to throw the broom at him while he was distracted. It struck his jaw hard, and he stumbled into Scot's body, snatching at it desperately in a effort maintain his balance. Then he and the corpse crashed to the floor together, and the surgeon gave a yelp of disgust as he tried to free himself from the cold, flopping limbs.

Meanwhile, Lisle raced towards Chaloner, brandishing his surgical cudgel. He swung it with all his might. Chaloner raised his hand to protect his head, and there was a sharp crack as the splint broke. Lisle lunged again, while Reynell moved groggily to grab Chaloner's foot, making him fall. The spy became aware of gagging sounds behind him, and wondered what was wrong with Johnson. He glanced around, and Lisle used his momentary inattention to strike again. The dressing took another monstrous blow that sent waves of shock up Chaloner's arm.

'That is enough!' came an authoritative voice. It was Wiseman. 'Desist immediately.'

'Thank heavens you are here,' said Lisle, lowering his weapon in apparent relief. 'We were preparing the subject for this afternoon, when Heyden arrived and began to run amok. You can see Reynell and Johnson covered in blood from his attack. Seize him quickly, while he is down.'

Chaloner sagged. There was no point in protesting his innocence, or in telling Wiseman what he had learned. It was so outlandish that he would be wasting his breath.

'Actually, I heard enough to know exactly what is going on,' said Wiseman haughtily. 'I have suspected for some time that the handsome specimens you use in your Private Anatomies are not from prisons, and I resolved to discover how you came by them. I set a trap, using Heyden as bait.'

Chaloner scrambled to his feet. 'What?'

The surgeon stepped into the vault, and continued to address Lisle. 'I told the porter to let me know when Heyden arrived to see you. I knew you would be unable to resist him – a man with transient friends and no London family. I applied an especially robust splint, knowing *he* would be desperate to be rid of it, and *you* would be equally willing to oblige him.'

Lisle glared at him. 'You abused a patient to entrap me?'

'To catch you in the act,' corrected Wiseman. 'And I have done it, too.'

'No one will believe you,' said Lisle, although there was an uneasy expression on his face. 'Most of our Company find you arrogant, disagreeable and rude, so no one will take your word over mine.'

Wiseman's smile was unpleasant. 'I do not care what my colleagues think, because I have him.' He gestured over his shoulder, and Chaloner saw Williamson framed in the doorway.

'I heard enough to hang you,' said the Spymaster coolly. He turned to the soldiers who were ranged behind him. 'Arrest them all.'

'And if Mr Williamson is not a powerful enough witness, there is always him,' said Wiseman, pointing to the floor, where Johnson was gasping for breath. Scot's corpse was on top of him, and Chaloner saw with a start that its hands were fixed firmly around the surgeon's throat. Scot was alive, and busily throttling the man who had tried to kill him.

*　　*　　*

'You should not have stopped me,' said Scot resentfully, sitting in Wiseman's chambers a short while later. He was pale, and there was a sizeable lump where Johnson had struck him, but he was quickly regaining his customary composure. 'The fate they had in mind for me was horrible, and I do not trust the law-courts to hand down a suitable sentence.'

Wiseman did not agree. 'They may not hang at Tyburn, but there are other means of dispensing with people, especially if you are Williamson. You should be aware of this – you work for the man.'

'How do *you* know that?' demanded Chaloner, immediately wary. Scot was ruthlessly careful, and did not confide in just anyone. Wiseman would be one of the last people to earn his trust, especially as Scot had said on several occasions that he was wary of the man.

Wiseman sighed impatiently. 'Because government intelligencers live dangerously, and I am a surgeon with a Court appointment. Williamson often summons me to help his people, and so does Lord Clarendon. I ask no questions, because it is safer that way, but I know what you two do.'

Chaloner glanced at Scot. 'Is it true?'

'He has been the unofficial "surgeon to spies" since the Restoration, and I am surprised you have never had recourse to call on his services.' Scot turned to the smug medic. 'What will happen to the Public Anatomy? Will you cancel it now Lisle and Johnson are unavailable?'

'There is no need for that,' replied Wiseman comfortably. 'Not when *I* – the Company's most accomplished practitioner – am ready to save the day. The demonstration will go ahead as planned.'

'On Willys?' asked Chaloner in distaste. 'You intend

401

to use him, even though his corpse was snatched from its grave?'

Wiseman rubbed his chin ruefully. 'Lisle was right about one thing. Dillon *will* bleed if we use him – his lengthy scaffold speeches mean he has not been dead long enough for the bodily fluids to settle. Meanwhile, the other corpses in the basement have been partially dissected already. Willys is our only choice.'

'You cannot use Dillon, anyway,' Scot pointed out. 'No one seems to know where he is.'

'Johnson does,' said Chaloner, 'but he is refusing to say.'

Wiseman was unhappy. 'I hope Williamson finds him soon. It will be bad for the Company if his corpse appears somewhere public. People will think we are careless with them.'

'And that would never do,' said Chaloner acidly. He was torn between anger at having been used as a tethered goat to entrap Lisle, and relief that Scot had risen from the dead.

Wiseman grinned. 'I suppose I owe you an apology, although, as Clarendon's man, you must be pleased with the outcome – you have successfully eliminated Johnson, one of your master's nastiest enemies. Perhaps I *should* have taken you into my confidence, and asked whether you minded lending a hand – literally, in this case – but I thought my plan would work better if you were kept in the dark. Besides, I mentioned several times that Lisle and Johnson had recently become inexplicably wealthy, but you did not take the hint and offer to investigate.'

'I did not know it was a hint,' objected Chaloner. 'I thought you were just talking.'

'I never just talk,' declared Wiseman. 'Everything I say is worth listening to – and acting upon.'

402

'Lord Clarendon *will* be delighted to learn Johnson is so spectacularly disgraced,' said Scot, when Chaloner snorted his disbelief. 'Especially if some of the mess can be made to stick to Bristol.'

'Perhaps so, but there was still no need to maim me. I would have helped to expose Johnson and his gruesome dealings, and performing bad surgery was both unnecessary and unethical.'

Wiseman grimaced at the reprimand. 'Well, it is done now, and to make amends, I shall remove the splint. You will play your viol this evening as though nothing has happened.'

'Good,' said Chaloner coldly. 'Because if I find I cannot, I shall return and brain you with it.'

'Do not be bitter,' said the surgeon with his irritating unflappability. 'We have just apprehended three very dangerous criminals *and* you saved your colleague into the bargain. If you had not arrived when you did, he would be down in the basement now, having his veins waxed.'

When he went to fetch what he needed for his operation, Chaloner turned to Scot. 'I thought you said he could not be trusted, but now it transpires that he works for Williamson, too.'

Scot shrugged. 'I do not trust *anyone* at White Hall, no matter what his credentials, and there *is* something sinister about the man. I was right anyway – normal people do not use patients to trap their errant colleagues, after all.'

Wiseman returned with a huge pair of shears. 'Tell us again what happened, Scot,' he ordered as he sat in front of Chaloner. 'How did Johnson come to wallop you on the head with his bone chisel?'

Scot touched the lump and winced. 'It is very simple.

403

Chaloner told me Lisle was planning to "help" him today, because you had bungled the original treatment. However, I knew you were unlikely to make the kind of mistakes Lisle had accused you of, so I decided to spy on the man and his domain. I was exploring the Anatomical Theatre when Johnson jumped me – to my eternal shame. I was in and out of awareness for hours, and only came to properly when he dragged me to the floor.'

Chaloner scowled at Wiseman. 'If you had not encouraged Lisle to want my corpse, I would not have agreed to keep an appointment with him, and Scot would not have come to save me. Your plan put us both in danger.'

Wiseman waved a hand to show he thought it did not matter, and began to ply his shears. 'Lisle did something right at least – this splint will be easier to remove now it is cracked. And it saved your arm without a doubt. I would have been amputating by now, had Lisle's blows done what he intended.'

Scot watched him. 'I thought you had invented some mysterious compound to dissolve your glue. Why are cutters necessary?'

'I lied,' said Wiseman. 'There is no compound on Earth that can dissolve a Wiseman Splint.'

'I do not understand much of this,' said Chaloner, talking to take his mind off the fact that a man he did not like was labouring over his arm with a very sharp implement. He was sure he could work everything out for himself, but he did not want to sit in silence. 'Can we go over it again? Webb was stabbed by Dillon and Fanning on the orders of their master. Who is he? Behn?'

Scot nodded slowly. 'I certainly think so, but we shall never know for certain, given that both assassins are dead and Behn is unlikely to confess without their testimony.

Meanwhile, someone must have witnessed the murder, and wrote to Bristol about it. Fanning and Dillon *were* guilty, but the other seven names were included for spite.'

'Because someone does not like spies,' agreed Wiseman, wiping sweat from his forehead. 'This fellow struck Williamson hard by exposing his people.'

Scot nodded. 'And I know you disagree, Chaloner, but I am sure the writer *did* mean Garsfield, not Sarsfeild. The confectioner was very unlucky.'

Chaloner was beginning to think it might be true, mostly because his favourite suspect for composing the note was May, and May would never pass up an opportunity to harm him.

Scot read his mind. 'May is not sufficiently clever. I think it is Behn again. There is something very odd about that man – just ask Eaffrey. She will not like it, but I do not want them together again. You know what I mean, Chaloner. I would rather be poor than see her in danger.'

'*I* have no idea what you are talking about,' said Wiseman cheerfully. He was panting heavily. 'But do not enlighten me – I am almost certainly safer not knowing. Lord! I did a magnificent job with this splint. It is as hard as a rock, and the secret ingredient I added worked better than I could have hoped. I shall be a wealthy man once I perfect it. Everyone with broken limbs will want one.'

Chaloner flinched when the blades gazed his arm, and hastily resumed his analysis. 'Behn *is* dangerous. Eaffrey said he killed some sort of accomplice in his office, and that man is now in the basement with his limbs cut off, ready to be anatomised.'

Scot's face was pale. 'You mean the fellow with the scarred throat? *He* is dead? Christ!'

Chaloner turned his thoughts to Webb again. 'All three men who were convicted of Webb's murder are now dead – although Fanning did not have gaol-fever and Sarsfeild did not kill himself. Dillon was hanged, though.'

'Was he?' asked Scot. He touched the back of his head again, and winced. 'I was not there, if you recall. Did you see the body? Feel for a lifebeat? Put a glass against his lips to test for breath?'

'*I* did not,' said Wiseman, exchanging shears for a saw and working furiously. The room began to smell of burning glue, and Chaloner hoped the dressing would not ignite. 'That was Lisle and Johnson's responsibility.'

'You let Lisle and Johnson pronounce life extinct?' echoed Scot incredulously. 'Then perhaps there is a good reason for Dillon's disappearance – such as he was cut down before he was dead and is now with his mysterious master. It is probably not the rescue he had in mind, but if it worked . . . '

'It is possible, I suppose,' admitted Wiseman, changing the angle of the saw. 'But let us return to our summary. Johnson admitted to killing Fanning, but denied touching Sarsfeild. I believe him. Why confess to one murder, but not another? We should have asked whether he dispatched Willys, too.'

'Then who did kill Sarsfeild?' asked Chaloner. 'Someone went to his cell disguised as a vicar and murdered him. If it was not Johnson, then who was it? Behn? May?'

'I have no idea,' said Wiseman, mopping his brow. His customary composure had begun to slip, and he looked sheepish as he gestured to the splint. 'I am afraid I was so determined to trap Lisle that I made my glue a touch

406

too hard, and you have compounded the problem by climbing walls, brawling and trying to play the fiddle. It is no way to treat these inventions.'

'What are you saying?' demanded Chaloner.

'That is stuck. I cannot get it off.'

'It is not stuck,' said Chaloner quietly. 'Believe me, you do not want it to be stuck.'

Wiseman bent to the task again. The soft menace in Chaloner's words seemed to have had an effect, because he renewed his efforts until he was red-faced and breathless. Then there was a loud crack. While Wiseman gripped the splint with both hands, Chaloner hauled with all his might in the opposite direction, and eventually managed to wriggle, pull and twist himself free. It cost most of the hair on his forearm and the skin on his knuckles, but these were small prices to pay for freedom.

'It is a good thing his bones were not really broken,' said Scot, as he watched. 'If they had been, the violent removal of the dressing would have snapped them again.'

'True,' mused Wiseman unhappily. 'My splint will hold a damaged limb immobile for as long as it remains in place, the only disadvantage being that it might have to remain in place for life.'

'I think you had better devise another way to make your fortune,' said Scot, laughing. 'You are liable to be sued by unhappy patients with this invention.'

'How does it feel, Heyden?' asked Wiseman, reaching out to examine him.

Chaloner pulled away. 'Like it no longer requires a surgeon.'

Chapter 12

The advertised Public Anatomy on the body of William Dillon, felon, was well attended, and Chaloner was astonished by how many people the Company of Barber-Surgeons had managed to cram into its theatre. He was even more surprised by how many he recognised, thinking it was not long ago that he did not know a soul in London.

Temple and Brodrick were among the first to arrive, talking and laughing to each other in a way that made them appear to be good friends. Chaloner was uneasy, wondering why Clarendon's cousin should so suddenly seek out the company of a man who was so open in his disdain for the Earl – especially as it had only been a month since one had hit the other with a candlestick, and only three days since they had sniped and bickered at Eaffrey's dinner party. Perhaps Thurloe was right after all, and Brodrick was not the loyal kinsman he claimed to be. Holles was with them, cautious and watchful. He spotted Chaloner and raised an eyebrow, although the spy could not tell whether the 'greeting' was friendly or otherwise. Chaloner nodded back, trying to decide why Holles should choose to attend such an exhibition; the colonel had openly admitted to being squeamish.

Williamson was also there, May at his side. May's gaze fell on Chaloner, and he muttered something that made the Spymaster laugh. Scot, clothing and manners adjusted to Peter Terrell, flitted here and there, exchanging bows with people he thought might speed his brother's release. When Eaffrey arrived with Alice and Behn, he went immediately to kiss her hand, and Chaloner saw her mutter a prayer of relief that he was safe. Without thinking, Alice ran to hug her brother, to show Eaffrey was not the only one who had been worried about him. 'Terrell' hastened to pass off the gesture as a joke, but Chaloner saw that Temple was suspicious. Realising with horror that she had almost given Scot away, Alice tried to pretend it was a case of mistaken identity. Her garbled 'explanations' were making matters worse, so Chaloner went to intervene.

'Did you enjoy yourself this morning?' he asked, saying the first thing that came into his head. It was meant to be an innocuous enquiry that would divert attention away from Scot, but he had forgotten she had missed the hanging because her clothes were caught in the seat.

She glared at him. 'Not as much as I would have done, had the condemned man been you.'

He winced. 'You have a savage tongue, Alice.'

'She is a tad sharp,' agreed Temple. Chaloner grimaced a second time; he had not meant his comment to be overheard. Temple turned to Brodrick, laughing. 'Did I ever tell you that her brother sent me a letter offering a vast sum of money if I agreed to leave her? I shall not take him up on his invitation, because it is common knowledge that Alice is the only Scot with any cash, and were I to accept his "generous" settlement, he would almost certainly default on payment.'

Alice gaped at him, while Terrell was suddenly nowhere to be seen. 'William was going to *pay* you to abandon me?' she demanded, aghast. 'Why did you not mention this before?'

Temple shrugged. 'It gave me cause to laugh for an hour, and then I forgot about it. He is irrelevant, anyway. I like you well enough, and your money will allow me to buy that plantation I want. What more can a man ask? Bristol spoke to the King on my behalf yesterday, and His Majesty said I can have you, should I feel so inclined.'

Alice's hearing became highly selective; she smiled broadly. 'You intend to marry me?'

Temple shrugged again. 'Why not? We each have something the other desires – you will acquire a hand-some husband with a glittering future in British politics; I will get a woman with plenty of ready cash. Well, what do you think? Shall we do it?'

'Yes!' she cried, eyes shining. 'I accept!'

'You old romantic,' said Brodrick to Temple. 'There is a silver tongue on you, no doubt about it.'

Temple inclined his head graciously, then sauntered away with his new friend, leaving his bride-to-be gazing after him in delight.

'I wish you much happiness, Alice,' said Chaloner, feeling he should say something nice to mark the occasion. He wondered what Scot would say when he learned his sister was lost.

'And I shall have it, too,' she replied, sounding as though there would be trouble if she did not. 'What are you doing here? Did you come because you heard us

410

talking about Webb's dissection at Eaffrey's party, and you wanted to see one for yourself?'

'How did the surgeons acquire Webb's body?' asked Chaloner, curious to know how such an odd occurrence had been explained to the spectators. 'It was supposed to have been buried in St Paul's.'

Alice watched Temple take his seat. 'My Richard made a joke to Surgeon Johnson, remarking on the irony of him commissioning a Private Anatomy, when a man who had tried to cheat him was newly dead. He asked whether it was possible to combine the two, and we were both rather startled when Johnson replied – quite seriously – that he would see what he could do.'

'Then what?'

'A few days later, he said he had devised a way to acquire Webb's corpse, but that it would cost extra. He said merchants' entrails are oilier than those of normal men, so more money is needed to clean up afterwards. I agreed to pay the difference, because Richard was so eager to see inside Webb. You look disapproving. Why? It was all perfectly ethical.'

'Was it?'

'Of course. Webb's body was *lent* to the surgeons after his funeral, and what is left of him will go back inside his cathedral tomb. That is what Johnson told us. He asked us not to mention it to Silence, though, because she was not invited to the cutting, and he did not want her to take offence. And now you must excuse me, or I will lose my place next to Richard.'

She slipped away, leaving Chaloner full of questions. He was watching Samuel Pepys and a host of navy commissioners ushered into seats of honour, when Wiseman approached and spoke quietly.

'Do not think too badly of our Company, just because of Lisle and Johnson. It is full of good men. Lisle is vocal about the amount of time he spends with the poor, but many others do an equal or greater amount of charitable work – they just do not brag about it.'

'We shall probably never know how many people Johnson killed,' said Chaloner, not of a mind to be forgiving about such heinous activities.

'No, probably not,' admitted the surgeon. He sighed. 'But the audience is growing restless, so I had better begin my demonstration before there is a riot. People are always impatient to see me at work. Are you going to stay? My invitation to you still stands.'

'I have seen more than enough surgery and anatomy for one day, thank you.'

Wiseman grimaced. 'I did what I thought was right, Heyden, and I would do the same again. Thanks to me, men can rest easy in their coffins tonight, knowing they will stay there.'

He went to stand next to the dissecting table, to make sure all was in order. Willys had arrived, and lay with a cloth bag tied firmly around his head. The barber-surgeons were taking no chances of it slipping off and revealing his identity. Then the lecture began, and Chaloner became interested, despite himself. After a while, he saw Eaffrey slip away from Behn, and indicate with a discreet flicker of her eyes that she wanted to speak privately. He waited a few minutes, so they would not be seen leaving together, then followed.

Outside, the air was clean and fresh, a pleasant change from the stuffy atmosphere in the Anatomical Theatre, where every man and some women puffed away on pipes, and the odour of overheated bodies, unwashed clothes

412

and the corpse mingled unpleasantly. In the sunshine, Chaloner could smell newly scythed grass and warm earth.

'Thank you for finding William,' said Eaffrey, when he joined her in the Great Parlour's cool, cloister-like undercroft. 'I knew you would not let me down. I cannot tell you how worried I have been. What happened?'

'He fell into the hands of men who wanted to make an exhibition of him,' replied Chaloner vaguely. His sleepless night was taking its toll, and he was too tired to embark on complex explanations. Scot could decide how much he wanted her to know about his escapade himself.

'Did you find your killer? The man who murdered Webb?'

'Dillon and Fanning did it, but on someone else's orders. I am inclined to suspect May, but Scot believes it is Behn.'

Eaffrey swallowed hard, but did not leap to Behn's defence. 'Your Irish alias *was* on Bristol's letter, Tom,' she said after a moment, raising her hand when Chaloner tried to speak. 'I visited Thurloe this morning, and he showed me the original note. He has a special glass that magnifies writing, and I saw quite clearly how the name had been changed from Garsfield to Sarsfeild. You obviously have a friend – someone who knows no powerful patron would step forward and provide *you* with a King's pardon or let you "disappear".'

'Why would anyone help me? Other than Thurloe?'

'Perhaps someone owes an obligation to the Chaloner clan. Perhaps you saved a life once, and that person found himself in a position to reciprocate. Perhaps someone did not want Lord Clarendon to lose his best spy. There are all kinds of possibilities.'

Chaloner tried to make sense of it. 'May wrote the letter, so the name must have been changed *after* he sent it to Bristol. But I doubt Thurloe was ever in a position to tamper with it – if he had been, he would not have asked me to steal it, because he would already have known what it said. And nor would he have let innocent Sarsfeild be incarcerated in Newgate on my behalf.'

'Lord Clarendon, then. At a time when half the Court is baying for his blood, trustworthy allies are important. However, your mysterious friend obviously wants to remain anonymous, or he would have made himself known to you, so my advice is to forget about him. You say Dillon and Fanning murdered Webb, and they are dead, so let that mark the end of the matter. We shall see Dillon dissected today, and then the whole affair can be buried with him.'

'It is Willys being dissected, not Dillon. Did you notice how the cloth is *tied* around the corpse's head, instead of being laid across its face? Many influential courtiers are here, and they might make a fuss if they learn Bristol's aide has been providing their afternoon's amusement.'

Eaffrey made a moue of distaste. 'Are you sure it is him?'

'As sure as I can be about anything on this case. I have answers to some questions, but not all. Who killed Willys? Who dressed as a vicar and strangled Sarsfeild? Why did May send that letter to Bristol, when the ruse could have misfired and seen him dismissed?'

'Actually,' came a voice far too close behind him, 'you are quite wrong about May.'

Chaloner spun around to see a tall figure wearing a cloak and a hat that shaded his eyes and the top half on his face. The rest was dominated by a sardonic grin.

*　　*　　*

There was a sword in Dillon's hand, and he held it in a way that suggested he was about to use it. Eaffrey gasped in horror, and Chaloner reached for his own weapon. It was not there, and he realised with a shock that he had neglected to retrieve it after Johnson had disarmed him. He backed away, looking for something with which to defend himself, but the undercroft was just an open-sided vault with pillars and a flagstone floor. And because it had been swept for the Public Anatomy, there was not so much as a twig or a pebble that could be lobbed.

'I saw you hanged!' breathed Eaffrey, aghast. 'Are you some fiend, to evade death?'

Dillon ignored her. 'I have questions, Heyden,' he whispered. 'My master wants to know—'

'That is a dismal attempt at deception,' said Chaloner contemptuously, stepping behind one of the pillars when he recognised the man's true identity – Dillon had no reason to harm him, but someone else did. 'You are too tall to be Dillon, your voice is too deep and the hat is at the wrong angle.'

May ripped the offending item from his bald head. 'It was worth a try.'

'What do you want?' demanded Chaloner, pulling Eaffrey behind him.

'I want an end to the trouble you have caused me,' snapped May. 'I want you dead.'

Chaloner balanced lightly on the balls of his feet, ready to jump one way or the other when May attacked. 'What trouble? Perhaps we should go to see Williamson and—'

May snorted. 'I do not think so! You will try to usurp my position – to have yourself hired and me dismissed, because you think you are a better spy than me.'

'He *is* a better spy than you,' said Eaffrey, eyeing May

in distaste. 'But he has no desire to work for Williamson or steal your post as chief toady. Why would he, when he is content with Clarendon?'

May sneered. 'Every decent spy wants to be in the government's employ, so why should he be any different? He has done nothing but tell lies about me ever since we returned from Ireland. But I shall have my revenge. First, I shall kill him, and then I shall sit back and watch his reputation destroyed. I have taken the liberty of hiding one or two documents in pertinent places, and when they come to light, they will ensure his name will always be associated with ignominy.'

'That is an ungentlemanly thing to do,' said Eaffrey angrily.

'Ours is an ungentlemanly profession. And do not think *you* will avenge his death, madam, because I know about you – your real lover is Scot, and you intend to wed Behn for his money. If you attempt to harm me, I shall tell Behn, and you will be poor for the rest of your life.'

'You are a pig!' spat Eaffrey in disgust. Chaloner glanced at her and wondered whether the threat was enough to buy her silence. She did not want her child born into poverty, and Scot would have no money once his sister – and her fortune – married the despicable Temple.

'What lies have I told about you?' he asked of May.

'About that letter to Bristol. I did *not* write it, and I resent the implication that I would expose the identities of my fellow agents. Your accusations have made my colleagues suspicious and wary of me. No doubt it is all part of your plan to usurp my place in Williamson's confidence.'

'It is nothing of the kind,' said Chaloner impatiently,

tensing when May made a practice sweep with his blade, making it whistle through the air. 'And what do you propose to do here? Kill me with half the Court within shouting distance?'

May smiled grimly. 'We both know no one will hear anything through those thick walls, not with Wiseman babbling about guts and bladders. You can holler all you like, but I will still skewer you.'

'Fetch Williamson, Eaffrey,' ordered Chaloner. He glanced around to see she had gone.

'She is a practical lady – and an ambitious one,' said May gloatingly. 'So do not expect help from that quarter. She will not risk a comfortable future just to save your miserable life.'

Before Chaloner could reply, May advanced with a series of well-executed sweeps. Chaloner ducked one way, then the other around the pillar, and May missed him by no more than the width of a finger.

'I should have dispatched you in White Hall', hissed the bald spy. 'I would have done, had Holles not stopped me. You had better draw, or this will be a very short fight.'

'I cannot draw,' said Chaloner, deeply unimpressed by the man's powers of observation. 'You can see I have no sword.'

May swished his blade triumphantly. 'Then you should have come better prepared. Are you going to duck and weave all day, or will you stand and die like a man?'

He darted forward, feinting at the last moment. Chaloner jigged away, but May's sword caught in the lace on his cuff. He knocked it free, then ran to another, thicker pier, hoping it would afford him greater protection.

'I waited outside your room last night,' said May, lunging hard and striking sparks from the pillar when his blade scored down the stone. 'But you have taken to sleeping elsewhere, and I wasted hours lurking in the darkness.'

'You ate a pie,' said Chaloner, remembering how a lack of peas had allowed him to conclude that it had not been Scot or Leybourn. 'You dropped crumbs all over the stairs. What did you want?'

'To kill you before you told anyone else about that letter.'

'Of course. Stealthy murder is no stranger to you, is it? You killed Willys and tried to have me blamed. You pretended to be a priest and strangled Sarsfeild in his cell. And it was you who ordered Fanning and Dillon to murder Webb.'

'There you go again,' snapped May, renewing his attack. He was furious, but although his blows were powerful, they were also wild, so Chaloner had no trouble evading them. 'Making accusations with no proof. I did *not* kill Webb, Sarsfeild, Willys or anyone else.'

'Then why did you shoot Fitz-Simons?' demanded Chaloner. He took a chance on an explanation. 'Because you wanted to stop him from telling Williamson what he knew – that *you* wrote the letter.'

'I did not even kill Fitz-Simons,' shouted May, exasperated. He grimaced and lowered his voice. 'I aimed and pulled the trigger, but the gun flashed in the pan. It was another man's ball that hit him.'

Chaloner did not know whether to believe him, and was puzzled enough that he was slow moving out of the way. May's sword caught him a stinging slash on the leg, although the sides of the weapon were too blunt to draw blood. He began to limp. 'You claimed credit at the time.'

'I did not *claim* it – it was given to me.' May grinned mirthlessly when he saw his blow had slowed his opponent down. He renewed his attack with greater purpose. 'One moment I was trying to work out why my gun had misfired, and the next I was being hailed as the hero who shot the King's would-be assassin. It happened so fast that I had no time to think. On reflection, I see I should have been honest, but it is easy to judge with hindsight and it is too late to do anything about it now.'

Chaloner remained sceptical, although his convictions were beginning to waver. He recalled the sizeable hole in Fitz-Simon's chest and his fleeting concern that it had been too large a wound to have been caused by May's handgun. 'If you did not kill Fitz-Simons, then who did?'

'I have no idea. At first, I assumed it was you, and was pleased when people started to give *me* the credit that should have been yours. Then Colonel Holles pointed out how the dag you had confiscated from Fitz-Simons was too filthy to work, and I knew you could not have been responsible. He witnessed the whole incident from the cathedral, you know.' May's voice was bitter. '*He* knows I did not fire the fatal shot.'

Chaloner's convictions wavered even more, mostly because he could not imagine May concocting a confession that showed him in such poor light. 'Then why has he not said anything about it?'

'I imagine because he intends to blackmail me. When I saw the body and recognised it as belonging one of Williamson's "occasional informers" I was appalled! I was obliged to hide its face with a bag to prevent anyone else from seeing. And then it disappeared, and I have been waiting on tenterhooks for the prankster – you – to bring it back in a way that will humiliate me even further. I have been living a nightmare this last week, and it is all your doing. But now you will pay.'

Chaloner jerked away from the flailing blade. 'You brought it on yourself by being dishonest. Put up your sword, May, and I will help you resolve this mess. We can talk to Holles, and—'

'You had your chance to do all that,' snarled May, 'but instead, you have concentrated on making accusations that harm me. Say your prayers, Heyden. The game is over for you.'

He changed the grip on his sword and his expression became fiercely determined. Chaloner made as if to run to the next pillar, but altered course at the last moment, and powered towards May instead. He saw the surprise in the man's eyes just as he reached him and snatched the weapon from his hand. It was absurdly easy, like taking honey-bread from a baby. May gaped in horror. Then there was a sharp crack and he crumpled to the ground. Chaloner spun around to see Scot standing there with a smoking gun, Eaffrey behind him.

'You cannot manage five minutes without me, Chaloner,' said Scot irritably. 'I warned you to be wary of the man, and what do you do? Allow him to entice you into a duel!'

Chaloner knelt to feel for a lifebeat in May's neck, but was not surprised to find there was none; Scot was a deadly shot. 'I was in no danger – I had just relieved him of his sword.'

'You sent me for help,' Eaffrey pointed out. 'So you were obviously worried about the outcome.'

'I sent you to fetch Williamson,' corrected Chaloner tiredly. 'I have no wish to see May dead.'

'The feeling was not reciprocated,' said Eaffrey tartly. 'He was going to kill you, and you had nothing with which to defend yourself. You seem sorry he is gone, but I am not. He was going to murder you and blackmail me to keep quiet about it.'

'I think I have done him a terrible injustice,' said Chaloner, sitting back on his heels. 'I am beginning to believe he was telling the truth when he said he did not send Bristol that letter.'

'Well, who did, then?' demanded Eaffrey. 'And why?'

'It was written in blue ink,' said Chaloner, rubbing his eyes. Fatigue was beginning to sap his energy and make him sluggish. 'Maude saw Behn in possession of missives scribed in distinctive blue ink.'

'So, I was right after all,' said Scot in satisfaction. 'I said days ago that the culprit was Behn.'

'What does this do to our plans?' asked Eaffrey, rather plaintively. 'Shall we devise another way to see our child raised in the manner of a gentleman?'

'Not necessarily,' said Chaloner, climbing slowly to his feet. 'The correspondence Maude saw was *received* by Behn, not *penned* by him – only very odd people write letters to themselves. So, the blue ink means he was *sent* notes from the same person who wrote to Bristol, not that he scribed them himself.'

Scot was becoming exasperated. 'Well, if it was not May or Behn, then who is left?'

'I have no idea. And nor do I know who shot Fitz-Simons. May was telling the truth about that, too, because I was surprised at the time that such a large wound could have been made by his dag.'

'But Holles *saw* May shoot him,' said Scot. He passed Chaloner his gun to hold, while he knelt to inspect the body himself. 'So May must have lying, although I cannot imagine why.'

'Put your hands in the air, Heyden,' ordered an imperious voice that made them all turn around. It was Spymaster Williamson. Holles and several members of the palace guard stood at his side, muskets at the ready, and Wiseman loomed behind them, his lecture notes folded into a bundle under his arm. 'Or I will give the order to shoot. Drop your weapons now!'

Chaloner did as he was told, letting May's sword clatter from his left hand and Scot's gun drop from his right. The Spymaster had chosen elite marksmen to accompany him, and Chaloner knew they would not hesitate to open fire. With weary resignation, he saw Williamson's gaze move from May, lying in a pool of his own gore, to the dag on the ground at his feet, and reach the obvious conclusion.

'May started it,' said Scot, also seeing the line Williamson's thoughts had taken. 'Ask Eaffrey.'

Williamson regarded Chaloner coldly. 'So, you decided to rid yourself of an old enemy once and for all, did you? Could you not have reasoned with him? Talked to him?'

'May was beyond reason,' said Scot, standing next to Chaloner, to indicate where his loyalties lay. 'You know what he is like once his temper is roused. He was insane enough to think he could disguise himself as Dillon – you can see that from his clothes – but he badly overestimated his talents. And *I* shot him, anyway.'

Chaloner could tell from the contemptuous expression on the Spymaster's face that he thought Scot was

422

protecting a friend with a false confession. He tried not to sag in defeat, suspecting Williamson would read resignation as guilt.

'*Is* Dillon dead?' asked Wiseman. 'Only I thought I saw him in the audience during my dissection. It gave me rather a shock, to be frank, and put me right off my stride.'

'That would have been May,' said Scot. 'Probably.'

Williamson continued to glare at Chaloner. 'Did May show you that letter before you gunned him down? Keep your hands in the air, or I *will* order Holles to open fire.'

'What letter?' asked Chaloner, hastening to comply.

Williamson nodded that Scot was to search May's body. Scot obliged, eventually locating a pocket sewn into the coat lining. He withdrew a piece of paper that was soiled and soft, as though it had been handled a lot. He scanned it quickly, then held it for Chaloner to read – the spy was not about to give Williamson an excuse to kill him by lowering his hands to take it. It was a brief note that said:

Noe Mann shoulde beare the insults of a Womann like Silens Webb. Lette her Husbande paye the pryce for her Vicious Tonge. If you succeede, the Summe of Twentie Pounds wille be Youres. And nor need you fear Reprisals against you. Youre Maister wille allow noe Mann to hange for Murdur, and God wille be Thankfull for your Ridding Him of this Devil's Sporn and soe wille I. Clarendon.

'It was among Dillon's possessions at Newgate,' said Williamson.

'Were there other letters, too?' asked Chaloner. 'In cipher?'

Williamson nodded. 'My clerks decoded them, but they all pertain to Fanning's attempt to leave Newgate via a barrel of poisoned ale. I cannot imagine why Dillon kept them.'

'Because he thought Fanning was wrong to escape,' explained Chaloner. 'Fanning offered to include him in the rescue, but Dillon declined, because he was utterly convinced that his employer would save him. He planned to show Fanning's letters to his patron later, to prove who had remained steadfast and who had not.'

Williamson was not very interested in Fanning's floundering trust. 'The important document is the one Scot holds, because it proves that Dillon and Fanning murdered Webb on *Clarendon's* orders. Dillon obviously kept the note to remind himself that salvation would be supplied – you can tell from the state of it that he read it again and again, seeking reassurance. So, now we know why he killed Webb, and why he thought he would suffer no punishment for it.'

'That is not Clarendon's signature, sir,' said Chaloner, disappointed in him; he had expected more from a man of Williamson's reputation. 'It is a forgery, and anyone can see it.'

Williamson raised an eyebrow. 'It looks authentic to me, and *I* see his mark with some regularity.'

'It is shaky and hesitant, because it was copied,' stated Chaloner firmly. 'His usual signature is free-flowing and confident. And that is not all. This note asks for someone to be murdered. Clarendon is not a fool, and would never append his own name to such an order.'

'That is true,' acknowledged Williamson. 'However, when I showed it to May, he pointed out that a man only exercises caution when there is a danger of his being

424

apprehended. His observation is a valid one; Lord Clarendon must have assumed he would not be caught.'

'I repeat: he is not a fool,' said Chaloner, thinking the same could not be said about May – or about Williamson for listening to him. 'He would never put his name to something like this, no matter how small the chances of discovery. And nor does he order a man murdered because he took offence at comments made by his wife.'

'It does seem out of character – he is not a violent person,' said Wiseman. His eyes widened in alarm when Chaloner shifted his position and six muskets rattled simultaneously as aim was adjusted. 'And *I* abhor unnecessary bloodshed, too. Will you put those things down before someone is hurt?'

'Not yet,' snapped the Spymaster as Holles started to comply. 'Not until Heyden has confessed to what he knows. And then we shall decide whether we shoot him here or he goes to the Tower. I would not stand in front of him, if I were you, Scot. Or you, Eaffrey. You both resigned today, so you are of no further use to me, and I do not care if I am obliged to shoot through you to reach him.'

'Move away,' murmured Chaloner to his friends. 'He means what he says. No wonder it is taking you so long to arrange Thomas's freedom, Scot. The man is ruthless.'

'I accept your reasoning, Heyden,' said Williamson, once Scot and Eaffrey had retreated to a safe distance. His face was cold and hard. 'Clarendon did *not* order Dillon to kill Webb. However, that means we are back to the beginning again, because we still do not know the identity of Dillon's master. So, *you* will provide me with the answer. If I am satisfied with it, I may let you live.'

'Me?' asked Chaloner uneasily. 'But I do not know—'

Williamson gave a nasty little smile, which put

Chaloner in mind of a lizard. 'Then you had better start doing some hard thinking. And if I am obliged to tell you *again* to keep your hands above your head, I shall order Holles to shoot them off.'

Chaloner knew he would carry out his threat, just to avenge May. He fought to shake off the weariness that was making his wits sluggish, struggling for an answer that would save his life.

'May,' blurted Scot. 'The master was May. He told Dillon—'

Williamson turned his reptilian glare on his ex-spy. 'May had invested a fortune with Webb, and Webb's death meant he lost most of it. He would *never* have killed the man. Try again.'

'I expect it was Behn,' said Wiseman with his customary confidence. Chaloner was grateful, because their suggestions were giving him time to assess his own conclusions and test them for flaws. 'Once Webb was dead, Behn persuaded Silence to make him a *gift* of Webb's ship. And Behn and Webb argued violently on the night of the murder – I saw them myself.'

'I think the killer is Silence,' countered Eaffrey, seeing what Wiseman and Scot were doing and eager to play her part. 'She is suddenly free and a wealthy woman.'

Williamson's smile was malicious. 'Not as rich as she believes, though. I saw Webb's last testament, and most of his fortune will go to the Guinea Company.'

'Company members, then,' said Scot, 'because they knew the terms of the will, and decided they wanted the windfall sooner rather than later. Further, Temple is without a serious business rival now Webb has gone, and—'

'Stop,' snapped Williamson. 'You are wasting my time

426

with your guesses. Well, Heyden? Let us hear whether your wits will save your life.'

Chaloner gestured to the letter, raising his hands again when Williamson's eyes narrowed. 'The note mentions an insult, and I think we can conclude that whatever Silence said to offend the writer was spoken at the Guinea Company dinner. We know it was busy that night, and that there were spats between a number of parties. However, Clarendon was *not* one of them, because he was not there. In addition, Silence likes the Earl, so would never have offended him. However, she did rail at someone by criticising his clothes and the way he smells.'

'You mean Bristol?' asked Williamson. 'Yes, I heard Silence gave him a piece of her mind about his old-fashioned costume and the odour of onions. He had made some jibe about women wearing an excessive number of face patches, and she responded in kind. Yet a powerful noble does not order someone murdered over such a trifling matter.'

'Silence brayed her comments to the entire Guinea Company,' said Chaloner. 'It would not have seemed trifling to Bristol. Besides, it was a good opportunity to have his arch-rival blamed for a crime, as attested by that ridiculous note. Can I put my hands down now, sir? They are—'

'No, you cannot. So, you think Bristol is Dillon's master?'

Chaloner nodded. 'Yes, but I do not think Dillon knew it. He told me he accepted commissions from a number of wealthy men after he betrayed Thurloe. Bristol was one, Clarendon was another—'

'Yes!' exclaimed Eaffrey. 'I saw Dillon's distinctive profile silhouetted in one of the Lord Chancellor's windows very late one night. I asked William to tell you about it.'

Chaloner continued. 'So, I think Dillon took the note at face value, and was anticipating that Clarendon would rescue him – the Earl is a powerful man, so Dillon had no reason to doubt his influence. Unfortunately for Dillon, Clarendon did not know what was being expected of him, because *he* was not the author of the letter. And Bristol – who *did* write it – could hardly show his hand by intervening.'

'Because that would lay him open to accusations of conspiracy to murder himself,' mused Williamson.

'There is a wine stain on the paper,' added Chaloner, pointing to it. 'I doubt it came from Dillon, who kept it safe, so it must have come from its writer. Bristol wrote it when he was drunk, without thinking through the consequences of his actions. It would not be the first time – he told Johnson and Willys to break into Clarendon's offices when he was drunk, too – and they went off and did it, as you know.'

It was some time before Williamson spoke. 'I shall compare this letter to Bristol's handwriting, and I imagine you might well be proven correct – this is a stupid note written by a man in wine-fuelled anger. I am sure he regretted it the following morning, when he realised Dillon had actually gone and done as he was ordered.'

'I expect he regrets it still,' said Scot wryly. 'The note promises the recipient twenty pounds, which is a colossal sum for an impecunious noble.'

'And it was definitely paid,' said Chaloner. 'Dillon was spending it on luxuries in Newgate.'

'So Thomas has solved your mystery,' said Eaffrey, making as if to leave and starting to pull Chaloner with her. 'And we have a lot to do if we are to sail to Surinam next week. We need to—'

'His insight does not make up for the fact that my best spy lies dead at his feet.'

'It was not—' began Chaloner, but what could he say? That the fatal shot had not come from him? Williamson had not believed Scot, and there was even less reason for him to believe Chaloner.

'I doubt Heyden killed May, sir,' said Holles. 'He is a poor warrior – I saw his incompetence myself, when May had him cornered in the Spares Gallery. One of the barber-surgeons' apprentices must have fired off a random ball, and then ran away when he saw what he had done.'

Williamson tapped his chin for a moment, thinking. 'I am about to turn a blind eye to the fact that Lord Bristol commissioned a murder. Meanwhile, Lord Clarendon will not want it put about that his spies go around shooting Grooms of the Privy Chamber. So, there is my solution: I shall spare Heyden's life in return for Clarendon's acquiescence about Bristol's antics.'

Chaloner sincerely hoped the Lord Chancellor would agree to the arrangement. The chance to strike a massive blow against his worst enemy was sure to be tempting.

'That is a fair decision,' said Holles, lowering his gun in relief.

'I suppose I shall get used to this kind of thing eventually,' said Williamson, 'although it goes against the grain to let a friend's killer go free in the interests of political expediency. Do not cross me again, Heyden. I swear I shall not be so generous the next time.'

Scot watched him stride away, the soldiers at his heels.

'That was close! You will have to come to Surinam with me now, Chaloner. You will not be safe here.'

Chaloner waited until Williamson was out of sight before making his move. He stalked towards Holles, ripped the man's dagger from his belt and held it to his throat. Holles's eyes widened in horror, and he looked around for his men. But they had followed Williamson, and he was alone.

'I spoke up for you,' he cried. 'I lied even – I happen to know you are very good with weapons. And I would never have obeyed his order to shoot you. What more do you want?'

'The truth about Fitz-Simons,' said Chaloner, not relinquishing his grip. Holles might have aimed elsewhere if the Spymaster had demanded an execution, but his men would not have done. 'You did not see May shoot him, did you?'

'I never said I did,' objected Holles, trying to free himself. He stopped struggling when the blade dug into his skin. 'I saw May take aim, but I could have told anyone that the fatal shot did not come from his dag – the angles were all wrong. But no one asked for my opinion, and Lord Clarendon told me to keep quiet about anything that might annoy May.'

'I do not think he meant you to keep *me* in the dark, too,' said Chaloner, exasperated with the soldier's literal interpretation of the order. 'You should have said something.'

'I did what I was told,' said Holles stubbornly. 'I have done nothing wrong.'

Chaloner was not so sure. 'Why are you here today? It is not to learn about anatomy, because I know you have an aversion to such things.'

430

'Brodrick is in the process of befriending Temple, to flatter him into confiding the details of Bristol's next attack on Lord Clarendon. I am here to protect Brodrick, because this feud has suddenly grown deadly.'

Chaloner released him. 'Then go and protect him.'

'He is a buffoon,' said Scot, watching the colonel stride away with his dignity in tatters. 'We should never have supported the Commonwealth all those years, Chaloner. It put soldiers in control of our country, and these military types are too stupid to make good leaders.'

'Yes,' said Chaloner bitterly. 'We are better with men like Williamson. He is an ethical fellow.'

The barber-surgeons' guests were milling about in the yard, waiting for the dinner bell to sound. Unhappy and flustered, Eaffrey went to join them, although Chaloner noticed that she avoided Behn and went to talk to the navy clerk – Pepys – and his friends instead. Then a bell rang, and the guests moved quickly towards the Great Parlour, eager to be at the food. It was not many minutes before the grounds were deserted again, and he and Scot were alone.

'Temple has asked Alice to marry him,' said Chaloner. He rubbed a hand across his face, now so tired he felt light-headed. 'She has accepted.'

'Damn!' muttered Scot, exasperated. 'She always was blind when it came to men, but Temple is by far the most unsuitable candidate to date. What should I do? Needle him into insulting me, so I can challenge him to a duel? Let her make her mistake and live a life of misery?'

'Arrange for some of her fortune to disappear,' suggested Chaloner, not pointing out that Temple was likely to live a far more miserable life than his new wife. 'He will not take her if she is poor.'

431

Scot slapped a hand to his forehead. 'Of course! I should have done it weeks ago. You always were good at devising non-violent solutions to problems. It is a virtue that will prove useful in Surinam.'

'I doubt it. From what I have read, Surinam is an unstable place, full of guns and knives.'

Scot took his arm, and guided him towards the now-deserted Anatomical Theatre, where Willys lay with his entrails neatly coiled on the side of the dissecting table. 'You should collect your sword and daggers before you meet someone else you want to fight.'

Chaloner had no wish to confront anyone else that day, although he knew his business was not yet done – he still did not know who had murdered Willys, Sarsfeild and now Fitz-Simons. He saw Behn lurking near the gate, and wondered why he had not gone for dinner with the other guests; Behn did not seem like the kind of man who would willingly forgo a sumptuous feast. Chaloner was simply too tired to think about it, though, and it was with leaden legs that he followed Scot down into the grim dungeon. He looked around for his weapons, but they were not there.

'Holles,' said Scot irritably. 'I saw his soldiers poking around after Lisle and Johnson were taken away. They must have stolen them.'

'Did Wiseman succeed in convincing everyone that Willys's body was Dillon's?' asked Chaloner. He leaned against a wall, and wondered when he had last felt so drained.

'Yes, he did. He even had an answer for when Alice demanded to know why there were no ligature marks on the neck. He spun some yarn about skin not bruising under certain chemical conditions. Can you bring yourself to

432

answer a few questions? I see now that the wicked master-mind behind Webb's murder was Bristol—'

'Not a wicked mastermind,' said Chaloner. 'A drunken fool who did something on the spur of the moment, and then declined to admit to what he had done. Poor Sarsfeild is the real victim in all this – Dillon and Fanning were killers, but the confectioner was not.'

'Quite so,' said Scot. He smiled kindly. 'But you are exhausted, and I can see you do not want to indulge my idle curiosity today, so we shall talk tomorrow, when you are feeling more alert. What will you do now? Join the barber-surgeons' dinner?'

'I am going home – to play my viol,' replied Chaloner, flexing his fingers. 'And then sleep.'

'You can play it all you like in Surinam. We will need something to entertain us in the evenings, because I under-stand there is not much to do once the sun goes down.'

'I cannot go to Surinam,' said Chaloner, not liking the notion of bowing solos for the rest of his life. 'London and its politics are bearable with music, and Surinam is humid – my viol will rot.'

'That is a pity. It is a chance for a new life.'

Chaloner nodded. 'And it will also ensure that I never tell anyone it was *you* who wrote that letter to Bristol – the one with the nine names.'

A gale of laughter billowed from the Great Parlour, followed by a cheer. The barber-surgeons were showing their guests a good time, and a distant part of Chaloner's mind recalled someone saying that watching dissections always gave men a good appetite. He regarded Scot with a mixture of disappointment and hurt, as the final pieces of the puzzle came together.

433

'You said you left African House early the night Webb died – you wanted to make the best of Behn's absence and be with Eaffrey. But Behn had quarrelled with Webb and stalked off in a sulk, leaving the dinner sooner than anyone had anticipated. So, you could not have been with Eaffrey, because *he* would have been there before you. You lied about that, and so did she.'

Scot gazed at him reproachfully. 'Why would we make up stories about such a thing?'

'Because almost immediately, I suspect Bristol regretted what he had asked Dillon to do, and sent someone to stop him: you. The landlord of the Dolphin recalled a second messenger asking for Dillon after the first note had been delivered. He said the man had a foreign accent, which put me in mind of Behn. However, you are skilled at disguises, and would never have gone on such a mission without donning one.'

Scot regarded him pityingly. 'Go home, Chaloner, before you say something you will regret. You are tired, and do not know what you are talking about.'

'And *that* is why you left the dinner early: to deliver Bristol's second note. But Dillon had already gone, so you went to Webb's home instead. Perhaps you were too late to stop the murder, or perhaps you decided it was in your better interests to let Webb die. Either way, you saw Dillon and Fanning kill him. Then you wrote that letter to Bristol.'

Scot sighed impatiently. 'Why would I do that? My name was on the list, too.'

'That is what May said when I accused him of sending it, and my answer to you is the same as the one I gave him: because it would have looked odd for it to be missing. And it was not your name, anyway. It was Peter Terrell's,

434

a man who can disappear today, if necessary, and be replaced by someone else. You risked nothing by including him.'

'This is rubbish,' said Scot warningly.

'You used blue ink,' Chaloner went on. 'The same kind you used to send letters to Behn – Maude saw them. You were doubtless working for him in another of your guises, making sure his money-making ventures came to fruition. After all, there is no point in defrauding a poor man, is there?'

'None of this is true. The messenger who went to the Dolphin was said to be a yellow-headed fellow. You can look among my collection of wigs – you will not find one like it.'

Chaloner was sorry. 'I told no one the landlord's description of the courier – and he swears I am the only one who has asked – so there is only one way for you to know about the fair hairpiece.'

Scot regarded him coldly. 'Why would I write that letter to Bristol? What would be in it for me?'

'Revenge for Williamson's failure to release your brother. You encouraged Thomas to turn traitor and give evidence against his co-conspirators, expecting him to be freed at once. Yet Williamson declines to keep his side of the bargain, and Thomas is still in the Tower.'

Scot scrubbed at his cheeks, making the pastes on them blur and mingle. 'All right,' he said softly. 'I did send Bristol the letter to avenge myself on Williamson.'

'Why Bristol?'

'Because he was the one who set a murder in motion, and it appealed to my sense of justice that he should be the instrument of its resolution. I made sure he received the note when he was with the King, so he would have

435

no choice but to share its contents. But so what? Dillon and Fanning *did* kill Webb, and they have received their just deserts.'

'What about Sarsfeild?'

Scot shrugged. 'A casualty of war. Why did you meddle? You made life very difficult for me.'

'And you reciprocated at every turn. You encouraged me to think Webb's murder was something to do with the Castle Plot, when it was nothing of the kind. You told me several times that I should not trust Wiseman, in an attempt to make me waste time by investigating *him* as the killer. And then there was Fitz-Simons. I thought from the start that he had been killed to prevent him from talking to Williamson, and I was right. *You* shot him.'

Scot shrugged again. 'Another casualty of war.'

'When Fitz-Simons murmured that Terrell "is not what he says", he meant more than I realised. Somehow, he had learned that you wrote Bristol's letter. Perhaps he saw you deliver it, or perhaps he recognised the ink. Regardless, you could not have Williamson knowing what you had done.'

'Blue ink,' murmured Scot ruefully. 'Using it was a stupid and unforgivable mistake on my part. I was obliged to send Fitz-Simons a few notes in his capacity as government informer. He attended Dillon's trial – dismally disguised as a milkmaid – and I knew that as soon as the law-court started to make an issue of the ink's unusual colour, he would associate it with me. I hunted him for days, and then he appeared at Westminster Abbey. I shot him.'

'Everyone – including Eaffrey – seems to think you included me in your list of names. Why?'

'Because I thought it would allay suspicion against me if I included an old friend. I care nothing for May, Willys and the others, though. All I wanted was to deliver a stunning blow to Williamson's little empire. Do not look disgusted, Chaloner. You were never in danger from my "accusation". You were in Ireland when Webb was murdered, and could have proved it to any law-court's satisfaction.'

Chaloner stared at the ceiling. Scot was wrong: a judge would have treated his alibi with the same contempt with which he had treated Sarsfeild's. 'You must have been surprised when Garsfield's name was changed to Sarsfeild. Do you know who did that? Eaffrey.'

Scot closed his eyes. 'I know. She does not share my confidence in English justice, and altered it before I had it delivered. She confessed to what she had done a few days ago – defiantly and unrepentantly, of course. She has always looked out for you. How did you guess it was her?'

'Because she demonstrated to Thurloe how the changes had been made – changes so minuscule they were all but invisible. But she identified them with suspicious ease.'

Scot grimaced. 'Another foolish mistake on our part.'

Solutions were coming so fast to Chaloner that it was difficult to analyse them all. Meanwhile, the enormity of Scot's betrayal threatened to overwhelm him, and he had to force himself to speak. 'It was you who disguised himself as a priest and killed Sarsfeild in Ludgate. You knew Thurloe and I had been investigating his alibi, and you wanted us to stop making efforts on his behalf, because we would have learned that he was innocent of everything except an unfortunate name and an unlucky address.'

437

Scot sighed. 'You are right – I knew that once you believed someone had changed the letter to protect you, the game would be up. You do not have many friends in London, and it was obvious that you would have looked to us. Eaffrey had no idea the trouble her tiny alterations would cause.'

'She virtually told me,' said Chaloner tiredly. 'Today, at Dillon's execution. She said someone had done it to benefit me. I should have made the connection then.'

'So, what happens now? Will you tell Williamson? I doubt if he will believe you. Or will you forget about our misunderstandings and come to Surinam?'

'I doubt I would survive the voyage – you have tried to be rid of me several times already.'

'That is not true,' objected Scot indignantly.

'The first time was at Bristol's house. You were ready to hand me over – a perfect opportunity to be shot of the nuisance I was becoming – but Alice arrived, and you did not want your beloved sister to see you betraying an old friend, even one she does not like. Then, after we left the garden, you wanted to turn right when it was obvious that if we did, we would run directly into Bristol's men.'

Scot's expression was harsh. 'You have a fertile imag-ination.'

'The last time was here, in the Anatomical Theatre. You said you came to investigate Lisle, but you knew he was no real threat to an experienced spy like me. You were here to kill me and leave me for the dissectors, but Johnson got the better of you.'

'That is an unpleasant thing to say.'

'But true. Johnson has already told me that the barber-surgeons accept corpses with no questions asked. That is

438

how you disposed of the man with the scarred throat – the man *you* killed in Behn's office. You brought him here and they obligingly chopped him up for you.'

'You cannot prove that.'

'I probably can – by asking Williamson whether any of his spies had a damaged neck. He is almost certain to say yes. What did the poor man do, Scot? Stumble across your plan to trick Behn into marrying Eaffrey for the alimony you are determined to wring from him?'

'Eaffrey,' said Scot, turning when he heard footsteps. 'Chaloner is making up all manner of tales.'

'I have been listening,' said Eaffrey. Chaloner was shocked by the dead, flat expression on her face. 'It is a pity, because we were almost through this hellish time: your brother's release is imminent, Webb's murderers are dead, and we had plucked up the courage to tell Williamson that we no longer wish to work for him. And he did not even *ask* us about his missing spy, so we are clear of that nasty business, too.'

Chaloner looked hard at her. 'And Willys is dead. You arranged the diversion with the horse, while Scot stabbed him in the back. Why was that necessary?'

Neither denied the accusation. 'He was threatening to fabricate evidence that would see my brother executed,' said Scot. 'And do you know why? Because of you.'

'Me?' Chaloner did not see how he could be held responsible for anything Willys had done.

'You suggested I investigate the Trulocke brothers, but it transpired that the man who oversaw the supply of weapons to the Irish rebels was none other than Willys.'

Chaloner frowned. 'But he said he *prevented* a shipment of arms from reaching the conspirators.'

'He was lying. Subsequent probing has shown he was

a close ally of Dillon's; they were drinking together on the night of Webb's murder. Dillon was a rebel, and he encouraged his friends – Willys, Fanning, Fitz-Simons and others to join him in Ireland. When I tackled him, Willys said that if I did not overlook the matter, he would tell Williamson that *Thomas* sold them the weapons. Unfortunately for Willys, he chose the wrong man to threaten.'

'And England is now minus a traitor,' added Eaffrey, a little defiantly.

'You made the mistake of stabbing him with your left hand,' said Chaloner. 'You did it, because you knew May would make an issue of the fact that I can fight with both, but you forgot about the splint. It was a clever idea, but you did not think it through properly.'

Scot sighed impatiently. 'Yes, I killed Willys and yes, we wanted you accused, so you would stop your investigation and leave us alone. But nothing would have happened to you – your master is Lord Chancellor of England, and he would have stepped in to save you.'

'And if not, we would have arranged your escape,' added Eaffrey. 'You were never in any danger. Damn it, Thomas! Why could you not leave this alone? Now what are we going to do? You have landed us all in a terrible mess.'

'I should say,' came a voice from the stairs. All three jumped in surprise, and turned to see Holles standing there, a cocked pistol in each hand. 'A terrible mess is a good description of what you have made of our lives, Heyden. Search him for daggers, Scot.'

'He is unarmed,' said Scot. 'I hid all his weapons before we came down here.'

Chaloner looked from one to the other in confusion,

440

then shook his head in disgust as Holles trained both dags on him. 'Wiseman said you could not be trusted, and he was right.'

Eaffrey spoke in a low voice. 'You have always been loyal to a single master, Tom – first Thurloe, and now Clarendon. The rest of us are rather more practical. Bristol is generous, and Holles, William and I have all accepted commissions from him – to see him victorious over the man whose bigotry against Catholics has deprived him of the right to hold public office.'

Chaloner was numb. 'Now what? Do we all go to Surinam together?'

Slowly, Scot took a gun from his belt, and aimed it at Chaloner's chest. 'I think it is too late for that.'

'Would you like me to turn around?' asked Chaloner softly. 'So you can shoot me in the back?'

Eaffrey stepped forward and snatched the weapon from Scot's hand. 'Let me.'

She took aim, and Chaloner saw the fierce gleam in her eye. Then, at the last moment, she swung around and fired at Holles. But the colonel was already bringing his own gun to bear on her, and he shot first. The two almost-simultaneous reports were deafening in the confined space, and Chaloner dived for the floor. Eaffrey stumbled against Scot, and both crashed to the ground, but it was not Eaffrey who lay still. Holles's aim had gone wide, and Chaloner saw a spreading stain of red under Scot. Eaffrey gazed at him and began a low, keening wail of distress.

Meanwhile, Eaffrey's ball had hit Holles, who lay on his side, gasping. He fumbled for his second dag. Chaloner scrambled towards him, but was too far away to prevent him from using it. A third shot rang out, and Eaffrey's cries stopped abruptly. Chaloner reached Holles and searched him, but there were no more weapons. The soldier was dying, and blood bubbled between his lips.

'I was testing them, to see if they really would kill you,' he whispered, trying to grab Chaloner's hand. 'I was going to shoot them before they could do it, and all that posturing was to make *them* show their true colours.'

Chaloner glanced to where Eaffrey and Scot lay in a motionless embrace. 'I do not understand. Eaffrey just said—'

'Of course I am not working for Bristol! He is a rake and nothing would induce me to spy for him, not even the fifty pounds he offered me. I have only ever served Lord Clarendon, but now you must take my place.'

'You have killed my friends,' said Chaloner, unable to keep the catch from his voice.

'They were no friends of yours.'

There came the sound of footsteps and people started to converge on the basement, alerted by the sound of the gunfire. Wiseman knelt next to Eaffrey and Scot, and shook his head at the clamour of questions. They were already dead, and there was nothing he could do to help them.

Epilogue

A robin sang in Lincoln's Inn, perched high in the ancient elm that threw cool shadows across the path. Thurloe looked up at it, and gave a rare smile of genuine pleasure

'We have won the war. There were casualties, but we won eventually, which just goes to show that God's justice does prevail on occasion.'

Leybourn breathed deeply of the rain-scented garden, strolling contentedly on Thurloe's left, while Chaloner walked on the right. 'The spat between Clarendon and Bristol *does* seem to have abated.'

'I am talking about my trees,' said Thurloe. 'I lost some to Prynne's axes, but a timely lightning strike – plus an oddly croaking voice that warned him of thousands of Roundheads – caused him to revise his plans. They will form part of the display now, instead of being removed to make way for grass. When all matures, Lincoln's Inn garden may even be better than it was before.'

'Did anyone else hear this "oddly croaking voice"?' asked Leybourn, bemused.

'Of course not,' said Thurloe. There was a hint of laughter in his eyes that made Chaloner wonder whether he was telling the truth.

'What will happen to Bristol and Clarendon now?' asked Chaloner. 'Will they call a truce?'

'Never,' said Thurloe. 'Bristol is insane with frustrated ambition, and Clarendon will not enjoy a long political career, more is the pity. England needs men with scruples, and that will not be found among the likes of Bristol, Buckingham and Temple.'

'You had better secure yourself another master, then,' said Leybourn to Chaloner. 'What about Williamson? Surely he must see you are the kind of man his intelligence service needs, especially as he is now deprived of May, Eaffrey and Scot.'

'He will never hire me,' said Chaloner unhappily. 'He thinks I killed May. Worse yet, he found some documents when he cleared May's room.'

'What sort of documents?' asked Leybourn.

'Ones that imply *I* stole Dillon's body, and was planning to sell it to the barber-surgeons. May paid Lisle and Johnson to write letters offering to buy the thing from me – they were discussing it in the Anatomical Theatre, although I did not understand what they were talking about at the time.'

'Surely Williamson cannot believe such a monstrous tale?' demanded Leybourn, indignant on his behalf.

Chaloner explained further. 'Someone – Johnson, probably – brought Dillon's corpse to Lincoln's Inn after the hanging, which explains its disappearance. He hid it near that wall we blew up, along with the clothes similar to the ones I wore when I was disguised as an upholsterer.'

Thurloe took up the tale. 'May had a written statement from a "witness" who said he saw the suspicious interring of a body here. His crude little plan was for him and Williamson to unearth Dillon together, and for May to point out the significance of the clothes – to prove Thomas's guilt. In the event, however, Williamson was obliged to excavate Dillon alone, and the upholsterer connection was overlooked – fortunately for Thomas.'

'So Williamson is not sure what to believe,' said Chaloner ruefully. 'He would like me to be guilty, but without solid evidence, he is erring on the side of caution, and has declared the matter closed.'

Leybourn paled suddenly. 'Oh, Lord! *I* helped May! When we went to that tavern together, he asked which Inn you had attended. Like a fool I told him, because I wanted him to fall foul of Prynne. I thought I was being clever! I should have known there was something more to his questions.'

'Yes,' agreed Thurloe. 'You should. The man was a spy, after all.'

Leybourn looked suitably chastened. 'I owe you an apology for declining to visit gaols when you asked, too, Tom. Thurloe tells me you have a better reason than most for wanting to avoid them.'

'Why did you refuse?' asked Chaloner curiously.

'Rats,' replied Leybourn in a low voice. He shuddered. 'I cannot abide them, and the ones in Newgate are notoriously bold.'

Chaloner went back to his analysis. 'I did not kill May, though, no matter what Williamson thinks. I hoped to resolve our differences without bloodshed.'

'That would have been impossible,' said Thurloe. 'May's hatred of you was fanatical, as attested by this ridiculous business with stolen corpses.'

'Why did Scot kill him?' asked Leybourn. 'I still do not understand. Was it to save you?'

'No – I had already disarmed him when Scot fired his dag. May had to die because he had just threatened to expose Scot and Eaffrey's plans to defraud Behn.'

'How did he know what they intended to do?' asked Leybourn doubtfully. 'He was a dismal spy, and could never have learned such a closely guarded secret.'

'I cannot prove it, but I believe the man with the scarred neck – who *was* one of Williamson's officers – found out by chance,' said Chaloner. 'Like Eaffrey, he had also been charged to monitor Behn's activities by worming his way into his confidences, and he must have overheard a conversation between Scot and Eaffrey in Behn's house. He told May about it, so Scot killed them both.'

Leybourn blew out his cheeks in a sigh. 'Tell me again what happened in Chyrurgeons' Hall last week. I should not have tested so many of Prynne's strong wines that day, because I still do not understand how the murder of Webb was connected to what those surgeons were doing.'

'It was not connected,' said Chaloner. 'Or not significantly so. It all started when Silence Webb insulted Bristol at the Guinea Company dinner. Bristol immediately decided to avenge himself. He baulked at harming a woman, but her unpleasant husband was fair game, so he ordered Dillon and Fanning to oblige. He wrote a note, spitefully signing it with Clarendon's name.'

'Then he had second thoughts, and sent Scot to stop them,' said Thurloe, who had not been drunk when Chaloner had arrived to tell them how the case had been resolved. 'But Scot decided to enact a little vengeance of his own – on Williamson for keeping his brother in the Tower.'

'Scot witnessed Webb's murder,' continued Chaloner. 'And then he wrote Bristol a letter, naming not only Dillon and Fanning as the culprits, but exposing several of Williamson's best agents.'

'Why did Scot pick your Garsfield alias for his letter?' asked Leybourn. 'Why not Heyden?'

'He was being clever,' said Chaloner. 'Or thought he was. He chose that name – which I have only ever used in Ireland – to strengthen the apparent links between Webb's death and the Castle Plot. That was probably why he included Fitz-Simons, too – like Dillon, he was a rebel. He had stressed the Irish connection in his letter, but it was suppressed – too politically sensitive, I suppose. Fortunately for me, Eaffrey intervened.'

'Why did she do that?' asked Leybourn.

Chaloner looked away, and it was Thurloe who answered. 'Because she was fond of Thomas, and was determined that nothing bad should happen to him.'

'She was complicit in trying to have him accused of murdering Willys,' Leybourn pointed out. 'That is not keeping him out of harm's way.'

'That came later, when Thomas's enquiries were coming too close for comfort. But even then, I do not think she would have left him to stew for long. She was a true friend and would have organised some kind of rescue or release.'

'And Scot?' asked Leybourn. 'Was he a true friend, too?'

'No,' said Chaloner softly. 'I misjudged him badly. I think he might well have shot me, had Eaffrey not grabbed the gun. Killing came easily to him, after all.'

447

'Who did he kill?' asked Leybourn. 'Other than May and the scarred spy?'

'Fitz-Simons, for a start,' replied Thurloe. 'Because he recognised Scot's distinctive blue ink. The ink was a stupid mistake on Scot's part, and shows he was losing his touch.'

'No wonder he was keen to resign from the intelligence services,' said Leybourn. 'The release of his brother was probably a factor, but self-preservation played a role, too.'

'Sarsfeild was another of his victims,' continued Thurloe. 'He dressed as a priest and killed him in Ludgate when he learned Thomas and I were investigating his alibi. He knew we would discover that Sarsfeild's arrest was a case of mistaken identity, which would raise awkward questions about the rest of the letter. He strangled Sarsfeild in the hope that it would bring an end to our investigation.'

'And the deaths of Fanning and Sarsfeild in their cells – for reasons unrelated to Webb – made Dillon think his master was tying loose ends,' said Chaloner. 'The reality was quite different, but it served to make Dillon more confident of his master's power. He was deceived.'

'He was deceived by the *name* of his master, too,' said Leybourn, recalling one fact that was not lost in the drunken haze. 'He thought it was Lord Clarendon, but it was actually Bristol.'

'Then Scot killed Willys,' said Thurloe. 'He had discovered that Willys had sold guns to Irish rebels, but Willys tried to blackmail him by threatening to say Thomas was involved – a mistake of monumental proportion.'

'Did he kill Holles, too?' asked Leybourn.

'That was Eaffrey,' replied Thurloe. 'In a ridiculous and pathetic misunderstanding, each was trying to probe the loyalty of the other. Eaffrey wanted to know whether Holles was going to be a danger to Thomas in the future – to find out whether he really had defected to Bristol. And Holles wanted to know whether Scot and Eaffrey would try to harm Clarendon by depriving him of a valued servant.'

'It all happened so fast,' said Chaloner unhappily. 'Guns were out, and they both jumped to the wrong conclusions without giving themselves time to think. I keep running through the scene in my mind, trying to see if there was a way I could have averted the slaughter.'

'There was nothing you could have done,' said Thurloe gently. 'Do not dwell on it.'

'Meanwhile,' said Leybourn, after a few minutes of silence, 'all the barber-surgeons are guilty of is making themselves rich from conducting these Private Anatomies.'

'Hardly!' said Thurloe with a shudder of distaste. 'Not only did they murder people for their corpses, but they were willing to accept any cadaver in good condition with no questions asked.'

'Behn and Temple are innocent of everything, though,' said Leybourn.

'They promote slavery,' said Chaloner. 'Plus there is the fact that Behn is a foreign spy. He sends dispatches to his government every Tuesday, which he writes in cipher. Furthermore, he gave money to the Irish rebels, to help the Castle Plot succeed.'

Thurloe glanced sharply at him. 'How do you know that?'

'Because, despite what Eaffrey believed, it was obvious

that there was something suspect about the man. Maude saw him with Fanning once, and Fanning – like Dillon – was a committed insurgent. I intercepted and decoded one batch of messages and passed the information to Williamson.'

'Behn is arrested for spying?' asked Leybourn.

'Unfortunately, he somehow learned the game was up, and escaped. Williamson is furious.'

'I have a confession to make,' said Thurloe sheepishly, when the Inn's cat approached and wound around his legs. Chaloner was pleased to see it recovered. 'It involves a certain tonic.'

'I already know,' said Chaloner. 'It was *you* who poisoned me.'

Leybourn gaped, while Thurloe looked reproachful. 'I would not have put it quite like that. It makes it sound deliberate, and I assure you it was not. How did you guess?'

'First, we suspected Prynne, but Will disproved that by drinking his wine. Then it seemed obvious that Yates had done it, but his remit was to spy, not to kill. You, however, are very interested in cures and strong medicines, and you are always willing to try new ones. I suspect your manservant stops you from doing yourself too much harm, but Yates had sent him away. You added a new cure-all called Goddard's Drops to one experiment, but those contain volatile oil of silk among other powerful ingredients. Wiseman says they are toxic in any quantity.'

Thurloe nodded unhappily. 'He was appalled when he knew what I had done. Still, I have learned my lesson and shall mix no more potions. I hope you bear me no grudge.'

'No,' said Chaloner. He sighed and looked up at the

450

leafy branches swaying over his head. 'I am not sure I want to work for Lord Clarendon any more. I cannot help him in his spat with Bristol, and it is only a matter of time before their followers start killing each other.'

'He is still a powerful man, so do not abandon him just yet,' advised Thurloe. 'However, the Queen has noticed you at White Hall, and she has a spot of bother she wants investigated. Clarendon happened to mention that you know Portuguese, and she would like you to visit her tomorrow.'

Chaloner regarded him uneasily. 'I hope she does not ask me to spy on the King's mistress. Lady Castlemaine is more dangerous than Williamson, May, Scot, Behn, Temple and Bristol put together.'

A few miles away, a ship was sailing down the Thames on the Early tide. It was bound for Surinam, and carried a number of passengers, as well as a cargo of wool for the new colony. Eaffrey Johnson stood at the rail, arm-in-arm with Johan Behn. Behn was wearing warm clothes against the stiff breeze, and he looked bigger and bulkier than ever. He sighed his contentment.

'We are finally on our way. These last few weeks have been tiresome, and I dislike being in a position where I do not know whom to trust. I did not approve of your friend from Holland, either. I think he might still be in love with you.'

'I think I have successfully destroyed any lingering affection he might have held for me now,' said Eaffrey, leaning against him. The wind was sharp, and made her eyes water. 'When shall we marry?'

'When we touch land in France. I am sure we will make each other happy.'

Eaffrey nodded, although her eyes still watered furiously. 'And you will forsake the Silences and the Maudes, and stay faithful to me? You have not forgotten the agreement you signed, which will see our marriage annulled to my advantage if you stray?'

Behn waved an expansive hand. 'They are nothing, a diversion. Did I tell you I paid that impecunious Wiseman five pounds to say you were dead when Holles shot at you? I had managed to spike one of the colonel's dags, but I could not lay my hands on the second.'

'Yes, you did mention it,' said Eaffrey patiently. 'Several times. You are very clever.'

Behn preened at the praise. 'I was terrified Heyden would catch on and tell everyone. He is too curious for his own good, and insisted on examining your "corpse", even though I did my best to stop him. Still, you fooled him, because he has no idea you are still alive.'

'Actually, Johan, he felt my neck for a pulse – and he has seen enough death to be aware that cadavers do not have one. He knows I am alive.'

'No!' whispered Behn, gloating triumph evaporating like a puff of steam. 'What shall we do? Hire an assassin in France to deal with him? We cannot let him live, not if you want to be safe.'

'Tom will not betray me,' said Eaffrey softly.

'How can you be sure?' asked Behn worriedly.

'Because I know him,' replied Eaffrey. She turned slightly, and glanced at the elderly man who sat huddled in an old-fashioned woollen cloak nearby. It hid his bandaged shoulder. He shot her a brief smile, and then turned his pale eyes to the book he was reading: *Musaeum Tradescantianum.*

Historical Note

The quarrel between the Earl of Clarendon and George Digby, earl of Bristol was public and bitter. They had been allies in exile during the Commonwealth, but it did not take not long after the King's Restoration in 1660 for their friendship to disintegrate. Their disparate personalities did not help. Bristol was gay, witty and fun-loving – a man of 'irresponsible brilliance'; Clarendon was pompous, staid, respectable and something of a killjoy. They clashed when Clarendon dismissed Bristol from a post at the University of Oxford – in the distasteful bigotry of the time, Clarendon objected to a Catholic holding the position – and they disagreed violently about which European princess the King should marry. One of Clarendon's most ardent supporters was his cousin, Sir Alan Brodrick. Brodrick was a Court debauchee, who never amounted to much, despite his kinsman's patronage.

Matters came to a head when the blustering Sir Richard Temple arrived on the scene in 1663. He offered to manipulate parliament on the King's behalf, and allegedly recruited Bristol to help him. Fur flew once details of the plan emerged. The King was furious at the presumption, and ordered Temple to explain himself in the House of Commons. Temple lost his official posts, but survived to side against Clarendon in another dispute in the late 1660s. Bristol did not fare so well. He made a desperate attempt to have Clarendon impeached for treason in June 1663, but it failed miserably – mostly because the charges were manifestly false – and the incident left his reputation in tatters. The Commons claimed its time was being wasted, and the King ordered Bristol's arrest. Bristol fled the country, and only emerged from hiding when Clarendon finally fell from grace in 1667. One of the charges of a later impeachment was that Clarendon had stolen black marble from St Paul's Cathedral to use on the fabulous new Clarendon House in Piccadilly.

The Middlesex County Records of 1663 tell of a case in which one Matthew Webb was stabbed in the chest with a rapier, and nine gentlemen of the parish of St Martin-in-the-Fields were accused of his murder. Of these, William Dillon, Thomas Sarsfeild (written as 'Garsfield' in some sources) and Richard Fanning were sentenced to hang; George Willis, Gregory Burne, Walter Fitz-Gerrard and Laurence Clarke produced a King's Pardon; and Richard Fitz-Simons and Peter Terrell disappear from the records altogether.

Shortly after his execution – with a silken noose, as was his prerogative as a gentleman – Dillon was dissected at a Public Anatomy demonstration at 'Chyrurgeons' Hall'. Samuel Pepys was among the audience, and professed himself very impressed with the lecture. He also enjoyed the dinner that followed, along with being given a private viewing of Dillon's corpse, which he touched.

Perhaps the most famous barber-surgeon of the 1660s was Richard Wiseman. He held a royal appointment, but was best known for raising the surgical profession to a level where it was considered equal to that of the physicians. He wrote significant academic tomes on his subject, and was elected Master of the Company of Barber-Surgeons in 1665. The Master in May 1663 was Thomas Lisle, who also held the post of King's Barber. Francis Johnson was paid an annual salary of £10 as the Company's beadle after 1659, and the clerk in 1658 (and possibly until 1685) was Richard Reynell.

The Trulocke brothers – William, George and Edmund – were gunsmiths with business premises on St Martin's Lane. William Leybourn was a mathematician–surveyor who drew maps of London after the Great Fire of 1666, and Adrian May was a Groom of the Privy Chamber. Thomas Greeting was a famous Court musician who made extra money from teaching – he gave Pepys's wife lessons on the flageolet.

John Thurloe was Oliver Cromwell's Spymaster General and Secretary of State in the 1650s, but fell from power after the Restoration. He lived quietly in Lincoln's Inn, where he was a bencher. A fellow bencher of this time was William Prynne, one of London's most repellent fanatics. Prynne had lost his ears for writing unpalatable nonsense in the 1630s, although the punishment did nothing to make him more moderate in the future. He wrote about two hundred books and pamphlets, many of them deeply unpleasant. On 27 June 1663, Samuel Pepys visited Lincoln's Inn, and wandered up and down the gardens that were in the process of being landscaped. The Inn's archives for that year contain records that detail tree-felling and the levelling of uneven ground for the remodelling.

Thomas Scot was one of Thurloe's predecessors. He was appointed head of the intelligence services in 1649, but fell out of favour until 1660, when he took over from Thurloe. He did not keep the post for long. He was one of the fifty-nine men who had signed Charles I's death warrant – as was Thomas Chaloner (1595–1661) – and was executed on 17 October 1660. Later, the running of intelligence matters fell to the clever Oxford academic Joseph Williamson.

Scot had three children. Thomas Scot the younger played a role in the disastrous Castle Plot – an attempt to seize Dublin Castle and its lieutenant – but managed to save himself by making a deal with the Royalists whereby he would escape execution in exchange for naming his co-conspirators. He was kept in the Tower, and not pardoned until 1666. His sister, Alice Scot, married one of Cromwell's wartime scoutmasters. And William Scot was perceived by the Royalist government as a dangerous dissident. He embarked on a torrid affair with another Restoration spy called Eaffrey Johnson, who later married a German merchant named Johan Behn. Eaffrey (or Aphra) Behn made a name for herself as a playwright, and some of her work enjoyed a twentieth-century revival – it had been discredited by the Victorians, who considered it too lewd.

The affair between Aphra Behn and William Scot may have taken place partly in Surinam, where her remit was to seduce him and encourage him to work for Williamson. Lady spies were probably rare in Restoration England, although historians disagree about Aphra Behn's effectiveness and importance. Some say she was clever enough

456

to take on men in a man's world, and others say she was not very good at it. Whatever the truth, she eventually returned to England – without Scot – and turned her attention to the stage.